NIBIRU'S CHILD

Book 1

Who Killed Cressie Moonchild?

Allegra Drakos

BENYA PUBLISHING

Library of Congress Control Number: 2025942446

First published in 2025 by Benya Publishing

ISBN: 978-1-968455-12-5 (paperback)
ISBN: 978-1-968455-13-2 (ePDF)
ISBN: 978-1-968455-14-9 (ePUB)

Publication data:
Allegra Drakos
Who Killed Cressie Moonchild?
Book 1 in the "Nibiru's Child" Series

Design and layout by Scribe Inc.

Benya Publishing
P.O. Box 799
Sullivan's Island, SC 29482

www.benyapublishing.com

Chapter 1

"That," Ms. Rooney said emphatically, "is the face of global warming."

She had projected a photo of an ice-free Antarctica on a screen rather than doing the American History lesson like she was supposed to. It would soon lead to race, class, gender, and the oppression of America's history, her usual pet topics.

"No," Samantha said tentatively. "Those are the McMurdo Dry Valleys. Ross Sea and McMurdo Sound. There's extremely low precipitation. They've always been that way."

Ms. Rooney looked at Samantha like some heckler at her political rally. Her nostrils flared.

Samantha—Sam to her pals—should have let it go. It wasn't easy being smarter than the teacher. In fact all of them were smarter. They had tested genius level back in elementary school and been swift-streamed into a special class. They were a wacky bunch of super brains. One-on-one, no teacher stood much of a chance against them, and collectively, it was a total walkover.

It was a university town and you get that kind of thing. Two intellects breed and a synergy results. Everybody with offbeat hobbies based on their parents' research areas. The thirty of them had been together since fourth grade and were like a big communal family.

Otherwise it was a typical American high school with slackers, stoners, student government ass-kissers, jocks, and a honey cheerleading squad. They hated and feared the smart kids who went about in a defensive pack.

Ms. Rooney was always angry because she was always being made to look ignorant, which she was. It would have been so easy to have said "Really?" and let Samantha talk. Sam was always polite about stuff she knew. Instead, Rooney had to challenge her.

"So how did you get so informed on this, Samantha Fitzhugh?"

Sam knew she was blushing. She didn't handle stress well. "My mom's there right now."

The teacher glowered at her, doing all but call her a liar.

"She sent me photos," Sam added.

Rooney was skewered. So completely that it seemed like Sam was being a smart-ass, which Sam hadn't intended at all.

Ms. Rooney snorted. "I see."

Sam felt tense. She had let out some potentially dangerous information. It was a big nanny state town. And she spent a lot of time alone. Her dad was who-knows-where, and Mom was an archaeologist frequently employed by the government. So she would jet off at a moment's notice.

Ms. Rooney flashed the famous hockey stick diagram of global warming on the screen. Began the diatribe they had heard so many times before. And then Nasar really put her over the edge.

"Actually, global warming has been totally debunked."

Her face turned beet red. "How can you be so anti-science?" she spluttered. "Anti-intellectual, anti . . . anti-anything sensible? And your father a physicist!"

Sam feared she was going to explode right there, but Nasar was oblivious. He was purely left-brain and seldom processed other peoples' feelings. He also was close to seven feet tall and all those emotional vibrations passed somewhere below him.

"The ice is actually growing in Antarctica," he insisted.

She slammed the flat of her hand on the desk. "You don't know that! It's just some corporate propaganda you've read on the web! All the polluters and greed-heads, they want you ignorant until it's too late. Profits over people right up until we go extinct."

"No, it's all a fraud," put in Kurt Jaeger. He was seated to Sam's right. The handsomest boy in the class, and she was too shy to look at him.

"Temperatures have been dropping for a decade. We may be headed into a new Ice Age. And the stable line of temperature to the left on the hockey stick deliberately leaves out the Medieval Warm Period when Norsemen lived in Greenland. And it was really green. For five hundred years."

Ms. Rooney's eyes actually bulged from her head, and Sam imagined she could hear her molars grind. The woman really was ridiculous with her butch-cut hair, motorcycle boots, baggy carpenter pants, and a t-shirt with "Well-Behaved Women Seldom Make History."

Then the flagpole fell over. Wham.

We have to back up here and tell you something about

the history teacher. The first day of class she announced she was a Marxist, an atheist, and a lesbian. She thought that would really rock them. In fact, the entire class gave a big collective yawn.

As previously stated, it was a university town. And even in the South, probably half the parents were socialists or communists or something even wackier like anarchists. Nobody was into religion unless it was Buddhism or Wicca or Rastafarianism. And gay rights had been preached at the kids since elementary school.

They moved towards their AP history exam despite their teacher whose only interests were trendy causes. One day it was the oppressive patriarchy, the next the threats to the teaching of Darwin or women's right to contraception. And the exam was going to be on actual history.

The flag was of course hanging upside down in the symbol of distress. America in distress. Racism, sexism, classism, homophobia. On and on. Blah blah.

The week before she was carrying on about Thomas Jefferson having slaves and how that made the Constitution a hypocritical document that ought to be abolished, completely excised from the law. Emerson had pointed out that James Madison had written the Constitution. Jefferson had written the Declaration of Independence, which was a founding document, but nonetheless, not part of the law of the land.

Sam thought Rooney was going to have a cow.

Emerson's father was in history. And yes, Emerson was black. His middle name was "X." Emerson's father had once been into black power. Now he was just an absent-minded professor who actually wore a tweed jacket with leather elbow patches.

Yes, the flagpole fell over with a crash. No apparent agency. It just went over.

Ms. Rooney leaped up behind her desk in confusion. "What? Wha—?" Then pointed a finger straight at Samantha. "You did that! How did you do it? Is there a thread tied to it?"

Sam thought why is she picking on me? She was just shy Samantha Fitzhugh. Living a studious and dreamy life with a mother who was seldom home and a house full of archaeological finds. She never caused any trouble. Never was in trouble.

Kurt took up for her. "She didn't do anything. We're all just sitting here."

She thought my God, Kurt took up for me. Kurt knows I exist.

Ms. Rooney was ranting at the class in general, but chanced to be staring straight into Sam's eyes when the next thing happened. She simply fell over backwards onto her fat rear end.

Skidded and fell as though she had stepped on a banana peel.

Of course the class laughed.

Well the shit hit the fan with that.

"It was you two. Get down to the principal's office and I mean right now and no delay. You are in trouble, you can't talk your way out of this time with your glib mouths."

"You're just picking on them because they're white,"

said Emerson. "You're worried about racial disparity in discipline statistics."

Ms. Rooney threw a book across the room in rage.

■ ■ ■

Townsend "Boo" Radley IV sat in his small stockbroker's office with one of his bigger whales as they were called in the trade. A fish on the line. A sucker. A patsy.

Marvin Pfiezer. Seventy-two years old. Sold a plastics extrusion factory in Belleville, New Jersey for twenty-six million and retired to a southern university town with a major teaching hospital and ACC basketball. Didn't know what to do with himself now that he wasn't bossing a pack of Puerto Ricans every day. Liked to imagine he could pick stocks and had a nose for hidden value with explosive growth.

"Well, down here with the grits and yahoos," said Boo, "nobody much likes the action."

"Bunch'a yokels," Marvin echoed. "How did they fight the Civil War?"

Boo made a forced laugh. "It's good to see a man who can take the torque of a rollercoaster ride on the market."

"No guts, no glory," croaked Marvin.

Sleazy old yuck with his dentures and foul cigar breath. It was just too funny to churn his account, make commissions on pointless trades. The man was in pre-Alzheimer's, had no short-term memory retention and wouldn't figure out he was losing money until tax time. By then he'd have forgotten how all the transactions had worked.

The Yankees got drawn south by the low taxes. They all

said it was the weather, but in fact their big government obsessions had ruined New York, Rhode Island, New Jersey. You hang on there, you're just paying lavish retirements for a pack of parasite-unionized civil servants.

So they flock south to a university town with "culture," not that you noticed it much, and a teaching hospital to keep your sorry carcass upright. Buy up all the nice real estate and drive the penurious faculty out of the town. Retired, nothing to do but carp with each other about how dumb the hicks are, how things were done so much better back where they came from.

Boo didn't feel bad about what he was doing. He was young and needed to make his way in the world, and Marvin had no use for the money. Just leave it to adult children who he constantly bitched about. Ingrates. Freeloaders. Moochers.

Marvin struggled to his feet, his brain already devoid of the trades the two had just agreed upon. Slapped a broad straw hat on his head like an Impressionist would use painting in the open air. Cataract glasses. He had one of those Medicare metal canes that you can adjust the height on. Couldn't even carry a stylish cane carved from exotic wood. What good did twenty-six mil do him? Better it belong to Boo.

Boo had been the bottom of his prep school class and couldn't get into the Ivies. One admissions director had actually laughed at him. Asked what "diversity" he would bring to the student body. "Old money wastrel? The vanishing New England WASP?" What a shithead.

So he had come to the university along with the rest of the bottom of his class. Administrative fools actually fawned on them, believed they brought style to the place. Branded the school a "Southern Ivy." Branding was big at colleges. What a joke.

Boo had been a lacrosse star. Had a mop of blond hair he could flip out of his eyes, wow the coed honeys. They all thought since he was from Greenwich he was rich.

Problem was, there was no Townsend family money. Or very little of it. During his college years, he liked to swank around in his fraternity and pretend he was a trust fund boy. But his father could barely pay the bills. And after he blew his brains out in the embezzlement scandal at his investment bank, there were no Wall Street connections either.

So Boo got his broker's license and stayed on in town. His high-performing pals from his prep school class had all been Dartmouth and Yale, now they were at Goldman Sachs. Always talking big deals. Who the heavy hitters were. The big swinging dicks.

He'd tell them he liked the low-key atmosphere of the South. Honey-voiced belles. Mint juleps. Said he was thinking of buying a racehorse stud. They were working eighty-hour weeks and sounded envious. They had no idea what a ratty state it was. Dead textile mills. Feedlot hog farms. Hillbillies in the mountains.

Boo played racquetball and squash now, liked to work out over at the medical school health center. Med classes were half women. Keep his eye peeled for hot young honeys in white coats with stethoscopes. He knew the income levels of the various specialties by heart. Interventional radiology was right up there at the top. Cardiology.

He could picture himself married to one of them. Scale back his business and just manage her personal fortune.

Take up fly-fishing. They'd travel to New Zealand, Iceland, and Chile. Make a regular thing of Christmas each year in Gstaad for the skiing.

A row of three-dollar signs began blinking in the upper right of his computer screen. Got him out of his reverie.

Good Christ, it had come in again. A cool million fucking dollars from a bank in Switzerland transferred once a year to Maeve McAlpin Fitzhugh jointly with her daughter Samantha. The sum was up to ten million now, and they never enquired about it, never withdrew any. They never fucking touched it.

And it just sat there in an account that paid maybe two percent. He always got a home office congratulations letter on his mismanagement of that one. The New York office got to play with the money and pay the Fitzhughs peanuts for the use of it.

He had only met them one time when the total was six million. Maeve Fitzhugh had seemed bored by the whole thing. Totally disinterested. Kept checking phone messages.

He pulled up the photos of mother and daughter. The firm always kept pictures in case of identity issues. The mother was what his mother in Greenwich would call a "handsome woman." Mid-forties. Clean face lines. Hair pulled back. Very outdoorsy. Wind-burned complexion. Did some kind of exploration thing.

The girl was just a junior in high school. But there was something compelling about her. Her eyes pulled you in.

He'd sit and stare at her for long periods of time. Picture her with her clothes off. She was only sixteen, had a rack on her like an adult.

Chapter 2

The principal's office was a place of queasiness. Nothing good ever seemed to happen there. At least there wasn't any sign of Ms. Rooney. The principal was murmuring something to someone in the hall. Mr. Peevey. What a name.

The wall had framed diplomas from a teacher's college and a PhD from a place Sam had never heard of. West Texas State.

Samantha sat giving Kurt shy glances. She was in trouble along with this beautiful boy. That couldn't be all bad.

What was funny was she'd known Kurt since elementary school, but they had not done much more than say "hi" and once in third grade they were on the same team in kickball.

His family summered in Switzerland, plus he seemed to miss a lot of each school year traveling that always got excused because it was educational. It was just since he had come back from the year in a Swiss *gymnasium*, or high school, that all the girls had started wetting their pants over him.

And it was major teenage lust. Cherry cute-butt, the head cheerleader openly talked about doing him on a bed covered in rose petals.

Principal Peevey came in for the grand inquisition. Seated himself carefully behind his desk. No friendly chat with his sitting at the edge of the desk in a chair with them. This was showing his authority.

His face was expressionless. Like he practiced the blank look. Or maybe he was just a complete dullard. Samantha thought what sort of person would choose such a career? Were there any high points? Any days you felt you had really achieved something?

All the same, he was managing to fill her with nervousness, doubt, and insecurity. She saw herself as a goody-goody. Obsessed with college admission.

He consulted a file with her name on it. The dreaded "permanent record" they had been threatened with since first grade. As in, this achievement test will go on your permanent record.

He put on half-glasses to read, then looked over the rims for the first question. Gimlet eyes. Totally cold.

"Is it true your mother is in Antarctica?"

"Yes."

Sam shivered, then reminded herself she was in trouble along with the most handsome boy in the class. And brilliant. He had been in school in Switzerland for the past year. Utterly fluent in French and German. Skied. Climbed mountains. Some insanely high level of karate.

"How long has she been gone?"

She hesitated. It felt like he was setting some kind of trap. But she had to tell the truth. He might check somehow. "About five days."

"About?"

"She left early one morning."

Without telling me, Sam thought. Per usual, her mother had left a note and a debit card for groceries.

"She is an archaeologist, I believe."

"That's correct."

"But she never got tenure at the University."

Did Sam detect a faint sneer? "True. She works off grants."

"Why would an archaeologist go to Antarctica? There are no human artifacts there."

"I really don't know."

"Are you mocking me?"

"No. I mean, I don't intend to."

More shuffling of the file. He was beginning to seem peeved. Peeved Peevey.

"Your father lives where exactly?"

"It's not clear. He travels around a lot."

"And what does he do?"

"I don't know."

He raised his eyebrows in his look of mock surprise. "Your mother hasn't told you?"

"I'm not sure she knows."

"Are your parents divorced?"

"No."

Throat clearing. Closing the file and resting both hands on it.

"I understand you carry a knife."

Sam thought how do they learn these things about you? Are there snitches in the school? She spoke cautiously. "I do on occasion."

"And do you have one here at school?"

"No, of course not."

"You know our zero tolerance policy for weapons?"

"How could I not?"

"You wouldn't by chance just happen to have one in your backpack in your locker? I mean you might have assumed that since you weren't actually carrying it in class that it was okay. The sort of hair-splitting that teenagers tend to do."

"No."

A faint smile played about his lips. "Answer carefully. Because your locker is being searched right now."

Sam suddenly felt like she was being suffocated. Was this some kind of frame-up?

Crazed Ms. Rooney came rushing in, her face glowing in triumph. She thrust out a knife at her. A stubby little paring knife with a serrated edge and plastic handle. "Here it is. Take it."

Sam sat on her hands. "Uh, no thank you."

"It's yours, you little malcontent! I said take it!"

Sam looked over her head not wanting to meet the crazy eyes.

"You know our policy," said Mr. Peevey sternly. "We've got a call in to the police. They should be on their way."

"I hope," said Kurt, "that they bring a fingerprint kit. Everyone has seen Ms. Rooney cut apples with that knife.

Every day she eats an apple and a hardboiled egg for lunch. The faculty and all the students have seen it."

"You wretched liar!" Ms. Rooney shouted. And in one swipe, she whipped the knife in the air and slashed the back of her other hand, blood splattering in a long string.

She screeched with the pain, dropped the knife.

And it hung just a second too long in the air before finally thunking onto the desk. It had appeared to be suspended for just a tiny moment of time.

The teacher sat there clutching her wounded hand, blood splattered across her glasses and her blouse, trembling, panting, squealing.

"Nobody calls me a liar! I didn't plant that. She stole it from me. I've been missing it!" Rooney was absolutely shrieking. Hysterical.

The school nurse appeared as though she'd been lurking in case of a need to do a strip search on Samantha. She practically dragged Ms. Rooney out of the room. They left behind a kind of sweaty oily smell like they had given off their tension.

Mr. Peevey was completely unmoved by what he had witnessed and went to his fallback position.

"Samantha, we're concerned about your being left alone for prolonged periods of time. The guidance counselor is phoning Social Services."

I'll bet, she thought. Hypocritical concern. God you could actually smell him as well. Some kind of floral scent. Emerson called him a smug popinjay.

"Actually," said Kurt, "she's staying with my family. It was all arranged before her mother left."

Yes, he had just lied, but utterly smoothly and for her.

The principal looked like he had indigestion.

■ ■ ■

"You're such a nice young man," said old Mrs. Ader as she stood up to leave.

"It's always a pleasure," said Boo Radley with his winning smile. He was thirty-one, but he could still do the nice young man routine.

Her husband had been a circuit court judge. Dead, but she still got his retirement. Boo had put her in annuities with flabbergasting management fees. She was over seventy. When did she imagine collecting the income? She never even asked. Never imagined such financial chicanery.

When she was gone, he sat back and looked around his dinky office. The silly framed certificates the corporate world loves to hand out. Plaques. Homilies from the brokerage's founder a century before. Bull and bear battling it out. A signed photo of Boo shaking hands with some cheesy politician he had given a five-hundred-dollar campaign contribution. Whores. They'd come running for pocket change.

When Boo started out, he'd still hit on coeds in the bars. Thinking they'd be impressed by his suit and expensive shoes. You always heard girls looked at your shoes first. But they were caught up with frat boys who still believed the world was theirs for the taking and projected that confidence that so snows women.

So he moved to the town gym with hairdressers and

schoolteachers, food and beverage girls with fake nails and orange skin from tanning beds.

But he kept hearing the voice of that asshole business law professor. Tyrannical shit. Always spouting his "iron laws." But they had a weird way of turning out accurate. "Men trade down while women trade up."

It was really obvious. Men so sex-obsessed that's all they can see. Rationalize anything for nooky. For some breathy creature to tell him he's Mister Big Guy.

And with these women he was trading down with a vengeance. All of them with credit card problems, car payment, rent problems. I mean just laying it out like a fee for prostitution.

That was when he had made the decision to get close to the medical crowd. But what were you talking about income-wise. A million-five max? And they had to work like dogs for it. Come home worn out, expecting him to listen to tales of abuse at the hands of self-entitled patients. Welfare scum. Old zombies on Medicare.

He deserved old, trust-fund money. I mean the Townsend Radleys had been in the social register until his father's felonies had come screaming out in the open. It would seem like the man's suicide would have cleansed the thing, but by his junior year in college he was no longer invited to deb balls.

He flipped up the pictures of Fitzhugh mother and daughter and sat staring. Ten million they had with another million next year, and the year after that.

Samantha's mouth looked pink and tender. Her eyes seemed to flare with passion. Was that possible? God such a piece of teenage tail. What if say, her freshman year of college she fell for him hard? Mature guy with an established business. Greenwich social connections.

She'd be eighteen. Legally able to manage her own affairs. They could go away together. Live in Italy. The Isle of Capri. Maybe the Aeolian Isles where they'd be harder to locate.

He would put his seed in her. She'd have a huge baby bump on her but wear a bikini. And he'd ram her from behind while she braced herself against a carved post in their stucco villa. Leave her breathless and glowing.

The phone lit up on the New York line. He snatched it up knowing it was that asshole Chirburg, who was always on him about something. Calling weekly to ream him out.

"Okay, pretty boy. What's with your staring at the Fitzhughs?"

"Huh?" Boo was rocked by that. "How do you . . . ? I mean what makes you think . . . ?"

Snorting laughter on the other end. "You don't think everyone's computer is monitored? Security has been onto your little peculiarity for the past four months. We're starting to wonder just why you have so much spare time?"

"I've made my numbers every quarter," said Boo defensively.

"Yes, but could they double or triple?"

Boo waited. There was no point in arguing with the jerk-off. You just had to eat dirt, eventually he'd hang up without saying goodbye. Just suddenly the phone clicks off.

"You're not thinking of getting cute with their account are you?"

"You mean like put the money in something with a decent return?"

Fatigued sigh. "You and I both know you aren't going to do that. If you know what's damn well good for you. All I know is security is bothered enough that they referred it to the psychologist. She seems to think you've got some sexual fixation on one or the other or both of them. Fantasizing a little mother-daughter action are we?"

"Am I allowed any kind of human dignity in this company?" Boo burst out. "Spying on me. Putting the worst possible interpretation on everything."

"Why don't you spare me your happy horse shit and tell me what I'm about to say next?"

Boo bit his lip, choking back his anger. This was the shit he was put through. He began to recite from memory. "Every year the university graduates hundreds of business majors who long to stay in their college town because they are immature and lack ambition. You could replace me in a day. Some of them would be willing to fight with knives for my job."

"And?"

"And what?"

"The rest of it."

"I went to a fancy-pants boarding school and you came off the streets of Brooklyn. I went to college and you didn't. You talked your way onto the trading desk and started making more money in an hour than I make in a year. Have I missed anything?"

"No, that pretty much covers it."

The phone clicked off.

Chapter 3

"That was certainly ghastly," said Samantha. She shivered at the memory of the blood spattered across Ms. Rooney's glasses. "You know I've owned all kinds of knives for years and never seen anyone slashed with one."

"What do you think happened?" asked Kurt.

"I truly don't know."

Sam couldn't believe that after that wretched day she was walking to her home with the most devastatingly desirable boy in the school. Pushing their bikes. It was an eco town for their class. No cars. Physical fitness. Out in all weather.

Kurt Jaeger who usually left early and took two college courses in the afternoon. Then went to teach little kids karate. Kurt who was lusted after by the entire cheerleading squad.

He'd stayed behind for her and was going to put her up in his home after she packed a bag. Cute little Cherry the head cheerleader was so jealous. The news had flashed through the school, and Cherry had been heard slamming locker doors and spitting out her wrath.

Sam wondered if she could be bright and appealing like a cheerleader. Perky.

"Were you looking at the flag when it fell?" Kurt asked.

"Yes, I think so."

"And when *she* fell?"

"I was looking directly into her eyes."

"Is there a history of psychokinesis in your family? Influencing the movement of matter through the power of the mind?"

"No. And I didn't want to hurt her. I don't think I even did subconsciously."

"A reflex then? A sort of push-back in defense against her wrath?"

She shrugged. "Maybe. I don't know. I don't know that I did that to her. How do you know about psychokinesis?"

"Dad's a Jungian psychologist. It's a fairly mystical approach to analyzing the human mind. And the subject bleeds over into the paranormal. And Mom, well, she's, shall we say . . . unusual."

Sam was five-ten, and still he towered over her. That swept back sandy hair. He always seemed to wear hiking boots and thick socks.

She bumped up against him, put her hand on his arm as a small pushing off gesture to maintain their space.

"Jeez, you're hard as a brick. Do you lift weights?"

"Isometrics. I do an hour every night. It's a form of meditation."

"Really?" she teased. "What do you meditate on?"

He laughed. "We'd have to know each other better before I'd entrust you with that secret."

"I fence with the university team," she said. "All I get is strong thighs."

He gave her a wry smile. She bit her tongue in embarrassment. Did everything in this world have to have a sexual innuendo? And her the lonesome virgin, never a boyfriend, never even a guy to hang out with.

She had always been gawky and tomboyish. Now she had curves and had grown . . . a frontage. But with the intellectual nerds in their genius class, no one particularly noticed.

Her house was in an old wooded neighborhood that dated to the 1940s and fifties. Hers was kind of fifties bohemian modern with funny angles and a teak wood deck out back that extended out over a steep gulch. Floor-to-ceiling windows in front. Flat roof. You went down a slope to get to the front door. Unlock the front door and then come smack up against the revelation of how the Fitzhughs lived.

Artifacts from digs in Spain, Italy, North Africa, the Middle East. A carved screen from an old house in Constantinople. Beaten copper trays and tea service from a *souk* in Syria. A bright yellow tent poorly stuffed into its bag. Orientalist paintings from nineteenth century France.

Kurt was filled with curiosity. He ran his fingers over casts of terra cotta tablets of cuneiform writing from Iraq, a bronze bull from Minoan Crete. He seemed to find an intangible loveliness in it all.

Sam apologized nonetheless. "Our house is kind of a junk heap. Mom basically runs her entire enterprise out of here. Expedition gear. Photography lab. Grant writing. Reports. Articles for journals. Sorting out what she digs up. All kinds of chemicals."

"It's conventional enough for this town," he said. "Wait'll you see ours."

She led him down the hall to her bedroom, the little spiritual paradise of every teenager. Books and pictures. Complete Roald Dahl collection. Beatrix Potter from when she was a little girl. A photo of Samantha on a donkey in Greece. Her mother dressed as a belly dancer for a costume party. Rack of fencing foils and masks. Girls don't fence with the sabre or the epée. Only the foil. Some of hers had the Italian grip with a quillon or crossguard, giving them a very Three Musketeery look.

She cringed at the thought of him seeing her pack her underwear in a tote bag. But no, he was looking at her knife collection.

There they were mounted in a glass front case in all their deadly beauty. Glistening with a slight sheen of oil. Straight, curved, and wavy blades. Some with beautiful inlaid wood handles.

Military, tactical, and survival knives. Gurka Kukri. Jambiya, the curved Arabian dagger. Indonesian Karambit. Navaja clasp that the Spanish shepherds used. SAS tactical fighting knife. Wavy blade kris from Malaya.

"Well, this is a secret side of you I'd never have guessed. The evil Rooney was onto something."

Sam laughed. "It's my one connection with my father. Each year on my birthday he sends me one. I don't know what the symbolism is. Mom enrolled me in fencing when I was seven. I think it was just a substitute for daycare."

Kurt kept studying each one in turn.

German hunting knife. The Fairbairn British dagger from WWII. Folding tactical knife. Russian recon knife.

"Do you throw these?"

"I've tried. Not very good at it. If someone attacked me, I'd be at close range and rely on surprise, just stick it in him. Not that there's any danger. There've been maybe two murders in the entire history of this town."

Kurt continued to marvel at the wicked lucent sheen. "Sheer fantasia," he admired.

It made Sam feel slightly proud that she'd so kept his attention. She thought of Cherry twirling her skirt at the basketball games to show her tights and little taut bottom to the rapturous male mob. Inciting their sobbing desires.

German hunter's short sword you used to dispatch a stag or a wild boar. WWI trench knife with brass knuckles on the hilt. Buffalo Horn Bowie knife. Marine Corps KA-Bar. And finally an eighteenth century sword cane.

At last he straightened up. "You saw Rooney's knife, didn't you?"

Sam knew exactly what he meant. "Yes."

■ ■ ■

Quinn Shaw parked his Harley with fourteen others in front of the motorcycle club out in the ratty rural area of a neighboring county. Junk cars on blocks. Hogs rooting in garbage piles. Feral chickens up in the trees. Metal Butler building with a front porch where Squirt, just out of the state prison for armed robbery, was grilling bratwurst.

In his navy blazer, faded designer jeans, and Gucci loafers, Quinn wasn't like the rest of the club. Quinn had walked in one day with a death wish. He had been denied tenure at the university, and his wife had left him. "Your life is a quilt of contradictions," she had snarled.

"I suppose that's an honest appraisal," he had replied. "I was always a deeply divided personality."

"Fuck you," she said. Not with great originality.

A third of his adult life trashed. Why not go out with a bang?

He had expected to be crucified or dragged behind a motorcycle. But oddly, they had all been quite amiable. Sensed he was a lost renegade looking for family. They didn't even laugh when he said he was a professor of ancient Middle Eastern history.

"Hey," said one. "You like books? I read one once. *Forty Yard Dash to the Johnny House* by Will E. Makeit and Betty Don't."

They all howled with laughter at the sixth grade joke. Quinn gave them a saturnine smile, knowing that they were virtually retarded. Like a pack of pitbulls, all teeth, appetite, and pea-brains.

They thought he had come to score dope and were quite upfront about the fact they dealt methamphetamine, muled it over four states. Over time he gained their complete trust, showed them how to keep account books, transformed them into a purely wholesale business, holding the retailers at a distance out there dealing at the truck stops, risking it all with the cops.

Leaning against a post was Jude somebody, the emaciated geek who cooked the meth for them. Clutching a beer, shivering and shaking, since the fumes had melted his brain.

One more educated dropout in the town. A children's librarian of all things. Fired because he did something nasty to a young boy in the restroom. He babbled lines from *Treasure Island.* "Bring aft the rum, Darby McGraw."

He might have been Long John Silver's parrot.

Inside, four of them were shooting pool. Another eight or so sat on high stools at the bar or around tables. One slept in a corner of the floor. For them, this was domesticity, their home away from the hours of open road where the wolves run free. To them with its setting among sighing pines, it was somehow darkly magnificent.

Hog Man saluted with his pool cue. Cut-off sleeves on his denim jacket, biker colors on the back. Skull and crossed camshafts. He was like an aging Tyrannosaurus, slow but brute deadly.

The first thing Quinn had gotten them to do was change their club name from Satan's Scum to Lucifer's Legion. It almost made them sound literate. Rebels, yet there was a yearning in them for obedience to some supreme authority. Now he was their leader. Rather like Captain Hook, the Old Etonian who went bad in *Peter Pan.*

Dealing meth didn't bother him. People destroyed themselves with it. But they destroyed themselves with booze and cigarettes and white sugar.

Skeeter, the skinny one with the full body tattoo, popped the top on a Blue Ribbon, and Quinn took it, sucked it down two inches. Skeeter filled the vacant space with Wild Turkey. A cocktail Quinn had invented.

Sometimes Quinn would stretch and yawn and imagine he'd been asleep for eight years. Three years for his doctorate at Brown, which was a near record, but not good enough for them to ask him to stay on the faculty. No, you have to come down to the big state university level. And spend five years grinding out learned articles here to convince the swine he was worthy to be among them.

Death and the denial of tenure. Funny how similar the two seemed. Condemned to some boondocks college where they'd put you through the same mill. Forced down still lower to a technical college.

"I was brave and true to my craft, and they pissed on me," he frequently said.

Such simpletons these bikers, it was so easy to dominate them. Get their smuggling on a business footing so the money was actually stacking up. It used to run through their fingers, leading to nasty arguments and knifings. Not good for maintaining the personnel roster.

Walking back to the porch, he laid an iron glove on the fire right over the white coals. It was from a suit of fourteenth century armor. He had stolen it from a museum at Brown when drunk after his dissertation got passed and he thought the academic world was his for the taking.

The gang exchanged vaguely uneasy glances. This was what made him the natural leader of a pack of killers. They knew he would heat the glove to cherry red and make a major point.

Hog Man looked at him anxiously, wanting to be in on the secret. Pouched pig eyes, big round bristly jowls with a fastidious mouth in the middle. He would kill instantly and without question. And there was killing to be done.

Quinn had had his rogue reputation in academe. Didn't like intellectual fads or ass-kissing the senior faculty. His very existence a red rag before the pompous old fart bulls.

Drip, drip, drip they dinked acid on his work. Rewrite this. Redo that. Come at it from another angle.

What a dry, antiseptic world, he thought. The total absence of beauty, of laughter and joy. Gerbils rattling on their wheels. Article after article he churned out. Published in class-A refereed journals. The crème-de-la-crème. And then he did the one negligent thing.

He needed fifteen hundred dollars. That was all. His wife with all her charge card debt. That ridiculous time-share she nagged him to buy on Hilton Head Island.

Fifteen hundred dollars. That's what they paid in the UFO magazine. So he wrote about the Planet Nibiru. How it orbited past the earth every 3,600 years. The Sumerians had named it. Carved it into diagrams of the solar system. The Annunaki came down from Nibiru in spaceships. Culture bringers. Teaching an ignorant people architecture and astronomy.

And they found the daughters of men fair and bred with them. They worked their way into the Bible as the Nifilim, "those who have fallen from heaven."

He wrote it in academic jargon. Footnotes. Obtuse language. The editor went ape-shit over it. Included his academic credentials. It got on the Internet minus the name of the UFO journal. And damn if *The New York Times* didn't pick up on it and treat it seriously. And every other newspaper in America trailed right along behind them.

And that was what they used against him. Utterly unprofessional. Bringing disrepute on the institution. As if he had single-handedly kept them from "reaching the next level." He could still hear them spluttering.

The pickup truck rolled up. Rust all over it. Busted

muffler. Oddball bumper stickers. "Keep It Weird." "I Brake For Boiled Peanuts."

A man with wild hair like a mad scientist climbed out. Jake Milroy, the crazed artist in his uniform of brogans and paint-splattered coveralls. Lantern jawed. Bulbous nose and ears sprouting hair.

A studio art professor at the university, Jake was a man of remarkable gifts. Naturally the talentless drones of his department hated him with their daubs flung at canvases. The man was into hallucinogens and when in a trance, he painted scenes not of this world. The bar was decorated with his paintings of the cosmos, infinite space, and night with zillions of glittering stars.

The filthy room seemed to accept the presence of high art. Hanging them was part of Quinn's program of cultural uplift for his hoodlums. Bringing a vein of fantasy, a power of enchantment.

And a lurking fear of what was to come.

"Welcome to our barbarous locale," laughed Quinn.

"Airy vistas and green pleasaunces," Jake said in a fake British accent.

"You mean a pustule that will soon be lanced."

"Should be smashed with a hammer."

Quinn asked the important question. "Is it complete?"

"You bet your sweet ass. The final revelation."

Jake had sought Quinn out one night in a saloon while a summer storm raged outside. Pulled up a stool beside him at the bar.

"Every sham shows there is a reality," he had said cryptically.

Quinn was in the early flush of his meth money. His cut of loot for his first month was greater than a professor's annual salary. He had had no problem buying drinks for an already drunk Milroy as the rain pounded the windows and gusted through the open door.

They talked of their hatred of toadying careerist professors. Killjoys and spoilsports. Eunuch men and the screeching harpies who had gelded them.

Drinks followed drinks. Jake's voice became slurred to the point of incoherence. Until he quite clearly said: "We sensitives know what's about to come down. Even if science is coldly ignoring it."

"And what's that?"

"Nibiru."

Then lay his head on the bar and passed out.

They had been friends ever since.

Jake fought with his creditors, lived off whisky and fried chicken skins, named his daughter Cressida Moon Child Milroy. She was something of a piece of teenage tail, all molten eyes and that emerging teenage sense of woman's elemental power. But of no interest to Quinn. She stared at crystals, did Zen meditation, hatha yoga, and talked to disembodied spirits.

Besides, Quinn knew his intended bride was nearby. A woman of cosmic consequence. Jake said he had known her personally since she was a little kid.

Jake hauled a big tarp-covered painting inside. The gang of bikers actually drew back from the fixity of his crazed stare. They knew him and didn't know him. A friend of Quinn's. The one with the paintings of stellar explosions and black holes. A mushroom eater and glue sniffer. Out of his mind talking in tongues.

He chalked a big circle on the floor, a perfect circle, yet done freehand. A mystic circle to guard against the riffraff. In the middle he set up an easel. Placed a frame upon it and unwrapped the canvas.

Such a painting. A work of human genius. The adolescent girl stood in perfect elegance. You could see the silkiness of her flesh. Her long slender neck. Mouth like a pink bow. A royal blue background deepened the richness of the flesh tones, giving it a perfect three-dimensional look. Eight-pointed star behind her russet head, the symbol of the Sumerian goddess Inanna. The morning and evening star. Ishtar to the Assyrians. One hand lifted a breast, as an offering of milk. The other fist was closed about a knot of reeds. Circular. Almost like a quoit. It symbolized the doorpost to the storehouse of life, all fertility and fruitfulness.

She was a prophesying priestess, a volcano about to erupt, and at the cleft of her thighs, woman's cosmic sexual power. The delta shape of hair. The entry to the cave of fertility. Occult symbols were carved into the golden frame. The signs of the Zodiac. Framing woman in all her lunar phases. Was there a faint glint of amusement in the girl's eyes? Like she knew her superiority?

A long shivering thrill went through Quinn as though he were having an orgasm. Filled with an overwhelming wanting. How her slim body would tremble to his touch. She was his queen and his destiny, and he would worship at the shrine of her body.

The bike gang stood in a kind of catatonia, eyes haunted, unable to move or make a gesture. A rapt, reverent silence.

Jude the meth cook, lips flecked with foam, began barking like a dog. The others joined in, sliding into howls as at the moon.

Perspiration beaded Hog Man's upper lip. "They's comin' back, ain't they? Jes like you said."

"They're coming back alright," said Quinn.

"And she's their queen, ain't she?"

"Yes. And I will breed with her. Only I am worthy."

Quinn took off his blazer and hung it on the back of a chair. Rolled up his sleeve. And slid his hand into the red-hot steel glove. Held it trembling aloft. Feeling no pain.

The men gasped in awe as ever. Stunned by the gulf that separated them, by his mystical powers over burning pain and mutilation.

Quinn placed his trust in this gang of cutthroats because they feared him. They were his wolf pack, his motorized Mongol Horde.

Milroy flinched as Quinn shoved the glove towards his face.

"How the fuck do you do that?" he gasped.

"Tell me her name, It is time I knew."

"Samantha . . . Samantha Fitzhugh."

Quinn rolled the name on his tongue. She would taste of the sweetness of wild honey.

And Quinn would kill anyone who got in his way.

Chapter 4

"You're on top of the Matterhorn?" Samantha said incredulously as she examined the framed photo. Kurt in goggles and a parka, wind-burn on his face.

Kurt shrugged. "I'm Swiss. You have to do that sort of thing."

She was half-thrilled, half-terrified to be in Kurt's home about to meet his parents. And then to find he did something so heroic. She had never really done much of anything. Follow her mother to some dusty digs on Greek islands in the summer. Swim in the Aegean.

"But you look so young in the picture. How old were you?"

"Thirteen."

"No!"

"We did the easy side. We climbed the overhanging face the following year. That's the real challenge. But you have to master it early if you're going to be any kind of climber. Like swimming or riding a horse, put it off and you get scared."

Kurt lived in a Cape Cod style house in a loop of 1930s homes that extended out on a ridge into a green wildwood park. An antique neighborhood, one of the most perfect in the town with its meandering loop of road and ancient trees. The University annually threatened to put big dorms in the park, but the town resisted fiercely.

Chintz armchairs and books and pictures, a hearth with an oak fire set to be lit if it got cold. Everything about it said good taste in the way that college professors never achieved. A life of culture and aesthetics. It smacked of inherited wealth.

And then the parents came. Sam didn't have time to get the jitters because they were so kind.

The mother had a pale complexion, a heart-shaped face and dark hair pulled back that she must have colored. She wore a tailored suit and seemed to exude some unexplained power. When she smiled, it was as if she were seeing into Sam's soul.

Professor Jaeger had short, iron-grey hair. He wore a double-breasted suit and polka-dot blue bow tie. Pocket handkerchief. He radiated calm. Sam had never felt such calm. As though nothing ever ruffled him.

Kurt told his parents all about their day. They exchanged curious looks.

"She doesn't look very poltergeisty," the mother said to Kurt with an amused smile.

"Oh she's not. Not in the least."

"Well, I'm glad to hear that." And to Sam, "Welcome to our home. What is ours is yours."

Samantha sensed a murmuring in her ears. As though something more had been whispered. She shook her head to clear it.

The woman was looking deeply into her eyes. Probing.

The parents drank sherry in the living room while Sam sat next to Kurt outside on a porch swing. The sun went down in a blaze, gilding his blond hair, shaping a halo. And then the light was gone, and she sat in the dark feeling like she was next to her fate, something she couldn't escape, didn't want to escape.

"So what kind of girls generate poltergeist events?" she asked.

"Withdrawn, sullen, moody ones. Usually dreadfully unhappy and filled with . . . um, sexual repression. You seem quite happy and balanced. I can't speak to the sex."

She knew she was blushing. Her face was hot.

He laughed aloud at her discomfort, and she could feel the shake of his shoulder against hers. He shifted, and his thigh touched hers.

"How many college courses are you taking?" she asked to change the subject.

"Two a semester. The dreadful freshman/sophomore courses they make you take that are nothing more than high school. I want to spend as little time in college as possible."

"Really?"

"Football games? Fraternities? Living in those hideous high-rise dorms on the South Campus? That's not me."

"How soon will you be through?"

She listened in amazement as he outlined a program of one year at the University and one year abroad in Zurich. He had advanced placement in French and German, an easy major for a native speaker. Then he would start his doctorate in psychology in Zurich where it was purely a research degree without tedious classes like in the US.

Sam marveled. "You've got everything all planned. I feel . . . I dunno, rudderless."

"Doesn't sound like you at all. I see you going to Antarctica like your mom. Maybe finding some lost civilization from the dawn of creation. From when the earth was on a different axis."

It turned cool so they went inside where the fire had been lit and gave off a comfortable warmth.

There was so much to take in. Sam's eyes lighted on the living room pictures. Well, you couldn't miss them really. The walls were completely filled—frame nearly touching frame—with paintings and drawings of standing stones. Menhirs they were called in Brittany. Dolmens. Megaliths. And many were arranged in circles like Stonehenge. Bronze age astronomy or an expression of the sacred. No one quite knew.

Sam knew all about these because of her mother's archaeology.

They exerted a powerful charm and yet were quite soothing. With their variety and concentration, it was as if the whole house possessed a secret.

"Okay," she said. "I'm going to ask. What is your interest in these ancient monuments?"

"Well, my mum is in an interesting trade. You'll learn about it later. And Dad is a Jungian psychologist. You determine people's personality and their emotional needs by their reaction to symbols."

"Well these certainly get you in the gut, and I've had my mom's artifacts around all my life. Some of those do send emotional ripples through you no matter how many times you look at them."

"I would say your knives are powerful symbols. They hold a power unto themselves that radiates."

As Samantha helped set the table, Mrs. Jaeger reassured her. "My dear, dealing with other people's food is always difficult. But we Swiss are all meat and potatoes. So you shouldn't be alarmed."

The dining room was dominated by a mahogany table with a vase of long-stemmed red roses. An oil painting by the Swiss artist Arnold Bocklin of two trolls fighting with boulders and tree trunks. Paintings of Alpine forests on the edge of black lakes with mountains like teeth in the background.

They ate what the Swiss call a raclette. A variety of sausage slices called charcuterie, boiled potatoes, carrots, leeks. Melted cow's milk raclette cheese poured over it. A golden Savoy wine. Just a small glass for Sam and Kurt.

"Welcome to our clan," said Prof. Jaeger. "We'll call this your official induction."

When Sam sipped the wine, she noticed that odor and flavor came together and reinforced each other.

Cheese ran off her chin. She dabbed at it with a cloth napkin feeling like a total slob, as if she had no table manners. They used paper towels in her home.

Prof. Jaeger gave off such an extraordinary charm. Samantha listened in amazement as he explained the core of his subject, running through the Jungian archetypes that symbolized the female personality. Queen, lover, mistress of useful crafts, huntress, mother, maiden.

"That's it? That's all women?"

"Oh there are some demons and sorceresses and

temptresses. But most women fall onto the first list. That's why behavioral psychologists don't like the Jungians. We make it all too simple."

"But how?"

"Each individual has an overriding primary need that shapes her behavior. Power and status. Romantic love. Achieving useful things. The society of women. Child birth and rearing. And the sad child who never grows up remains an eternal maiden.

"You determine your most important need and pursue it. Do anything else and you're miserable. Fall into all the neuroses that the behavioralists so love to classify. If you follow your heart, everything is fine."

Samantha's brain was all awhirl wondering what her primary need was. Girls wanted all these things in a way.

"You want to do useful things," the mother purred. "Great intellectual achievement. And in your sub-archetype you're a huntress. The virgin goddess."

Sam gaped at her. Mrs. Jaeger had spoken to her directly, but it was as though an elusive frontier separated them. As though the woman was behind a veil that kept her in a pale obscurity.

"Are you serious? You know just like that?"

"Well, I could observe you a tad longer before coming to such a conclusion. But I'm pretty sure I'm correct." She gave an approving smile as though this was the most perfect archetype one could be.

Rather than stripped bare, Sam felt flattered. As though for the first time someone understood her. It was only later that she realized she had said nothing aloud. The woman had read her mind.

After dinner they listened to a recording of classical music, Francis Poulenc, a clarinet sonata which gave off a kind of glad sorrow.

Sam marveled at the scene. So many of her classmates' parents were divorced. She had never even known her father. And here she was in this warm little family tableau where everyone seemed to be totally loving and the best of friends.

No need for speech. Thoughts just flowing among them like telepathy.

She looked into the fire until the shifting flames made her woozy. Then she focused on bits of the room. A Persian carpet that depicted hunting and court scenes, a tree populated by falcons. Deep carved vegetal designs framing the door.

An hypnotic thread ran through the room as though it was weaving a magic net that Sam was only too happy to be caught in. In some vague and unspecified way, her entire life had changed.

After twenty minutes, the father cut off the music, said don't want to make this tedious. And besides children have homework needs.

Kurt's and her bedrooms were at the upstairs front of the house with a bathroom in between. Not wanting any embarrassing conflict over the bath, Sam put on her nightgown, brushed her teeth, ran the water furiously as she peed.

She sat reading US history for an hour, having a lot of trouble concentrating. There was so much on her mind. The flag falling over. The knife hanging in the air. The incredible boy just on the other side of the bathroom. The magic of his personality.

She went through the tiny bathroom and rapped lightly on his door. Peeked in.

He was doing isometrics, one straight arm supporting him with his body forming a triangle with the floor. His shirt was off. Muscles tense.

He didn't budge an inch. "This is how I study. I try to concentrate ferociously in class. Then go over it in my head at night."

"I'm sorry. I didn't mean to disturb you."

A half-smile curving his lips, he looked her steadily in the eye and seemed to be tugging at her with his will. "Not at all," he replied.

She thought, I . . . I would do whatever you wanted . . .

Sam broke eye contact, said goodnight, closed the door to her room quietly and stood with her back against it, her heart pounding.

God she would give it up to him. Give him anything he wanted, and she hadn't even kissed him. She hadn't kissed any boy.

She cut off the light and lay down in bed. Her emotions seemed intensified. She could actually feel her eyelashes flutter.

She lay in bed imagining their limbs intertwined. Their bodies writhing with the passion of helpless desire. The total anguish of desire. What was it like?

The night grew colder, a watery moonlight filtering through the window. The park ravine filled with a ghostly mist. The dense trees sighed like a distant sea. They made her feel very tired.

A light still showed under the door.

My gosh, was Kurt still in that isometric trance?

A lone owl hooted.

And she fell asleep.

■ ■ ■

"Why are you doing this to me?" croaked the old woman in the cold, ghostly dark.

"For sheer pleasure," said Quinn from the darkness at the edge of the fire. He was wearing a navy blue Melton wool overcoat, notch collar, triple back vent.

The sun had been down for two hours and a sliver of moon was rising above the black wall of pines deep in the woods behind the motorcycle club.

Sybyl Colfax—Dr. Sybyl Colfax, if you please—was tied between two saplings that were bent over and staked to the ground. When the ropes were cut, the trees would spring up and yank her arms and legs in opposite directions tearing her to shreds.

She always was a troll and now was even worse. She was virtually bald, her skull showing through wisps of blue rinse hair. Eyebrows painted on crookedly. Lipstick smeared outside her mouth.

She had evoked some arcane rule of procedure to actually come out of retirement so she could lead the vote against his tenure. She didn't have to do it. She did it for sheer meanness.

Seven years ago. He could remember like yesterday how they gave him the letter in his box. Didn't have the guts to face him. Not a one of them.

You have been denied tenure. You will have one more year to teach. We will do what we can to find you placement at another college. A much smaller college . . . more suited to your level of research.

It had been simple to carry her off. She lived alone, house in a heavily wooded lot. Fed by Meals on Wheels. The neighbors ignored her. She was a nasty old bat after all. As he well knew.

"I've been retired for years," she protested. "I . . . I haven't harmed you."

"You don't even remember do you?"

"I can't remember. My memory fails me. Who are you?" She sounded desperate.

"Hogging the department travel money for your little trip every summer to Ireland. All your so-called research that never got published. While no matter how many articles I did, it was never enough. Or not in the right journals. Or not cited by enough other authors."

"Our standards were rigorous but fair. The demands of academic excellence continued to rise. We couldn't sit dead in the water."

Quinn snorted. He knew from firsthand accounts how she had been so red-faced adamant before the big tenure committee. The one with all the biologists and sociologists and all the other dipshit-ists on it.

She had gotten a unanimous vote against him in the

history department. And she wanted another at the next level so the provost would have no weasel room. Quinn would have to go down. She would brook no disagreement.

It was reported that at the meeting she was virtually levitating in her blinding rage. As though his very existence on the earth were an affront to scholarship, good manners, and the consumer price index.

The bikers were all getting hammered on a variety of beer, whisky, and speed. The whole interchange was over their heads, but they took everything Quinn did as part of his awesome mystery. And they always enjoyed a good killing.

Quinn's voice purred. "There were those on the big committee who could smell a vendetta. Some even held human feelings towards me. They knew you were leading the charge to get me shit-canned. They waffled. They demurred. They raised points of order.

"And then you produced your trump card. You brought out the Nibiru article. Accused me of deliberately hoaxing the sacred *New York Times*. What greater blot on the university than a professor with a sense of humor. And to smear egg on the face of the *Times*. Unforgivable. Why it's the 'paper of record.'"

Her face changed at that moment as though a mask had slipped away. Or it was made of putty that had been reshaped. The deep throaty laugh that emerged was soul-petrifying. The voice of a demon.

"I couldn't let you stay. You were onto it all. You were too close."

Quinn was stunned at her transformation, at what she was saying. "Too close to what?"

"We thought you had somehow penetrated The Circle. Oh the frantic searching for leaks. The encrypted email exchanges on four continents. Pure hysteria. Utter frenzy. But no, you had arrived there all on your own."

She gave a throaty chuckle. "Sure. Kill me. I'm old. And it's a blessed release next to what is coming for you and all the rest."

"What? What are you—?"

That was when Skeeter came drunkenly stumbling forward waving a machete. "Let's get this show on the road!" he shouted.

And slashed the ropes.

"No, you idiot!" Quinn yelled.

But it was too late.

Chapter 5

Samantha and Nasar sat on the school steps in a brief moment after lunch. Nasar wore a t-shirt that said "But for the police and the laws of physics, I'd be invincible." Hush-puppy suede shoes with trousers too short. He was still growing and slept a lot but he could look through a math book and just say "yes" like he had totally grasped it all.

Nasar closed his advanced placement physics text. Sighed thoughtfully.

"What is it like being a girlfriend?" he asked.

"How should I know?" Samantha shrugged. "I've never been one." She shrugged again, put up her hands. "Never even been close."

"You and Kurt?"

She gave him a narrow look. "I spent the night at his house. That's all. Separate rooms. His parents were there and everything."

"It's all over school that you two are an item. Wild speculation about how far you let him go."

"Oh good grief. Do I deserve this?"

Nasar lay back on the steps. "I don't imagine I'll ever have a girlfriend," he said a bit wistfully.

"Well maybe not high-school style. But one day your parents will bring a girl from India for an arranged marriage, and she'll be so beautiful everyone will be totally jealous."

He sounded surprised. "Really?"

"Of course."

"Oh, she'll be an accountant," he scoffed. "Or working on a doctorate in nuclear physics."

"Well, what would you talk about if she weren't? Reality TV? Her new layered haircut?"

Nasar looked thoughtful. "You have a valid point. You always are quite astute, Samantha."

The bell rang and the kids settled noisily into the US History class. Ms. Rooney came in slowly as though wading through snow. She seemed unnaturally calm. Like she was on meds.

"Master suite, master bedroom are terms that are both racist and sexist," she pronounced in a monotone. It seemed to be her talking point for the day.

"Racist?" said Emerson indignantly. "Where do I sleep? The slave cabins? I can't be the master and have my own bedroom?"

"And what," posed petite, beautiful Drusana Shelley, being a real provocateur smartass, "if you're a real mistress? Like a sugar baby, and he's keeping you in luxury? Wouldn't it be a master suite then?"

Dru was Sam's best friend. Also the other black kid in the class. Mixed-race. One assumed. Father unknown. Mother's skin quite dark, but Dru was the color of café-au-lait. Coffee with milk. Violet-blue eyes.

Ms. Rooney stared at them balefully. Too tranked to get angry. Her eyes roamed the room, rested on a big FedEx box on her desk. It was open, filled with manila envelopes. The genealogy results had come.

The project had nothing to do with US History and everything to do with Ms. Rooney's relentless campaign against racism.

That is when she wasn't extolling locavore food and bemoaning society's failure to put enough money in food stamps so the poor could buy nourishing veggies at farmers' markets.

For this project, she wanted to demonstrate that they all came out of Africa. Everyone had done a saliva swab and sent it off for DNA testing.

DNA composes the genes inherited from parents. Mitochondria is a tiny structure in cells that help them use oxygen. mtDNA is inherited only from the mother and can be used to trace maternal ancestry in an unbroken line for thousands of years.

All people on earth can be traced back to one of thirty-six "clan" mothers. And those women can be traced to an African Eve about 200,000 years ago. And her ancestry could presumably be traced back millions of years. Of course the literature was at great pains to explain there was no such thing as Adam and Eve even though the evidence sure seemed to point to it.

Emerson handed out the envelopes, and everyone tore them open to see what clan mother they were descended from. General chatter broke out.

"You see," Ms. Rooney pronounced. "There is no such thing as race."

Everyone looked at Federico's black La Raza t-shirt with the clenched fist. He was a sawed-off little firebrand who was perpetually vowing violent war against the Anglos. That is when he wasn't openly weeping over a blond girl from Florida he had met on a family vacation in Majorca.

His father was in the university Spanish Department. As gentle and nice a man as you could meet. A specialist in the love poetry of Garcia Lorca. In class he switched between two pairs of glasses, and at home had taken in about thirty stray dogs. His wife made pottery.

Sam looked up to find Ms. Rooney riveted on her.

"And Samantha, what is yours?"

"Mine . . . mine says 'unknown mtDNA strand. Send second sample.'"

"Yes!" hissed Ms. Rooney, punching her fist in the air.

"Yes? Yes what?" Sam stammered.

Ms. Rooney was actually bouncing in her chair. Her eyes bored into Samantha.

"Yes I knew it! I knew it! I knew there was something wrong with you!"

Then she had the knife, that familiar paring knife, out of the long drawer on her desk. She got up and moved carefully around the desk, keeping touch with one hand as though fearful to lose its protection. Her voice hissed like a snake.

"I want to cut your legs and lick the blood from them."

She took two and then three steps across the space towards Samantha.

Sam stood up reflexively. "You want to what?"

Ms. Rooney took another step. Then another.

"I . . . want . . . to . . . lick . . . the blood . . ."

She lunged. But she was incredibly easy to dodge. Sam just feinted to one side and then back. And Kurt was up and there.

He grabbed Rooney's wrist with one hand and just held it. Not hard. Not painfully. Just firmly.

Ms. Rooney started screaming she was being attacked. "They've got me! They're all over me! Help! For God's sake get them off! There are too many!"

And in an instant, there was Ms. Frissel from across the hall. What a gargoyle. Slobber coming out of the corners of her mouth. Shouting, "Unhand that woman!" like someone from an old vaudeville drama.

Kurt let go. And stepped back.

Now Ms. Frissel was running down the hall shouting for help. Flat feet slapping. Voice cracking with her exertion.

From the opposite direction, Principal Peevey came running up the hall, necktie up in his face, nearly knocking her to the ground in passing. Held to the door frame as he swung into our class.

"What is the meaning of this? What are you—? What is this—?"

Authority totally in a flap.

Ms. Rooney dropped back behind her desk waving the ridiculous little knife in the air. Ranting about defending herself.

"They were coming for me! Coming for me I tell you! Both of them!"

The principal was gathering his indignant stance. Put his hands on his hips and glowered at the class. "What is going on here? Who is going to explain to me? Hmm? What is behind this? I want to know right now."

"She's completely losing it," said Kurt firmly. "Everyone in the class saw what happened."

"They're all lying!" shrieked Ms. Rooney. "They're all out to get me! They've gotten together and cooked up this story!"

"That's preposterous," Samantha argued.

The principal's gut instinct was to back his teacher. Except when he found it convenient to roll over on one. He actually stroked his chin as though lost in contemplation. Which way to go.

"I've seen instances where students set out to get a teacher," he said sternly. "A kind of pack behavior takes hold."

"What is this travesty?" demanded Emerson, slapping both palms down on his desk. "Now we're all being accused? Am I going to have to call my father?" There was an edge of a threat in his voice.

"Um, no. No. Everything's fine," the principal soothed. "Of course not. Of course you don't call him."

"If this interferes in any way with my getting into Princeton!"

Principal Peevey was seriously backpedaling now. "No, no. That's our top priority with you."

Samantha almost laughed. Being black and an intellect—wearing your pants up on your waist with a belt—got Emerson a free pass on pretty much everything in a liberal cocoon town like theirs. It was like being the rich kid somewhere else.

Emerson wouldn't be mollified. "The woman's *non compos mentis*. Lick the blood off Samantha's legs. I threw up in my mouth when I heard that."

"This is . . . this is all going to be resolved," the principal reassured in a jittery voice. "There's no reason for any of this to go outside the school."

"That maladroit mess Rooney. Why does she have to bring her LBGTQ obsessions into the classroom? Isn't Samantha supposed to be free of sexual harassment?"

The principal was practically whimpering. "Yes, yes," he agreed. "It will be dealt with. I promise."

■ ■ ■

Boo introduced himself to Samantha Fitzhugh as she came out of the gym still in her fencing costume, a bag with foils and mask slung over her shoulder. He was nervous and put on his brisk, all-business manner.

"Boo Radley?" said Samantha. "Like in *To Kill a Mockingbird*?"

He laughed. "I'm amazed. You're one of the few people to understand. I got saddled with it in prep school, and it's kind of stuck. I'm actually Townsend Radley IV, but that's pretty pompous, even from where I come from."

He always liked to get in a prep school reference. Let her know he came from a proper background. It worked wonders down South where the girls were so unaccustomed to it. Up North you might run into flak from feminists and social-justice bitches. Call you "preppy" as an insult.

"I can walk whichever way you're going," he offered.

"Well, I'm not sure where I'm going. What's on your mind?"

Was she giving him a slanting gaze? Was it meant as flirtatious?

He glanced past her at the other members of the fencing team coming out of the gym. A weedy bunch. Geeks and creeps and Jews. God what a sport. None of them seemed to be paying any attention to him.

He had been watching the girl in the gym for a half hour. All slim lines, curves, and rippling thigh muscles. When she would take her mask off and laugh she was positively radiant.

He found himself drawn in despite his contempt for the sport. Clashing blades, great leaps. When she lunged, her right tit would come down to kiss her bent thigh.

He knew her fencing jacket had metal cups to protect her bosoms. Imagined her shivering as he unsnapped it and pulled it back over her shoulders, pressing his chest against those twin globes. As he kissed her gently, her hair would come loose and tumble down in flowing auburn curls.

He was trying to be decorous, keep his lust contained. Told her he was her broker. She had visited him once with her mother. The little office on Chastain Street. Dinky nature of it was deceptive. He handled big accounts. Mostly foreign so he didn't need a lot of space for walk-in customers.

She was looking at him gravely. A teenager in the presence of adult authority. He was wearing a suit of course, prep school rep tie, expensive shoes from Bally of Switzerland.

"Why do they deal with you instead of New York or . . . I don't know, Chicago?"

He tried to hide his shock. She had seen straight through him. No one else did that. They just sucked up his bilge.

"Well . . . I travel a lot. People I know up North introduce me. Round Hill Club in Greenwich. The Union League in New York. You form a network. Most of the Europeans, the Latin Americans want someone who can take an unhurried look at their investments. They don't like being hustled."

Of course it was more lies. His father had belonged to those clubs and his grandfather. Both of them dead now. Boo had tried for the Union and been blackballed. His father had bilked a number of the members.

God he wanted to kiss her throat. He'd kiss her feet, her belly-button.

Boo rubbed the back of his neck. His hand was trembling. Took a deep breath.

"I know I'm violating every fiduciary rule . . . do you know what that means?"

"The big word?" She laughed. "Yes, it's a relationship of trust where you owe a hundred percent loyalty. The sort of thing brokers have with their clients. Like between you and my mom." She paused, made a deprecating face. "Sorry. We're taking the SAT soon. Am I right about the word?"

"Yes . . . yes. I didn't learn it until b-school. I was in business school here at the university before I . . . yes, you're right, it was a big word we had to learn in business law. That jerk-wad baldheaded law professor! The grief he put us through. Daily preparation. My God. Did he think we were out in the private sector?"

"Well, you are now, aren't you? Isn't this called 'working for a living?'"

"Some people don't call it work. If you have the feel for the way the market's going . . . and I have to confess I had something of a reputation as a stock picker as an undergrad. Could out-guess the S&P just sitting on the can in the morning. Whups. Sorry to sound vulgar. But there was some talk of me actually joining the faculty."

There was no such thing. But curiously, for a doofus Southern state university, the MBA program was nationally ranked in the top ten. He had somehow gotten accepted, he never could figure out how. Maybe they thought his family would give a donation.

Signed up for the law course thinking it would be the easiest. And there was that evil bastard who had taught him as an undergrad. Just flat failed his ass this time, and an "F" put you out of the program.

"Well, those who can't do, teach," she said. "Isn't that the old saying?"

He drew a deep breath. Those soft pink lips. He wanted . . . he wanted to kiss them. A long hungry kiss.

Did she have hungers? You always read in the lads' mags that women had emotions that would start to flow uncontrollably. Any man who could channel them would have total power.

He cleared his throat. "What I need to talk to you about is . . . well . . . you are a very wealthy young lady. And at your age, you need to begin to understand the responsibility . . . you see, all this money mysteriously flows into your account once a year and your mother doesn't do anything with it."

He suddenly stopped. Looked at her intently. Her eyes . . . were otherworldly . . .

"I . . . I want to touch you," he whispered. Afterwards he couldn't believe he had said it. A total compulsion. Madness. Counter-productive. Self-destructive. But irresistible.

She stepped back, startled. "Uh, no. What for?"

"To . . . to see if you're real."

Color had come into her cheeks. Her eyes hashed a warning he couldn't grasp. He was too intoxicated.

She would relax when she realized how gentle he could be. Her hands trying to push him off would slowly shift to a caress. Her hurried breathing would show the urgency mounting in her.

"No. Absolutely not."

"I just want to see . . . your fingernails."

"What? Are you crazy?"

He couldn't endure it any longer. He closed the space between them.

She leaped back, flung her bag down. At the same instant she drew out what looked like a walking stick. Cleared three feet of steel from it in a flashing arc.

A sword cane poised inches from his chest.

"Now listen to me . . ." he began angrily. And like a complete idiot snatched at the blade.

She twisted and drew it back smoothly. A searing pain ran through him. It was sharp as a razor!

He screamed, fell to his knees flinging blood as he waved his hand in agony.

She stammered in fear at what she had done. "Oh, God, I'm sorry! I didn't mean . . . I really didn't mean!"

"Ohshitfuckinggod!" Boo wailed. He had never imagined such pain.

She snatched up her bag and ran.

"I'm sorry. I'm sorry!" she yelled back over her shoulder.

Boo was weeping with the pain. "Make it stop!" he wailed.

Chapter 6

Quinn was so furious he wanted to just tear apart everything in the old biddy's house. Rip out the walls even. But he knew he had to search cautiously. Make a pile of things and you'd overlook something.

That dumbass Skeeter cutting the ropes, he fumed. Sybyl Colfax yanked into pieces and he hadn't even gotten to savor it, and she was telling him things. What did she mean by "The Circle?"

The place was a total mess. Disgusting the way old people lived. Newspapers. Dirty dishes. Dirty cups and glasses. Boxes from Meals on Wheels.

And a cat of course. Filthy litter-box in the corner. Quinn would like to have drop-kicked the beast into the ceiling. Instead he poured out some sour milk and opened a can of wet food. Couldn't have it acting up while he searched. It had been starving for days and was actually grateful. Rubbed up against his leg and purred.

Here was her office. Built-in bookcases loaded with books in helter-skelter order. The detritus of a professor's life. We all turn to dust, but Quinn wasn't about to leave rubbish like this behind for others to heave out. His life wouldn't be buried like that. Pointless scholarship on the trash heap of history.

He turned his eyes slowly about the room. Some heavily tooled leather-covered books. No one made them anymore. Myths of Ireland. A nineteenth century oil of Irish peasant cottages, the sea, and scudding clouds. An antique clock ticked softly. Some postcards stuck in the edges of a mirror. Kilclooney Dolman. Tory Island. That was where Sybyl used to go for her alleged research. That chunk of the Irish Republic that wraps around Northern Ireland to the west. County Donegal. The forgotten county.

The file cabinets were unlocked. He went through the drawers methodically. Confused bills and correspondence from Medicare. Photocopies of journal articles dating to the Xerox days. Good grief, even faded stuff from carbon paper.

He racked his brain. She was always taking the grant money to go to Ireland. Doing "research" that somehow never got published. What was she doing there? At the time he thought she was just taking a series of vacations.

And then he came across his file: Quinn Shaw— tenure vote. He thumbed through it.

List of his publications with derogatory remarks beside each one in her crabbed handwriting.

Acceptance rate way too high.
Not a tier-one journal. Is it even peer reviewed?
This has page charges. It's virtually a vanity press.

Then there was a letter with what were talking points for tearing him to shreds.

Unprofessional must be stressed repeatedly. Childish practical jokes on a major newspaper. Mockery of his own subject matter. Scholarship has never been first rate. Theories out of the mainstream. Some major questions of originality, perhaps even plagiarism. No presence in the wider academy. Unknown internationally. A virtual nonentity.

As long as he is banished from academe he will not be taken seriously. He can join the Cassandras and cranks of the world giving dire warning of UFOs. Oh perhaps he will eke out an existence as an academic vagabond. A series of adjunct teaching positions. Maybe a technical college. But the journals will not publish him. We can certainly see to that.

And so she had thrown the chum in the water and brought the sharks circling.

Quinn laughed harshly. That people this wicked could exist was totally plausible to him. Anyone who has lived in the world of college teaching knows this to be true. And so they had cold-bloodedly sealed his fate.

Their malice is boundless. They come together in casual savagery like the boys in *Lord of the Flies*. My scholarship is more profound than yours and you are a stupid-head and you get out and go die.

He could picture them in conclave all shouting and gesturing like a Soviet show trial. But now he was judge, jury, and executioner. He'd show them death, and therein would lie his unspeakable triumph.

He found a letter from someone at Trinity College. Dublin.

"We rely upon you to achieve our objective. It is imperative that Shaw be silenced."

Quinn was dumbfounded. He had interested people outside the university. The Circle was that widespread. Then he found some fuzzy photos of humanoid-looking creatures coming out of water on a rocky coastline. He guessed that was what he was seeing. It was black and white photography, maybe even from a much earlier time. Blurred like a Loch Ness monster photo.

Quinn thought he heard something, peered, and listened. Went back to the file.

"Find anything interesting?"

Quinn whipped around to see an old man hunched over a metal walker shuffling into the room. Dome bald head and goggle glasses with his eyes swimming in the lenses. Incredibly, he held a medium-barrel, maybe .38 caliber revolver, with crabbed fingers along with the rubber grip of his walker.

Quinn let out his breath. The spectacle was about as unthreatening as the sight of a gun could be.

"Sybyl's gone to visit her sister," he ad libbed. "She asked me to feed the cat."

The stranger gave him a long stare. "The sister in Ohio?"

"Yes."

"That's funny. Because she doesn't have a sister." His eyes squinted and his voice had that sly old man tone of "I'm quicker'n you, you young whelp."

Quinn snorted. "I got the request third-hand. I do what I can to help the sick and shut-ins."

"You're Quinn Shaw, aren't you." Again the tone was certain. As though he had out-thought him several chess moves ahead. "She said you'd probably be coming around. To keep an eye peeled for you."

"I'm afraid you have me at a disadvantage. Are you a retired professor?"

"Irish Literature." A big drool of slobber ran down the corner of his mouth. He wiped at it with his gun hand.

A light bulb came on. "Tobias Smollett. You wrote *Lord Dunsany, Lost Worlds, and the Celtic Twilight.*"

Smollett, as indeed it was, made a gummy smile of pleasure at his recognition. "We wrote books in my day. None of this endless churning out journal articles. You spent your career and produced the one opus sometimes long after you had retired, but it went on a shelf in a real library and became real knowledge. Not this 'in the cloud' horse pucky of today."

Quinn almost warmed to the man. Then he remembered that old Toby had been on the campus-wide committee for his tenure vote. Sat there with an insincere smile plastered on his face while Quinn made his presentation. The man was in his seventies even then. Still teaching herds of bored undergrads. Had questioned him pointedly about . . . about what exactly?

And now his cackling old voice rose in diabolic mockery. "What do you do now? Junior college? Public high school?"

Quinn's muscles went taut. "I am the business manager of a fraternal order." He almost sounded huffy.

Smollett's face was radiating malevolence. "It's a good thing they got rid of you. You would never have made a decent historian."

Quinn gave him a violent backhand blow that bounced him off the wall. The pistol clattered to the floor.

■ ■ ■

Samantha could barely stop herself from bawling as she told Kurt and his parents what had happened. She covered her face with her hands. Wiped her eyes repeatedly.

Mrs. Jaeger rested a hand on Sam's arm. "Well, I don't hear any police sirens. I suspect it's not as bad as you imagine."

But it was every bit as bad. Sam knew how sharp the sword was. Remembered vividly the slashed red mess of his hand.

All the same the woman's touch made her feel so calm. Made the blood course smoothly and warmly through her veins. Like a glowing vision of peace and perfection was shimmering before her eyes.

Sam looked at her slantwise. She was wearing a grey wool dress and black pearls. She seemed like such a gracious lady. Like someone from a vanished social order.

Mrs. Jaeger got up, taking her hand away, but leaving Sam still feeling calm. "Well, perhaps we need to close the curtains tonight. Nothing definite. Just a feeling."

She walked briskly through the house drawing the curtains across the windows. The outside world was totally blotted out.

"They're blackout curtains," Kurt explained. "What you would use in a war to prevent light-attracting enemy bombers."

Sam raised her face. "Why do you have them in your house?"

"Well . . ." He hesitated. "It's mom's business. It provides a minor protection from spying eyes. And it . . . it keeps out psychic attacks."

"What?"

"I'll have to explain it to you when we're alone. It's hard to believe."

He put a hand on her shoulder. Squeezed. Sam felt this incredible restorative. Like a tonic. Or the best massage ever. Were these people magicians?

Car headlights appeared outside then were turned off. Sam looked out to see a red Thunderbird. Cherry Stobbs, head cheerleader and all around bitch, was tripping up the walk.

Kurt answered the doorbell ring.

"Kurt, I need to talk to you," she said in her perky little voice.

He invited her in. She smiled sweetly at Sam. Saccharine sweetly. "Hello, Samantha. I heard you were a guest here. How interesting that is. Everyone's talking about it."

She contrived to give Sam a look that said she was so utterly beneath her contempt.

Sam made no reply.

Cherry's smug gaze passed over Sam's head. She blinked and her eyes went wide. She put her hand to her mouth in alarm. It was like a hatch had been opened deep in her brain and forgotten fears crawled out.

She spun around in a circle. "Omigod, what are these pictures?"

She was staring at the menhirs and stone circles, and she was aghast. She shivered. They were actually affecting her emotionally. And not in a nice way. She hugged her elbows.

"You've seen them before," Kurt said, puzzled.

"I know I must have. And yet I swear I haven't. I was thinking of other things at the time I guess."

"They're pretty harmless, Cherry."

"Please, Kurt, can we take a walk? I can't seem to think with these . . . *staring* at me. It's just too creepy."

"This is my home," said Kurt. "It's how we live." There was something serious there. Like he was challenging her to dislike how he lived.

"I know. I'm sorry. I just feel like I'm going to cry." She put her face in her hands. Gave a faint sob. Was it fake?

Ordinarily Sam would have pronounced it a total fake. But something was getting to Cherry. She was not her normally perky in-control self. The bright flame of her self-confidence had been snuffed out.

Cherry tugged at Kurt's hand. Drew him outside. He didn't look back at Sam in any sort of explanation.

"Put your arm around me," she said. "I'm cold."

Sam sat there with Mrs. Jaeger feeling utterly crushed. She knew she was nothing to Kurt. Just a charity case he had taken under his wing. The little girl whose mother ran off at unexpected times. The Fitzhughs who lived in jumble and squalor.

Time passed. A clock dinged. Sam tried to concentrate on her book.

What were they doing out there?

"I imagine they're being hormonal teenagers," Mrs. Jaeger said. She gave one of her incredibly conclusive smiles.

Sam thought, Oh God she read my mind. What was whirling there that she could see?

"I'm sorry. Please excuse me. I've got to do homework." Her tone held a faint desperation.

"We should all go read," said Mrs. Jaeger decisively.

Sam took the stairs two at a time.

Of course she knew what they did. Kids had been talking about next to nothing but sex since sixth grade. Some much earlier because they came from intellectual families. Then sex ed started in seventh grade. They showed it to them. Diagrams. Condoms on cucumbers. Oral sex demonstrations. The creeps who loved to do that. Leering at the students.

Cherry was down there in her cute little T-bird blowing him with her cute little painted mouth. Face flushed, voice incoherent.

It made Sam so furious and jealous and disgusted all balled up in one. She punched the pillow. She tried to read but found herself incredibly sleepy.

When she woke in a daze, someone had turned the light off in her room. She fell back asleep and dreamed the Jaegers were beside her bed. She could feel their physical presence. Opened her eyes and saw them there, their faces swimming into focus.

Mrs. Jaeger sat down on the bed, stroked Sam's face.

"It's all right," she soothed. "There's nothing to worry

about. He has no real interest in her. She's a little love god-dess. Every boy, every man will be *the one,* until she finds the next one, and the next one after that."

Sam rubbed her eyes. When she opened them again they were both gone like wraiths. Had they even been there?

Chapter 7

Boo was being prepped for surgery—lying on the bed in the curtained off area, IV in his arm—when Chirburg called.

"The fuck's happened to you?"

Boo was filled with painkillers and was feeling pretty blasé. "Do you have some new method of spying on me?"

"The hospital put in a claim. Wanted to make sure your health insurance was in force. Brokers come and go with such regularity they've learned to be careful."

"I got mugged."

Chirburg snorted.

Boo could imagine his condescending lecture. Mean streets of Brooklyn. Rough high school. Learned to take care of himself.

"You know if you're not able to do the job, you might want to retire."

"Fortunately, it was my left hand. Soon's I'm out of here I'll be back fishing for whales."

"I can't believe what a pussy you are."

"Yes, I'm sure you would have stomped them blind-folded and with your hands bound behind your back."

"You know I was a Navy SEAL."

Boo paused. "No, I didn't know that. I appreciate you sharing such wondrous details."

"When you were throwing balls around with a stick with a little net on it, I was kicking ass big time. Under water demolition. SEA-AIR-LAND. The works."

"Do tell. Did you serve with Thomas Magnum or Mitch from *Baywatch?*"

"Are you gettin' . . . what'cha callit? Sarcastic on me?"

"Perish the thought."

"You butt-fuckin' loser."

He hung up the phone.

Anesthesiologist came in all smiles. Told him what drug they were using. Asked his full name and date of birth.

Boo got a warm feeling all through him. He was following a thread out of a labyrinth. He could feel damp stone walls. Stone fitted perfectly together without mortar as ancient people built. Hand over hand he went along the thread. A faint light in the distance glowed brighter and brighter.

The image of Samantha was swimming through the haze. Her eyes showed golden as though lit by the light behind her.

She wore a gauzy dress which slid slowly to a puddle at her feet. She ran her hands down her naked body. Her breasts seemed swollen as though filled with milk. There was a distinct mole on her left breast.

He reached to touch her with shaking hands.

Overwhelming sorrow filled her voice. "I didn't mean to do this," she said. "You frightened me."

"I know. I'm sorry. I deserved it."

"Nibiru," she whispered. "Nibiru."

The nurses paid no attention to what Boo was mumbling. People talked gibberish as they went under.

■ ■ ■

"Damn your eyes!" screamed Tobias Smollett. His feeble fists beat the floor.

He was so frail, Quinn didn't even need to bind the man. Just smack him across the face if he tried to get up.

Quinn had stones between two of the old fart's toes, twisted them with the handle of a spoon in a thick rubber band. Tightening. The pain was excruciating.

"I wasn't good enough to dwell among the oh-so-learned beings of the Academy. You smirking at me like you were some fucking index of civilization just before you cast the blackball that heaved me out into the gutter."

"We had to maintain the highest standards in scholarship," Smollett protested. "We're a Southern Ivy. We couldn't see you making the sustained effort of scholarship required."

"Why did you care? You just now told me you were a defender of the old ways. The leisurely life of contemplation. The magnum opus at the mellow end of life."

He had him there. The old man blinked at a glazed blur of Quinn. His glasses had fallen off leaving him virtually blind. His eyes ran with tears.

"Were you part of 'The Circle?'" Quinn demanded. "Were you afraid I was getting too close?"

Smollett stared in naked horror. "I . . . I . . ."

"That was two questions. Answer them one at a time. Were you part of 'The Circle'?"

"I don't . . . don't under . . . stand . . ."

Quinn gave the spoon a vicious twist, and Smollett squealed until it ended in a strangled croak. He had fainted.

In frustration, Quinn bound Smollett's hands with duct tape and began searching the room again. He could spend years going through a house of rubbish like this.

"If I were Colonel Mustard," he muttered, "would I beat him to death with a lead pipe?"

Then he had an inspiration. He took down the Irish painting, and there behind it was a wall safe.

Chapter 8

"Mom is psychic," explained Kurt.

It was after school, and he walked beside Samantha in the wooded park down the steep hill to where a small creek meandered. The ground was uneven with roots and rocks. He wore an orange backpack with some of her knives in it and the top of a shoebox.

"It's hard to miss," said Sam.

"Really? It goes right past most people. And if you slip up and tell them, they're totally skeptical. I mean they can get angry at the idea like you're trying to hoax them out of money."

"When she put her hand on me I went all calm. It was just her hand, but it was like warm arms were enfolding me."

"She can do that. I've seen her calm people when they're in a manic frenzy."

"Plus she read my mind."

"Really? About what?"

She met his gaze briefly. "Oh nothing I want to share. She just did."

Kurt gave her a curious look. "As a kid I just assumed it was normal. Even traveling with my parents to the dolmen sites. It wasn't until I was maybe six that I realized we were different."

"What was it you said you'd tell me about your mom's business? You said you'd tell me when we were alone."

He looked thoughtful, then stopped. His gaze swept around the woods as if verifying they were alone. Then he let his eyes settle on hers. "Mom works for some secret part of the government. It sounds crazy to say the CIA. But that's the secret part so it must be. She's not a spy or anything that I know of."

"What does she do?"

"Psychic research. Science scoffs at it, but governments have never given up probing. Trying to find some truth. Or whether it could be useful for espionage or war or mind control."

Sam felt an odd tremor in an eyelid.

They walked on in the deep rich silence of nature that isn't really silence but birdsong and chattering squirrels.

Down along the creek, Kurt set down the backpack and laid out the three knives on the canvas. He walked down ten yards to a Basswood tree.

"Just kind of toss it lightly. See what happens. Focus on a particular spot on the tree."

Kurt stood well out of the way.

Sam had looked at a knife throwing video on the web. She put her right foot forward. Stared at the tree, narrowed her gaze. Held the knife by the point and gave it a little flip.

Ker-thunk. It stuck firmly in the tree. Held. Didn't drop to the ground.

"Woo!" Kurt yelled jubilantly.

Sam seemed puzzled. "I could never do that."

The next time she really whipped it down straight past her head. Ka-thwang! It vibrated, half of the blade sunk in wood.

She felt like her lips were trembling. "Something's happened. Something's come over me."

Over the next half hour, she threw while Kurt fetched. And she hit the mark on the tree solidly. Over and over.

A vein seemed to be pulsing in her forehead. She knew that something had emerged from her that would change her life.

Kurt drew a circle with a magic marker on the top of a shoebox. He stood to the left of the tree holding the box top against the tree. "Now focus on the circle," he said.

She knitted her brows in intense concentration. The world around the cardboard faded like an old photograph. As she let fly, he moved the cardboard six inches more to the left. Out of the trajectory of her aim.

In the last second, the knife altered course and squarely impaled the cardboard to the tree.

Stuck deep in the tree. And dead center in the circle.

They both stared in amazement.

■ ■ ■

Cooter was a shifty, skinny man with Lucifer's Legion. He could crack any safe made. The one in Sybyl Colfax's house was child's play. It might as well have been a toy. Even Quinn could hear the tumblers click.

Quinn pawed out the papers stuffed in there. Hurriedly

shuffled through them. Here was her last will and testament, the names of the members of The Circle, with contact information, and a nasty letter about Samantha's mom to a tenure committee. So they did the same to her, he thought. Before his time, they'd gathered like wolves for her as well.

The desiccated old scumbag Toby Smollett lay bound on the floor. He stank from having wet and defecated himself. Quinn imagined he took a raft of pills. Blood pressure. Cholesterol. Toby had been without them plus food and drink for two days now.

"I'm so thirsty," he moaned.

"Why did my article on Nibiru upset everyone so? It wasn't just the usual vicious glee of it. It was over the top."

"Please give me something to drink."

"Answer me."

Toby gulped like a goldfish. "Because . . . because you knew that earth was the seventh planet to the Sumerians."

Quinn stared at him.

"The Sumerians said the solar system was twelve planets. Incredibly, they knew all the planets yet had no way to observe what we would call the last three. Uranus was only discovered by telescope in 1781, Neptune in 1846, Pluto in 1930. Now the eggheads have decided Pluto is not a planet, but no mind. The way we see the solar system is with the sun at the center. We would count out Mercury, Venus, Earth."

Quinn leaned close to the old man. Whispered: "Because they counted from the outside. The Annunaki came from another system and counted inward with the earth as seven and earth's moon as eight. Pluto, Neptune, Uranus, Saturn, Jupiter, Mars, Earth. They counted our moon as a planet as well as the sun. That made eleven. Nibiru was the twelfth planet."

Toby smiled feebly. "You knew . . . too much."

"What did you care? I was ancient Middle East. You were Ireland. Sybyl was Ireland."

Toby had closed his eyes. His breathing was labored. Almost a snore. Had he had a stroke?

"Wait a minute! What does this have to do with Ireland?"

Quinn shook him violently.

"The Fomorians . . ."

Chapter 9

In the early afternoon of a Friday, Samantha was surprised to get a text message from her mother saying she was back in town. Nothing more. Just that.

At school she couldn't find Kurt to tell him. He had left for one of his college classes. She went home to find her mother hunched over the computer with her hair tied up. You could see the wind burn on her neck. Arctic gear was thrown hither and yon in the room.

She gave Sam the briefest of hugs, went back to what she was doing.

"How's school?"

"The usual." Sam didn't know where to begin to tell her all the turmoil in her life. "How was the trip?"

"Well it was certainly a momentous one. Your mother is now privy to something that . . . well, it's not clear."

She was looking on the screen at an array of objects from the ancient Middle East. She zoomed in closer on one.

"Actually," said Sam, "some odd things have been going on."

"What do you want for supper? Want to call for a pizza? I don't care what you get on it."

"Mom, we never see each other."

"Nonsense. We're seeing each other right now."

"Some really odd stuff is going on, and—"

"I'll say. Out of place object, Sumerian."

"What?"

"Ta-daa!" She held it up a small black stone statue maybe eight inches high. It appeared to be a nude woman in a helmet. Or if you let your imagination run, in a space helmet.

"Very significant find in one of the dry caves. This is the only thing I could pilfer before the inventory was done."

Maeve put her nose back to the screen like stealing from others was all part of a day's work. When she flicked onto another picture, it showed a goddess with wings and bird feet, hands holding her breasts, not in modesty, but in a proffer of the milk of life. Maeve was talking to herself as much as to Sam.

"I'm pretty sure the stone is diorite. Which you get in Antarctica."

Sam was puzzled. "It couldn't have been made in Antarctica. And it's not like some polar expedition would have brought it along."

"That's what's always such an enigma about out-of-place objects. They don't make the least sense. So the scholars just shove them in drawers and try to forget about them."

"You mean this won't be big news?"

"Oh they're going to try to hide it alright. That's what they always do. Anything that doesn't fit their narrow little dogmas. But this is big. Tenure at a class-A university level big. Not that I want such a thing anymore. I can, however, see it taking me to a major nonprofit."

She flicked through more images.

"Mom, there's apparently a lot of money in our brokerage accounts. I know I'm not supposed to know about it, but I do. Some really strange man . . ."

Her mother looked up, eyes puzzled. "What's money got to do with anything?"

Samantha was dumbfounded. Her mother truly lived in another world. Then her brain clicked again. "Mom, what else did they find?"

She didn't answer because just then a rattle-trap pickup truck came down their drive spluttering and backfiring. Sam's mother jumped up startled. Shoved the sculpture into a drawer and slammed it. Crossed to the front window. For a brief moment she had a hunted look on her face. Then she saw who it was and relaxed.

Sam thought Cressie Moon Child herself. Please no. Just what I don't need.

Cressie was wearing a long floral skirt, a peasant blouse, and enormous yellow plastic beads. Her hair was dyed henna and frizzed.

Bursting through the front door, she threw her arms around Sam in a girly hug. "Sam, Sam! It's been forever! I just had this like total compulsion or irresistible impulse or something. I just had to come see you. Are you singing a siren song that lures the unwary?"

Sam thought what on earth? They weren't particularly friends. They hadn't been friends since elementary school and then only because her mother forced her into play dates as a substitute for a babysitter. The father always gave Sam the creeps.

Cressie was the leader of the local Wiccan group. That little gang of fruitcakes were always chanting to the full moon or meeting in misty meadows at dawn to greet the morning star. Good grief, she was wearing a belt made of ham bones threaded with a leather cord around her waist.

Cressie burbled on with an enthusiasm so wild the bones at her waist rattled. "We have so much to catch up on! I want you to spend the night at my house. Just like we did when we were six."

Sam didn't have any fond memories of that. The house had been dirty. The parents fought openly in front of them. Threw things. That was before the mother took off with a guru and moved to India.

"Please let her go, Missus Fitzhugh. Please, please, please. It'll be such fun!"

"I think that's a glorious idea," said Sam's mom. "I have so much to do here it will be ideal for me as well."

Sam thought did they rehearse this? What the heck was going on?

Sam protested, cited overwhelming homework. An essay to write. Chapters and chapters to read. French irregular verbs to memorize. But her mother wouldn't accept it.

Maeve said, "You need a night off. A chance to be girls together and catch up on gossip."

"Mom!"

"I've got so much to do, I don't need you underfoot. Now go on. Shoo."

"Do you want me to order you a pizza?"

"No. I'm good. Must concentrate."

Sam packed her toothbrush, some clothes, the Fairbairn fighting knife.

The truck almost wouldn't start, and Sam had a brief flare of hope. But the engine eventually took hold. Backfired a few times. Cressie clashed the gears and backed up the drive. Almost hit a fire hydrant.

"Here we go," she exclaimed. "Two girls in a truck. We could make a raunchy road movie."

Then Sam remembered Kurt, frantically called Mrs. Jaeger, and explained her mother had come home. She wouldn't be returning to their house that night, then thanked her over and over trying to be gracious. She knew she had laid it on too thick, but the woman was so polite and urged her to come back whenever she needed. She was now part of the family.

Oh shit, thought Sam. Is that possible? Could I be part of them?

"Well that was certainly laying it on thick," said Cressie.

"Thanks, Cressida Moon Child," said Sam dryly.

"Well, I can understand your mood. Giving up the über-stud Kurt Jaeger. I mean I'd be . . . I don't know what. I mean really jacked out by the twists of fate. Your mom coming back inconveniently. Just when you were poised to jump his bones."

"Stop, please."

"Okay, I can't wait. You talk. Provocative storytelling time."

"Have you been sent here to dig gossip out of me?"

"No one sent me," she said with a kind of surprised innocence.

"Really?"

"I'm not some spy for the cheerleaders. Anyhow, come on, give."

"Give what?"

"Quit playing dumb. What happened? Did he sneak into your bed after the parents were asleep?"

"No, certainly not."

"Oh come on. The guy makes me wet my pants."

"Give it a rest, Cressie."

"You went into his room when he was doing aerobics. Is he really hung?" She drove with her wrists on the steering wheel, holding her hands a foot apart.

"What? Were you outside spying?"

"Me? No. Why would you think that?"

■ ■ ■

Boo was in his office in the evening dusk, lights on, the secretary gone home. He was woozy with painkillers. Big bandage on his hand, which he feared might never really function again and be like a club.

Chirburg on his ass. Saying he was going to send down someone to keep the business going. Boo said that was fascinating in the abstract.

"The fuck's that mean?" growled Chirburg.

"I'm sleep-walking right now. You can't pin me down on anything."

Chirburg hung up.

Obsessed with Samantha. She seemed to float in front

of his eyes like an optical illusion. He'd take her to a remote isle. Make her his Mediterranean goddess.

He kept telling himself not to be a fool.

He had printed out the picture of Samantha and her mother so he'd never have to put it on the screen again. Then the new client came in. Quinn Shaw. Maine accent. Or 'down East' as they called it.

He said, "Boo Radley. *To Kill a Mockingbird*. Right?"

"You're correct."

"The character was supposed to be modeled on Truman Capote. Little midget faggot."

Boo kept his business smile on. "You've confused it with Dill. Boo was a recluse. Symbol of goodness greatly abused by the evil of mankind."

"Like a New England prepster exiled to the South?"

Boo saw Quinn was looking at his prep school diploma hanging just above the university one. When Quinn named his obscure prep school in Maine, Boo felt instantly superior. There was, after all, the prep school status pecking order. St. Paul's and Groton at the top. Then the so-called St. Grottlesex group. Then Boo's level. And dear God where Quinn went was almost beyond the pale.

"Hamilton and Brown," Quinn added. "I got a doctorate. Very unprep. Should have known better."

They stood there feeling a sense of communion. Enchanted by a mystic vision of their adolescent past. The American copy of British schooling, each school a sector of the sacred. The green sward lawns. The buildings donated by this or that great fortune. The chapel with its arcading and niches and incrustation of crocketts and doo-dads.

They talked like they were exchanging secret passwords of a privileged society unknown to the sweaty masses.

"Sport?" asked Quinn.

"Lacrosse and handball," said Boo.

"Sailing and squash," said Quinn. "As they say, when preps play with balls, they're small balls."

Boo laughed. "Is that what you've got in the bag? Squash racquets?"

"Hardly."

"Summer?" asked Boo.

"Campobello."

Boo pictured that edge of Maine that went from Mt. Desert Island over into Canada. Crisp nights where you wore a sweater. Days of sailing with the chop on the water.

"Lake Saranac," he said. "Upper Saranac."

Quinn smiled. "The eternal debate. Which is more prep? Ocean or lake?"

Boo laughed at that too. It was an ancient joke.

"Clubs?" said Quinn.

"St. Anthony Hall here at the university. Union League. Round Hill Club." The last two were lies. "Yourself?"

Quinn closed one eye. A smile played at the edges of his mouth. "Lucifer's Legion."

Boo actually took a step back. "Wha—? The bike gang you see driving through the county in pairs? Forty of them strung out in a long line nobody dares pass."

It didn't compute. Quinn was wearing a blue blazer with piping around the lapel like he was in a rowing club.

Quinn opened the duffel bag and showed all the cash. Street money. Truck stop money. Wads of dollar bills with rubber bands around them.

"I need to invest some bucks. A considerable sum."

Boo worked hard to recover. His hand hurt like hell. He needed a Vicodin, an Oxycontin. Whatever they had given him. "Well, you're in the right venue. You'll need to run it through your bank. Bring us a cashier's check. Or just a business check. While we wait for it to clear we can talk about various products we promote. Flocks of new ideas come in from New York like starlings overloading a tree."

"It would have to come in cash."

Boo shook his head with sardonic sadness. Thinking Lucifer's Legion, well, it all makes sense. Several guys from his prep school class had taken to dope running in daddy's big yacht. Of course they're now in the federal pen.

"You can't just bring quantities of cash in here. There are all kinds of IRS reporting requirements."

"So how do I launder it?"

Boo winced. "Let's not use that dreadful word. In fact after today, let's not talk about this step at all. Let's just say if you were the agent for a foreign company that wanted to invest in the US, then you wire it from a known bank in the Netherlands Antilles. You stroll in soon after and look at the array of possibilities."

Boo hesitated. Stared at him for a long time. Was this some FBI stooge? Was he wearing a wire? Maybe Quinn really was a grad student gone bad. But didn't grasp the most basic concepts of disposing of ill-gotten gains. Odd.

He spoke in a whisper. "The whole Caribbean is set up

for hot money banking. Get a lawyer down there to form a company. Move the money to the Cayman Islands or really any island. Then wire it here. We'll be in business. That's all I'm going to say on the subject."

Quinn zipped up the bag and slung it over his shoulder. Paused at the door.

"Your old man knew everything but restraint. Bet long; bet short; covered his bets with client money. Then blew his brains out. Sent the maid home first. Spread newspaper on the floor. Drank a last glass of a favorite scotch. You found the body. Harrowing."

Boo froze. This strange person knew everything, had him thoroughly checked out before making his approach. Knew he was half-way *louche*. Ready to grasp at shady possibilities.

"I was going to lie to you," said Quinn. "Make up a mythical past like Scott Fitzgerald's Gatsby. Say I was raised in Bar Harbor, son of the idle rich. Father crewed in the America's Cup. I've been doing that act since I went off to college at eighteen.

"Fact is I washed dishes at Hamilton. Went into student loan hell for Brown. Neither of us belonged in the Ivies. I didn't have the brains or the background; you didn't have the brains or the drive.

"So we end up on the peripheries with the other prep n'er-do-wells. Go to college here. Or Colby and Sewanee and Vanderbilt. SMU. Rollins. Hang with our kind. Keep our little social set tight like we would soon be returning to take our rightful places at the mystical center.

"Someone might look at Boo Radley and think the prep schools just turned out third and fourth generation trust-funders. The effete on a downward spiral. Can't really hack it in a modern world of Silicon Valley geniuses.

"Oh the preps still turn out the élite," Quinn continued decisively. "Sons of CEOs of the Fortune 500. Daddy pulling down forty mil a year. Writes out the tuition check like it was pocket change. And sonny boy is that infuriating composite of brilliant, athletic, and incredibly beautiful to look at because he's the son of the trophy wife. He has no trouble getting into the Ivies, making the varsity crew, captain of rugby. The right dining club at Princeton. Tapped for a senior society at Yale. Going straight to Goldman for two years and then Wharton."

"But you said you went to Brown . . ." Boo stammered.

Quinn snorted. "Grad schools will take anybody who will pay the bill. You want to be a Yalie? Apply for a master's in liberal arts.

"Listen, my old man was a cook in a prep school. I went for free. Crept around hoping no one would particularly notice me. Go to college and start playing 'let's pretend.' Pop the collar on your Izod shirt. Wear corduroy trousers, LLBean waders, and boat shoes. Talk about spinnakers. It wasn't hard. Even the commonality in Maine ski and sail."

Boo had to sit down. He was dizzy and this breast-baring was coming too hard and fast.

"Academe is a lower-middle class profession," said Quinn. "Little worms who got praised by the professor for being smart. Think there's some status there. My mother kept books in an auto parts store for Chrissake. You figure to be the final word on art or architecture. Get invited to grand estates to pronounce on rare books or silver.

"Find out it's just playing patty-cake with sneering

undergrads. The rich ones condescend. Tell you they have to cut class because they're flying home to sail in a regatta. Expect you to envy them their youth and perfection. And the big estate invites somehow don't come.

"One day you reach a new vantage point in time, real-ize in a flash of rage that cultivation is all bullshit. Learn that Satan's lucre is the beating heart inside the body of all social pretense and grace. You decide to get out and get yours like in the days of the giants. Frick and Stanford and Harriman. Rockefeller and Flagler and Rogers. But it's not just the money. That's just how you keep score as they say. It's whether you can have . . ." his voice dropped to a sibilant whisper . . . *"a cosmic impact."*

Quinn went out and got on a Harley. Incongruous with his blazer and loafers. Slung the duffel bag across the gas tank in front of him. Kick started the engine and drove off with a muted growl.

Boo shoved some pain pills in his mouth and swal-lowed them with mineral water. God his hand hurt.

Boo wondered how much money they were really talking about. The image of Samantha came back before his eyes. Her lovely face, her chiseled nose. "She walks in beauty like the night," he whispered.

■ ■ ■

"Life is harsh in the Milroy purlieu," said Cressie dramat-ically, the back of her hand on her forehead.

The house sat one row back from Chastain, the old main street of town, clapboard one-story bungalow with a squat columned front porch. Inside it was low ceilings and grimy surfaces loaded with dumpster found objects, broken clocks, bits of machinery.

Skeleton of a dog. Smashed musical instruments. Giant Buddha with burned out incense sticks. Bicycle with flat tires. Dead plants hanging in pots from the ceiling. A knocked over cactus, pottery shattered, sand all over the floor. Deeply scuffed wood floors and ramshackle salvage furniture.

The electricity out and the house was filled with ghostly shadows. Cressie lit candles. She said her father always forgot the light bill.

Cressie offered Sam a drink of Old Crow. Sam declined. Cressie knocked back two shots. She said her father drank so much he'd never miss it.

"He breaks things up in his violent moments. He says his alter ego won't be chained up. He'll come back drunk tonight. Thrash all around."

Sam knew she looked alarmed.

"Hey, it's okay. I'll be your guardian angel." Cressie laced her fingers under her chin and put on a silly smile. "If only we had Kurt here. We could share him. He'd protect us from all danger. You know he's some insane level of belt in karate."

"Yes, I heard."

"The Chinese army actually sent observers to see if he possessed *qi*."

"What on earth is that?"

"It's a flow of vital energy, a life force. What the Hindus

call *prana*. The Chinese believe that certain adepts can channel it so effectively the force itself blocks the blows of an opponent."

"So what was the result?"

She shrugged her bony shoulders. "It was inconclusive."

Sam looked at the paintings on the walls. Blue-black outer space done with astonishing depth. Constellations. The Milky Way. One showed the earth with a dark planet approaching like it was on a collision course. It held a frightening sense of the void of space.

"You know," yacked Cressie, "Kurt has an older sister in Switzerland. She's a shrink. She wrote a really graphic sex guide. Some people say it's about sex magic."

Sam looked at her. She didn't want to hear a discourse on sex magic.

With no power, the refrigerator was sour milk and spoiled food. They ate trail mix and brown bread, drank tap water. The kitchen was hung with Indonesian devil masks and smelled of old grease and garbage that spilled out of the can.

"Mostly I'm a juicer," said Cressie.

"Is that some drug term?"

"No, fruit juice. Beet juice. Spinach, lemon, and ginger. That kind of thing."

Sam realized Cressie was borderline anorexic not from throwing up, but because there was probably never any food in the house.

Cressie said, "What do you think Kurt would be like in the sack?"

"I don't know." Sam shook her head. One minute Cressie

was all mysticism and next she was crotch jokes and jabber about torrid sex. "I don't know anything about sex but theory. Have you had intercourse with a guy?"

"Once. It was kind of weird. My mom decided we were going to have a nuclear war, and she wanted me to know the bliss of sex. Or she didn't want me burdened with ignorance or something."

"Did she tell you how to do it?"

"Not really. She just said to take the training wheels off."

"So how was it?"

"I emerged victorious."

"What does that mean?"

"I got rid of my virginity."

Sam was hungry and cold, and she didn't know how much longer she could tolerate this bohemian dingbat. Did Cressie have any endearing qualities? Her thrift-shop wardrobe was so pointlessly theatrical, and her hair looked like it had been put through a blender.

Sam got up and walked around the living room, saw the door to the room the father used as a studio. A skylight brought in enough illumination to see. Easels with works in progress. Paint splattered all over the floor. Squeezed out tubes. Old brushes in jars. Sam froze.

"Cressie, what is this?"

Cressie came in behind her, shrugged. "Some of Dad's work."

It was a portrait of Sam. There was no question of it. The face was a true likeness. But the biggest shock was the body was incredibly exact. Dimensions. Proportions. It was as if he had worked from naked photos of her. Exact right down to the shape of her navel, size of her nipples and a mole on her left breast. Spectacular detail.

She was holding up her breasts in offering. Above her head was an eight-pointed star. "I'm not my mother's daughter for nothing. That's Inanna. He's painted me like a Sumerian goddess."

"What? The hold-the-tits thing? I think it hints at inner turmoil."

"What?"

"Anyhow, it doesn't present any new information about you."

"What are you saying? Is that rubbish artist talk?"

"The torso is quite supple, but then so is yours. You've got big knockers. I wish mine were like yours."

"Maybe you should eat normal food."

"Anyhow it's one of his more ambitious works."

Sam drifted out of the room feeling something terrible was brewing. Cressie's eyes had been darting hither and yon, not meeting hers.

"Dad will appreciate your feedback," Cressie said from behind her.

God this was unhinged. The father, a lunatic with only the barest veneer of the college professor. How did he produce her image so perfectly? And why?

Cressie blew out the candles in the main house and lit one in her bedroom. It was stuck on a genuine human skull.

Sam followed her in. The ceiling was a deep, deep navy

blue with glittering stars painted on it that were luminous in the dark.

There was a four-foot tall reed or willow statue of a man. Crude, obviously woven by Cressie who had then stuffed it with Barbie Dolls. She said the ancient Celts burned prisoners alive in such things. On the summer solstice she would sacrifice the Barbies in the backyard.

Cressie was artistic like her father and had filled the walls with paintings of stone circles. It was remindful of Kurt's house.

"Do you smoke?"

"Smoke? Oh you mean weed. No. No, I don't."

Cressie had the plastic baggie out and was rolling a joint in paper decorated with little half moons and stars.

It was so bizarre. All her little health kicks, but no exercise. And snorting or sucking down any drug someone offered.

Cressie licked the edge of the rolling paper. "This is my coping mechanism. My father does more drugs than me."

Sam felt like saying she could believe it.

Cressie lit the joint with a kitchen match and sucked in the smoke deep into her lungs.

"Do you know anything about ancient Ireland? I mean in the mythic times."

"No, my mom's Middle East. Just what I've picked up from her."

Cressie gave her a haunted look. "There's something so compelling about you. It's an elusive emotional charge. It comes over me like velvet."

Sam shifted uncomfortably.

Cressie sucked deeply on the joint again, held it in her lungs, blew it out her nose. Then she started talking Ireland again.

"The Formorians were a divine race that came from the sea. Now you might think that meant came in ships, but they, in fact, were sea demons. They were later defeated by the Tuatha Dé. Their last stronghold was on Tory Island. We don't know what became of them or of their ancient knowledge."

Sam thought when would this all be over? For crap sake, ancient knowledge. It sounded like her mother. She was so sick of it.

"I sometimes think all the answers to the mysteries of life can be found on Tory Island."

Cressie held the last bit of joint with her fingernails and sucked the final hit. "When I smoke this, your face becomes all abstract."

"It would tend to do that."

"I perceive things that others don't."

"Okay."

Cressie's outbursts of enthusiasm, her one-sided conversation, were dying down as the weed took hold on top of bourbon. She yawned repeatedly, making Sam yawn in turn.

Without any explanation, Cressie stripped down to her underwear. Celtic tattoos ran down her spine. Whorls and interlaced knots. She licked her fingers to pinch out the candle and climbed into the bed.

Sam realized with dismay they were going to have to

share the bed. She decided she'd sleep in her clothes on top of the covers. She lay down with great reluctance telling herself she'd go to sleep and morning light would come and all this horror would be over.

"I feel this deep rush of affection," said Cressie in a drowsy voice. "I want to tongue kiss you. We Wiccans all kiss each other on the mouth."

Then she suddenly zonked out. And within minutes was snoring.

Sam tried to turn an emotional off-switch and lay there stiff as a board. Try to think nice thoughts and pray for the dawn. The ceiling glimmered down seeming to make hypnotic patterns. When she closed her eyes, they moved behind her eyelids.

Kurt's mother came and brushed her face and slid away into mist.

Sam must have slept because she distinctly remembered waking to the sound of motorcycles. Not loud and raucous to wake the neighborhood. Muted. But quite a few of them. They stopped outside the house.

The front door opened and closed. She could hear men's voices whispering. Someone lit a candle. The light showed under the door. And then the door to the bedroom slowly creaked open. Flickering light covered her face. Her heart was pounding. She held her breath, tried desperately to still her eyelids from flinching. An intense feeling of malevolence crept over her. Who were they interested in? Her or Cressie? Or both?

The light went away and the door closed.

Sam listened intently. The front door closed. A wave of relief went over her.

Time crept by. And more time. And then Sam suddenly had an urgent need to take a pee.

She crawled out of bed as silently as possible. Listened at the door. Opened it a crack. The house was dark.

She crept across the living room and stopped short. The father was in the bathroom with the door open taking a loud piss. One hand bracing himself against the wall. He seemed to hit in and out of the toilet bowl.

He was wearing only boxer shorts. His broad white back was completely tattooed with the classic Renaissance work of art Saint Sebastian martyred by being shot full of arrows.

Now he was bending over throwing up. She could hear and smell it.

Sam flew back into the room and bolted the door. She was convinced she was going to be sick as well.

The window. She struggled to get it open, clambered out to crouch in the yard. Fought to get her jeans down before she wet herself.

A light flicked on, its beam right in her face. She put up her hands to ward it off.

Then another and another came on. She was blinded by the headlights of motorcycles.

The men on them began howling like dogs or wolves.

Then the cycles revved their engines and peeled off one by one leaving her in darkness.

Sam sat on the grass hugging her knees and trembling. Sobbing quietly. Convulsed with terror.

Chapter 10

Cressie was snoring with slobber running clown her chin when Sam slipped out. The father was snoring at the other end of the house.

Sam walked back across the green sward of the big quads of the campus with dew on the grass and no one around. She wondered if she looked like a coed doing the walk of shame.

Just as she went through the front door of her house she happened to check her messages and saw her mother was off again.

"The statue is you-know-where. Don't tell anyone and don't fiddle with it. Thanks. Luv, Mom."

Sam was furious. She couldn't believe her mother. Just wander out again. Why couldn't she have a normal family? At school they had had it drummed into their heads that the nuclear family was an artificial construct, but there was something awfully nice about it. An actual father who she knew. Who loved her and kissed her goodnight. Came to watch her fence and told her she was perfect in every way. A mother who made dinner so they could all sit at the table together.

The house was dead silent. Sam wanted to make bacon and eggs, take a bath, and scrub every inch of her to get the Milroy dirt off. And then sleep all day. Or maybe bathe first and then the bacon and eggs. Fry bread in the bacon grease and damn the health of it.

When she heard the busted muffler outside she closed her eyes and said oh dear god spare me.

She wouldn't let Cressie in the house. They sat on the steps.

"I thought we'd go out to breakfast."

"I'm really tired, Cressie."

"What, you didn't sleep?"

"It didn't help that your father and someone else kept looking in the room. And then all those motorcycles outside."

"Oh, that. Yeah they all wanted to see you for some reason."

Sam stared at her shocked. "Is that why you insisted I come over?"

"Sort of. But I really wanted to spend time with you. Find out the down and dirty on you and Kurt."

"Cressie, I am the complete nerd. I pursue life in all innocence. You're the one with the sex experience."

She shrugged and looked a bit despondent. "That. Well, it wasn't real nice. I had to put my hair in pigtails and dress like a Catholic school girl. And he actually spanked me really hard. Said he was punishing me for being a bad girl."

"I thought this was supposed to be a blissful moment before nuclear death."

"No. Not really. My mom pimped me out. I learned it later."

"She charged the man money?"

"Yeah, she had a big bill with her dealer. He didn't need to threaten. Just cut her off, and she was climbing the walls in a day."

"Who did she sell you to?"

"I don't dare name him. A professor. He wanted a virgin. I have to see him from time to time which is pretty disgusting."

"Cressie, why do people want to see me?"

She looked bewildered. "I dunno. Dad did that painting of you . . . I guess he wanted to check it against reality."

"How did he get me in such detail?"

"He has visions. Goes into trances, particularly when he does LSD. I think the painting's kind of like Burne-Jones' Andromeda. There's that feeling of sentimentality. He should have had you chained to a rock."

Sam almost shouted at her. "No, it's not. It's the goddess Inanna. She's Sumerian. I should know. It's my mom's subject. Now you tell me what's going on!"

Cressie actually condescended. "I think you should move on past these negative vibrations you're experiencing. It's really not good for you."

"Your father knows how I look right down to moles on my body! A motorcycle gang comes over for a viewing! And my attitude isn't good for me?"

"Why are you acting so upset?"

"Acting? You're the actress! You're doing an uncanny imitation of a dingbat!"

Sam stormed into the house and slammed the door.

Then she heard the grinding engine noise outside. Cressie couldn't get her truck started.

Sam wanted to scream. She jerked open the front door.

"Do you want me to call a tow?" What she meant was please get the hell out of here.

Cressie was on her cell. "No, Dad's coming."

Jake Milroy arrived on the back of a Harley driven by an ugly brute with one side of his teeth knocked out and tattoos of a spider web on each of his elbows.

They opened the hood of the truck and began tinkering with things inside.

The motorcycle animal kept turning and looking back over his shoulder at her. His cut-off sleeve denim vest said "Lucifer's Legion."

Sam went inside without saying goodbye.

■ ■ ■

Quinn had stopped in the lower end of Chastain Street to gas up the van, when his ex-wife Lorraine pulled up on the opposite side of the pump in her own van.

When she got out, sunglasses on the top of her head, Diet Coke in her hand, she spotted him. Quinn Shaw in a van with Hog Man and a ton of money, charter boat ready and waiting down in the Florida Keys.

Lorraine looked with disgust at Hog Man behind the

wheel, unkempt beard, hair like a lion's mane, scorpion tattoo on his neck.

"A man's known by the company he keeps," she said in a deliberate taunt.

Quinn sighed. Towards the end of their marriage her voice had begun to resemble the crack of a whip. Once a hot-bodied Italian bitch, now gone majorly fat. Just packing away the junk food. Never without some screw-cap soft drink in her hand. Roaring around in a van pretending she was a big real estate magnate. Six-pack of Diet Coke in the little cooler she had in the console.

What a pig. Condescending to him. The failed professor. Mr. Big Loser she called him at the divorce hearing. She couldn't even guess the sum of money in the back of the van in Hefty Bags. Here he was with this big animal with a .357 magnum and a Mossberg pump, who'd blow her fat ass away if he told him to.

Incredible that he had married her. He had always fantasized about marrying for money. A truly tasteful wedding in a rustic chapel on an island off the coast of Maine. The bride would have a summer home there. Giant shake shingle Queen Anne from the nineteenth century. Been in the family for three generations just like the money.

A few close friends as groomsmen. White duck trousers, blue blazers, bow ties. Bridesmaids who had gone to Smith or Vassar together. Farmington before that.

Some dotty old relatives from the bride's side. None from his. If the weather turned cool, the old women would have full-length minks. The men would all drink Scotch.

That tense little moment the night before when his soon-to-be father-in-law would spring the prenuptial agreement on him. Watch intently, expecting Quinn to cut up nasty, give him an excuse to call off the wedding. Instead, Quinn would readily sign. Fully intending to stay with Miss Moneybags through thick and thin. Well, no thin. Her money would see to that.

In the depths of despair of grad school, he had married Lorraine in a registry office with no witnesses, no friends. She was a waitress in an Italian restaurant where he ate because it was cheap and they gave you huge bowls of spaghetti with red sauce and meatballs. Momma Monza's with red check tablecloths and candles stuck in old Chianti bottles.

He took her to his crummy room one night, shoved his hand down her underpants and gripped her tight, black curls. Fucked her like nobility bestowing a favor. She responded to it. Thought she was coming up in life. High school diploma girl going to marry the important professor.

Why had he lacked the courage to go it alone, the knight errant he had always been? Was it the power of regular nooky? Or sheer desperate loneliness? They say men trade down in life, and he did it in spades.

She took a job as a receptionist for a law firm. Had to pick up the phone a zillion times a day and say "Horvath, Horvath, and Horvath. How may I help you?" Shyster father and two sons, all of them with giant egos. Couldn't call it the Horvath Firm. Each had to make his personal presence known.

When Quinn would go to pick her up at the end of the day one of them would dream up some pointless chore for her so he had to sit around reading a book. Then they'd find a way to condescend. Make it known that he was a worthless history grad student and they were pulling down big bucks.

She was pumping her own gas now. "So what are you doing exactly post-academe? I knew they would bounce your ass. If ever anyone didn't fit in. So what is it? You've found your level in life?"

Hog Man lay his log-like forearm on the open window. Grateful Dead teddy bear tattoos dancing down it. Lifted his shades and looked Lorraine straight in the eyes. "If'n I weren't a Christian, I'd get out'en this car and smack the livin' dog shit out'en yew."

Lorraine looked genuinely scared. Southerners in general terrified her.

Quinn didn't fit in? God the horror of her at faculty dinners when they came to town, him the lowly assistant professor. Despite the grad school years, she hadn't absorbed anything. Talking about playing the ponies, pari-mutuel betting. The time she hit a trifecta. Her cousin Vince who was into warehouse break-ins. How she never lacked for "Channel" No. 5 perfume.

His original plan had been to make a pile of loot out of Lucifer's Legion and disappear one day. Buy a house in Bar Harbor and be quietly genteel. Be vague about the source of his wealth. Say he had "hit it a couple of good licks," but decided to go on a different life journey. He'd meet that wealthy girl of his dreams. Divorced and lonely. A little pudgy. Her trust fund a bit strained. But distinctly WASP culture. The sort of girl he'd imagined he was worthy of all through prep school and college.

But everything was different now. An accidental academic article. Banished into the wilderness by shit-heels academicians. The chance meeting with Milroy. The painting of Samantha and the whispered tale of Nibiru.

Now he was catapulted into the greatest of all mysteries. And he approached it with a genuine sense of wonder. He had the membership list of The Circle. Sybyl had named them all as legatees. To what exactly? Did she own anything?

One thing was certain. Samantha was his legacy. She was to be his. She would arch her mound of Venus and moan in longing.

"Hey, Quinn!" Lorraine yelled. She was safely inside her van with the engine running.

"Yeah?"

"Get fucked!"

Chapter 11

When Samantha went home to her normally quiet neighborhood, she found the front door broken open and a crowd of six or eight old people pawing through drawers and cabinets searching for something.

And they were old. Cataract glasses. Wattles under their necks. Skinny arms and legs. Sagging muscles. Women with blue rinse hair. An old man with a walker was pushing his way over the litter of things thrown on the floor.

"Who are you?" Sam gasped to the room at large. "What are you doing?"

"What say?" The voice was that harsh New York Bronxish. The speaker was on all fours looking under the skirt of an armchair cover. He got to his feet, his joints plainly bothering him. Knees painfully swollen. He had a pallid face like he lived in the dark. A big canker in the middle of his dome of a forehead.

"The door was open. We just walked in."

"Are you being facetious? You jimmied the lock."

"Oooo! Listen to Miss Big Vocabulary, everybody. Put her on a TV quiz show. They still got 'College Bowl'?"

Then Samantha recognized him. "You're Tyndall Cranmer.

You were the head of the anthropology/archaeology department when . . . when . . ."

He fingered his canker with liver spotted fingers. "When your mother didn't come up to the mark. Unfortunate. But we had to think of our place in the Academy. I guess your mom points me out and hisses."

"Why are you ransacking my house?" she demanded. "There's nothing you would want here."

"I think ya got insufficient reflection, kid. We came by to see our old colleague. We just found the place a mess. I'd think your mom would hire a maid or something."

"Stop that!" Samantha shouted.

A rabbity little man jumped. He had been rummaging through a desk drawer. His hands shook either with nervousness or palsy. "I'll only be a minute. Then we'll be on our way."

A hump-backed old woman tipped over a bookshelf with a huge crash. Books spilled in a heap.

"Boy, somebody here sure likes to read!" she said in the loud voice of the near-deaf. She had hearing aides in both ears.

She flopped clown on the floor and began flipping through the pages of each book in turn looking for a secret hollow space. Afterwards, she'd toss it over her shoulder.

An old woman in a shower cap, flowered housecoat, and fluffy slippers was dissecting a tangerine, dropping the peel. It was like she had brought a snack.

"Get out of my house," Sam ordered. She tried to tug the woman towards the door, but instead the woman fell to the floor with a thud.

"Ooo we got ourselves a lawsuit here," said Tyndall. "You didn't break a hip did you, Jewel?"

The woman going through the books had stockings rolled down to her thin ankles. "No respect for the elderly. Just disgusting. I witnessed the whole thing."

Sam wanted to scream in despair. It was like a loony bin had been emptied into her home. She went outside and called the town police. They didn't seem terribly interested, but said they'd get to it.

She called Kurt who was coming out of his college stats course. He said keep clear of them and he'd be right over. He was unlocking his bike.

Sam paced furiously. Had her mom come upon something significant? It had to be linked to her mom's find in Antarctica. But why would these geriatrics be interested? They should be in front of the TV set in an old folks' home.

Things crashed inside the house. Sam turned and started back in the door when the cop car drove up.

A hush fell. They had sensed it. Or seen it.

"Everybody act normal," Tyndall instructed.

Totally blasé, he signaled them to evacuate the house. Led them up the walk. Smiled blandly. "Good afternoon, officer. Turning out to be a beautiful day."

The cop was young and hard looking, probably lifted weights. His name tag said "Buck." "We had a report of trespassing," he said.

That brought a chorus of indignant voices from the old creeps.

"Rash assumptions."

"Stuff and nonsense."

"Unconvincing bunch'a asseverations," said Cranmer in his Yankee rasp. His nose twitched.

They kept slowly filing past. Shuffling. Teetering. Hobbling. Walker. Cane. One supporting another. Hands claw-like with arthritis. They looked like they lived on pain pills.

Tyndall ushered them all past and into a van with the name of a nursing home on it. Then he turned back to the cop.

"Looks to me like a couple a' teenagers had a big party, their friends wrecked the place, and now they're trying to blame us."

"They were rooting through the house when I got here," Sam protested. "Look at the door."

The wreck of the living room registered on the cop. "What on earth?" The age of the people Sam was accusing totally confused him.

"Oh, hey, it was like that when we got here," said Tyndall. "Like I said. All the earmarks of wild party. Prob'ly on dope. You know kids today."

Kurt came up on his bike. The cop looked from him to Sam.

"So you had yourself a little party. While the cat's away . . ."

"Evident absurdity," said Kurt. He explained they were both staying with his family. Tried to get his father on the phone in the psychology department but failed.

The cop was skeptical. Said they would have to come to the station if they wanted to file a complaint. He didn't seem real interested in them doing it. Told them they better get the place cleaned up before their parents got home.

"And if you're gone do the usual threat of going over my head to complain . . ." He pointed at his name tag. "It's Officer Buck, spelled with a 'B' and not an 'F.'"

Sam and Kurt went in the house and surveyed the damage. It was total destruction.

"You can't stay here," said Kurt. "This is becoming insane."

"Shhh," Sam cautioned with a finger to her lips. She closed the broken door, went to the edge of the carpet and rolled it back. Prying with her fingers, she lifted a secret door.

Reached out the Sumerian sculpture.

■ ■ ■

The days were getting longer, light still at six o'clock.

Boo's hand was bandaged and stiff. He didn't like looking at the network of stitches. Whenever he did, he could feel the blade slashing into him. It gave him an ugly twinge down in his balls.

There was still a March nip in the air, and he was wearing a russet chamois cloth shirt with two flap pockets on the front. Sun-faded chinos. Glen plaid sport jacket in Italian silk-linen. Oiled leather ankle boots.

He stared at the printout of Samantha. He wanted that girl like he had never wanted anyone. He was no longer willing to wait until she was in college. Somehow he had to have her now. He had to convince her to flee with him.

He had actually had a wet dream last night like a teenager. She came to him in an unknown landscape of mist and dark trees. Yew trees?

No, it was the golf course at the Round Hill Club. Where he had banged Tippy who went to Rosemary Hall. The one whose daddy his father had ripped off. Old money. The daddy did nothing but collect priceless furniture for the Metropolitan Museum collection. Killed himself when he realized he was broke and his life of nonprofit board sitting was over and done.

But Samantha. She had . . . she had an owl on her shoulder. The fuck was that about? And a watery crescent moon shone behind her head.

She wore a slip. Or a gauzy gown. Sleeveless. Tied at the shoulders. It wasn't clear. She drew it up to show her shaved bare pubis. Pushed it at him in challenge.

"Inanna," she whispered. "Isis. Astarte. Ashtoreth. Ishtar. Aphrodite."

He was awkward, his hands going over her wildly, wanting to grab at her tits, to jam his fingers into her. Thinking the more roughly he handled her the more he would arouse her passion. Really fire his fingers in and out of her with piston force.

"Stop," she breathed. "Be patient. I'm only sixteen."

"You were beyond ready in ancient times," he urged.

Yielding, she pulled him down to rest his chest on her bosom. Her thighs spread. Her arms laced about his neck. Her lips parted in moaning passion as he kissed her throat, thrust violently into her and came in three strokes.

He sobbed. Premature ejaculation. He hadn't had that since freshman year when he could impress the Southern honeys with his prep school allure and they wanted their first college fuck.

"I'm sorry," he gasped, pulling out of her and dribbling semen on her flat belly.

"Nibiru," she whispered as she faded away, leaving him bewildered and humiliated. "Nibiru."

Boo touched his office desk to ground himself. Closed his eyes against the painful memory. How could a dream do this to him? How could a dream be so lasting in his mind?

In his youth, Boo had had a rich aunt who moved about Italy renting elegant ruins. A palazzo in Venice. A villa in Capri. A farm in Tuscany. She never married, kept a string of lovers, threw them out with a fancy wristwatch and a monogrammed cigarette case when she tired of them.

Boo and his mother often used to visit her on his spring breaks and summers. That had all come to an end when his father had pillaged the woman's money, and she, unable to face destitution, had taken an overdose of pills in the bathtub. He had found her there. Just like he had found his father.

But Boo could still vividly remember the sun-soaked landscapes and the sound of cicadas among the olive groves. And the food. It was the only Italian he had learned. The traditional meat skewers called *arrosticini*. *Nocette di pescatrice in umido di asparagi*—monkfish and asparagus in a buttery broth. He could taste each one.

Samantha was a teenager, a child carrying his child. He saw her in her bikini, her baby bump round and taut, her bellybutton popped out. Carrying his child, she would be ravenous, eating for two. He planned the meal. Braised lamb shoulder with spring peas and a kind of lid of egg yolk over it. A nice bottle of Castello Monaci from the vineyards south of Bari in Salento. For himself of course, she would be forbidden alcohol.

The dollar signs dinged in the upper right of his computer. A trust account he had set up was receiving a stream of money in $100,000 amounts. The sender, a bank in Curaçao, said the account should be designated El Macho Buggaron GmbH & Co. Boo sat watching fascinated. The sum totaled two million dollars. And it was still mounting.

Then Chirburg called. Did the man never go home? Did he have a home to go to? Some sleazy row of houses in Queens. Some chain-smoking slattern of a wife.

"The fuck's goin' on?" he growled.

"I've got money coming in as you can plainly see. I'm a champion producer. Hitting my stride."

"El Macho Buggaron. Does that last word mean what I think?"

"I wouldn't know. I took French."

"Hinky dinky parlez-voo."

"How creative and cosmopolitan we are tonight."

"You're getting a smart mouth on you, preppie boy."

"When you produce, management holds no fear."

"You're a real swingin' dick. Don't be in a hurry to put that money into a fund. Even one of ours. Let's leave it in cash for awhile."

He hung up.

Chapter 12

Ms. Rooney had disappeared from AP history. It was said she was in a hospital bed heavily dosed with lithium. A substitute took her place.

He was strange and scrawny with a lot of facial tics. His face was only shaved in patches. And he seemed to be wearing the "colors" of a motorcycle gang—denim jacket with the sleeves cut off and a skull and crossed wrenches on the back. It actually said "Lucifer's Legion."

Everyone thought he said his name was "Dude," which made sense because of his appearance. But Samantha heard it as "Jude."

Had anyone actually looked at this man before hiring him? His teaching ability was limited to asking the class questions out of the teacher's manual for the text. He kept dropping into a strange voice like he was playing "Talk Like a Pirate Day." He actually said, "Avast, ye swabs."

The lesson was the Compromise of 1850 and the Fugitive Slave Act. As you could imagine, Emerson was in his element. He threw around big words like manumission and sophistry and casuistry. He quoted chunks of Daniel Webster's "Reply to Hayne" on the topic of South Carolina's nullification act for US laws the South disapproved of.

"Liberty *and* Union, now *and* forever, one *and* insepa-rable!" Emerson pronounced in a resonant voice.

The teacher was twitching and squirming the whole time. Tattoos of skulls and crossbones on his scrawny neck.

His eyes would blink fiercely. His mouth would twitch. Then he would jerk his chin to the side as though trying to touch his shoulder with it. Claw at his face.

"Ohmigod," said Francie. "That's meth face. The man's speeding so fast he's going to launch into the stratosphere."

Francie's dad was a major cardiologist at the medical school. She had scored so high on the AP Biology exam that the testing authorities decided she had cheated and launched a fruitless investigation.

"I've a yen to splice the main-brace with a doxie like thee," he said.

And Sam knew he was staring at her. Not Francie. Leer-ing even.

Now he began to shake and shiver all over. He staggered to his feet and took a few steps around the desk straight towards Sam.

"You came from among the stars. You're a descendant of the Annunaki. You're divine. Or semi-divine. One of those. I want you."

Twitch.

"Sure, you're scared. You know what they said about me. I only went to the restroom with the little boy to help him winky-tink. He said he needed help. So I stopped the story. *Treasure Island.* Told them all to wait. I'd be right back."

Twitch.

"And then all those big butt Birkenstock librarians came busting in. Accusing me in loud tones of vile things. Thunderous tones. They wanted me to dance the hempen jig. Their calumnies weren't true. None of it was true. I like girls. Little girls sometimes, but at least they're girls."

Then he pulled out a screwdriver and rose slowly to his feet.

"You're mine," he said, eyes glaring at Sam. "I'm taking you with me, and I'll kill any man-jack that objects."

Kurt stood up, positioned himself between Jude and Sam. "You've really picked the wrong classroom for that," he said.

Kurt kicked the screwdriver from Jude's hand and then spun in the other direction and kicked him up into the air and bouncing off the wall.

Kurt seemed shocked at what he had done. Without any revulsion he went over and felt Jude's chest for a heartbeat. Peeled back an eyelid.

"I don't even know what I'm looking for," he said, gesturing helplessly. "They just do that in movies."

"His eyes are rolled back," said Francie, going over to join him. "It just means he's unconscious."

"God I feel terrible about this. But there are no half measures in karate. I know I've broken his ribs. I hope I haven't given him a concussion."

He motioned everyone out behind him. Sam got caught in the mob exit and couldn't even say "my hero."

The whole class was instantly on cell phones to parents and the police. Immediately the school was in a full-throated uproar. The fire alarm went off.

Ms. Frissel went squawking down the hall in terror banging on the principal's door. She found it locked. The principal was on the intercom hysterically babbling "Lockdown! Lockdown! Gun in the school!"

Principal Peevey stayed in his office until he heard the sirens. He didn't feel like eating hot lead to protect students.

The cops seemed right timid as well. They took forever to surround the building, radios crackling, hovering behind cars. Meanwhile all the students were outside milling around ignoring the orders bellowed out of a bullhorn. It was school holiday time for them.

Samantha hung with her class. They knew they were even more apart from the rest now. Cherry was leading the football team in a fatuous cheer. She danced and twirled.

"Lockdown! Lockdown! Guns in the classroom!"

At last some overweight cops in SWAT gear rolled up in an armored personnel carrier. They had come from the county seat. Flak jackets, helmets, AR-15s. Moving by hand signals.

Randall rolled his eyes. "The current militarized American hayseed cop force."

His father was dean of the law school and as such heavily connected politically. Randall could out-debate any teacher and find a loophole in any rule.

"Boys will play with their toys," chimed in Dru Shelley. Her mother ran Women's Studies and had given her the middle name Wollstonecraft for the early English women's rights advocate. Dru found it an enormous embarrassment.

The SWAT team found the fire door locked so they

actually set an explosive charge. "Fire in the hole!" bellowed the bullhorn.

At that moment, Principal Peevey opened it from the inside and poked his head out.

"Get back, you damned fool!" barked the bullhorn.

The principal fell back just as a big BOOM blew the door off its hinges and up into the air to clang on the ground.

Then another cop fired a grenade launcher that exploded a magnesium-based pyrotechnic commonly known as a flash-bang inside the building.

KA-WHAM!

One hundred and eighty decibels and a blinding flash of one million candela.

"Hold your fahr, yew re-tard!" ordered the bullhorn.

"They's noncombatants in theah!" protested the cop. "I'm incapacitating 'em!"

At that moment, Principal Peevey staggered out, his eyes glazed, face in rictus, arms in front of him like a Frankenstein monster.

"Good grief!" said Francie. "Flash blindness, deafness, tinnitus, and inner ear disturbance."

"What's tinnitus?" asked Nasar.

"His ears are ringing like his head's been used as the clapper in a bell."

The SWAT team charged in, knocking the principal down and one of them tripping and doing a face-plant as well. His rifle clattered across the floor.

The classroom was empty.

When Kurt tried to turn the screwdriver over to the

cops they wanted to arrest him. That was when Randall informed the chief there were thirty witnesses to Kurt saving them from mayhem at the hands of a dangerous lunatic.

It took the rest of the day to interview the kids from the class. The initial adult reaction was to think it some hoax. But the kids were adamant, and Randall got his father the dean of the law school on the line with the police chief. That got their attention.

Sam was thoroughly depressed by the madness that was invading her world. And now she'd have to be the subject of Cherry-driven gossip.

Sure enough, as she left the school Cherry came crooning up. "Sah-man-tha. I understand you have an admire-ah."

Sam put on a feigned concern. "Cherry, have you finally managed to pass Algebra I? Your poor head, does it hurt?"

Then she saw Kurt waiting and the sun came through the clouds.

■ ■ ■

A nasty March wind was blowing outside, whipping branches up against the windows of Boo's office.

Boo sat staring at the print-out of Samantha and her mother, imagining a crumbling villa he would buy. He was shifting the fantasy to France. Perhaps near Avignon.

Windows facing the road shuttered against the sun. Cool interior shrouded in half-darkness. Rooms practically bare but for some fallen ceiling plaster. A few old wicker chairs.

An old wrinkled crone would come twice a week to do minor cleaning, make them a meal. *Brandade de morue,* the salt cod and pureed potatoes. *Daube de boeuf with* herbs and a nice lemon zest on the beef stew and olives. Capers and olives chopped up in the appetizer called *tapenade.* Spread over crusty bread.

"Wine," he murmured. What would be on point? A rosé Bandol? A white Cassis?

As the heat of the day turned tepid at dusk, he and Samantha would sit naked in the cool water of an old cistern. Watch shadows lengthen and Venus appear glimmering in the sky. Bats fluttering and night birds swooping.

He always saw her as pregnant. She never failed to arouse him. His cock would grow and stretch like a great beast. Lengthening and stretching. Her breath would catch, her eyes widen. She would hold up her wrists as though in manacles. "I am enslaved to your manhood," she would lisp.

Boo suddenly jerked back to reality. Quinn Shaw was looming there with some enormous galoot of a motorcycle hoodlum.

Quinn wore a green Barbour jacket. Houndstooth linen shirt. Corduroys. He stood there like a dark prince come to claim Boo's soul under their compact.

The hulk wore a leather jerkin, motorcycle boots, filthy grease-stained jeans. He stank of BO, tobacco, stale liquor, bad breath. It was totally repulsive.

The contrast couldn't be more absurd, yet these two seemed completely relaxed around one another.

"I forget my manners," said Quinn. "Boo, meet my sidekick Hog Man. Tonto to the Lone Ranger."

Hog Man shoved out his hand which Boo took tentatively although the animal didn't try to crush it. Just a solid grip with big fingers like a baseball glove. "Pleased t'meetcher."

Boo couldn't believe that in a town so overrun with outsiders the actual Southerner he would meet would be this creature out of a cesspool.

Then Boo noticed they both had deep suntans.

"You've been in tropical sun," he observed.

"Male bonding. Two pirates of the Caribbean on our maiden voyage. I trust the cargo came through."

Boo flicked on his computer, tapped some keys, showed them the deposit to El Macho Buggaron. Seventeen million dollars.

"Any directions as to its disposition will have to come from the Curaçao bank. We'll need a paper trail from a legit financial institution to justify our not looking too hard at the origin."

Boo tried to slide the photocopy of Samantha and Maeve Fitzhugh into a drawer. Quinn put his hand on it. As he reached, Boo could see the grosgrain watchband.

"And who are these people?" Quinn asked, but it was clear to Boo that he knew.

"They're clients."

"Do tell. I suppose it's all confidential hush-hush et cetera."

"Correct."

Quinn gave him a very strange and penetrating look. Returned to the screen.

"So, it's all in cash. What are we getting for it? A half percent?"

Boo put on a studied casual air, but knew his voice was strained. "That much coming in at once . . . home office wants to make sure it's safely accounted for. Tucked up nice and warm in bed."

"How hard would it be for you to withdraw our money and skedaddle?"

"Next to impossible," Boo lied.

Hog Man spoke. "You look to me like the kinder b'wa what'd sneak into a can of mixed nuts when nobuddy was lookin' and eat out all the cashews."

"No," said Quinn. "If we go by paternal heritage, our brave lad here would take the whole kaboodle and run. Wouldn't you, Boo? Make the big score. Think you could disappear?"

"Uh . . . no," Boo protested.

"Your problem is you can take the boy out of Greenwich but you can't take Greenwich out of the boy. Let's say you decided to go to ground. You simply couldn't stand it in Alaska or Saskatoon or some place. You might last six months.

"Then it would be Jackson Hole. Or Nantucket. Maybe Taos."

Quinn slapped his forehead. "No, I see it. Europe. Oh, you'd imagine Scotland. But it's too damn cold in the winter. No, you look like the south of France or Italy to me."

Boo sat frozen.

"And we'd be there. I'd try to dress Hog Man here up in some kind of cheap suit.

"You'd have the money in a Swiss account. All we'd need from you would be a number. Put a hot iron to your feet. You'd lie about it the first time. Make it a digit off. Think you can play for time. Surely someone would come along to rescue you. We go to Zurich and find it doesn't work. When we'd come back we'd be really mad."

Chapter 13

"She's emanating something," said Kurt to his mother. "These weird nuts are coming at her out of control."

He related what had happened that day.

Mrs. Jaeger gave her soothing smile. "Kurt, I need to talk to Samantha. Alone. So scoot."

He hung in the open doorway.

"Close the door, please."

Mrs. Jaeger put her hands on either side of Samantha's face. Instantly, the calming ran through her.

"Samantha, do you know your blood type?"

"Yes, I've always been made aware of it because of blood transfusions. I'm O-negative. I can give blood to anyone, but only accept blood from group O."

"Rh-negative. No Rhesus monkey proteins."

Sam laughed. "Yes, I guess I'm not descended from apes."

"Actually Rh-negative is most prevalent among Europeans. Particularly the Celts. And you are a Fitzhugh. But there are other things I'm curious about. May I hold your hand for a moment?"

Sam said sure. Sat down in a chair next to her. Mrs. Jaeger

told her to close her eyes. Took her hand with the familiar soothing effect.

Sam had a sudden vision of a purple planet hurtling through space trailing moons and space debris.

"Goodness!" said Mrs. Jaeger, releasing her hand quickly.

Sam opened her eyes to find the woman looking quite startled. "What?"

"Sorry. I had an odd effect. There's only one other person I know who does that to me. A woman in Scotland. We . . . well, never mind."

She made a temple of her hands and pressed the fingertips along the bridge of her nose. "Russet hair. Deep green eyes," she mused. "May I count your ribs?"

Sam agreed and kneeled in front of her. Mrs. Jaeger began by probing around the collarbone. Then moved under her armpit and started down, counting silently. Sam flinched.

"Don't be embarrassed about your bosoms, dear. They are nature's way of attracting men. Although in your case . . . you might want to remain chaste."

Sam didn't ask what she meant. It only became worrisome later.

"Just as I thought," the woman said. "You have an extra rib."

Sam stared amazed. "How did you guess?"

"And it's not in the normal place of extra ribs which is above your very first rib. This one is down at the bottom of your rib cage. Really unprecedented."

Mrs. Jaeger looked thoughtful. "Samantha, I'm going to ask you to do something quite embarrassing."

Sam got to her feet. "I don't mind. For you. What is it? Touch my nose and rub my stomach at the same time?" She laughed lightly.

"No. I want you to face the fireplace mantle, legs together, and take your underpants down just to below your hips. Just pretend you're at the doctor's."

Sam knew she was beet red. But she did it. She felt she could trust Mrs. Jaeger on anything.

Fingers brushed down the lower spine and touched the fleshy pad at the base of the tailbone. "As I suspected. You may dress now. I'm sorry to do that."

"What is it?"

"You have scar tissue there. Did you have any kind of an accident?"

"No. Never."

"Please sit down. I don't want to upset you."

Sam did as she was told. Her mind was racing, her breath coming fast.

"You were born with a vestigial tail."

"Vestigial? You mean like useless—stunted? A throwback to reptiles?"

"Yes. It was removed surgically, probably right after birth."

■ ■ ■

Soon after Kurt called her name and came down into the ravine where Sam sat on a log weeping quietly.

He said, "My mom's really sorry she upset you. She wants

you to come back to the house. It's getting dark, and, well, who knows what's out here?"

"Your mother tells me I was born with a tail. I'm some kind of monster. And I shouldn't have children because they'll be monsters."

"That's not what she meant."

Sam lashed out at him. "Do you read minds too? How do you know what she meant?"

"Sam, plenty of people are born with bits of a tail. Or with webbed feet or toes. Or earlobes fused to their heads. Male nipples are vestigial and every guy has those. They don't serve any purpose. Sometimes people have three nipples. It just happens. But when you put it together with other traits, it means you have enormous psychic potential. Believe me, Mom is an expert on this kind of thing."

"But I can't ever have a lover or a husband or children?"

"You're only sixteen. That's for down the road. Right now you have to . . . remain chaste. And it's not because you'd give birth to a freak."

"Well, why then?"

"Because the greatest occult powers are possessed by virgins. The Roman vestal virgin. The Greek seeress called Pythoness."

"Bullshit. Kurt—you and I—we're taking AP chemistry. I can't believe in that."

"Sam, you saw what you did with the knife. You altered its path with your mind. I told my mom about it and she said we should wait and see. But all these fruitcakes coming at you . . . you're giving off something."

"Great. I'm a bitch in heat for the low life degenerates of the world. I can take that geek to the senior prom."

"Do you want to lose your virginity?"

"I've passed puberty for God's sake. Of course I want to have sex with a man. I'm moiling in all the teenage confusion. Afraid of disease. Afraid of pregnancy. And all the time burning with desire."

"You can't give it up if you want to develop your full range. Something lies latent in you and is beginning to emerge. We have to see where this is going."

"I don't want to develop my full range. I want to be normal. And don't tell me there's no frickin' normal. You'll sound like Ms. Rooney."

"Sam, you're not normal. Just look at the day-to-day facts. You've been in a class of brainy nerds since fourth grade. You're one of the class beauties, but you don't seem to know it. You've never tried out for cheerleader or volleyball. Fencing is a dork sport. You go off fencing with college dorks older than you. You've never had a boyfriend. Never even had a date."

Sam's temper flared. "Is that supposed to make me feel better?"

He put up his hands. "Sam, Sam. Do I run with the cool kids? We're outliers you and me. Everyone in the class is. If we were mixed in with the normal kids we'd be so intimidated we'd be afraid to be pals."

Sam scoffed. "I can't believe you'd be intimidated by anything."

He laughed. "Cherry cheerleader scares me."

"Get out!"

"She's Aphrodite. There's something volcanic inside her that's all wrapped up with passion. No rational thoughts whatsoever."

"No argument on that," Sam said. "She has the brain of a chipmunk. Is that why she appeals to you?"

"Hey, I haven't laid a hand on her."

Sam snorted. "Given her proclivities, you wouldn't have to."

A tear ran down Sam's face again. She couldn't hold it back. She was so furious and jealous and miserable. "I'll never have a boyfriend. Hold hands. Have a first kiss. Shit. Lose my cherry."

"I could be your boyfriend," Kurt said quite solemnly. He was looking straight into her eyes. No wavering.

"What?"

She felt like the ground was rising and falling beneath her feet.

Chapter 14

Tyndall Cranmer lived in a shabby, run-down house in one of the old neighborhoods in town behind Chastain Street. Not snapped up by the Yankee invasion because it was too close to student bars and their permanent raucous revelry.

Quinn browsed the living room, turning over objects, opening drawers. The sun was at four o'clock, trending towards five. He didn't need to turn on lights.

"You won't get away with this," said Tyndall in his awful Borough of New York accent.

Quinn said, "You ought to get that fatty tumor taken off your forehead. It's not dangerous, but it sure is unsightly."

"You can't keep me like this," Tyndall whined. "It's not comfortable."

Old fart professor. One of The Circle. And Quinn knew because he had the list. But what a tangled tale it was becoming.

Tyndall was held helpless with metal thumb cuffs. $10.99 over the Internet. Leave virtually no marks.

"I can't feel my feet," whined Tyndall. "My circulation's shot."

"Well, we all have our tribulations," said Quinn.

Quinn was giving him sips of a blended Scotch. Disgusting cheap whisky, but all Tyndall had in the house. This seemed to be working better than torture. The man was getting tipsy. As old as he was, he had probably lost his tolerance for booze.

Quinn kept looking. Worn Turkish carpet. Broken down furniture with the springs coming out the bottom. Smudged glass cabinet with stone axe heads, chisels, polishing tools. On a mantle a stone effigy of the mother goddess Cybèle. Above that a framed photo of Tyndall in shorts and a broad brimmed hat standing next to a stone inscribed with archaic symbols.

And there on a bookshelf was the New York Social Register lined up back to 1900. He took down the last volume, leafed through it. Then went back a volume and found a listing for Cranmer. *"Tyndall Stuyvesant Croxdale Cranmer IV. Dalton School. Columbia, BA, PhD."* No clubs. No dynastic marriage. No list of multiple homes. Zilch.

"You were in the New York social blue book up until the 1980s."

Tyndall brightened. "Mother was a Stuyvesant. Father from one of the original families in the Bronx. We had intermarried with Pences and Pells, but it all kind of ran out when the parents died."

Quinn nearly said leaving you a nobody professor. But he didn't. He was trying to play this man through something other than fear. And no matter how low they fall, they always remember when they were somebody. And will remind you of it in a second.

"The Dalton School," said Quinn. "How progressive of your parents."

"They were New Dealers. Interior Department under Harold Ickes."

"Ripped off the Indians, did they?"

Cranmer chuckled. "As a matter of fact, you're correct. All that lease money for oil and gas on reservation lands. Grazing rights. It goes into federal trust and then all disappears. The redskins get a pittance each month. But, hey, they'd only blow it on firewater."

"So you grew up in the West? That would explain your attraction to anthropology."

"Yeah, the old man wore cowboy boots every day. To friends back East, he could pretend to be bohemian. That's a respectable society path as long as your children come back into the fold. Problem was he didn't steal enough, so the fold was barred. I had to find my own way to suck on the public teat."

"You're a baby boomer?"

"Front end. Born during the war. Old man dodged that of course. Come 1960, I was JFK all the way. First draft of Peace Corps volunteers. Went to Turkey. Made my first find. Came back to Columbia to get the doctorate."

"Columbia," Quinn said. And he couldn't keep the disparagement out of his voice.

"Don't get snooty about your credentials. Columbia's an Ivy. And in many cases it's the preferred choice for old New York families."

Quinn gave Tyndall another drink of whisky. He knew he had to dial it back. Get chummy somehow. Then he saw the picture that astounded him.

A bearded Tyndall as a young man in a hole with the

skeleton of a giant. An ink inscription said "Hacilar, Turkey, 1967."

He fixed Tyndall with his almost wondrous gaze. "You found a Nifilhim skeleton."

Tyndall smiled. "Bingo."

"How did you get permission to dig?"

"I was Peace Corps. We didn't do anything useful. Just spent money on the local economy. So we could do what we pleased. Plus there was a local industry in looting ancient ruins."

Quinn sat down in a chair opposite Tyndall, gave him another drink of whisky. Took a swig himself from the bottle. Disgusting. He hated blended Scotch.

"So you trotted back to Columbia thinking they'd be all over your research, practically hand you a PhD, beg you to stay on the faculty."

Tyndall snorted. "You know the drill. Dire threats about sending me to prison for jeopardizing a dozen international treaties on antiquities. Interrupting their flow of grants and precious research."

"Then they played good cop?"

"Precisely. We could forget the whole thing. I could crawl through the program like the usual worm. Do a dissertation on the domestication of the dog in Neolithic times."

"Not the broad topic of course."

"Oh no. A narrow bit of it. A virtual footnote to some senior faculty member's seminal work. Filling in here and there for his revised edition. No daring speculations for Tyndall Cranmer."

"And then you were banished to the South to teach."

"'Think of it as a civilizing mission,' they told me."

Quinn got his own glass and they sat in the settling dusk drinking more whisky. Becoming right convivial.

"I want you to go back in memory," said Quinn. "To something you'll enjoy recalling. Everyone you ever denied tenure to. You should take a macabre relish in that. A little *tour d'horizon* of all the pain you've dealt out."

"Ah, now that . . ." Tyndall's face seemed to light up. "Broad subject."

"I'll steer you. Maeve Fitzhugh."

"Disgraceful scholarship," he spat without a second's hesitation. "Woeful. The pits."

"You're breaking little fresh ground."

The liquor was taking hold. Tyndall seemed to take on a jocular familiarity.

"I wanted a closer intimacy with her. Inherently improbable with this new breed of rad-lib women. Think their pussies are some kind of goddamn natural resource that needs to be preserved. She threatened me with a sexual harassment charge. Then got nervous, said of course she wouldn't but we had to keep things on a professional basis."

With another drink of whisky, Tyndall warmed to his tale of revenge. "We got the bitch good. All her grants and trips to Iraq. Published articles. Thinking she could show us up. We knew how to take care of some eager beaver like that.

"She just excelled herself in arrogance there towards the finale. One article after the next. Preposterous. Couldn't be of any quality there were so many. Probably self-plagiarized."

Quinn said, "And The Circle is made up of people who have somehow come upon evidence of Nibiru."

Tyndall repeated the word meditatively. "Nibiru." Then, "Maeve's got something, it's hidden there in that house. She stole it from Antarctica."

■ ■ ■

Sam heard a click of heels outside and peeked out of the blackout curtains. The night was clear with a few scudding clouds going across a half moon. The air had turned chill. Mrs. Jaeger was walking around the house making peculiar signs.

Sam got undressed and stood looking at herself in a full length mirror behind a closet door.

Long legs. Blooming young womanhood. A russet bush the exact color of the hair on her head. Cherry and all the in-crowd girls shaved their twats and talked about it endlessly. This cream and that razor. Some of them even "sexted" pictures of it to boys when they were freshly smooth. They were so trashy.

Sam tossed her head, tried to look saucy. To feel like a cheerleader. Shook her shoulders in a little shimmy that made her breasts jiggle.

When would they have the first kiss? Would Kurt put his lips on hers and press gently? What did you do exactly as a girlfriend? Was it something you could study and lay out in a business plan?

For the first time it dawned on Sam that the room had belonged to Kurt's sister. Photos of her in skiing and climbing gear. Gosh she was beautiful. Group pictures from college and in medical scrubs. A conch shell. An antique doll with porcelain head and arms, cloth body, dressed in a Swiss peasant costume.

She opened a drawer to find sex toys. A variety of dildos and handcuffs with padding inside to not chafe the wrists. She quickly shut it in embarrassment.

Book cases with books in foreign languages, many of them medical texts.

And then she saw *the book*. It had the name Jaeger on the spine. The rest was in German, and she couldn't read it. She gasped when she opened it.

It was so beautifully printed she was afraid of leaving fingerprints. Swirling rich decoration of roses, poppies, violets and green stems around the edges of the pages and a gold margin.

Sam quickly shut the overhead light, turned on a lamp and crawled into bed.

It was a how-to-do sex book, no doubt about it, with extreme devotion to detail. The hard bunched muscles of the male back. The twining female hands. The men were craggy and handsome, the women pre-Raphaelite looking beauties with wavy serpentine hair and long, swan-like necks.

Twisting bodies in sex positions. There were so many variations. And then cut-away anatomical illustrations showing the position of the sex organs in each. A text that no doubt described how to reach the Nirvana of orgasm. Never had she seen the sex act so beautifully illustrated. It was absolutely spiritual.

It made the trash teenagers looked at on the Internet seem utterly tawdry. Painted whores with pneumatic boobs being hammered by hideous looking men.

Every seventh page or so was an embossed painting with brilliant color and an almost jewel-like transparency. In the nature scenes, the leaves and roots and climbing, twisting vines were in bright sharp focus. A pale-skinned girl in a dark forest, rump thrust out taking it from behind while braced against a tree. Lustrous wavy blond hair billowing against a nearly black lake.

A wood paneled room with stained glass window and candles. Flowing rich gown stripped off and abandoned in passion. The woman with her thighs raised and ankles locked around the man's back, the pair wrapped in sweet fusion. The obvious symbolism of a velvet jewel box, a glimpse of fire in the heart of the stone.

She turned more pages. Another lush room with drapes and carved wood, light filtering through a Gothic window with a noble crest in the center.

The woman was lying on her back spread out over the man. Radiant flawless skin. Navel a narrow slit with her belly taut as she arched her back. Thick lustrous wavy mahogany hair spread out like a soft sea. Her hand stroking him or rubbing her clitoris or both. Her wet red lips, her entire face open in perfect ecstasy.

His hands held her hips. Could easily stroke her swollen breasts. She was at the same time passively entrapped and filled with her own vitality and potency and frantic desire.

It made Sam wet. She could feel the lips of her vagina swelling, spreading. Her hand slid under the covers. Touched the vegetal tendrils of her bush. So like the gleaming tresses in the pictures.

A light tap on the door. Sam shoved the book under the covers and pulled the sheet up to her chin.

Mrs. Jaeger walked in and sat on the edge of the bed, looked at her with affection. "I didn't mean to imply you were a freak. But it is of interest that the biggest concentration of Rh-negative blood in the world is found among the Basques of Northern Spain. They are believed to be the descendants of the original Neolithic people of Europe. Their language is related to no other on earth. Some believe they settled the British Isles and then were later submerged by the Celts, another ancient people."

"Neolithic?" said Sam.

"My husband and I have spent time among them. They are extremely beautiful. Not the kind of caricatures of Neolithic that might come to mind. And I'm sure with a name like Fitzhugh you're aware of the unnatural numbers of Celts who possess second sight."

"Yes. But I thought it was superstition. Like horoscopes. Predict the future so anything fits."

"Hardly. Do you ever have visions of things that follow very shortly afterwards?"

"I . . . no. Not really. Kurt's told you about the knife, I'm sure."

"People have no idea of the power of the mind. They live starved in the midst of plenty. I think that your mind has the capacity to conceive of transcendent things. You have a potential mystical fervor inside you that just now burns with a smokeless flame."

She tapped the book under the sheet. Smiled. Sam could feel herself blushing. Busted looking at sex pictures.

"It's a bit of a shock I know," said Mrs. Jaeger. She laughed softly.

"No," Sam protested. "We have the Internet." Then she felt abashed.

"My daughter is a talented artist and a brilliant doctor. She mostly works with victims of rape and abuse, tries to help them learn to enjoy sex."

"I . . . I didn't know."

"Lisl—my daughter—her patients are filled with great shame, guilt, some with fear of damnation. She wanted to design something elegant to remind them of innocence and first love. Of the true sweetness of romantic love."

"It's a beautiful book," Sam said truthfully.

"Sex is a marvelous gift. As marvelous as producing children and watching them grow and develop.

"People separate physical sex from the emotion of love. But a magnetism that comes from Nature runs between couples and uses them as the poles use the compass and binds them to a larger whole. When you are truly in love and making love, you will feel that you are all women and he is all men."

Sam was stunned. No adult had ever talked to her about sex like that. Her mother had been too embarrassed. Had her watch a movie.

"Roll over, Samantha. Yes, I know you're naked under the sheet. Here. I'll just turn it down a tad. Arms up, hands under your face. Now try to relax. I'm going to rub your shoulders. My daughter always liked this. You're very tense."

"Mmmm," Sam murmured. It felt so soothing. Like butter being rubbed into her muscles.

"We want you to be one of us, dear. Let us share in the awakening of your powers."

Sam felt suddenly groggy. Her defenses lulled, she mumbled her innermost mind. "I want to be Aphrodite and love a boy. A man. And be adored in return."

"Aphrodite is a potential in every woman. When you are in love, she bubbles up from the subconscious like Aphrodite rising in her birth from the sea. But you are something much stronger. Athena may emerge. Or wise Sophia.

"But the goddess of love will come when it is time. If I may say this, you have curves and beautiful breasts. One day you will bare them to a man in the age-old way of ensnaring the male gaze. Provocative with trancelike force. Making woman both temptress and victim.

"Now let your heart and mind be a clear crystal spring. Peaceful oblivion. Let Aphrodite come to you in dreams."

Sam slept for she didn't know how long. She woke in darkness. She felt as though she were smelling incense and could feel music rippling through her body. And she levitated. Drifted out of her body in silence and through the bathroom door.

Briefly heard the drip of the spigot in the sink. Felt a cool sensation of the porcelain. Then another door.

Kurt was lying there asleep. With the lights out, he had opened his curtain so the objects of the room showed ghostly gray.

Her hands solid and then dissolving. Sliding over his silky skin. Feeling the flesh and then turning to water.

Lips pressed upon one of his nipples. Sucked gently. Her mouth hardened and pressed more strongly. Worried its stiffness with her teeth.

He moaned in his sleep.

And then she dissolved and was no longer there. The music died away.

Birds were singing. She got out of bed and opened the curtain. It was a bright new day. Her first day with a boyfriend.

Chapter 15

When Samantha came downstairs, Kurt was scrambling eggs. Toast had popped out of the toaster and the air held the aroma of coffee.

She poked him playfully. "Are you out of sorts?"

"I had a visitant in the night."

He had said "visitant." Not "visitor."

"What happened?" she asked cautiously.

"Nothing I care to share." He gave her a forced smile. Went on with what he was doing.

"A visitant? You mean like a succubus or something?"

Reluctantly, he pulled up his polo shirt and showed her his nipple marked with a large hickey.

Sam gasped. "I dreamed I did that to you. I . . . I don't . . . I refuse to believe I did that. You can't believe it."

"My mom sealed the house last night. I'm glad it wasn't something that penetrated it."

"You think there are ghosts out there? Spirits or something?"

He gave her a wry look. "Sam, you've seen my family. We are passing strange. We have witnessed and believe in a great number of occult phenomena."

"Where are your parents?"

"They went away. I heard them in the night. A car came for them. They just go away. That's the way it always is. Kind of like your mom."

Suddenly the possibilities seemed endless. She began to have wicked thoughts. Alone in this cocoon of a house with a beautiful boy. Her actual boyfriend. Like "The Blue Lagoon" or something.

"Do they leave instructions or anything? Turn down the thermostat when you go out? Beware of busy-body neighbors?"

Kurt held up a note written in a beautiful cursive handwriting like no one did anymore.

Tell Samantha to be patient. The road will open before her as she advances. Do not tamper with the seals around the house. Do not compromise Samantha's development. Her destiny forbids it.

Love,

Mutti

"What does the third one mean?"

"Keep my hands off you."

"Do you have to be told that?"

"Probably. You're a very attractive girl, Sam."

She stood very close, put an innocent look on her face. "Thank you, kind sir. Do you really want to keep your hands off me?"

"Not in the least. But one doesn't buck my family. Oh, this came FedEx today."

Sam opened it to find six throwing knifes. All steel. Leaf shaped blade perhaps two inches across at the widest point, four inches long.

"Well," she said with evident pleasure. "How utterly thoughtful of you."

"I thought they'd be easier to play around with than your ornate killer commando ones."

"Is this our first exchange of gifts as a couple?"

"Sure."

"But what do I give you?"

"Nothing is required."

"How about this?" She threw her arms around his neck and kissed him hard on the mouth. Emotions wild inside her.

Her first kiss.

■ ■ ■

The incident at the school dominated the local and even statewide news. TV film of the cops made them look as incompetent as they were. And Jude was nowhere to be found.

The county school superintendent had been heard exiting Mr. Peevey's office threatening: "You better get a grip on this school, Peevey, or you'll be back in the classroom. Where you were a complete disaster I might add."

All the kids knew it was coming. What does the career

educrat do when confronted by the need to show he's in control? He puts on a battle-against-violence dog and pony show.

First up was a toy gun buy-back. Everyone was to bring in a toy gun—no BB guns—someone might get hurt. They would be piled up in an oil drum, set ablaze to melt down. In exchange you would get a slice of vegetarian pizza on artisanal gluten-free crust.

A total of one gun came in. A rubber tipped dart gun. And it was loaded. Mr. Peevey handled it gingerly, dropped it with a clunk in the drum. A fat kid waddled off shoving pizza in his mouth. Boxes of pizza went untouched.

Next up was a day of mandatory pink t-shirts to show opposition to bullying. You were given your shirt in home-room. A class assembly had a professional "facilitator" who proclaimed them united in celebrating diversity and raising awareness of the need to accept differences.

She lectured them on how a third of people with eating disorders in America were men. No, not overweight, beer gut type disorder, but full-blown anorexia. And there was no support group to help them with their body image and inadequate public mental health care and blah blah blah.

The entire school sat there in glassy eyed submission, reading text messages, surfing the web. Nasar tweeted to the genius class: "When limp-wristed utopian dimwits drown you in doctrinaire goo #boredwitless."

Laughter broke out in the group. The facilitator put her hands on her hips and glared at them.

When it ended, there was a virtual stampede for the doors. Samantha went out with Nasar and ran smack up against a big lug of a football stud. "Bo." As in "Hey, bo'. How's it goin'?"

He said, "What's kickin'?"

"Going to class," she said, trying to slide around him. He moved to block her path.

"Want to hook up on Saturday, and like, get weird?"

"Um . . . no. I can't imagine doing that."

"Why not?"

"Do I need a reason?"

"Yeh. You do. Cause you're talkin' to the one and only Bo."

Sam sighed. "Got your swagg on? Just all freakin' awesome on the field and off. Can't figure why I'm not weak at the knees confronted by your mackin' skills."

"Yeaah," he said. His brain was working slowly, not really believing she was making fun of him. No one made fun of Bo.

"Kurt Jaeger and I have decided to date exclusively."

He snorted. "That's not what I heard."

"And what is dear Cherry spreading maliciously around the school?"

"I heard you ride with a bike gang. And we all know what that means."

"Do tell," she said acidly.

"Hey, the girls I hook up with know what I want and know I've got to have it."

"You're odious." She tried to step around him again.

He looked confused. Sniffed his armpit. "What're you talkin' about? I took a shower."

She shook her head in despair. "Odious means inspiring hatred. Not being smelly."

"You think you're so smart," he snarled. "Don't you lay your haterade smarty shit on me. If all them perfessers are so dam' smart, why ain't they rich?"

"Do you enjoy being dumb?" she said with disgust. "Keep the brain blank. Read a few sports stats each morning and forget them by noon."

He shoved his bulk up against hers. "Don't you talk down to me. You and them fencing fairies. You like to priss-pot around with them? Get up to hinky-winky-tinky?"

"I can't pretend to understand your idiom," Sam said.

"Leave her alone," said Nasar.

The hulk turned on him. "What are you going to do about it, stork?"

Nasar had never conceived of being in a fight. Got furious when people asked why he didn't play basketball. Would say, "Why on earth would I want to throw a round orange ball through a hoop?"

Sam was furious. And her throwing knife just came into her hand. It just appeared. Animal instinct.

The lout looked down at it. Sneered. "You don't have the guts to use that."

"Try me."

He reached and took hold of her breast. "Wooo! Big kow-a-bonga!"

With one quick slash Sam opened the back of his wrist. Ker-swick. Blood splatter.

A look of total shock came over him. Then the hideous

smile of someone about to cry. He let out a wail, blood running down his hand.

"I'm going to the prince-pul 'bout you," he sniveled.

"Sure. Go ahead and tattle. That's what bullies always do when they lose. You'll be a hero for the whole school. Beaten by a girl and runs crying to the principal. That's prin-ci-pal by the way."

She left him with his hand clutched between his legs. Crying openly. Big round shoulders heaving. Blood spreading across his jeans.

As Sam cooled down she knew that had been a mistake. She sat in chemistry class dreading what was to come. Text messages were spreading the story all over the school.

It wasn't long before Principal Peevey came storming into the class.

"Where is it? You hand it over this instant! And this is it for you, young lady. You're expelled. And you'll probably get jail."

Kurt gave her a look like what have you done now?

Sam thought, why do they persist in calling you "young lady" when the whole school ethos was to eliminate ladies and gentlemen from the landscape.

From the middle of the class, Randall cleared his throat and stood up as though addressing a court. His father was dean of the law faculty after all.

Randall had taught himself to read at age six with a set of Southeastern Reporters. Hundreds of pages of appellate cases. In fourth grade he could explain summary judgment and *res judicata*, legal stuff like that, to the class. Typically talked in complete paragraphs.

And he was the embodiment of acne-covered, pencil-neck geek. But at that moment he was never more heroic. He polished his thick glasses on his sleeve, taking a dramatic pause. Dangled them from his fingers.

"Well actually, if I may address this issue, there are a number of points in Samantha's favor. To wit: Complete and utter failure on the part of school administration to provide even minimal protection from sexual harassment first from Ms. Rooney, then from a biker hoodlum, now from a meathead football jock; failure to provide even minimal physical protection first from Ms. Rooney with a knife, then from said hoodlum with a screwdriver, then from said jock with his paws; failure to do even minimal background check on said hoodlum including total and unconscionable ignorance of the fact he was on *a sex-offenders'* list."

Randall came down hard on the last, and had actually used the word "unconscionable." Against conscience. It was so lawyerly as to be overwhelming. The principal looked like he had been kicked in the stomach.

Then Randall put in the final blow. "My father taught the state's attorney general. He never tires of saying it."

When Mr. Peevey actually stumbled out of the classroom—yes, stumbled, he was not walking straight—Sam went over and hugged Randall and planted a big kiss on his fairly revolting forehead. Ruffled his greasy hair.

She felt like a teen queen for the first time in her life. She had a boyfriend. And now random guys suddenly wanted to be her protector. The whole idea of her as a complete sweet-sixteen babe was catching on.

Emerson stood up and started applauding Randall. The whole class joined in.

Chapter 16

Incidents kept escalating at the school. Someone had been stealing from the girls' lockers during gym, and ever-the-activist Drusana squeezed into a locker to ferret out the culprit. She was quite tiny and it wasn't much of a squeeze.

And who should come along but the football coach Donny-Mack Wade. A man in the girls' locker room. Pilfering food and money. Looking at data on cell phones. And yes, sniffing underwear.

Dru got it on film with her cell phone video and took two other girls as witnesses to present it to Principal Peevey. He studied it very carefully, turned in his chair and looked out the window for a long time. At last he turned around again.

"I'll deal with this . . . issue," he said grimly. "Now I want you to delete that film."

Dru did as she was told even though she could smell adult treachery. It didn't really matter because she had already put it on YouTube.

When that got all over the school, Dru was frog marched down to the office to confront a truculent hulk of a coach glowering in the corner and a red-faced principal.

She was hit with loud jumbled threats of expulsion over

lying and spying that could get you sent to jail and duplicity and how dare you. The coach chimed in from the corner with grunts and finally "Yew don't know that's me on that there film."

Dru wanted to laugh and ask him if he had been to college. But she had been raised in a tough school of gender conflict and knew her rock solid position was to say nothing and do nothing that could be twisted into belligerence. She had uncovered a thief. She was in the right.

At last she was dismissed with threats of thinking about whether to bring in the police about this unauthorized taping and "you better think hard on what you've done, young lady."

Dru felt pretty good about the whole thing and called her mother expecting praise for her masterful performance. Instead, her mom—Rhoda Shelley—came storming over from the campus in full ball-buster mode.

She was a holy terror at the university, running her department and any committee she was on with an iron fist in an iron glove. She resembled a women's basketball coach with buzzed hair, and male slacks and a golf shirt. Rippling biceps. It was hard to see petite, pretty little Dru in her.

She demanded to see the principal, and when given the standard "he's in a meeting" had flung open the door and strode in.

He looked startled and stricken.

She slammed her tote sack down in the chair and stood looming over Principal Peevey. "You listen to me, you pathetic eunuch!" she roared.

That was the last anyone heard because the secretary closed the door of the outer office.

Except for the loud bam of an object striking the desk a terrific blow. Rhoda was rumored to carry a metal *bocce* ball in a string bag as a weapon, and it seemed to be true.

While this was going on, Dru and Samantha sat eating their lunch out on the lawn. Dru had a vintage Ororo Munroe lunch box with a spring vegetable lasagna she had seen on the food channel and made herself.

"It's so mortifying," said Dru. "She always wants me to stand up against men. And the first thing that happens, she has to butt in."

"Maybe you're lucky. Maybe she actually loves you in a kind of fierce momma lion way. Mine barely knows I exist."

"You really think that? Fiercely protective and all that?"

"Sure."

They sat in thought.

"I'm so jealous of you," said Dru. "You've got Kurt beating people up for you. Randall acting like your personal attorney."

"This is a new departure for me," said Sam. "I'll have to get back to you one whether it's a good thing or not."

Dru asked, "Do you think anyone will ever describe us as 'smokin' hot'?"

Dru was wearing baggy mom jeans with red alligator clip suspenders and a blue denim work shirt that said "Ray's Garage" over the pocket. Glasses with lime green frames. Black high top tennis shoes. Her hair was parted in the middle, tied off with scrunchies in Afro pigtails. From a distance it made her look like Minnie Mouse.

Sam smiled. "I seriously doubt it."

"When I was seven I was at a friend's house and we got into her mom's vanity, made ourselves up. I guess we looked like child hookers, but we were just children. Her mom thought it was hilarious. Mine went through the roof. She whipped me so badly I'm surprised DSS didn't take me out of the home. It's no lipstick and eyeliner for me. I have to wear jeans to hide that I shave my legs."

She tugged up the ankle of her jeans above lime green socks to show that her legs were scraped bare.

"Did you know your father?" asked Sam. "I've never seen mine that I remember."

"No. He was just a sperm donor. My mom dreams of a world without men. Her only child had to be a political statement."

"Mine just dreams of dusty old ruins."

They sat pensively.

Dru held up the backs of her hands. "I presume he was black. He must have been a pygmy. I'm only five-three."

"Well, you don't have to wear sunscreen."

"Do you ever want to dress in slut-wear?" asked Dru. "Uber-tight dresses that barely cover your ass. Give guys come-hither looks through inch-long false eyelashes."

"It's not high on my list of desires."

"My mom expects me to be a dyke." She shuddered. "God, the hutches she brings home. Giving me the lascivious eye. Making lewd propositions when she's out of the room. It's enough to make you run away from home and become a pole dancer."

Sam laughed. "I hardly think that's you, Dru."

"Well what am I then?" She sounded slightly tearful.

"You're flippin' beautiful for starters. You're like a teen version of—who's the actress from *Carmen Jones*?—Dorothy Dandrige."

"Seriously?"

"For true. And you're totally literary. You'll grow up to be a famous writer like Jacqueline Woodson. Intelligent. Independent thinker."

"Really?"

"I see you at Oxford or Cambridge, maybe St. Andrews in Scotland where Prince William and Kate Middleton went. You study English lit where they still do that rather than political indoctrination. Chaucer. Shakespeare. Byron, Keats, and Shelley."

"Mom would never go for that. She wants me at Berkeley or Chicago."

"Your mom is an education snob. She'd be a sucker for a foreign degree. It's three years for British degrees instead of our four. Our prestige universities are so outrageously expensive that she'd come out cheaper. Pony up the money without objection."

Dru sounded thoughtful. "She would fall for that, yes."

"Old gothic colleges with cloisters. Every girl serious about her studies so you're not a freak. They wear academic gowns and dine at long oak tables each night in a wainscoted great hall hung with portraits. Soup course.

Gristley meat and watery vegetables. Pudding dessert. Very British.

"And you're surrounded by cute kind of gawky guys with cute British accents. They'll wear corduroy and their socks will fall down, but they'll have those boarding school mops of hair. Dreadlocks if they're African. Like something out of Harry Potter. You'll adore them."

Dru's eyes seemed to be seeing distant horizons. "Gosh," she said.

■ ■ ■

After school, Sam sat on the bleachers in the university gym studying French while taking glances at Kurt teaching karate to seven-year-olds. Black pants, green t-shirt, black belt. He really had a chest and arms on him.

The kids adored him. Hung all over him. Swung on his arms. Begged for special attention. He held a kicking bag like a huge catcher's mitt while they let fly.

Some girls would have thought his obvious ease with children would have made him THE ONE. In fact, Sam had thought very little about children. Never imagined herself as a mother. Never even considered being a school teacher. She just liked watching Kurt be totally in charge of the situation. See him demonstrate the moves that he had done with such mastery when she was in danger.

Afterwards they walked across the campus towards his house. She grabbed hold of his bicep with both hands, briefly rested her head against his shoulder. They had been a couple for nearly a week. He had saved her from a meth-deranged creep that the police couldn't seem to locate.

Sam laughed. "You know after you took down that Jude creature, I got swept out of the room with the rest. I didn't get to throw my arms around you and say 'my hero.'"

He smiled slowly, his eyes twinkling.

They came to the meandering road that made a circle in his neighborhood, wooded park all around.

Sam got in front of Kurt and put her hands against his chest as a blocking movement. Looked up at him quite seriously. "I'll do whatever Cherry does to you."

"Cherry doesn't do anything," he said, but his eyes cut away evasively.

"Kurt?"

"Well, sort of. But it doesn't count."

Sam held back her flare of jealousy. She wanted nothing more than to adore him, to feel his hands going over her while his voice whispered in her ear.

For dinner, Kurt made balsamic-vinegar braised chicken with garlic, onions, raisins, Italian bacon called pancetta. He brought it to a boil, simmered it for forty-five minutes while it gave off the most delicious odor.

"I continue to be amazed," said Sam, sitting in a ladder-back chair at the kitchen table. "You slay my enemies, control fire, put food in front of me. What can't you do?"

Kurt sipped from a big wooden spoon. "I dunno. Fathom the mysteries of eternity?"

She propped her face in her hands. "We could work on that together."

Kurt sat down at the table. "Right now you're just a fluffy chick pecking her way out of her shell. We have to see how you grow."

Sam got up, straddled Kurt's legs, sat down and stretched her arms out over his shoulders. She pressed her forehead against his. Her bosom was very close. She could feel his strong vitality.

"Did you mean it when you said I was one of the class beauties?"

"Of course."

"Really?"

"Do I have to put you in front of a mirror?"

She held his face in both hands. "I'm pretty grown, you know. I certainly have big girl hooters."

She couldn't have been more blatant. Kurt's mouth opened, but he was speechless.

They heard the purr of the engine as Cherry drove up in her T-bird and tripped up the boxwood-lined walk. The doorbell chimed.

Kurt gave Sam an inquiring look. "Shall we just ignore this?"

Sam shook her head. "You know she knows we're here. If not now then she'll come again." She didn't tell him to get rid of Cherry. No huffy ultimatums of it's her or me. She slid to the dining room table where she had left her school work.

Cherry put on her bright cheery face. Asked Kurt to "come with me into the night." He declined. Invited her in. Cherry took a step forward and then stopped.

She seemed first disconcerted, then puzzled, then genuinely frightened. She couldn't seem to go forward. She was stymied by something.

"What? What's happening?"

Then she saw Sam sitting at the dining room table. Doing nothing. Pretending to work on chemistry.

"So that's what's going on!" Cherry shouted, furiously indignant. "I see you there, Samantha Fitzhugh! I'll get you for this! I'll get you!"

She ran down the walk in tears, gunned her engine and squealed off.

"What is going on?" Sam asked, alarmed.

"Mom sealed the house," Kurt explained. "I told you this morning. Ordinarily you can invite someone past it. Cherry must be very susceptible to occult powers."

"If I didn't know you and your mother," said Sam, "I'd find this really scary."

Chapter 17

"Boo? Trey Wallingford. From school? Squash team?"

Boo recognized the name right off. Rutherford Hanford Wallingford III. Trey had gone to Yale and studied art history. The prep school alumni report, which Boo read religiously looking for clients, had Trey working for a big art auction house in New York.

"I'm holding the phone away from my ear. Do you hear the uproar?"

"Yeah, what is it? A brawl?"

"Abso-fucking-lutely! A donnybrook-slash-brawl-slash -free-for-all. Art dealer pussies hammering each other. The cops are here. Arrests. Injuries. It was like Tucky's deb ball at the St. Regis. Remember how out of control that was?"

"I was there," said Boo. Thinking it was his last before he was blackballed from society.

"We had this trash lot of contemporary work. Mostly figurative. Very over-sized. Fifteen by twenty-five feet. That sort of over-size. They gave it to me to handle. I figured yuppies might buy it for loft apartments down in Soho. There was the usual viewing day before. And then at seven tonight all hell broke loose."

"Explain."

"Big time art dealers showed up. Agents representing undisclosed principals from Colombia, Argentina, Tokyo, Europe. Crazy bidding. Fistfights. Full-throated uproar over cell phones to get directives. Then it turned to fistfights. Did I mention that?"

"Did you sell it?"

"Somebody in Tokyo. Want to know the price? Fifty million. For an absolutely unknown, never heard of nobody. No big art dealer hype. Nothing. Nada."

"What's the painting of?"

"It's a nude girl. Kind of academic. What the French call *Pompier* school. Might have been done by Bouguereau or somebody late nineteenth century. Except it's contemporary. She's holding one tit. A hook-shaped twisted knot of reeds in the other hand. Eight-pointed star behind her head. A lioness is rubbing up behind her."

"So who's the artist? And what's this to do with me?"

"He's somebody in your town. Jake Milroy. A professor or something. I'm sending you a photo of the painting from my cell phone right now. And I'm catching a flight down tonight. Pick me up at the airport at ten. I got a direct flight. Don't tell me you're not my fucking chauffeur. You're going to want in on this. I don't forget my old *compadres*."

Right thought Boo, hanging up. Which is why we haven't talked since prep school.

Boo clicked on the photo of the painting. Holy shit! It was Samantha Fitzhugh.

■ ■ ■

"It does look like a spacewoman," said Kurt, holding the statue in his hand. "But you say it's Inanna?"

A breeze brushed leaves against the kitchen window. The sky was lavender and filled with birds. The simmering chicken smelled wonderful.

"I really should have paid more attention to my mom's lectures," said Sam ruefully. "Once in seventh grade when I needed a last-minute paper on mythology, she practically dictated one on Inanna's descent into the Underworld."

"Ah," said Kurt. "The quest for inner understanding. Sorry. I'm interrupting."

She cocked her head quizzically. "You know all this."

"I doubt it. Go ahead."

"She meets her sister Ereshkigal, the Queen of the Underworld, who fixes the eyes of death on her. She can only be saved by offering up a substitute. Angry at her husband Dumuzi who seems indifferent to her absence, Inanna gives him to Ereshkigal.

"Eventually she feels bad, repents, and makes Dumuzi immortal. And she allows him to come up for half the year. It's a myth that is supposed to explain the seasons."

"A Jungian would say Ereshkigal represents the dark side of the goddess. Inanna goes there to face it. The dark forces of the subconscious. She emerges reborn and emotionally whole."

"Rats," said Sam. "You know everything."

"Just my narrow area. It's what I hear at the dinner table."

"Yeah, but I don't have any profound knowledge. Not even narrow. I feel like a dunce." She gestured at the stove. "I can't even make dinner."

Kurt pressed her hand. "Sam, my mom is convinced you're in a stage like Inanna before the descent. You're about to be made complete."

"Great," she fumed. "I get to go down into hell. But from the way things are going, it's like hell is coming up to greet me."

Kurt took the chicken off the stove and served the plates. They ate at the dining room table in silence. Sam put down her fork.

"Have you ever heard of Tory Island?"

"No. Never."

"It's in Ireland."

Kurt shrugged. "Nothing."

"Cressie was talking about it that gruesome night I spent with her. I looked it up on the web. It's off the northwest coast. It was the last home of some sea people—possibly sea monsters—the Fomorians."

"It's pretty common in mythology to characterize the other side as monsters."

As darkness set in, strange chanting came from across the road on the edge of the park. Kurt peeked out of the curtains.

"Good grief. It's the Wiccans."

Neighbors lights came on. Kurt knew they were calling the cops.

It wasn't long before the patrol car rolled up, lights flashing. A muscular cop got out slowly like he was having trouble with his knees. Hands on his hips, he stared at the Wiccans. They were wearing some kind of sack dresses with leaves in their hair.

"We're levitating the house, officer!" Cressie shrieked with laughter.

"If this house is rockin' don't come knockin'!" yelled some other girl's voice.

What he said to them couldn't be heard inside the house. But the girls were loud. They were drunk or on drugs. Everything seemed hysterically funny to them.

"They're in there cohabiting! Isn't that against the law or something?"

"Yes, shouldn't they be arrested and put in cells with murderers and rapists?"

Again the cop said something unintelligible. Then turned and slowly came up the walk. He rang the bell.

"Don't go to the door," Kurt ordered. "We haven't done anything. And with the curtains, he can't tell if there are lights on."

BAM BAM BAM! A fist was hammering the door. "Open up! Police!"

Reluctantly, Kurt opened the door. The light flooded out. It was the young cop Buck from the incident at Sam's house.

"So it's you two again."

"I live here," said Kurt. "Sam lives at the other house that was being ransacked."

"Where are your parents?"

"They're out for the evening, sir."

"I'll bet."

"Do you want to come in and search? They're not hiding under the bed."

The cop didn't like that sarcasm one bit. "Well, since you've waived any Fourth Amendment fol-de-rol, I think I will."

He hitched up his gun belt like he was about to make some huge effort.

But he found he couldn't get past an invisible barrier. Something was holding him back. He waved his arms at it, but they wouldn't penetrate.

"Well mully-fuckers!" he exclaimed in astonishment.

He tried to bull his way through. But was invisibly blocked.

"What the . . . ? What are you two doing to me?"

"Nothing," said Kurt innocently.

The cop dropped back cursing under his breath. The world had turned weird on him and he felt distinctly like a fool.

To make things worse, the girls were shrieking with laughter as he came back down the walk. He began bellowing at them to go home.

"I thought you asked him in," said Sam.

"I sort of did. Mom must have really laid something heavy on."

Chapter 18

Boo picked Trey up from the airport in his Range Rover at nine as instructed.

Trey was wearing a perfectly tailored suit, Knickerbocker Club tie, and shoes with soles so thin they looked like they should only be worn on carpet.

In "catching up" Trey pretty much let Boo know his trust fund was more than adequate, but big commissions in the art world were starting to excite him. Of course he had an apartment on the East Side and a weekend house in Croton-on-Hudson. Summers he usually shared a house with some friends in Sagaponack—or Sagg as he called it— in the Hamptons.

He allowed the Range Rover was okay for its purposes, but he had a vintage Jag he kept up the Hudson. Go up by train and had his wheels waiting for him. Out on Long Island he'd rent a Beemer. The traffic was too bad to drive all the way there. He usually shared a helicopter.

Boo thought with gratitude the status seeking he had escaped. Zoned out completely thinking of Samantha and his ultimate escape from everything.

In a tree-shaded neighborhood, they found Milroy's house, and a totally stoned teenage girl told them he was at his club. Gave them directions along with some vague gestures into the night.

"You into underage sex appeal?" asked Trey when they were back in the car.

Boo gave him a skeptical look. "That girl? She seemed to have leaves in her hair."

"Any girl. Jail bait type girl. You should see them in the night clubs of Manhattan. Barely there ensembles. They do not keep their goodies under wraps."

Trey said he'd take one back to his apartment. He had a sex swing there.

Boo couldn't comprehend this. The prepster trying to be urban and hip. It was almost obscene.

They drove on in the dark on two-lane blacktop until they came to the end of the directions. A falling down shack with heavy metal music blaring from a juke box. Light provided by hurricane lamps sizzling on the floor in an eerie circle.

"His club?" said Trey. They were facing the falling down building with Lucifer's Legion on a sign above the overhang.

A fire was glowing in a charcoal grill. The whole effect was sinister.

"I think maybe we should come back in daylight," said Boo. "If even then."

"No, we're getting this done."

Trey got out. Boo cut the car engine aware that he was making a big mistake.

Back in the shadows behind the lamps, paintings of the

cosmos lined the walls. But for the brilliance of the painted stars, they would not have been noticeable.

Boo had known he was dealing with hoodlum meth dealers. But he never imagined walking into their lair. One misstep . . . *my God they might be taken for narcs or something.*

And there was Quinn. He looked puzzled only for a moment, stepped forward offering his hand to Trey.

"I haven't had the pleasure."

Trey took it distractedly.

Boo introduced Trey, named their mutual prep school.

Quinn stated his. Quinn wore a summer weight Field Coat, jeans, chukka boots.

"Is that a Knickerbocker Club tie?" Quinn queried.

"Yes, it is," said Trey, pleased at the recognition.

The pair sized each other up. Privileged backgrounds. Men of the same kidney.

And yet it was insane, Boo knew. The scene was surreal.

Hog Man loomed large bringing his stench with him. Quinn said to Boo, "You of course know my chief lieutenant. Mr. Smee to my Captain Hook as it were."

Hog Man spat tobacco juice on the floor, wiped his chin. He was weaving drunk. Chortling in a kind of snuffle.

"Yore funny as shit. Yew know that?"

Despite the continuous drinking and the awful music, the room held an expectant air. They had interrupted something.

There must have been thirty men there outside the circle

of the lamps. Lurid shadows on their tattooed faces. Reptilian eyes glinting.

Flanked by guards on either side, a skinny twitching man sat on a straight chair, his head in his hands. He was shirtless, knobs of bone showing in his shoulders.

"I'm keeping you in cruel suspense," Quinn said blithely. "We're having a bit of a kangaroo court here. Or a show trial. Whichever you prefer. Of Jude. Dear Saint Jude. Our chef as it were."

"That karate kid nearly killed me," Jude whined. "My ribs are busted in. I think my head is broken open. I been punished enough."

"Jude presumed to play at substitute teacher," Quinn explained to Boo. "And there dared to make a pass at . . . Samantha Fitzhugh."

He gestured towards the painting on the easel set in the chalk circle.

Boo's jaw dropped. Samantha. They had a painting of her in the nude. God she was exquisite. He wanted to embrace the painting. To fall to his knees before it.

"She's for all of us," whined Jude. "You can't just have her by yourself."

Barrage of cursing and jeering.

"Leetle shithook!"

"Pissant dumbass!"

"Presumptuous chap, wouldn't you say?" Quinn addressed to Boo. "His ratiocinative processes are so limited."

Boo realized they were about to do something violent to this poor geek. And they didn't care whether he witnessed it or not. Which meant they might kill him too. Or they were absolutely certain of his harmlessness.

But what about Trey? How could they be sure of him?

Jude was babbling at random. "Sure I liked the library. Go online and chat with a twelve-year-old girl. She was kind of advanced from what I remember at that age. Take a nekkid picture of herself and put it over the web. Lived in a little box of a house with a mother who fucked around. Got her cues there. Little bud tits next to mom's huge hanging down honkers."

"You liked the library, but the library did not like you," Quinn said.

"But I fit in *here*," Jude said ingratiatingly. "I'm one of the boys. Got a chemistry book and learned to cook meth. Where would you be without me?"

"And so you do fit in," Quinn agreed. "We are a powerful protector. It's part of our benevolent aspect. Providing in good faith useful goods and services demanded by society at large. Looking after our own with total loyalty."

Another chorus of approval.

"Yeh-bwa!"

"Yew done said it!"

"A-men to that!"

Boo looked at Quinn thinking it was like a civilized man who had been shipwrecked on a cannibal isle and had found himself made chief. Because he had a ticking watch that mesmerized them. Or predicted an eclipse of the sun.

"You presumed to aspire to the love of a child of Nibiru. Then you must pass the ordeal. Perhaps you are worthy of her. I am a fair man. Stern but fair. This consideration now guides my course of action."

Quinn used big blacksmith pliers to lift a glowing steel gauntlet off the Green Egg grill.

Jude shook in naked terror. He tried to scream but it came out a screech due a hysterical constriction of his vocal cords.

Hog Man held him from behind just above the elbows.

Jude's voice was high and hoarse. "I don't deserve this! I don't want to do this!"

"I'm afraid you have no choice in the matter," Quinn said rather mildly.

Hog Man lifted Jude's trembling arm by the elbow in a vise-like grip. Jude closed his fist in resistance, but the gauntlet was big enough to accept it.

He didn't scream at first, lust fell over twitching. Hog Man kicked the gauntlet away.

Jude's hand was charred flesh burned down to finger bones that looked like tree twigs. The screams began. Went on and on. Legs and feet kicking.

"Please God *makeitstop*!"

He frothed at the mouth. Until he was still but for some last shakes of his head beating the floor. His open eyes were opaque as marbles.

"No," Quinn pronounced. "Not worthy of the goddess. I really didn't think so."

Boo stumbled outside vomiting. His head swam. Blindly he found the Rover, got inside and started the engine.

Hog Man leaned inside the window, bathed him in his filthy breath. "Hey, don't be a stranger."

"No . . . we won't," Boo gagged. "We know the way now."

Boo drove off, his mind racing with fear. Would they come after them? Did they just not care what had been witnessed? Quinn was a monster. He could have expected any kind of animal behavior from the others. But Quinn was educated.

Trey's brow was furrowed, thinking hard. His voice came out in a panting rush. "Did you see that painting in there? It's like what I sold in New York. The thing is worth millions."

■ ■ ■

The clock struck eleven. Sam yawned. Kurt yawned.

Sam thought how warm and cozy it was. Books and paintings in their closed, sealed world. No one could come in due to some magic she was simply taking as part of her life now.

They brushed their teeth together at the bathroom sink. Looked at each other's face in the mirror. It was very intimate.

"Your family is really open about sex aren't they?" Sam asked, more as a statement than a question.

"You've apparently seen my sister's book."

"Yes. And the dildos."

Kurt laughed lightly. "Tools of her trade."

They stood there knowing they were about to exit the bathroom by their own doors. Hesitating. Feeling something should happen.

Sam didn't know how to be provocative. It was not

something ever witnessed around the Fitzhugh house. Did she wet her lips and leave them half parted?

Kurt's mother said you thrust your breasts at him. That seemed rather obvious. But she had done just that when she sat on his lap in the kitchen.

Finally she said, "You're the boyfriend. Aren't you supposed to grab at me and thrust your tongue down my throat? Try to get to various 'bases' with your hands?"

"No," he said. Did he say it ruefully?

She pressed herself up against him. He was so big and desirable.

"We're all alone in this cocoon," she said slyly. "Aren't you going to try to talk me into sleeping in your bed? Promise you won't do anything, but of course you will."

"Sam, my mother would know the instant she walked in what had happened."

"How does she know? Read your dirty mind?"

"She feels the vibrations of emotions people have left behind. That's what she's hired for. By yes, the CIA. It's a great secret. If police agencies knew her powers, she'd never be left alone. And it exhausts her when she reads a scene of murder."

"So sex would catch her attention?"

"Very much so."

"I really don't think she'd mind."

"Yes she would. And you know why, and we've been over this."

"I'm sixteen. I'm more than ready."

He gave her a peck on the forehead.

She tried to snake her arms around his neck, but he backed up, raising his hands in denial. "The bathroom's free."

Sam was left holding empty air. Kurt closed and locked his door. She distinctly heard the lock click.

She got undressed down to her underwear and turned out the overhead light. Left a reading lamp on.

She couldn't stay away from the book. Opened it at random. A woman was lying on a man's chest, impaled on his rod. Making them one. Her breasts squashed against him.

Her hands were in his hair. She kissed him sensually. Sam guessed it was sensually. Maybe it was passionately.

She had lowered herself onto it. Taken as much as she wanted. She was probably moving slowly. Grinding the base of his cock.

Sam was in such a lather. She put the book on the floor and cut out the lamp. The room was in utter pitch black. She slid out of bed and hooked one of the curtains back admitting a gray light. Crawled back in bed.

The familiar owl hooted from the park. Sam slept.

And at some point woke to a groggy awareness. She had heard a voice.

"Please Samantha. I'm cold. Please let me in."

Samantha abruptly sat up in bed, stopped breathing. She couldn't breathe.

Cressie's face was floating outside the window. Her arms seemed to reach out in an icy embrace.

"Please let me in."

Sam ran screaming to pound on the further bathroom door. Calling Kurt's name desperately.

He jerked open the door, pushed past her into her room.

Cressie's face was slowly drifting away. He whipped the curtain back into place.

"I'm so cold," cried a plaintive fading voice.

He turned to Sam. "You didn't invite her in did you?"

"No!"

He enfolded her in his arms.

"No no!" she wept.

Clung to him desperately, shivering with fear, shivering uncontrollably. Cressie's face was still swimming before her eyes.

He took her into his room, made her lie on the bed and wrapped the duvet tightly around them both.

"We're fine," he soothed. "We're safe in here. Mom has made certain of it."

"What's going on?" she begged to know.

"Something bad has happened to her. That was her spirit."

"How can you know that?"

"I've seen this sort of thing before."

Her heart was pounding in her throat. But she realized for the first time he was wearing nothing but boxers. She could feel his hard smooth flesh. Her cheek rested at the base of his throat where a faint pulse beat. She ran her hand down his side, felt his strong thigh.

She could feel his tool all long and hard against her stomach. She had aroused him. It was that easy.

She touched it and felt him quiver. "Stop, Sam," he ordered. "Just lie still."

She held to him tightly. "Make love to me."

He said nothing. Surely her offer tempted him.

She forced him over on his back, climbed on top of him. Reached behind to undo her bra. Peeled it off. Hung her bosoms down in his face.

"You want me. I know you do. Just like I want you. Just like the pictures in the book."

It was easy for him to throw her off, wrap her in the duvet like a straitjacket. Imprison her in his arms and legs.

"Shush, Sam," he whispered into her hair. "We're going to try to sleep."

She struggled against it, and he held her tighter.

Kurt's mother brushed her cheek with her hand bringing the soothing effect.

"Shh," she whispered. "You are like me. You must develop your powers. One day he will make a union of your bodies. For now you only dream of it in your sleep."

"Please tell me," Sam murmured, already asleep.

"Your supple body. The narrow waist that joins your swelling hips. His hands grip your curves . . ."

■ ■ ■

Sometime around 1:00 a.m. Boo woke to a banging on the door of his apartment. Boo had drunk himself into a stupor, passed out in his clothes on the couch. He stumbled to the door.

Trey was there. He had gone away or something. It was

all very foggy. Boo shook his head trying to clear it. The memories of Jude being fried . . .

"Have you been gone somewhere? What . . . ?"

He was so excited there was spittle coming out of his mouth. Pulse racing. Eyes wide. Hyperactive. Just seething.

"I need you to drive me to the airport. I've got to get out of town. If you don't want to, I'll just leave your car there and you can pick it up tomorrow."

Boo stumbled downstairs. The painting of Samantha was in the back seat. Sam in her spell-binding beauty. He touched it disbelieving. It stood the test of reality. It dawned on him. Trey had gone back to the club and . . .

"You stole it from Lucifer's Legion?"

"They don't need it. Anyhow, Milroy can paint them another one."

Boo went into a panic. "I've got to live in this town. I can't be looking over my shoulder for those animals. What we were witness to—!"

"Hey, you wanna be clueless, that can be endearing sometimes. Maybe around women. But this is top-tier money. Not hedge fund level. But still, we're talking Napa Valley vineyard. Bronze driveway gate. Full size gym. Indoor saltwater pool. Hydro-massage room."

"Have you lost your mind?"

"Caesarstone countertops. Grohe faucets. If you're going to have an olive orchard, you've got to have a *frantoia*, a traditional olive press."

Trey was jabbering out a litany of status symbols he felt he deserved. He was out of his mind.

Boo looked at the painting lovingly. She was everything. Sex and life. Eternal love.

Now Trey was babbling about the painting. "Look at that beauty. Light radiating from her. The layers involved in it. The reflected light in the glazes. Emotional resonance. An aesthetic marvel."

"There are two of them," said Boo. "Where did the second one come from?"

Trey didn't answer.

"I've got to get these back to New York. And you've got to deal with Milroy one-on-one. I want to be his exclusive agent. You'll get a cut of the loot."

"Did you kneel in something? What's on your pants?"

"Nothing. Don't worry about it."

Trey shoved Boo in the Rover and ran around to the driver's side. Got in and cranked the engine.

A dim line of lights approached like psychological themes coming out of the dark. Evil incarnate. A column of motorcycles slowly surrounded the car.

"Yew lost yore way?" said Hog Man.

"No. No, I'm not lost," Trey insisted.

Hog Man jerked open the car door. "Squeeze over," he said, his huge bulk getting under the wheel.

"I didn't do anything!" Boo yelped.

"No, but yore little buddy did." He put the Rover in gear and they set off in a long cavalcade.

Trey was desperately bargaining with Hog Man. Telling him how much the paintings were worth. "Millions," he said. "I'm on the level. I'm not shitting you."

"What's that on yore knees?"

"I . . . I fell in paint."

"Looks like blood to me."

"No. No it's not. It's paint. Most definitely."

They reached the biker club, dragged Trey out into the woods while Boo followed along, afraid of what was about to happen, but too afraid to run.

Quinn was in a clearing with a bonfire lit. He was wearing an Orvis signature sweatshirt in dark navy with a band of nautical signal flags across the chest. Red sailcloth pants. Sperry top-siders.

Trey seemed more concerned about the loss of wealth than he did what was about to happen to him. It was as if he had not witnessed the death of Jude. Or his greed had blotted it from his memory.

"You fools! Don't you realize the money? We'll divvy it up. We'll all be rich."

Hog Man slammed him up against a tree. "We's already rich," he said, leering with a gold tooth. "We's rich in spirit."

"I'm afraid we've got to take you outside your comfort zone," said Quinn.

Three of them hefted him up off the ground, crossed his wrists, and nailed them to a tree with a railroad spike. Hog Man wielded the mallet, drove the spike in two blows.

Trey began screaming uncontrollably. His feet kicked wildly until Hog Man gathered them together and nailed them as well.

They lashed the hands and arms to keep his flesh from tearing off the spike.

"Man, that's some high octane bleatin'," said Hog Man. He turned to Boo seeking agreement. "You think he's taking performance enhancing drugs?"

Boo felt like he was gagging on his tongue.

"Fiercely eloquent," said Quinn.

"You know, there's nothing like a crucifixion to deliver a message," said Skeeter. "What say?"

There was a chorus of agreement.

Trey was weeping hysterically now.

"I guess he's got a few more gallons in the tank yet."

"You don't look real festive," Hog Man said to Boo. "Want a beer?"

Boo's knees crumbled as he fainted.

Chapter 19

Sam woke in the morning to find herself alone in the bed. She pulled open the curtains to flood the room with golden light. The park was bright and cheery.

The shower ran in the parents' bathroom. Sam followed the noise. She could see the watery outlines of Kurt's torso through the frosted glass of the door.

She could fit what she was feeling in no category of any previous experience of the world. She knew she could come to no conclusion about it. Could only follow instinct.

She peeled out of her underpants and dropped them on the floor. Opened the shower door and got in with him. She closed her eyes against the pounding water, pressed her hands against his chest. Molding herself into him. Soft and docile. He was starting to grow fine blond hair on his chest.

Her hands slid down his body and closed around his erection. The fullness of it.

She said, "I'm not particularly ashamed of how I behaved last night. I was really scared. And then with you holding me . . . you make me melt. Coherent thought just sort of goes away."

He took her hands away, entwined his fingers with hers.

"Fear and sexual desire are so close. It was natural you felt that way."

"I feel that way now in clear daylight. Desire I mean. And so do you from the look of things."

"Of course I do, Sam. You're . . . you're exquisite." He gestured helplessly. "I'm struggling to keep my hands off you."

She pressed her breasts into him. "I want to wear down your defenses."

"No," he protested.

"I want to do what Cherry does to you."

"Why Cherry?"

"I see her as my competition."

He turned her around.

"Good grief, forgive me. You're impossible, Sam."

She turned back around and smiled roguishly. "I'm worse than impossible. I'm incorrigible."

She soaped up her hands and began to stroke him.

"Stop," he said, but she didn't.

■ ■ ■

Cressie's body was found by her father, and the news was all over town by lunch time. Everyone at school was buzzing about it. The Wiccans were crying and consoling each other. Going into random hysteria in their classes.

Naturally the school had an assembly and laid on grief counseling. The woman counselor was a "nondenominational spiritual culture healer," an adjunct faculty member from the university psych department. Sam couldn't imagine what course she taught.

She was gaunt, dressed in black with dyed jet black hair. Spindly legs and large feet in Birkenstocks.

She had brought life-sized clay heads representing the stages of grief from the university art department. Some senior student's project left behind upon graduation. They lined the stage in a grotesque way like severed heads you might find scattered at the base of a guillotine.

"Grief is an 'issue,'" she began in a fierce voice. "You either own the issue or it owns you."

She sounded vaguely threatening, but no one was paying attention.

All the students began checking their cell messages. Cressie's death didn't seem quite real. No one knew any details. And all had been "counseled"—read nagged, lectured, bullied—so often before on sustainable this and green energy that and carbon footprint the other. Supportive, inclusive language. Reaching out. Listening to others.

She stood behind the first clay head in the row. The eyes were squinted, the lips grimacing. "There are stages of grief," she said. "Everyone goes through the same pattern. The first is denial. Denial is not a river in Egypt."

Sam knew that was meant as a joke, and everyone was supposed to laugh. Instead, a football player called out in falsetto, "Oh nooo! Say it ain't sooo!"

It was the most tasteless and crude behavior you could imagine. And the cheerleaders giggled. Which of course egged the jocks on.

"Nooo! I dooon't buh-leeve it!" another one crooned.

Principal Peevey leaped up on the stage and glared. No one paid much attention. They were now laughing and talking among themselves.

One of the Wiccans, purple hair with hair clips, eyebrows dyed blue, stood up and shouted out: "I know where to start looking for the murderer! Cressie was blackmailing a professor because she had underage sex with him. Find that professor, and I'll bet you've got your killer!"

Well that bombshell got everyone attention, but she was interrupted by the entry of Cressie's father. Jake Milroy came stumbling out from the fire curtain, weaving as he walked, voice slurred. Paint spattered on his coveralls. Combat boots.

"Nibiru is coming!" he warned. "And the Annunaki will come down in their space ships long before that as a final warning."

"Hoo-boy, he's drunk as shit!" yelled one of the jocks.

"Shut the fuck up!" Milroy bellowed.

The auditorium fell dead silent. He was a large man, and looked wild-eyed dangerous like an old time anarchist. Beard bristling. Hair disheveled. A laborer's thick hands and neck.

His voice became surprisingly clear. He surveyed the auditorium from side to side.

"Yeah, now you fall back on civility. When you're good and scared. It happens so seldom. Nibiru is concealed now. But by the time it appears on the horizon larger than Venus, it'll be too late.

"You think you're so in control with your little Facebook world. Your undisturbed lives. Looking at dog tricks on youtube. You'll know different one minute after a rogue planet whips past trailing space debris. The fall of the shit hammer. Jerking the poles in reverse. Typhoons. Earthquakes. Volcanic eruptions."

Cherry stood up making a squeaking noise. Something about this lecture was getting to her. She seemed to be trying to shriek.

Milroy kept going. "They've found algae fossils on a meteorite that landed in Sri Lanka. Life came from outer space. We were seeded. Either by accident or some divine mover. But we were ape men until the Annunaki brought us culture."

Samantha's mind was filled, overflowing. Remembering that night at the Milroy's. The motorcycles. Seeing Cressie at her window. The pleading.

She had a flash image of Cressie being strangled by picture hanging wire. Eyes and tongue bulging. Blood splurting.

The clay heads began to explode one after the next in perfect sequence down the row. Pow pow pow! Shards of pottery went everywhere.

Milroy got hit in the temple by a lump and went down flat.

The kids all ducked behind seats screaming and yelling. The counselor fled squealing in terror. Principal Peevey knocked her down trying to get away himself.

Sam pressed her hands over her eyes and the very last head failed to go off.

Chapter 20

The rest of the clay was devoted to waiting outside for a bomb squad to come from SLED in the state capital to look at the unexploded head. The kids milled around or lounged on the lawn.

"You know, Nibiru is really quite impossible," said Nasar.

"What is Nibiru?" Sam asked.

"It's supposed to be a twelfth planet known to the Sumerians that comes around every 3,600 years. It's on an extreme elliptical orbit so we have never seen it. But it will crash throughout solar system causing cataclysms."

"What?"

"Not to worry. Kepler's Law makes it impossible. Planets orbit in ellipses with the sun as a focus. A line joining a planet and the sun sweeps out equal areas during equal intervals of time. Nibiru would have to go around the sun, not come in a tight ellipse and blast past the other planets."

Sam was astonished. "Did you not see what went on in there? Cressie's father?"

"Yes, he mentioned Nibiru. I started doing calculations in my head. You see the square of the orbital period of a planet is directly proportional to . . ."

"Nasar."

"... the cube of the semi-major axis of its orbit."

"Nasar!" she shouted to get his attention.

He blinked.

"You didn't see the clay heads exploding?"

He looked at her blankly. "I guess I was absorbed."

Then Sam noticed he had the bottom of his trousers tightly rolled to show about an inch of plaid lining and socks with black and yellow bands like a bumble bee.

"Nasar, why are your pants rolled? They're too short as it is."

"I believe the Italians call it *'sprezzatura.'* A carelessness or artful dishevelment. Not being too perfect to conceal that one is too perfect."

Sam asked, "Nasar, are you interested in a girl? I mean, like, a particular girl?"

He looked down abashed. "Well, I know you're taken. But I find your friend Dru quite lovely. Her face is like a Renaissance cameo of an African queen."

Sam shook her head in dismay. Dru was exquisitely beautiful. And tough and brave and smart. But Nasar?

"Nasar, you need to face the reality of the parallel universe you live in. The girl who will be drawn to you will be one who thinks working equations is a fun way to spend an evening. And maybe her life ambition is to look through the Hubble space telescope."

He looked thoughtful. "You do paint an attractive picture."

"Nasar, roll your pants down. The socks are embarrassing."

■ ■ ■

The bomb squad hadn't come by 2:30 so the kids were all sent home. Sam had been so caught up in menacing events she had lost track of where Kurt was. College course day or karate day? Why wouldn't he answer her text messages? Had he been at the assembly?

She let herself in the silent house, spread out her homework on the dining room table and set to it. Then she thought about Nibiru and looked it up on her iPad.

Mostly it was found on UFO sites, but then she ran across an article in *The New York Times* by an assistant professor here at the university. It was five years old. The author was Quinn Shaw.

She went to the university website to see if he was still on the faculty. No. She googled him. Found no other university location. Screens of titles of scholarly articles on Sumeria, Babylonia, Assyria, Canaan. She recognized the journals as first class.

She went back to the *Times*. It was about as dry as the things her mother wrote. It seemed to be a creation myth of the Sumerians. Nibiru was a twelfth planet that crashed into our solar system, struck the earth, shattering off a big chunk. The largest piece became our moon, the smaller fragments the asteroid belt. It explained why our continents are mostly on one side of the earth, the other being the vast gouged-out Pacific ocean.

There were pages of hideously dull stuff. Apogees and perigees and perihelions. Sam doubted she could ever be a professor. Ever take such a deep interest in anything.

Then it got her attention again.

Nibiru was the home of the great god Anu, the mightiest of all the gods. Inanna was one of his consorts.

Anu's abode was far in the deep regions of space. Its orbit was 3,600 years. The Seven Heavens were the seven planets beyond the asteroid belt.

Her eyes fixed on the symbol of Inanna. Lions as symbol of power. Bird feet and wings because she flew through space. Reeds twisted in a circle. All of these resonated with her. Felt deeply meaningful.

Sam felt very tired.

A goddess stood before her. She was nude to the waist with a diaphanous gown barely covering her *mons venus*. She held two twisted reeds in circles.

Her eyes were smoky whorls behind glittering glass. She pointed at the bright point of light that was eternal Venus. Or Inanna to the Sumerians. Ishtar to the Babylonians. Astarte to the Assyrians. Aphrodite to the Greeks.

She turned and walked into the mouth of a cave. A breeze was whispering in a language Sam couldn't understand. Sam followed her. The smoke curled around her ankles.

Cherry's face was filled with ecstasy. She was lying back with her butt at the edge of the dining room table, Kurt between her thighs. Her underpants were in a little pink puddle on the carpet.

She shook and kicked and wrapped her thighs about him tightly, wild with emotions set loose inside her. She moaned and threshed.

Kurt and Cherry were doing what Sam had never seen except on the Internet.

"Do it oh do it! Please don't stop! Please don't stop!"

He pulled her blouse open. His mouth closed over her pink erect nipple. Her sounds became incoherent squeaks rising in their tone. She shook her head from side to side, her mouth open in ecstasy.

Sam woke with a start, her whole body shivering at the shock of what she had seen. She rubbed her eyes.

Kurt was sitting there across from her at the table. He had come in without waking her, sat watching her sleep. He smiled.

"Are you okay? Bad dreams?"

"Let's talk about you and Cherry back in the fall," she said abruptly.

"Let's not." He tried to touch her hand, but she snatched it away.

She looked him straight in the eye, her whole body flaming with jealousy. "How far did you go with the little tramp?"

"Please, I said let's not discuss it."

"*No*, let's *do* discuss."

He looked abashed. "It's not something that's easily turned down. We . . . we didn't do much."

"Much? You banged her right here on this table in *your* house where *your mother* could and would know everything. I know it was here. I could see the objects in the room. She was begging 'don't stop don't stop'. She was wearing her pleated cheerleader skirt. White bobby socks."

"You could see . . . ?"

"Yes. The pictures were on the walls. The silver salt and pepper shakers were right there. One had been knocked over and slowly rolled to the floor."

Kurt looked stunned. But not for the reason Sam would have thought. "It's started," he said, almost awed.

"What?"

"What mom predicted. You're starting to have the second sight."

Sam clapped her hand over her mouth. Stared wide-eyed. "During the assembly . . ." she began carefully "I saw . . . Cressie's face as she died. She was being strangled by picture hanging wire. The sort of thing you'd expect to find in the Milroy house. And then the heads began to explode."

Kurt let out his breath. "Not a vision you can report to the police without a world of hassle. And they know what you know anyhow. So far."

"What do you mean *so far*?"

"You'll probably see more."

Sam had a sudden horrible thought. "You mean I could be walking past the murderer and just know it was him?"

"Yes."

Sam put her face in her hands.

"I don't want second sight. I don't want to be weird. I want normal. Is that too much to ask? A husband. Two children. I've never thought about children before. But now I suddenly want them."

"It's your destiny, Samantha. You must not avoid it."

"So I'm just some helpless prisoner of this? Is that your position?"

"Yes."

Sam was furious. The Jaegers were just shoving her into this like she had no choice in the matter. Her voice shook.

"Cherry was faking it," she said maliciously. "She has an orgasm face she puts on. The cheerleaders practice them."

Kurt looked taken aback. "How do you know?"

"Girls can tell."

■ ■ ■

Quinn listened intently. Someone had knocked on Tyndall Cranmer's door. After a time, footsteps went away.

Quinn had stopped the newspaper, would dutifully collect the mail after dark. When he came for his interrogation visits, he would spend a half hour searching the house. Looking for hidden compartments. Leafing through books.

Then he opened the bathroom door, unlocked the thumb cuffs, and made Cranmer take a shower. Let him out of the bathroom. Made him do stretching exercises, then jumping jacks, run around the room in a circle.

He told him to sit at the desk. Gave him two barbecue sandwiches and a Dr. Pepper.

"You could improve my diet," Cranmer carped. "Nothing but fast food. You're gonna give me a fatty liver."

"You could quit stringing this out. Make a clean breast of it all."

"I get the impression this is all that's keeping me alive."

"But I enjoy our little intellectual chats so much."

"Bullshit. I'm still one of those who denied you tenure. Your hatred eats you like a cancer."

Quinn waved a file of correspondence with a professor in Germany. "Who's Hans Dietrich?"

"University of Marburg. Anthropology professor. Africa."

"What does he study in particular?"

"The Dogon. They're a tribe that lives in Mali near Timbuktu. Believed to be of Egyptian descent. They've really jacked the scientific world around because they have ancient oral traditions that contain astronomical knowledge that would be impossible to obtain without modern telescopes. This was uncovered by two French anthropologists starting in the 1930s."

"What did the Dogon tell these Frenchmen?"

"The star Sirius is the brightest star seen from earth. We now call it Sirius A because in 1862, via telescope, a white dwarf star—Sirius B—was found that rotates around Sirius A. Sirius B has a super density. The Dogon both knew of its existence forever and believe that Sirius B is the heaviest thing in existence. They also believe there is a second companion. Which we have never seen.

"They believe that life was seeded by extraterrestrials who came from the Sirius star system. They called these people Nommos. They were amphibious. They descended in a space ship, dug a great hole and filled it with water. Then lived in the water."

"I see," said Quinn. "And you track this with Sumerian and Babylonian myths. The fish god Oannes."

"They had knowledge of Saturn's rings and Jupiter's four moons. This information came from the Nommos. Their planet rotates around the second dwarf star, which if we knew it existed, would be called Sirius C.

"The establishment scientists have to explain it away of course. Claim that French missionaries told the Dogon about it before the anthropologists arrived."

Quinn said, "Why would a French missionary have known about Sirius? Or cared?"

Cranmer shrugged. "I agree."

"Sea creature myths are pretty widespread."

"Yes. But consider the culture-creating ones. Like Oannes. Or consider the ancient Greeks. They're the ones who left us the best records. Cecrops."

"The mythical founder of Athens?" asked Quinn.

"Yes. If it's a myth."

"He was a culture bringer. True."

"Teaching them marriage, reading and writing, and ceremonial burial. And navigation."

"And there was something funny about him wasn't there?"

Cranmer did a saturnine smile. "Cecrops is not a normal Greek name. It means serpent-tail. Or fish-tail."

"Fish symbolism," Quinn mused. "Dagon was worshipped from the time of Sumeria through a couple thousand years of history to the Phoenicians and the Philistines. The name sounds threatening because it's used in horror novels and movies. In fact it just means 'fish.' He was a culture-bringer because he brought grain to the people. Yet he was a fish-god. The biblical Samson destroyed the temple of Dagon."

"Amphibious peoples," said Cranmer.

Quinn stared at him. "Don't tell me you found one of those too."

"Reptilian. Close to Mount Ararat."

Chapter 21

"What do you know about blowjobs?" Sam asked Drusana in the middle of their usual lunch outdoors.

Dru gave her a searching look. "No more than what you can see on the web. Why? You thinking about giving Kurt a treat?"

"I can't really."

"Why not?"

"His mom."

"He doesn't strike me as a momma's boy."

"He's not. But she's psychic. She can read minds. She can read events that have happened in a room from the emotional residue."

"Get out!"

It's true. I've witnessed it. It's pretty uncanny.

Dru looked up "Blow Job Technique" on her iPad. Turned it to Sam. Said, "So, if she can read rooms, why don't you go out in a car like teenagers are supposed to?"

"I imagine I'll have to. And yet it's so nice there in their house. All snug and tucked up. Like a magic world that's safe from everything."

"Your eyes are getting kind of dreamy."

"You best believe it. I've got it bad, Dru."

"How marvelous," she enthused.

Sam closed her eyes and bit her lip. "The emotions that are roiling through me . . . I've never felt anything like it. I'm eager, I'm desperate. I'm frightened, I'm jealous . . . I feel like crying at odd times. It just comes over me."

"Jealous of whom?"

"Of that little bitch Cherry. You know she did him back in the fall. The whole way. Middle of her period. No condom. And who knows what she's done since. And yet I do know. It's disgusting. But he's a boy of course. So it's somehow okay."

Dru was looking at her with awe. "Wow," she breathed. "Real emotions. I didn't think you had them in you. Now I'm jealous of you. I mean really jealous."

■ ■ ■

After school, Sam went down in the wooded dell with her throwing knives. Sun was bright on the trees, and where it penetrated, sparkled on the slow moving stream. Islands of dead leaves formed in eddies. Sam could smell the coolness of the water and damp earth.

But the peace of nature left her unmoved. She felt murderous. Cherry doing Kurt right there in his home. Kurt not caring that his mother knew. Or else too brain-fogged by the offer of sex. What was wrong with boys? Didn't they know who really loved them?

And how did he know how to do it? From what she read, it wasn't a talent that really came naturally to boys. Or men.

You read they were all desperate and impatient and came in two strokes.

And Cherry. My gosh, the girl was sixteen and like a raging whore. What erotic perversity drove the engine of a girl like her?

Sam had lied. Cherry's pleasure had been genuine. It made her sick to think about it. And she was supposed to be the prim virgin to develop her powers. She wanted to spit in disgust.

But she wanted him so badly. She didn't care about his conquests. All those little high school ding-bats. God knows what there had been in Switzerland. Were they beautiful ski-bunnies? As long as he loved her. If he would just hold her and kiss her.

She threw two knives together. One from each hand. Focused on placement, and one stuck two inches above the other in a tree. Shivered with the impact.

She walked over and wrenched them free. Thinking she was supposed to just burn with desire because that's what vestal virgins did. Then she could throw knives. Explode clay heads. What was the point of that?

She threw again, this time sticking them side-by-side about an inch apart.

Two strange men stepped out of the woods. Sam would later know them as Quinn Shaw and Hog Man. They were so out of place in the park as to seem threatening.

Sam hesitated, the blade of a knife between her thumb and forefinger.

Quinn put up a hand. "Whoa! Hey don't stick those in us." He wore a double-breasted blue blazer, Wayfarer sunglasses on top of his head. He was handsome. Strong jaw. Dimple in his chin.

The other was a motorcycle gang animal. Unwashed. Filthy really. Holes in his jeans.

"Down," Quinn ordered.

Then to Sam's shock, the filthy one knelt down to her. One knee on the ground, the other knee up propping an arm. His head bowed.

She felt like she was in some Medieval movie. Her standing there armed. A churl kneeling down in obeisance. Had she walked down into the woods and stepped into another dimension? This natty, attractive man like a noble. He should have a cloak and a hat with a feather.

His eyes danced with light. Or pleasure.

"Does Tory Island mean anything to you?"

Sam was nettled. "No, why should it?"

"My apologies. We're being intrusive. Yet you bear all with grace. It is fitting. No personal vanity. No fussy details of adornment in your attire."

Sam began to back away. Leaves rustled beneath her feet. Who were these creeps? Why did these kind of people keep coming at her?

The motorcycle brute got to his feet. "Ma'am, no disrespect . . . but did you have a tail when you was borned?"

In a fury, Sam flung the knife at Hog Man, sliced open a gash across the top of his head. The blade thunked in a tree.

He wiped his head, looked at the blood on his callused hand. Looked up at her in amazement. His eyes were a pale, washed-out blue.

"You could'a kilt me," he said. And then in admiration: "Far out."

Went and fetched the knife. Knelt down and offered it to her. Blood still running down his head. Bright red. His fingernails were like tortoiseshell.

Chapter 22

"I've sent you a personal assistant," Chirburg barked over the speaker phone. "He went to some candy-ass prep school too. You should get on great."

Boo looked across the room at the assistant in question, lounging with a leg over the arm of the chair. "Chip" Trafford. Could anyone be more prep? St. Paul's and Yale. He was like a mirror being held up to Boo's face, reminding him of his inferior status and lack of money. And barely in his twenties.

He had flown down and leased a racing green Porsche, was staying at the University Inn. All on the company tab. If Boo ever asked for any largesse like that, the answer was "no" in advance.

Tailored charcoal suit. Econ major at Yale. Intense, driven. A lot of interests, all competitive. Tennis, sailing, and rock climbing. Apartment on Central Park South. At ease with spreadsheets and financial analysis. Claimed to be an expert on e-commerce start-ups.

"I don't really need any assistance," Boo protested.

"There are those who are wondering if you're trustworthy," said Chirburg.

"So he's a spy? A class monitor?"

"I think we've heard enough of your malarkey, 'burgie," Chip said to the room. "Go check on what your brother-in-law got in the warehouse break-in last night."

Chirburg hung up.

"I can't believe you patronize him like that," said Boo.

"Why not? The man is like something scraped off the bottom of your shoe. I usually bait him by correcting the grammar in his office memos. I've got him so frightened he won't put anything in writing anymore. Provides a satisfying aspect to our dreadful office life."

"He's pretty powerful," Boo warned. "He could wreck your career."

Chip scoffed. "I don't want a career here. Perish that dire thought. I just have to put in two years to get the necessary work experience for Wharton. It'll be Goldman Sachs after that. I'm not about to spend my life flogging equities."

Boo thought why have you come here to taunt me with my personal failure? Do I deserve this? If God would just strike Chirburg dead I could amble along in my quiet little life.

Then he thought of Samantha, and desire surged through him. Her soon-to-be ripe body. Her fertility goddess aspect. It was time for him to sire a child. He would have to take the Lucifer's Legion money.

It was still in cash. Wire it to the Caribbean. Then fifteen more bank accounts to confuse the trail. Singapore. Tokyo. Zurich. Isle of Sark. Then lights out.

They couldn't really track him down as easily as Quinn claimed. He'd take her to Tasmania. Or the south island of

New Zealand. Resilience against long odds, but he'd win through.

"Are there squash courts in this benighted town?" Chip drawled. "I feel positively deracinated without squash."

Boo recognized the Locust Valley lockjaw accent. Talking with the jaws together, lips barely moving. The old money part of Long Island. Wooded rolling hills. Two-lane roads. Oyster Bay. Matinecock. Mill Neck. The Creek and Piping Rock golf clubs.

"I . . . yes, there are. Somewhere. I can't seem to think right now."

"Yeah, dealing with a moron like Chirburg just sucks the gray matter right out of your head."

The secretary announced the arrival of Marvin Pfiezer. The old man hobbled in with the kind of rushing momentum he used to get around. Broad sun hat. Black cataract glasses. Crashing up against the desk, dropping his metal cane. He flopped down heavily in a chair.

"Got a goddam frat house down the street from me," he complained. "Fuckin' redneck shit-for-brains kids. Partying seven nights a week. Can't sleep for the racket. Broken glass all over the road. Used rubbers."

Boo commiserated aloud about life in a college town. Silently wondering why the fool hadn't moved to Florida like he was supposed to.

Marvin got out a list of stocks. Then couldn't find his reading glasses. Threw the list on the floor, declaring fuck it he knew what he owned. Bent down to pick up the list and his big sun hat fell off. Had to fumble for that.

Went back and forth with Boo about how the economy was royally fucked, and those geniuses in Washington were doing fuck-all to fix it.

Boo had Marvin's investments up on the screen. Talked over and around Marvin's rant. Advised buy this, sell that, hold the other.

Marvin would say "Yeah, yeah, what-the-fuck-ever. Hey am I shrewd or what the fuck?" Marvin had nothing else to do, so all this took nearly an hour. Finally he got his hat and his cane, struggled to his feet and launched himself out the door.

Chip sat there looking very smug. "May I be candid?"

"Sure," said Boo, sensing a trap.

"The man has early-stage dementia. And you're churning his accounts. Total rip-off. You're a real gem. Just like your old man."

Boo thought, did everyone know about his father? And was he some bad seed? If so, could he redeem himself by saving Samantha?

■ ■ ■

Samantha washed her hair and showered until the hot water ran out. She still felt unclean from her contact with the men in the park.

She came out of the shower, her head wet, a towel wrapped around her body. Through the open bedroom door, she saw Kurt napping on his bed. Lying on his side with his hands under the pillow. He had been at karate. Jacket off. Only the black trousers on, held by a drawstring.

A blue dusk was settling outside. Sam felt calm and voluptuous. Filled with a kind of glad sorrow.

Kurt lay there in his heartbreaking beauty. Like the sleeping shepherd of so many myths. Discovered by Venus or Inanna.

Sam had a cunning thought. Slipped barefoot into her room, silently slid open the drawer and got out the padded handcuffs. Crept into his room and cuffed him to the bedpost.

He woke with a start. Blinked his eyes against the gathering dusk in the room. Regarded her as an apparition.

"Samantha? What are you . . . ?"

"Your sister's toys," she explained coyly.

He was angry. He shouldn't have been ambushed like that. "You know I could kick you even chained. Hurt you really badly."

She caressed his thigh. Teasing. "Why would you do such a thing?"

"Maybe to knock some sense into you."

She peeled off her towel. Let it slide to the floor. Her bare torso illustrating the great L words. Love. Lust.

Her flesh was on display. Her natural self-flowering.

Just as Mrs. Jaeger had promised, the goddess was inside her. Without her willing it, her body was faintly undulating.

She looked at him seductively, her face asking the crucial question. Should she spread her naked body on his?

Pushing back her tangles of wet hair, she bent over him and kissed him openmouthed. Drew away breathless. Knowing her face was shining.

She could smell the sweat on his body. A masculine tang. It stirred her deeply. She stroked his chest. Went lower with her hands to untie his pants and pull them down.

Heat burning inside her. Wanting so badly to join their bodies, make them one.

She climbed on the bed and straddled his thighs. Took hold of his vital stiffness.

"Don't you put that inside you," he ordered. "I'll come in two strokes, and you'll get knocked up. I can't deal with a teen pregnancy. We're supposed to go to college."

"You seemed to hold it back pretty well with Cherry."

He sounded almost desperate. "That was different. She . . . I wasn't . . . in love with her."

A slow smile spread over her face. "No danger then. My virgin status will remain intact. This is all about you. My boyfriend. My man."

The smile hovered at the corners of her mouth just as she went down.

Outside, the owl hooted mournfully.

Chapter 23

"So did you swallow?" asked Dru.

Sam looked down bashfully. "I did actually."

They were having their usual little conclave at lunch outside.

"How was it?"

"Kind of icky. But it gives him so much pleasure you don't mind. You have total power. And yet you're showing profound love. Your whole . . . your bosoms hang down . . . your ass is . . . up in the air . . . kind of wagging . . . you feel so female. Like all of female nature is infusing you."

"Wow. What did he do to you?"

"Nothing."

"Nothing?"

"Well, he couldn't really. He was handcuffed to the bed."

Dru's jaw dropped. "Jeez. That's pretty advanced for a high school junior."

"Oh, it's not what you think. He wouldn't have let me do it otherwise. I had to trap him while he was asleep."

Dru looked wistful. "Sam, do you think if I actually went to Oxford . . . I know it's a fantasy, but *if* . . . and I had no sexual experience . . . I could kind of pick it up there? With some cute boy whose socks fell down?"

"Sure. I'm not finding it difficult so far."

"I mean my mom. If she thought I was spending time with a boy . . . the shit would hit the fan."

"You'll be away in England. And I refuse to believe she hasn't at least contemplated you being interested in boys."

She rolled her eyes. "My mother. Who knows what's in her twisted brain. Even when she claims she's doing something positive for me . . ."

"What?"

"About a year after I hit puberty she took me to some women's gathering on a mountaintop. We sat in a circle holding looking mirrors up to our vulvas and talking about how beautiful they were. I've never been so mortified.

"And then they started chanting 'I've got the pussy.' Over and over. It was supposed to make me feel empowered and a part of a continuous chain of women of all ages. I was the blossoming maiden. The others represented young mother, middle-age career woman, the crone rich in wisdom of the ages. There were eight or ten of them, but those were the categories as I recall it.

"And naturally, one of them tried to get me off in the bushes for further initiation. A crone. Long gray hair and hanging down flat jugs. I was thirteen for shit sake. She was moaning about craving my skin color."

"Think Oxford, Dru. The cute English boy. He'll play rugby. Or pull an oar with the college crew. You'll sit across from him at dinner giving him shy glances. He'll notice you and be immediately smitten."

"I'm not letting you cheer me up. I'm like a teenage old maid. I am so jealous of you I could spit."

■ ■ ■

On his Harley, Quinn stopped at the end of his dirt road to look both ways on the two-lane blacktop. A brown-skinned girl—mixed-race, might have been a coed—was jogging back towards town. Luminous pink nylon shorts, fancy shoes, t-shirt. She was more than jogging. Running. Hitting it pretty hard really.

He had never determined the mileage to his house, but he knew he lived a fair piece out of town. The girl had to be awfully tough.

A jeep went past Quinn, drew up beside the girl and slowed. The top was down. Four college boys keeping pace with her, giving her a raft of shit. Baseball caps turned backwards. Hip hop music blaring in that strange mix of country club and ghetto gutter of today's fraternity culture.

They were drinking beer. One of them chucked an empty up into the air trying to drop it on her. Missed. She kept focused straight ahead, shot them the bird.

Quinn drove his bike slowly out onto the road, wondering if he would need to intervene. He noted the license number and fraternity letters on the jeep. A sticker that read "Golf Naked," and "Golfers Putt It in the Hole."

The boys fell back, then sped up and bounced her off the hood. She flew over into a weed-choked ditch and lay still. They looked around, exhilarated, but also panicked at what they had done. They sped off whooping.

Quinn stopped his bike, climbed down in the ditch. She

seemed to be knocked cold. But she was breathing normally. Some scratches on her face and legs.

Quinn lifted her up easily, remounted his bike holding
her pressed against his chest, and drove the short distance
back up the dirt road to his house. He lifted her up the
porch, opened the door.

She was barely 5'2". What they would have called "a
spinner" in prep school. Not that any girl ever did it. It was
just a fantasy.

He laid her on the couch. Pulled up a chair to examine
her. She was incredibly pretty. Dark cupid's bow mouth.
Thick eyebrows like a raven's wings.

She had a faint smell of human sweat.

One knee was pointed up towards the ceiling. Scuffed
a bit from her fall. Her inner thigh looking soft and tender.
Skin was caramel—no—café-au-lait.

He ran his hand gently down it, stopped at the edge of
her running shorts. Drawing back from a violation.

He wanted her to wake, hold up her arms to him. Draw
him down to press their lips together.

How long had it been since he had had sex? His wretched
wife? One day into the marriage it was like a switch had
been flipped. Utterly cold. Always an excuse. It was his fault.
He was a lousy lover. She should have married the plumber
who was so hot for her. At least she'd have a decent house.

The girl slowly opened her eyes as though she were
merely drowsy. Her irises were the deepest aquamarine
blue.

For some reason she reminded him of a playing card.

The Queen of Clubs. Symbolism: summer, youth, irresponsibility. But also intellect, literature, Earth.

She smiled at him faintly. Unafraid. Not startled by her surroundings.

He told her what had happened. She insisted she was okay.

"Frat boy shitheads," she said, sitting up on the couch. "They're frightened to death of girls. So they roam in packs. Suzie Tri Delts will drag them to the altar spring of their senior year. They'll all be divorced seven years later. Hypergamy. The desire of the woman to trade up. She'll find someone with more money while she's still desirable. He'll have a nervous breakdown. He won't call it that. He'll call it getting drunk in bars and being beaten up."

"That's pretty insightful."

"My mom. She's Women's Studies."

She rubbed her muscles, got up and wandered about the room without any motor difficulties. Looking at the objects.

Mission furniture. Oil paintings of Monhegan Island, Maine. Crossed canoe paddles. Moose antlers. A trout suspended in an aquarium-like box tinted glaucous green as though under water—a Victorian sporting display.

What version to give of his life? Did it really matter? Everything was the future now.

"Is that painting a Rockwell Kent?"

"Yes. He lived on Monhegan for a time."

"Like, an original?"

"Yes."

"I'm impressed. We just have crappy 'goddess art' by some friend of my mother's. Pastel women being mystical and feeling the fertility of the earth. Women celebrating the loss of their breasts from cancer. Hideous."

She ran a hand over piles of books and papers. He still had his scholarly ways. Much of his day was spent in reading and research in arcane books. It gave him far more pleasure than when he had to churn out articles.

"Are you a professor?"

Was she giving him a coy glance? "Used to be. Found a better path."

"Subject area?"

"Ancient Middle East. Sumer and Ur."

"You're in the same field as Samantha Fitzhugh's mother?"

Quinn was startled by that. "Maeve Fitzhugh?"

"Yes, that's her name. She got denied tenure. But she does all kinds of digging and research all over the world."

"She was at the university before my time. But I know her reputation."

"I'm sixteen," she said, apropos nothing. She was looking him straight in the eye. Drinking him in.

"What is the take-away on that?"

She shrugged. "Just thought you'd like to know."

What was she telling him? That she was a child and he shouldn't have any ideas? Or she had reached the age of consent, and he could feel free to have ideas?

He knew he was playing with fire, determined to get her home. He made her put on some brushed leather chaps that were way too large. She had to turn the legs up a lot to not trip. She walked out of the house holding the chaps up so they wouldn't fall down.

As Dru put on a helmet, she looked back, noted the house was a converted tobacco barn. Looked at the big Harley. Looked back at the house. Looked like she wanted to ask a question but didn't.

"Yes?" he said.

"This does put a different slant on things."

She got on the bike behind him. Wrapped her arms around his waist. He drove slowly over the dirt track. Not wanting to give the impression he had some juvenile idea of frightening her. Or impressing her.

He could feel her small breasts pressed against him. Knew her snatch was vibrating with the engine.

Why did this virtual child fill him with such desire? It consumed him as they covered the ground back into the town.

Dru got right off when they arrived at her house, pulled off the helmet, started peeling out of the chaps. "You've got to be careful of my mother," she said. "She's not real friendly with men."

Quinn shut off his engine just as the mother came storming out the door. She looked like a muscular diesel-dyke. Like Leslie Jones in *Ghostbusters*. Or a basketball coach. The kind who would prey on the girl players. Stood there sneering like she expected him to flinch.

But Quinn didn't flinch. Women held no more fear for him. He had tasted blood.

He got slightly too close so he could look down on her,

knowing he was invading her space. She stepped back an inch as though threatened.

He introduced himself, told her what had happened. Dru echoed all that he said. Thanked him effusively. Stood too close when she handed him back the chaps and helmet.

"Thank you," Rhoda said brusquely. She had already turned her back on him when she said it and was pushing Dru into the house.

Quinn stood still. He could hear them inside the house.

"Mom, can I start ordering clothes from Anthropologie?"

"No."

"It's just that I'm developing this kind of . . . thing . . . for a girl in my class."

"Samantha Fitzhugh?"

"Yes."

"I'll take it under consideration."

Samantha Fitzhugh, Quinn thought.

Chapter 24

"Do you feel ripped off not having a father?" Drusana asked at lunch.

"I don't even have a mother," said Samantha ruefully. "I may as well be an orphan."

"Better than being raised by a bull-dyke. There are times when I really hate her."

"Dru, you're one of the more normal people I know. I don't mean vapid normal like Cherry. But in touch with reality. When Cherry starts getting crows' feet around her eyes, her whole vital self will disintegrate. I predict a husband in real estate who fucks around on her. A middle age of pills and booze. Drunk every night when he comes home."

"I can't argue with that. But I have my problems too."

Sam raised her eyebrows. "Like what?"

"Jungian psychologists believe there's a male element in each female. It's called the animus. If there's no father figure in the home, the animus gets control of a girl's psyche. Her romantic ideal becomes a dangerous, mysterious man. Heathcliff in *Wuthering Heights*. A masked highway man. Bluebeard who killed his wives. A prince turned into a wild animal by witchcraft, waiting to be redeemed by a girl's love."

Sam just stared. She was used to this kind of erudition out of her friend. But still, this was pretty deep.

"Sometimes it's a group of dangerous outlaws," Dru continued. "Or wreckers who lure ships onto the rocks and kill the crew."

"Where'd you get this?" Sam asked.

"From Kurt. His dad's a Jungian psychologist. Don't they talk to you about stuff like that?"

"When were you talking to him?"

"Hey, I'm not trying to cut in or anything. I was just curious about my own mental state. Wondering if I'm under the control of my animus."

"Why would you think that?"

"I've got an older admirer. And I'm really drawn to him."

"Seriously?"

"Not old, old. Maybe in his thirties."

"Get out."

"I'm not lying to you."

"You're sixteen."

"True."

"Why do you think he's an admirer?"

"When he thought I was passed out, he ran his hand down the inside of my thigh. It was really exciting. Like a wave of fire and ice went through me."

"Did you start in the middle somewhere? What are you talking about?"

Dru told her the whole story. Sam was amazed.

"He took you home on a Harley? And your mother didn't hit him with the *bocce* ball?"

"She didn't take it very well. Lot of storming around the house afterwards. I've let her think I've got a yen for you."

Sam cut her eyes at her friend. "Ooo-kay. But who is this man?"

"I'm not really sure. I'll probably have to stalk him on the Internet. But I know where he lives."

"You can't tell me anything about him?"

"Well, it was funny. He was once in ancient Middle Eastern history. He seemed to know all about your mother."

■ ■ ■

Sam's phone rang with the name of a stock brokerage on the caller ID. She answered. A voice said he had to talk to her. Could she come into his office. A secretary would be right outside the door. All she had to do was scream if she didn't like something.

"What? Who are you?"

He was speaking really rapidly. "I'm your broker. Your mom's broker. But yours too. You cut my hand with a sword cane. I deserved it. I behaved like an idiot. Please don't hang up."

"Are you crazy? What do you want with me?"

"I have to warn you. You are in great danger. Mortal danger."

"From what?"

"There's a motorcycle gang that's built a cult around your worship. They regard you as a goddess."

Her blood ran cold. The motorcycles outside the Milroy house. "What is the name of the club?"

"Lucifer's Legion."

Sam pictured the weird substitute teacher. That's what his jacket had said. Then she thought of the men in the woods. The ugly brute of a giant.

Boo's voice was emotional. "I don't know. I don't understand it. It's connected with Sumeria. And some lost planet."

"Nibiru? Is that the name of it?"

"Yes, I think so."

"Does Ireland have anything to do with it? Tory Island?"

"Ireland? I . . . I don't know."

"How do you know any of this? What is your role in it?"

"I . . . I can't explain over the phone. Someone's come in. You must come and see me."

He was crying on the other end as he hung up.

■ ■ ■

Around 10 p.m., Lucifer's Legion snatched the fraternity boy when he went to take a leak behind "The Shack," the favorite watering hole in the town for his breed.

They let him finish pissing, then threw the burlap bag over his head, drove off in his own jeep.

"Okay, guys, very funny," he said from inside the bag. "If this is a pledge stunt, you're gonna regret it big time."

They said nothing in return. Quinn wondered if the

boy could smell the gorilla stench of his men. Surely he couldn't miss it.

Way out in the county, they pulled onto a dirt track, bounced over potholes, stopped, and heaved him out. He jerked off the bag and stood up ready to fight.

There were twenty of them wearing Guy Fawkes masks like some Occupy Wall Street or Anonymous group. Formed a large ring around him so he couldn't run.

Quinn pulled the fuse on a highway flare and tossed it at the boy's feet. He reeled back, shielding his eyes.

The fear set in the second he realized he was dealing with big hulking adults and this wasn't a fraternity kidnap prank.

"You mother-fuckers better let me go, and I mean right now!" His voice hit some high notes.

They said nothing, just stood there solemnly. The flare sizzled, painting the boy in lurid orange.

"My old man's a lawyer! He'll sue your asses off!"

"That should be interesting," said Quinn. "I wonder what I would look like ass-less."

"I mean it! You don't fuck around with my old man! And in the meantime I'll get the brothers on you. We'll kick the dog shit out of you!"

"Curious thing, fraternities," Quinn mused. "All the guys swanking around like they're kings of the earth. Majoring in Business Administration. Chucking a football in the yard like they were top athletes or something."

"You're just jealous. That's all," blurted the boy.

"Not really. I have nothing against private clubs. Belong to one myself. In fact the wealthier a man becomes the more he needs one. Can't just join the Kiwanis and be part of the booster crowd. Everyone would want a piece of you. Expect you to pick up the tab on each occasion. You have to limit your associations to those of your class."

"That's right then."

"Except what's always puzzled me is most of the frat boys don't really have any money. Have to work summer jobs to pay their dues. They're just in because they were cool in high school and their reputation tagged along."

"We're very carefully selected," the boy argued. "We've been identified as heading for success. It's for future networking."

"Well, that's what's said. But I've yet to see an adult world example of it being any benefit. The only purpose it serves is impressing some very impressionable young girls for a couple of years."

"Well we get laid a lot. That's for dam' sure."

"But meanwhile you piss off the entire faculty and the ninety percent of the student body that couldn't be in a frat."

"That's their problem. Not mine," he said belligerently.

"You say that because you're young and you feel bullet-proof. You don't realize that their animosity might come back to bite you in the ass. All your little secret hand-shakes. But you have that universal haircut that identi-fies you with the larger order. And you keep it as long as you have hair on your head. Old men coming back to the reunions with their hair white but still piled up in a heap."

Hog Man threw the boy to the ground and put a boot on his neck. Grasped the boy's hair with his left hand.

"Yore real pleased with this hair-do, ain't cha? Jes' kinder says 'frat boy' from a mile off. Let all the honeys know you've arrived in the room. Just git their panties wet enough to stick to the wall."

"Yes," Quinn agreed. "I think it's time you changed to a new hair style. We're doing this for your own good. You'll probably thank us later."

Hog Man took out his Bowie knife, tested it on the hair of his forearm. Then went to work. Zip zip zip. It was very quickly done. Ripped upwards. He held up the blood-dripping scalp for all to admire.

The boy was screaming and thrashing. White skull showed in a big circle where the flesh and hair had been removed.

"You bastards you shit heads!" he wailed. His hands were shaking like he had palsy.

They lifted him to his feet, set him in the jeep.

"Now yew keep it between the lines on the way home," cautioned Hog Man.

The boy drove away weeping uncontrollably. A few miles down the road he became so blinded with tears and pain that he ran off the edge into a ditch. Headlights jutting up into the air.

A county cop found him there a couple of hours later. No one had ever seen someone scalped before. The newspaper carried the story cryptically. The editors had never dealt with a scalping either and didn't know the journalistic etiquette. But the frat brothers spread it all over town.

Chapter 25

When Boo got to his office at 7:30 on Friday, Chip was already there, three newspapers—*The Wall Street Journal, Financial Times,* and the local rag—coffee in a big paper cup with a lid.

He was doing it deliberately. Getting there each day before Boo so he could make some calls to the home office, talk about the market, let drop that Boo still hadn't dragged in.

"Did you read this local fanfaronade about the kid being scalped? I mean it's not in the article, but the word is all over town. Heard it when I got my coffee. Talk about wild. They don't even get up to hijinks like that at Columbia, and they're on the edge of a slum."

Boo sat down and tried to gather himself for the day. Chip always had to get in some comment on the pecking order of the Ivies. Columbia of course was rock bottom. Bordering Harlem. Cornell barely above it. That hotel management school. Utterly déclassé.

He had read the article, and it filled him with great fear. Abduction by a gang of grown men in Guy Fawkes masks. He knew it was Lucifer's Legion. It had to be.

His left hand fingers were still stiff. Would they ever be right?

But he was obsessed with Samantha. He wanted to stand naked with her in a warm summer rain. Her hair plastered to her face. Lie in the mud and screw with impatient lust.

"Y'awake yet, pussy mouth?" growled a familiar voice. "Or is it still sleepy-time down South?"

Boo jumped thinking the speaker phone was on. But Chirburg himself was looming there like a bad dream. He looked like he had slept in his clothes. His breath and armpits smelled. Christ, his tongue was white.

"Jeepers, look what some ill-wind blew in," said Chip. He didn't bother to stand up. Sat there with his feet crossed on his desk. Continuing to read.

Chirburg ignored Chip's familiarity, did the obligatory complaining about the difficulty of getting an air connection to this mother-fucking tank town.

"Every mother-fucking room at the University Inn is taken. I've got my bag out in the rental car. What are they doing? Having a hayseed convention?"

"Well, I'm certainly not sharing space with you," said Chip, turning a page. "You want to do your little ambush visits you're so famous for, you need to get a room in advance."

Seeing he couldn't intimidate Chip, Chirburg turned on Boo. "Get on the mother-fucking phone and find me a room, numb-nuts."

Hog Man and Quinn came in quietly and stood in the doorway as Chirburg continued to rant. You could smell Hog Man's stench, but Chirburg didn't notice.

"What the fuck do I pay you for, preppie-boy? To fuck me up the ass?"

"Jeez," said Quinn. "I sure hope you don't work here. Did you even go to college?"

Chirburg whipped around. "No I didn't jack off for four years with a pack of pansies. Wanna make something out of it?"

Quinn was wearing a gray silk tick weave sport coat over a starched madras shirt with the tail not tucked in. Cotton chinos. Hand-sewn leather loafers. Hog Man was his usual motorcycle hoodlum self.

Quinn didn't back off a bit. "Well you might want to go take a course in basic grammar. Maybe get a vocabulary list to memorize. Have something to say besides 'fuck' and 'shit.'"

"So what're you? Some Mister Professor Know-it-all or something? Or are you Mister Emily Post Junior? Gonna lecture me on my table manners?"

Quinn gave him a level look. "You don't have any idea who I am do you?"

"Okay, so who the fuck are you?"

"This is Mister Shaw," said Boo edgily. "He's my biggest client. I know you're familiar with his account. El Macho Buggaron?"

The light came on. "Oh, the Cayman account. Hey, all is copacetic. I'm giving it my special attention."

"Really?"

"Yeah really."

"Really and truly?"

"It's too early for word games. You're gonna have to take my word for it."

"Really?"

"Hey, don't start that shit again. You got a specific question, I'll answer it. I'm not doing some Polly-wanna-cracker echo routine."

"Okay, specific question. What I'm wondering is when it's going to get out of cash and into something with a return."

Chirburg didn't miss a beat. "I'm holding you in cash. It's called market timing. The market is about to have a major drop. I mean big ka-blooey. Turd dropped from a tall cow. I want you positioned to buy in heavily when big-cap stocks are at the bottom."

Quinn crossed his arms. "You really have no problem lying to a client do you? It's just like the public caricature of the avaricious broker. Really, when you think about it, a fireman's about the only career that you can't instantly think anything bad about. Our friend the fireman. Our friend the car salesman? The lawyer? Doesn't work so well.

Our friend the broker? Not a chance. Shithead thieving broker is more on point."

Chirburg could never control his temper. "Hey dip-wad, I give top returns. You ask any big swingin' dick on the Street."

"Language, language," sighed Quinn. "If you won't go to charm school, I think we'll have to bring it here to you."

He nodded at Hog Man who leveled Chirburg with one blow. Just hammered him right to the floor. Then picked him up by his belt and the back of his jacket, rammed his head into the wall and dropped him face first.

Chirburg lay still. Blood had splashed out from his face in a starburst pattern on the floor.

"Oo-ee," said Hog Man. "He do look like a turd dropped from a tall cow. Or is that something he said? I hate to not be original."

Chip had half gotten to his feet. His mouth was hanging open. In his privileged existence he had never seen anyone beaten like that.

Boo covered his face with his hands. He felt desperately sick.

■ ■ ■

At school in American Literature class, Dr. Lenny Clearwire was doing his usual rant against Western Culture. Neo-imperialist, hegemonic, racist, sexist, homophobic, heteronormative tripe. The voice of women and people of color never heard. Blah blah.

The class all rolled their eyes. Clearwire had a PhD and made them call him Doctor. He had failed to get tenure at a former junior college that now called itself a university. Since there was nothing lower in the academic food chain than that, he was reduced to the public schools. Hatred of the foundations of your own subject is pretty standard now in liberal arts. And naturally this had nothing to do with learning US lit.

He was so skinny his shoulder bones showed through the message t-shirts he wore. Although nearly forty, when he came at the beginning of the year, he wanted to be thought of as cool. Wore a Kangol "vent-air" cap indoors and hipster glasses. Made jokes about his weed habit. Grew a goatee.

Clearwire ranted we needed to be in sync with our environment and live in a cooperative peace with one another where we share scarce resources instead of divvying them out under a brutish and unequal capitalist system.

Emerson raised his hand to say that noble savages were not but so noble and did not live in utopian bliss. On a per capital basis, savages killed far more people than civilized ones because war was relatively rare in civilization while it was an on-going event with tribal societies—or small-scale stateless societies as anthropologists like to call them now. If you counted all the wars of the twentieth century, you'd only get sixty deaths per 100,000 people. Among tribal societies it was 500 per.

And anyhow, how did he expect 350,000,000 Americans to live as hunter-gatherers? Especially since he had gone on record as being against hunting. Was it all to be gathering acorns and berries?

Dr. Clearwire turned bright red and tore paper into tiny strips under his desk. He had already dictated they would not be reading *Huckleberry Finn* because it was racist rubbish. Now he announced they were going multicultural in their literature studies and would be reading the Gilgamesh Epic, the first epic poem in history.

It was the story of a god-king of the city of Uruk in Sumeria, a city state which lasted for 2000 years while America with its dreadful history of slavery and oppression had lasted a mere 224 or so, and was coming apart at the seams. And he felt certain Emerson would like to read something that wasn't written by some ghastly white male like Hawthorne or Melville.

And then he stared at him triumphantly, like take that you little upstart shit.

And of course Emerson couldn't let it go.

"You are aware, that Queequeg in *Moby Dick* is a South Seas Islander, and one of the first persons 'of color' as you say in American lit. And as a harpooneer, quite a hero.

"And if you want real color issues, James Fennimore Cooper's *Last of the Mohicans* has a mulatto, or in the new lib-speak, a 'person of mixed race.'"

"What are you talking about?" Dr. Clearwire demanded.

"Just what I'm saying. There are two daughters of the British colonel. The blond girl Alice is the child of a Scottish woman; the dark girl Cora of a black woman when the father was stationed in the Caribbean. The Indian Magua goes off his nut over Cora."

Clearwire thought he had his opening. "Don't you mean Native-American?" he demanded.

"No, 'Indian' is back in vogue. I got it from a friend of my father's who's an enrolled Comanche. But the point is, Cooper was dealing with racial issues that were touchy even then. And Hollywood for all its love of a racial theme has ignored it in every version of the movie. Probably because no one reads out there."

"You're making this up," Clearwire accused, giving him an unrelenting glare.

"Haven't you read the book?" said Emerson. "Or do you just see the movies? It's not mentioned in the Classics Comics version either."

Clearwire was boiling over. He stood up shaking with

fury. "You . . . you are totally inauthentic! You . . . you *negro*!"

Then he stormed out of the room.

"You forgot to add 'uppity' to it," Emerson called after him.

■ ■ ■

"I hope we don't have another Rooney on our hands," said Emerson after class.

"At least he doesn't want to lick blood off Samantha's legs," said Nasar. "Yet."

"What did he mean by inauthentic?" Sam asked.

"I'm not an angry young black radical. I don't demand an all black state in Alabama or convert to black Muslimhood or something. When he saw my middle name was 'X' he must have had his hopes."

"Their stereotypes are certainly patronizing," said Nasar. "Julie Huang wants to play rock-n-roll guitar, and she keeps getting sent to the guidance counselor to talk about careers in organic chemistry."

"White liberals are so screwed up with their pecking order of victimhood," said Emerson. "O.J. Simpson chops up his wife and the waiter. The waiter doesn't merit a thought because he's a white man. But the white wife doesn't become a 'women's issue' meriting the return of the electric chair because O.J. is black. Race always trumps gender. There's some real equal justice before the law."

Sam was pretty ticked that they wouldn't be reading *The Scarlet Letter* and *Moby Dick*, but Kurt said forget it. They'd learn around the teacher as they always did.

Anyhow, Gilgamesh should be right up her alley. Ancient Sumeria. And it was filled with enough profound symbolism to warm any Jungian heart. His father would delight in guiding them through the term paper.

"Anyhow, I remember when you read those books. It was back in the ninth grade. It's not like Clearwire has anything meaningful to add to your understanding of them."

"What?" she said. "You noticed what I read in the ninth grade?"

"We all did," said Nasar. "I remember when you read *National Velvet* in fourth grade."

"What?"

"You're quite beautiful, you know."

Chapter 26

On Saturday morning, Quinn sat alone in Starbucks having a café latte and perusing *The Wall Street Journal*. It wasn't a paper you saw in there frequently, the place crowded with college kids and their socialist fantasies.

Of course most of them didn't read at all. Constantly on Facebook. Checking texts and tweets and bullshit.

"Hey, you," said a cheerful voice.

Quinn looked up, recognized Dru holding an iPad to her chest. He stood up in a mannered way.

"Are you leaving?"

"No, I'm standing because a lady has come to my table."

"Wow. Manners. Old school. I'm impressed. No sarcasm intended whatsoever."

He held the chair for her, asked what she would like, went and bought her a hazelnut macchiato.

"Golly, I'm not sure how to take this," she said.

"You say 'thank you.' It used to be traditional."

She took a sip. Wiped white foam from her lips with a napkin. "Were those all pictures of Maine on your walls?"

"Yes. I'm from Bar Harbor."

"We used to summer on the Cape."

"Very stylish."

"Not really. It was some dyke nudist colony near Provincetown. My mom . . ." She rolled her eyes.

"As they say, we can choose our friends, but not our families."

"We're reading Gilgamesh in class. So, tell me all about ancient Sumeria. I want to write a risqué paper that will scandalize our dork teacher."

Quinn grimaced. "That's a long ago part of my life."

"I don't need a semester lecture. Just tell me about temple prostitution."

She was looking at him with bright eyes. Trying to tease him. How instinctive their coquetry became the moment they hit puberty. They knew their power. And were quite amoral about ruining a teacher or some other adult if it struck their fancy.

And she was turning her eyes on him. She had even pulled a hank of her hair in front of one eye to look seductive while he was up getting her coffee. A pang of desire ran through him.

"You can Google it on your iPad," he said.

"I'd rather hear a lecture. I bet you were a terrific teacher." She cupped her face in her hands, giving him total attention.

Quinn sighed. "In Sumeria, Babylonia, Assyria, even parts of Greece, sacred or temple prostitution was performed as a holy rite. Every woman was obliged once in her life to go into the temple and accept silver from a stranger and engage in intercourse.

"It's roundly condemned in the *Bible*. And a growing gang of revisionist scholars are saying it never happened.

An odd mix of politically correct prudishness and arrogance. No one's ever done anything bad but Americans. And somehow they know more than Herodotus or the authors of the *Bible*."

"How can they deny it when it's right there on the Uruk vase?"

Quinn didn't comment on the fact that Dru had clearly boned up on the topic. He couldn't believe he was having a conversation on this level. Moron coed chatter swirled around him.

"Things are really cray cray."

"Chillaxin."

"Fo' shizzle."

Peabrains. Had any of them even heard of Sumeria?

"You'd be amazed at what the Academy can deny," he said. "Anyhow the rite was a form of sacred marriage ritual or *hieros gamos*. In Sumeria, the king himself performed it with the high priestess of Inanna on the tenth day of the New Year festival of *Akitu*. Inanna was the goddess of sex, fertility, love and curiously also warfare."

"You've left something out, haven't you?"

He looked at her.

Dru said, "Inanna was the goddess of love but not of marriage. Sensual intercourse among lovers. The ritual marriage was only for the purpose of ensuring fertility, not marital happiness. The King was taking the place of Dumuzi, the beautiful shepherd who was her usual fuck-mate."

Quinn thought they can be foul-mouthed, the young. Even when they're as bright and educated as this one.

"Why do you find that significant?"

"It's so prevalent in mythology. The most famous one we know is Venus and Adonis."

"Yes?"

She paused, ran her pink tongue tip along her upper lip. Raised her eyebrows suggestively. "Few men can be kings. But any man can be the chosen beautiful shepherd."

Quinn kept silent. Her knee rested against his. He left it there long enough for her to know he had registered her little signal. Then moved it away.

"Dumuzi is associated with the zodiac sign Aries." She paused. "Which is yours. The ram."

Quinn still didn't speak. The Internet was so thorough, particularly with professors and their piles of bogus research, their resumés on display.

She said, "Did you happen to notice that the boy who got scalped was the one who bumped me off the road?"

She was watching his face. "No," Quinn said blandly. "How did you determine that?"

"They had a picture of his jeep in the paper. Those dirtbags got in front of me for a time, then dropped back. I remember the bumper stickers."

Quinn tugged on his earlobe.

Her eyes bored in. "I think you're a very violent man. But also righteous."

She stood up and tousled her hair into tangled locks. Then bent down and took his face in both her hands, kissed him on the lips. A slow melting kiss.

The whole room was staring at them.

Chapter 27

Chirburg came into the office Monday morning with his head and nose weirdly entwined around and around with a continuous bandage. Almost like a space helmet. Concussion. Flat smashed nose set with a steel splint. Violet bruises all up blackening his eyes. He had spent the night in the hospital. He sat down at a desk.

Chip smacked him in the top of the head—right where it had been rammed into the wall—with a rolled up copy of *Forbes*, the financial magazine.

"Hey, Burgie, how's tricks?"

"OW goddammit!" Chirburg put his head down on the desk. He might have been crying with the pain. "What the fuck are ya doin'?"

"Greeting the dawn. Gamboling on the spring grass. Have you ever seen grass before? I mean in Flatbush or whatever cement cesspool you come from?"

Chirburg clutched the edge of the desk tightly. "You little prepster shit-ass. I'll get you for this. I don't care whose dick you're suckin' on."

"You don't say. What are you going to do about it, Burgie? You get the shit smacked out of you by multi-millionaire clients. Is that our fault? They're big-bucks clients. You're the one with no interpersonal skills. You're just a perennial douche."

Chirburg stood up clutching his crotch. "Oh man I gotta piss somethin' awful." He rushed out of the room.

Chip followed him out, then came back in shortly, flopped down in his chair, just howling with laughter.

"I came up behind him at the urinal, grabbed his shoulders and shook him so he peed all over himself. Jeepers it's sooo funny! I haven't done that since St. Paul's."

Boo looked up with shock. Standing tentatively in the doorway was Samantha and a small, light-skin black girl. He was suddenly having trouble breathing. They were creating some kind of psychic synergy together. Light and darkness. Sun and moon.

"Urn . . . are we interrupting?" said Sam.

"Chip?" said Boo. "Can I have the office. This is kind of private."

"I don't think so," said Chip. "I need to sit in. Learn your masterful technique for client relations." He was staring at the two. Barely keeping himself from drooling.

Boo got up. "Girls, I was just going out for coffee. Come along with me. My treat."

"I'll come too," Chip insisted. "I am just dying for some handcrafted layers of delicious. The bold pick of the day."

Boo thought my god he's trying to be witty. Like a college boy with a freshman girl.

"Holy mother-fuckers!" Chirburg burst out. "That's the Fitzhugh girl. The one you're obsessed with who has all the money." He was standing in the doorway with a big urine stain on his crotch.

Sam looked at him with wide startled eyes. Then back at Boo. A throwing knife slid into her hand. She held it down next to her thigh.

Boo held up his hands defensively. "No, please. We really need to talk about your account."

Sam grabbed the dark girl by the arm, and they both ran out of the room. Through the window they could be seen weaving through the traffic on Chastain Street.

Chip looked quite indignant. "Burgie, you are such low-life. *Mother-fuckers*. You can't be taken out in polite company. You belong in a Bowery saloon sweeping out the sawdust on the floor. Emptying cuspidors."

He rolled up the *Forbes* magazine and hit Chirburg squarely in the broken nose with it.

Chirburg's eyes bulged, and his mouth formed a tiny round O, unable to fully express his excruciating pain.

"Don't you ever do that around a client again," Chip snarled, smacking Chirburg all over the bandaged head again and again.

Chirburg tried to protect himself with his hands. He was squealing and weeping with the pain at the same time.

Chip turned to the window to see the girls jump the low dry-stone wall and run across the grassy old quad of the university.

"Kow-a-bonga," he breathed in rapt admiration. "What a duo. Did you feel the vibes they were giving off?"

■ ■ ■

"I don't know," said Sam. "I don't understand any of it."

They unlocked their bikes from a rack on the campus. They knew they were going to be late to school.

"What did the old man say?" asked Dru. "Someone's obsessed with you?"

"A lot of people seem to be."

"Ooo aren't we pleased with our little sex-bomb self."

Sam stared at her. "Are you serious? Ms. Rooney? That creep Jude? You think I want these people slavering over me? And that broker . . . Boo Radley, he's the one I slashed with the sword. He wanted to kiss my toes."

"I think," mused Dm, "it's about time someone started to obsess over me."

Sam looked at her. Was her friend losing her mind?

Sam's phone rang. When she answered, her mother said: "No names please. And we can't talk but a second. But did something funny turn up on a DNA test?"

"Yeah, but mom, where are you?"

"I can't really say. But everything's okay. Not to worry. Just don't talk to anyone about your DNA until I return. Okay? Promise?"

"Mom . . . !"

But she had hung up.

Chapter 28

Quinn was back questioning Tyndall Cranmer. The morning was really the best time. Those who went to work had gone, and any oldsters around were on the commode with a laxative in their coffee.

Quinn dragged Tyndall to his feet, got him out of the bathroom where he kept him imprisoned. Unlocked his thumbs and listened to him moan about his aches and pains. His face was gray, lined and unshaven.

Amazingly, it hadn't broken him. Quinn figured the CIA torture pros ought to make a study of the man.

He set him down at a table with a bucket of fried chicken.

"Am I eating alone?"

"I already had breakfast. Didn't want to risk having to run to the can while we had our regular little chat. Coffee goes right through me."

Cranmer shoveled the watery white slaw into his mouth. "Is this the only green veggies I get?"

"We'll be through the interrogation before you get any deficiency diseases."

"Then what? I get deep-sixed?"

"Ohhh I dunno. Maybe we'll be pals by then. Maybe you

and I will walk out of here arm-in-arm and go looking for giant skeletons."

"We could go look in the Fitzhugh house. There's something hidden there."

Cranmer chewed chicken while Quinn browsed the room wondering what secrets were hidden in some innocuous nook or cranny.

"You know the truth," said Cranmer with his mouth full. "The Annunaki created mankind to work as slaves and mine gold. That's why there are Eve mothers in pockets. Why there are different races. And some Annunaki—what the Hebrews called the Nifilhim—found the women fair and bred with them. Their offspring were giants."

"Which is what you found in Turkey."

"Yeah."

"And there are others?"

"A lot of them. They're stashed in museums like the out-of-place objects that turn up. Things science has to deny."

Quinn pulled a scrapbook off a shelf and sat down at the table to look at it. Photos of homely girls. Geeks with glasses. Some of them real dogs. They all had their clothes off. It was a trophy book of Cranmer's conquests.

One was sitting naked on the john, knees together, ankles apart. Giving him the finger. Another was holding a sheet over her boobs while giving him the finger. Another leaning across the kitchen table, boobs hanging down. Finger with each hand.

"There seems to be a theme here."

"Yeah, they liked to imagine they were empowered,

strong women. Nuts and sluts. Academic style of course. Talk current events while you were humping them."

"Do these start at Columbia?"

"You know how it is. You were once a grad student. Is there one alive who doesn't imagine having casual sex with undergrad coeds? Picture them doing it for a grade change. And they do. At least up there.

"The ones at Barnard and Columbia are all rad-libbers. Lie down in the road chanting 'Two four six eight! Organize to smash the state!' That sort of bullshit. Fuck as a political statement.

"A lot of Jewish princesses. Spoiled rotten bitches. You know she's had an orgasm when she drops her nail file.

"But then I got exiled down here. Not a rad-libber in sight. Little Southern honeys sweet as nectar. Interested in professors? Maybe a creative writing type for a brief fling. One of life's trophies. Figure to get written into a novel.

"But not anthro. I had to make do with grad students. They were the same breed as Columbia. Just lower down the food chain. Hairy-legged harlots.

"Get one as an advisee, now you had a sex slave. Tell her to fuck as if your approval of her dissertation depended upon it. One of them was even married. Some twerp in Renaissance history. He'd sit and puff on a hash pipe while I did her in the bedroom. I'd make her change the sheets first."

Quinn started at the last picture. "This one's awfully young. Wait a sec. That's Jake Milroy's daughter. Cressie Milroy."

Cranmer snorted in mild laughter. "Yeah, her mom

needed some money for her drug habit. Rented her for a night. The kid kind of got into it and came back for more. She turned out to be a little . . ."

"A little what?"

"Nothing."

"You're really pretty despicable, you know that?" said Quinn.

A smile grew on his face. "Yeah, I've come to grips with that fact late in life."

■ ■ ■

Nasar told Sam, "I was having a talk with my father, and he happened to mention the discovery of Fomalhaut b."

"Which is?"

"It's a zombie planet. A giant alien planet about the size of Jupiter. Huge debris belt around it maybe 20 billion miles across. But what's of interest is it has an unbalanced orbit which scientists are struggling to explain. It has wild extremes between its closest and furthest point from its parent star—its sun. 4.6 billion miles at closest; 27 billion at farthest. A real ellipse."

"So it violates that whatever-you-told-me-about law?"

As ever, Nasar's gaze seemed to be turned inward. Not looking at the person he was speaking to. "Yes. It is speculated that it might have a sling orbit hurling it around two suns. A 2000 year orbit."

"A sling orbit?"

"Yes. As it goes around one sun it builds up speed and then is flung towards the other one."

"This is Nibiru?"

"No, it just means Nibiru is possible."

"Whoop-de-do. The end of the world."

"Hey, not to worry. It's not due until 2090."

Samantha's phone went off. It wasn't the dial tone of any of her friends. She pressed it on.

"Samantha Fitzhugh?" said a woman's voice.

"Y-ess," she said guardedly.

"Wilhelmina Shattuck. Dr. Shattuck. University of Michigan—Ann Arbor."

Sam's heart quickened. "How did you get this number?"

"Does it matter?"

"What do you want?"

"We understand you had a very unusual DNA reading. We'd like to know more about it."

"How do you know about my DNA?"

"We just found out. That's all. Look, I can fax you my bona fides. I'm on the web. We have grant money. We want to fly you up here and do our own genetic test. We'd get permission from your parents of course."

"I don't know you. I don't want to talk to you."

"Aren't you interested in your genetic origins? We're frankly quite excited about this and thought you would be too."

"I'm not. Now get lost."

Chapter 29

Nothing had been done about the football coach. He was too vital a part of the high school function. But the video Dru had put on the web had gone internationally viral. A Japanese animé outfit had done a cartoon version of him stealing money and food and sniffing underwear.

Coach Wade taught moron-level world history where he pronounced Versailles "Ver-sallys" and Trianon "Try-non." Half the hour was typically spent talking sports with the guys, the other half he'd tell them to write out answers to the questions at the end of the chapter.

He came in tense, knowing he was an object of derision. His opposing coaches had all phoned to ask how his spring practice was coming along. Making not-so-sly digs. "Wooo! Sumpin' smells reeel good!" said one, laughing raucously.

He opened the long drawer of his desk to find it filled with girls' underpants and dollar bills. Slammed it shut and looked around like a hunted beast.

Fully half of the class roared with laughter. The other half were Bo and the jocks. Bo jumped to his feet flailing his arms.

"Whut's so dam' funny? Yew can't make no fun of Coach

Donny-Mack Wade! He's a role model for the young chil-lun of this town!"

This incident was texted all over the school in minutes, reaching the genius class last. Dinorah Greenberg had a head of glistening black curls and an aquiline nose that hooked slightly over a mouth like a red flower. Her parents taught sociology and had once lived in a gypsy camp.

She opined that everyone who wasn't given an heroic role in the dominant athletic culture—which was to say everyone but the jocks and the cheerleaders—were living in a state of alienation due to social inequality. They would be made a deviant social group, ostracized and severely punished, unless they conformed and accepted their low status in the stratification.

The genius class was exempt because none of them played sports, and they clustered together in their pack. In the rest of the school, only the Wiccans had had the cour-age to be the "other." They openly refused the degradation ceremony of being assembled to stick a finger in the air and yell "We're number one!" Now all the subcultures of the school were spontaneously united in a coalition of total rebellion.

At the class break, the coach shoved his way through the crowded halls with eyes like hot coals, sweat beading up on his forehead. A grinning student had had the nerve to stick a sign that said "Panty Sniffer" on his back, and it took him an hour before he noticed and ripped it off. None of his colleagues had bothered to tell him. They resented the coach's high status as well.

The mockery advanced to students sliding up behind him in the hall and throwing loose change on the floor in his path. He'd whip around and roar at them. Expecting them to quail. But they'd grin from ear to ear. Snicker at him. Or openly laugh. A girl dropped a pair of underpants with three dollar bills and a bag of Doritos tucked in it on his desk. Right in front of him.

■ ■ ■

The following morning, a cop car and EMS came to the school, lights flashing, and Coach Wade was taken away in the ambulance. The student text message hive buzzed, but no one knew what had happened.

No one except for Dru who told Samantha during their lunch.

"Mom got this ugly letter this morning from a lawyer threatening to sue us for my defaming the coach. There was a bunch of other stuff Randall could explain. All kinds of invasion of privacy. Public disclosure of private facts. Intrusion into seclusion."

"That takes some gall."

"Yea-uh. I mean he was the one stealing money. Going into cell phones."

"So what happened?"

"You know my mom. She doesn't let grass grow under her feet. She drove me to school just steaming the whole way. Muttering about some meeting she had to be at later. Took me down to the coach in his smelly athletic office. Threw open the door.

"He jumped up like we had caught him at something. Shut his desk drawer in a hurry. I thought he was looking at a skin magazine. I found out it was far more creative."

"Don't keep me in suspense."

"Mom just slammed him in the ribs with the *bocce* ball in the string bag. No preamble, just wham. Clubbed him like a baby seal. He fell to the floor, rolled over on his stomach fighting back screams. His ass kind of up in the air. Those disgusting gray sweat pants he wears with the stain in the crotch. Giving her a target. So she kicked him in the nuts. She was wearing her Doc Martins."

Sam's hands involuntarily covered her mouth. "My gosh."

"He was lying there shrieking. And I'm thinking, Mom, I have to go to school here. And she went up and took one of his hands before he realized what she was doing and scraped it down the side of her face. He's got these thick fingernails he doesn't trim. She cut a slice down the edge of her face in front of her ear. There was blood oozing out. Totally gutsy. She said she'd probably get hydrophobia."

"My God."

"Wait. It gets better. While she was calling EMS and the cops, she opens the desk drawer. And pulls out this much thumbed copy of *Hustler*. Kind of a year end compendium of all the women." Dru shook her head in amazement. "He had cut girls' faces out of the yearbook and pasted them on naked bodies of the women."

"Get out!"

"The magnitude of the scandal . . . Mom didn't even need to fake his attack on her. But she went through with it anyway. Just lied through her teeth to the cops. Claimed he attacked her when she caught him with the magazine. Showed it to them but refused to hand it over. When they got pushy, she got her lawyer on the line. That had them kind of sulky and huddling off together. Muttering threats."

"Dru," Sam said in admiration. "I think your mom has some redeeming qualities."

Dru shrugged. "She doesn't like men, Sam. You know that. They put her in a rage."

"So whose faces?"

"Cherry's face was on one of the nudies. All the cheerleaders were. The volleyball team. Girls' basketball. And yours."

"Mine?"

"Of course," she said in disgust. "One with big gazongas naturally." She held her hands cupped in front of her chest.

"Dru . . ."

Dru turned away, fighting tears. "No one will ever lust after me. No man anyway."

Chapter 30

Chip cursed and threw his racquet up against the white wall of the squash court. He had missed a drop shot; the ball hit so gently off the front wall that it dropped immediately to the floor. Chip had charged at it, physically bounced off the front wall.

Boo couldn't believe how he had run Chip all over the court. He knew it wasn't old to be in your thirties. But Chip was such an Alpha-male that he had intimidated him. The younger man. Totally cocky. Waiting for Wharton. Now everything seemed different.

Afterwards they sat in the steam room their loins wrapped in towels. Sweat running down their chests, dripping off their noses.

"Do you want to take a flutter with that Buggaron money?" Chip asked, eyeing Boo speculatively.

"No. Absolutely not."

"It's pretty clear it's hot money. What could they do about it?"

"*What* could they do about it? Perhaps drag you behind a motorcycle until all the flesh was flayed off your body."

"Oh come on."

"Did what happened to Chirburg make no impression on you? Have you ever seen someone beaten senseless in an office setting before? These men have no fear."

They went through the showers and dried off in the locker room. Got dressed. Chip was thinking hard the whole time.

"A social media initial public offering is coming. Chit-chat. We could capture a big block of stock and then flip it. Make a killing. They'd never know how much we traded. Wouldn't know how to look or ask. Put a bundle in our pockets. Claim we were trading on our own behalf."

"No."

"They want it invested. They said so."

"No. You let Chirburg take the heat on that. I fear there are worse beatings yet to be meted out."

"But it's a sure thing," he insisted.

"No."

Chip looked off into space pensively. "I could go for a craft beer right now. How about you?"

"I'm going back to the office."

"Phone that girl? What were their names?"

Boo said nothing.

"By the way, someone called from New York."

"The home office?"

"No, it was an art auction house. They were looking for a guy named Trey. He seems to have disappeared down here. Or down a rabbit hole."

"Don't know him," Boo lied. And immediately wondered

if it was smart to lie about that. Knowing his eyes had cut left when he said it.

Chip was inspecting him. Trying to read him.

■ ■ ■

Setting sunlight was flickering through the canopy of the old trees of the neighborhood behind the businesses on Chastain Street. Sam and Dru lay their bikes on the grass and confronted Jake Milroy's ramshackle dark bungalow with peeling paint and weed choked yard.

Deep overhanging eves with decorative brackets under them. Front porch under an extension of the main roof. Outside chimney of clinker brick. Windows with large lower panes and small upper ones. Probably built around 1925.

Bats and swifts flitted after insects.

"Why do you want to do this?" Sam asked for perhaps the fifth time.

"Finding who killed Cressie is a challenge," said Dru, looking straight ahead. "Something I can achieve on my own without my mother bulling in. She just thinks I'm a bratty gadfly. I intend to prove otherwise."

"And why am I involved?"

"Because you're my friend."

Dru opened the screen door with a creak that sounded like it could be heard down the street.

"We've come to grieve with him," she said.

"What?"

"If we're caught, that's our excuse."

"What will we do? Hold hands and weep?"

"Shhh. Leave it to me."

Sam marveled anew at Dru's sheer nerve. She must have inherited it from her *bocce* ball mother. Neither of them imposed any restraints on themselves.

The interior smelled of dust and fried grease and turpentine. All the rubbish, the Milroy dreams and delusions. It filled Sam with a great sense of loss.

Sam was nervous and kept glancing at the open front door. Expecting to see the hulking Jake Milroy framed in it. He made her skin crawl.

Dru went straight to Cressie's bedroom and started searching like a practiced sleuth. Under the bed. In the closet. "Paydirt," she hissed. She held an open cigar box with a big wad of money in it bound in a red rubber band.

"I'm not touching this money," she said. "But take a gander at this."

It was a photo of Cressie bent over a chair with her bare bottom up in the air, underpants rolled down. Plaid skirt pulled up to her waist. Knee socks. She was looking back at the camera with a pouting duck face. She was not an unwilling participant.

Underneath were post cards of Ireland. Harmless bucolic scenes of emerald green fields and sheep. Stone cottages. A Celtic cross at a crossroads.

Beneath that a little ledger book with dollar amounts and some kind of code notations. Her blackmail book?

And beneath that, a sun bleached sepia photo of something . . . people . . . creatures coming out of the sea.

The water of a bay was black and the tide seemed to be pushing small waves into a rocky shore.

The . . . *things* . . . were slick with water. Dripping. Their skin seemed scaly. Their limbs . . . were not entirely intact. One seemed to have flippers for arms.

Clomping and crashing in the outer room. Sam froze. The scalp tightened on her head.

Jake Milroy had gone into his studio and was busying himself with a large canvas on an easel. Straightening it. Jabbing at things. Squeezing paint tubes. Doing it all in the growing dark.

The two crossed the floor silently to try to escape. Sam kicked an empty Tequila bottle. Clatter-cling. Froze. Milroy continued to paint, paying them no notice. His brogan-shod feet were planted squarely facing the canvas, his right hand raised with the brush. Moving with authority.

Sam tried to pull Dru towards the door, but she tore away. Moved up behind Milroy. Cold blooded insanity.

Dru clapped her hands. No reaction from him. She put her hands next to her mouth, lifted up on her toes and whooped. Still nothing.

They stepped carefully around to his side. Staring in disbelief.

He smelled of liquor and sweat. He was unshaven, his hair sticking up in patches. His eyes were glazed. The pupils dilated and black. He painted mechanically but surely. With total precision. Unaware of them, of anything around him.

A line of drool ran down his chin. He smiled as if in pleasant contemplation of his work. Seeing it through his sightless eyes.

Then they saw the painting. Samantha and Drusana against a flat sea-blue background. Full frontal nudity. Photographic detail. Subtlety of tones. Dru's navel was a perfect slit . . . my god. Uncanny.

Sam dragged her friend outside. They walked their bikes under the trees in the chill breeze, the beginning of stars overhead.

"He painted me," said Dru, her eyes looking at the sky. "Did you notice the detail?"

Sam's hands were trembling. Her heart rate would not go down nor her breathing slow.

"You were Erishkigal," she said. "Lady of the Great Below. The goddess of Irkalla, the Land of the Dead. She rules the Gate of the Land of No Return. The Guardian and Judge of Deeds and Beings."

Dru's eyes seemed to dance with starlight. Her mouth was wet and open like a blossoming tulip.

"I am a goddess," she breathed.

Chapter 31

Quinn's phone rang. He punched it on.

"Hey, you," said a girl's voice.

Was the voice sultry? The caller I.D. said "Dru Shelley."

Quinn was sitting on his front porch, Plymouth gin and tonic in hand. Half a green lime. Looking at some pencil sketches of a girl on heavy paper. The light was still strong at six PM. Music played through the open front door.

"Is that Brahms playing?" asked Dru quietly.

"Yes. Piano and strings."

Quinn was unsettled by the culture level of the girl. "So," he said. "How did you get this number?"

Her breath was audible over the phone. When she spoke, the voice was definitely sultry. "Off the Internet."

Quinn paused in frank astonishment. He engaged in large scale multi-state racketeering, cops and DEA never even getting close, and a sixteen-year-old girl could find his private phone number.

Milroy had given him sketches of a girl he said was emerging from his subconscious. Brought them to him during their regular drinks evening at the Dingo Saloon.

Laid them out on the bar. Startled, it was all Quinn could do to keep him from spilling booze on them.

Milroy didn't care. They were just sketches slithering out of his head. He said once the vision starts it moves quite fast. He thought it was a girl from his daughter's high school. A classmate like Samantha Fitzhugh.

Quinn knew her as Dru Shelley. It was obvious from the drawings. They oozed power and sexuality. Heavy-lidded eyes. The girl was alluring. A temptress. Delilah. Circe. Salome. Her kiss lingered in his memory.

"Did you know," Dru asked, "that men much more than women relate to their lover through the sexual act?"

He took a sip of his drink. "I can believe that."

"That's why they suffer from a deep fear of rejection. And have performance anxiety. It's their desire to please, to dominate with their love."

"Did you read that in a girls' magazine? Self-help column?"

"No. *The Wall Street Journal*. Health and Wellness section."

She had floored him again. "Seriously?"

"I have an app for it on my iPad."

Quinn found his heart rate was up. He hadn't had this reaction to a girl over the phone in . . . when?

"Thinking about a career in finance?" he asked.

"I'm not that far along. But right now, I'm thinking Oxford for college."

"Creative choice. But whatever you do, avoid academe as a career."

"Believe me, I know."

"You don't apply to the university for admission. You apply to a college. New College is lovely. Great gardens. Magdalen—pronounced 'Maudlin'—has the deer park. Worcester has the cricket grounds right there within the walls."

She said, "I'm looking them up on the web as we speak. Wow. New College certainly has beautiful gardens. Wonderful advice. I've always wanted a mentor. Someone older and wiser telling me what to do."

"Is that from a Broadway musical?"

"I believe so." Her voice was coy. She was bantering.

Quinn caught himself. Was she Eve? Or the snake? Or both? "You know I really don't like to stay on the phone too long. We live in an age of electronic snooping."

"Before you hang up . . ." said Dru.

"Yes?"

"I think you're diabolically clever."

A slow smile spread over his face. He was smiling in spite of himself.

Sixteen-years-old. The little bitch was a sexual predator. She was trying to draw him to doom. And she made it seem very attractive.

■ ■ ■

Just as Samantha stepped out of the shower, a bolt of lightning struck the yard in a huge flashing boom. She jumped and steadied her nerves. She knew what she wanted, what she had to do.

They were hermetically sealed against the world. She would realize her desires.

She put on a sleeveless dress that tied at the shoulders and fell in Fortuny pleats. This simple garment she bought one summer in Greece to wear over her bathing suit at the beach. Sometimes she used it as a nightgown. In ancient Mesopotamia it was called a "pala dress."

She only owned three pieces of jewelry: a chunky Byzantine ring, an Egyptian eye of Horus necklace called a pectoral because it lay on the chest, and lapis lazuli beads. She put them all on.

The beads were worn by Inanna on her descent into the Underworld. They symbolized fertility.

Sam painted her eyelids with Mrs. Jaeger's mascara, sprayed on her perfume. She couldn't remember ever making up her face before. The kohl with which Sumerian women painted their eyes was named "See me, men."

When she came downstairs, Kurt had pork cutlets cordon bleu sizzling on the stove. Cutlets pounded thin, deli ham and melty Emmertaler cheese stuffed between two of them. The whole thing coated in egg and bread crumbs.

She set the table with him at the head and her beside him. Put the goddess statue between their two places.

She felt ravenous and ate rapidly, but then slowed down. Chewed deliberately, savoring the food. Making eye contact with Kurt. Rubbing her bare knee against his thigh.

"You smell good," he said.

"Thanks. It's your mom's scent."

"Is that it? Am I feeling Oedipal?"

She smiled but said nothing. Trying to convey erotic yearnings through her silence.

The black stone statue lay between them, giving off a radiance, its improbable presence a portent of what Sam intended to do.

As they ate, she told him all about the Milroy painting. The photographic detail. About Milroy in a trance. About Dru seeming to go crazy.

When she finished, she said solemnly, "I can't take this any longer."

Kurt looked down at his plate. Feeling her emotional burden. Not knowing how to help.

The statue was opaque yet luminous. Luminous with eternity.

Sam put her bare foot on his under the table and pressed down. "I only know one way out."

Kurt understood her meaning.

"I am going to be the painting," she said in a thrill of eagerness. "I am Inanna."

Kurt shook his head, his face filled with consternation.

"I'm having my period," she insisted. "It's safe. Like with Cherry."

His eyes lingered on the swell of her bosoms. They didn't move away. She knew the temptation was strong.

Outside, the first fat drops of rain fell. Followed by a torrential downpour.

"No, Sam," he pleaded.

"You don't control me!" she lashed out. "You don't own me."

His face looked scorched. "True. But I won't destroy your powers. They're too much a part of you. They're your destiny."

Rain beat against the windows. Another clap of thunder seemed to rock the house.

Sam stood up abruptly. "I am the goddess," she asserted fiercely. "I can feel the pulse beating in my wrists. My heart is quickening."

And as Kurt watched, she underwent a transformation that no sixteen-year-old American girl should be able to accomplish. An alluring smile turned up the corners of her mouth. She touched the lapis lazuli beads at her throat.

"This is the symbol of fertility and of my rapture."

Her face was filled with purpose. "This is a pala dress, worn in Sumeria." She pulled the bows at the shoulders and let it drop in a puddle at her feet.

She folded her arms beneath her bosoms. "This is my pectoral, an eye of Horus worn on the chest. The eye is not passive, but an agent of action. The pectoral was translated in Sumerian as 'Come, men, come'."

Kurt stared at the ancient eye flanked by her two round, rosy nipples. He was mesmerized.

She backed towards the living room. Stood there in the middle of the floor. Trees were whipping in the wind. The gutters brimmed over with water that fell in a cascade.

"This is my garment of ladyship. The modest covering of my sexual role." She rolled her underpants over her hips and down, knees together, until they fell at her ankles. Stepped out of them one foot at a time.

"Put your hands on me. Touch me."

"Oh god, Sam," he moaned.

Then her voice spoke verses that Kurt did not know—Sam never knew she knew. They came out of her subconscious memory.

"Make your milk sweet and thick, my bridegroom.

My shepherd, I will drink your fresh milk.

Wild bull Dumuzi, let the milk of the goat flow in my sheepfold.

Fill my holy churn with honey cheese.

Lord Dumuzi, I will drink your fresh milk."

"Samantha?" Kurt said aghast.

But Samantha was gone, released from earthly bonds, and an aggressive love goddess had taken her place.

"Stop," he begged one last time.

But their world had begun to explode in color and emotion. They were rolling on the floor as she covered him with fierce kisses and ripped his shirt out of his pants, tore open his trousers, pulled him between her thighs.

"I want it. I need it so much."

Lightning crashed.

Sam felt a buzzing sound inside her head. Her ears popped like she was descending in an airplane.

She sat up. "Shit! It's your parents. They're home."

"How do you know?"

"I can see things. Remember?"

Frantically, she grabbed up her dress and ran upstairs like any stricken teenager caught going too far.

She stood with her back against the bedroom door, her

chest heaving. Rain and tree branches slashed against the glass. She heard the Jaegers run from the car through the rain into the house. Laughing. Happy to be back home. Calling good-bye to their driver. Hello to Kurt.

Then Sam realized with mortification that she had left her underpants downstairs on the carpet. Her mind was tangled with shame and frustrated desire.

Kurt knocked on the door and handed her the underpants in a wad. "She didn't see them," he whispered.

Sam closed her eyes and sighed. "No, but she knows."

He held her shoulders and looked her in the eyes.

"Sam, downstairs your flesh was burning hot, and your face altered completely. It was as if you had become . . . something else. A priestess. Or a goddess."

■ ■ ■

Mrs. Jaeger lightly rapped on the door and came in. Sam, deeply ashamed, stayed turned to the wall, her naked body covered by the sheet.

The rain was clicking down more slowly.

Mrs. Jaeger sat down on the bed and put her hand lightly on the rounding of Sam's hip.

"When we were not far away . . . in the car . . . I heard your voice. Don't ask me to explain how. I just did. You were reciting the 'Courtship of Inanna and Dumuzi.'

"Inanna's brother weaves the coverings of her bridal bed, and urges her to love Dumuzi, a mortal shepherd, while she prefers a farmer. Eventually he persuades her.

"This symbolizes a point in civilization where nomadic

herdsmen merged in union with stationary raisers of grain. It symbolizes the role of family in forming unions.

"It was the most beloved love story of ancient Mesopotamia. It is likely the inspiration for Solomon's love song to the Queen of Sheba, the only romantic-erotic piece of the Old Testament.

"It is the tale of a *hieros gamos*, a sacred marriage, and was reenacted ritually. Once a year the king and a priestess representing the goddess joined in sexual union to make the land fruitful. They lay down on 'the fragrant honey-bed'."

"No," Sam protested weakly.

"I know. Kurt has assured me nothing happened. But let me finish.

"In the New Year's ritual, the king was taken in a procession to the temple where he was transformed into Dumuzi. The goddess Inanna entered into the body of the chosen priestess. Intercourse gave the king a bridge to the gods, and he achieved intimacy with the divine for another year. The king imitated the gods, and the people were to imitate the king which they did through temple prostitution. Thus all was made whole.

"Inanna was the goddess of both love and war. In the poem, she says 'In battle, I am your leader, your armor-bearer.' Kurt tells me that you throw a knife with uncanny accuracy. That you can focus your mind and make objects explode."

She said this as if it were unusual but not unheard of.

Sam had begun to cry. She was completely miserable. "I don't want these things. I only want to love. But in the normal way."

"But it's all normal. It's just taught us through myths. Inanna mixes love and rage, erotic attraction with combat. Physical love is a search for our inner wholeness. The connectivity of love and the fierce energy of libido are unified. A harmonious whole is made of the two dichotomies."

Sam formed herself into Mrs. Jaeger and let the woman hold her and smooth her hair. A slow warm glow spread through her. The trees were dripping in the yard.

"I don't understand this. I'll have to think about it. All I know is my mother has left me. I want to be your adopted daughter."

Chapter 32

"That auction house called again," said Chip. "Their man has totally disappeared. Unused return air ticket. They're quite distressed about it."

Boo shrugged, tried to ignore him.

"Funny you saying you didn't know Trey. He was in your class at prep school. I checked the alumni list."

Boo cut his eyes at him.

The phone rang, and Chip jerked it up before the secretary could get it. Said hello. Announced it was the art auction house.

"I'm not in," said Boo.

Chip said into the phone: "He says he's not in."

Fuming, Boo booted his computer.

There was some gabble at the other end. Chip said he'd relay the message.

He turned to Boo, said blithely: "They say they're calling the local cops. Maybe it's an idle threat. Or maybe . . . who knows?"

"Who's calling the cops?" growled Chirburg, coming through the door. He was unshaven, smelly, the same slept-in clothes. Grease on his face like an oily sheen.

"Nothing that concerns you," said Chip. "A little imbroglio our Boo has gotten himself into."

"The fuck's goin' on, preppie boy?" Chirburg demanded.

"Nothing that concerns you," said Boo, studying the computer screen. "Did you find a hotel room?"

"I spent the night in my mother-fucking rental car. Those peckerwoods stole my wallet in the hospital. I can't even get the car out of the parking garage."

"Actually, I took it," said Chip blithely. "When you were on the floor knocked cold."

Chirburg stared aghast. His chest heaved like he was going to explode. *You took it?*

"Yeah, I thought it was kind of funny. See if you could live off the land. Like a Boy Scout ordeal or something."

"Well where is it?"

"Gone I guess. It might have fallen down a storm drain. Who knows? Say, weren't you a SEAL? Don't you know how to kill for food?"

Chirburg rounded on Boo. "You little prep school dicksucker. You come across with some walking around money and find me a hotel room. And I'm talking toot-sweet or your ass is fuckin' grass."

Boo got up, came around the desk and gave Chirburg a ferocious open hand blow across the chops. Knocked him back into the wall to hit his head with a big whack.

He fell to his knees bawling. "You're gonna put me back in the hospital." Sucking air, sobbing. "You're gonna kill me. I gotta have a place to stay." Blubbering. "I can't sleep in my car. I don't have money to eat." Sob. "I need to take a crap. I'm fucking constipated."

Boo really enjoyed watching Chirburg cry. He was starting to feel he could pull off the enterprise of spiriting Samantha away. Along with a bunch of money. And the Italian sun and wine was waiting.

■ ■ ■

Dr. Clearwire spent the first thirty minutes of the class ranting about how poorly teachers were paid and telling the kids to pressure their parents to vote "Yes" on the new school bond issue. It was the usual blah blah blah. A sick society with its values utterly skewed. The internal contradictions of capitalism that would eventually rip the country apart.

Twenty minutes into it, Dinorah started spelling the states and capitals backwards and the class got into checking for errors. She made none. And had gotten from New England down into the Mid-Atlantic states before Clearwire decided to do the lesson.

He called on Samantha to read aloud from *Gilgamesh* where the priestess of the Temple of Ishtar is to be brought to seduce the wild man Enkidu.

She began hesitantly.

"Take her . . . to the wild place
Where animals gather at the waterhole
Strip off her gown and have her lie
Naked, ready, legs apart."

Sam knew her face was red. But Dr. Clearwire was staring at her intently. A bead of sweat trickled from under his cap and down the side of his face.

"Oh lord," said Emerson. "Is this starting again?"

"Why are you interrupting?" Clearwire demanded. "Are you unable to take a positive view of sex? Are you caught in some Judeo-Christian fear of our most basic needs?"

Emerson rested his chin in his hand. "I'm not bothered by it in the least. You chose to have it read aloud when we're all capable of reading it on our own. And you deliberately chose Sam to read it. It's so transparent."

"What are you talking about?"

"You've got sweat rolling off you. Your hands are doing something under the desk."

Clearwire stood up in a rage.

"Are you going to call me a 'negro' again?" drawled Emerson.

Clearwire was barely able to control himself. He talked through gritted teeth. "You know there are those on the faculty who want to help you advance in life."

"Is it 1950?" Emerson asked in a bored voice. "Am I some barefoot sharecropper's son, and you're going to introduce me to a world of books and help me dream of attending the segregated Ag & Tech College?

"You get to identify the promising darky and pick which one is allowed to rise as long as he doesn't get too above himself. Those days are long past. And the absurd racial quota manipulations of white liberals are past too."

Clearwire really started to lose it, spluttering, stammering. "You . . . you impudent . . . rude . . ."

"Am I deprived? In a sense. Afro-American History doesn't pay much. There are two PhDs in my family and one car. Personally, I intend to work on Wall Street and be able to afford to shoot grouse in Scotland."

"Don't you ever dare . . . ever presume . . . to talk like that to me in here!" Clearwire roared. "I am a proud Progressive! I don't apologize for my views on affirmative action! I am on the right side of history!"

Emerson gave a light laugh. "The day of the white liberal is over. All the Chinese and Indian immigrants coming into this country . . . they'll eat your lunch."

■ ■ ■

Coming back from fencing at the gym around five p.m., Sam encountered Professor Jaeger returning home as well. They walked together into the tree-bowered neighborhood that jutted into the densely wooded park. Like the campus, it was an immaculately clean world with no litter of wind-blown paper or plastic bottles.

She took his arm without quite knowing why. He was like a patriarch, or the father she never had. It seemed to please him. Perhaps he missed his daughter. Perhaps he liked young girls.

"Are myths true?" she asked.

"All myths are true because they tell us about our subconscious. And it is the subconscious that directs our actions. So we in fact act out myths."

"What about a myth of a descent into the underworld?"

"It is a spiritual initiation. You abandon old values—fundamental illusions about life—and become empowered by making the descent."

"The Sumerian Inanna descends."

He almost became animated. "Ah, now that's a profound myth. The first descent we have in cultural history. But the fourth in her cycle of emotional development.

"In the first important myth, she acquires a throne and a bed. She sheds her subconscious fears and desires and becomes worthy of her queenly throne and the . . . the bed of great men. Sovereignty over mortals and sovereignty of her bed.

"In the second myth she acquires the tools of civilization—agriculture, architecture, astronomy—their secrets written on seven tablets, and bestows them on her city of Uruk.

"In the third myth she takes the shepherd Dumuzi as a lover and bears his children.

"In the fourth she goes on the journey to the underworld. She wears symbolic artifacts of civilization: crown, earrings, robe. At each of the seven gates she announces herself as 'Inanna, Queen of Heaven, traveling to the East.' And at each gate she is stripped of something: beads, breastplate, girdle, measuring rod. Until at last she stands naked before Erishkigal. Who strikes her dead.

"Inanna lies a piece of rotting meat for three days, a universal number in the occult. The period of the Dark of the Moon. And then is rescued in a complicated manner. It is the first example of a dying divinity who sacrifices to redeem the earth."

Sam wasn't sure she had followed it all. "And how does a psychologist relate to this tale?"

"It's spiritual because she lets go of the mundane facets

of life and undertakes a path of initiation. She finds her higher self."

"But she goes back to the way she was before?"

"Ah, very astute." He seemed genuinely impressed. "But when rescued, she must provide a substitute. Thus she can never close the gate to her subconscious."

"It's so amazing being a guest of your family," said Sam wistfully. "I just wish I knew about my mom."

"We're quite concerned about your mother as well. We're going to try to find her."

"How?"

"We're having a séance tonight."

Chapter 33

Before dinner, Kurt took Sam aside.

"Sam, you don't have to participate. You could just go upstairs and read." There was genuine concern in his voice.

"But I want to," she insisted. "This is about my mother."

Two other faculty couples came over brimming with departmental chitchat. Together, they ate a thick soup with sausage and celery in it, crusty bread, drank a Tokay wine.

Afterwards, Kurt got Sam out of the room and onto the porch. The sky had turned a wine purple. Whippoorwills were calling. He gave her a last warning.

"You have to steel yourself. When Mom goes through the ether some strange things come out. Whatever you do, don't move. Don't interrupt her trance. It can be quite dangerous."

With the dining room table cleared, they seated themselves, Mrs. Jaeger at the head, Sam and Kurt on either side. The others completing a circle of sorts. All holding hands. Waiting intently. The only light was a solitary candle.

Mrs. Jaeger took a series of deep breaths as though rallying her strength. Her eyes were closed. She seemed totally absorbed in her thoughts.

Someone shifted in a seat. The candle flame flickered and went out as though puffed by a breath of air. In the darkness, the temperature seemed to drop.

The faintest tingle of electricity ran through their hands, making everyone start.

Sam got the distinct feeling that Mrs. Jaeger had become a focus for the elemental forces of the universe. That invisible powers had converged on her.

Her head rocked back looking at the ceiling. Was she in a trance?

Sam felt the room dissolve around her, then steady. She closed her eyes. Colors like pieces of broken stained glass began assembling themselves behind her eyelids.

A woman in a pala dress stood before her. A crown upon her head. Eyes as green as emeralds.

She beckoned Sam to follow towards a horizon where a lone silver star hung.

Sam felt she was standing at the point of the concourse of great forces. She was surrendering to it.

The goddess disrobed but for a girdle. It was not like our corsets. To gird is to encircle. In ancient times a girdle was a wide band about the waist, metal with precious stones. Both a lure and a totem over the womb, the site of fertility, decorated with fertility symbols. Fertility magic.

She beckoned to Samantha. Urging her to follow into the subconscious.

Mrs. Jaeger was murmuring. Then she began to speak in a clear voice: "Oh dear god put it in me. I want it. I need it so much."

The voice was Samantha's. Her ardent longing for Kurt. Coming from Mrs. Jaeger's mouth.

Sam let out a shriek and jumped up, breaking the circle. She fled out the front door, across the narrow road and went tumbling down the hill on dead leaves, bouncing off trees.

Kurt was a split second behind her out the door. Tackled her. Held her weeping on the damp detritus of the woods. Wet leaves sticking to them.

Sam's hands pressed against his chest. "She thinks I'm a whore! I only want to be in love. To love completely."

"There's a limbo of forgotten things out in the ether," Kurt explained in a whisper. "They use my mom as a medium. She does nothing but relay messages."

"But why me? Everyone has dirty thoughts."

"She opened up a layer of memory of what was right there. The first thing she encountered was your emotions."

Sam couldn't stop crying. "I feel like such trash for natural god given urges!"

"No one means to hurt you. We only want to help."

"I'm sorry. I'm sorry. Your mother is so nice. How do you separate the human in her from the magical in your mind?"

"I don't. Any more than I do with you. You're like her, Sam. You're going to be a version of her."

Kurt was kissing her. Deeply. His tongue in her mouth. His arms wrapping her tightly. She melted. The deepest springs in her nature were being fed. Her thighs locked about his. She humped convulsively against him. Hot with desire. Wanting total surrender.

"Love me, Kurt, love me," she begged fervently.

A falsetto voice called out: "No no, don't do it without a rubber!"

Sam knew the voice in the dark. It was Bo. And two other football bruisers with him. Bandy legged fireplugs. They advanced, crackling in the undergrowth.

Kurt jerked Sam to her feet and put her behind him. The jocks closed in, but Kurt didn't budge an inch. He was actually taller than they were.

"Don't make me have to hurt you, Bo," he said calmly. "Your coach would not be pleased."

"Oooo I'm scared."

But there was another presence. A shuffling in the leaves.

Sam knew who it was. She could smell them. It was so familiar. She felt a flutter of fear.

Ghostly white blobs swam up out of the dark and resolved themselves into Nancy Pelosi masks. There must have been ten of them.

"Who the fuck'r you?" Bo demanded.

No one answered. The stench was noticeable. Like rotten meat and sweat and unwashed clothes.

Bo reached to jerk off a mask. Hog Man just kind of popped him in the side of the head with brass knuckles that flashed in the moonlight.

Bo doubled up in sharp skull-splitting pain. "Ow goddammit you sum'bitch."

"We got us what you call a predickyment here," said Hog Man. "These boys been spying on the house up there."

"You can't stop us," said one of the jocks. "We can do whatever we want, and you got no right to interfere. And anyhow, you stink like pig shit."

"I'm not real big on criticism," said Hog Man.

He turned to Sam and Kurt. "Now you kids go on back up to the house. We got this all taken care of. We'll see these boys get home and all tucked up in bed."

Suddenly he knelt on one knee before Sam. "M'lady."

Chapter 34

"I took him back to the airport," Boo told the cop over the phone. "He went inside. He had a carry-on bag. That's all I know."

He saw Quinn standing in the door, waved him into a chair. Dusty red trousers. Madras shirt. Double-breasted Navy blazer.

Quinn edged around the scuffle between Chip and Chirburg. Chip was winning of course. He had tripped Chirburg, and whenever the man would try to get to his feet, he'd kick out an arm that was propping him. Hook an ankle.

Chirburg was pleading, "Lemme alone, goddammit! I'm trying to get outta here!"

"So. Where are you off to this fine morning?"

"I'm not tellin' ya. Lemme alone."

"No, I barely knew the guy," said Boo. "We were in high school together he claimed."

Boo made a shushing noise with his hand, but Chip went on tormenting Chirburg. It was bullying on a level Boo hadn't seen since he was fourteen.

The cop didn't seem terribly concerned. Hadn't bothered to even come to the office. But he wouldn't get off the phone. His name was Wally Butts of all things.

Boo said Trey—was that his name?—Trey had been here looking for an artist. Boo didn't know who. Didn't know where he stayed. Just picked him up and delivered him back to the airport. Apparently his expense account didn't run to rental cars.

"Can't get up until you tell me," said Chip in a singsong voice.

Chirburg was close to tears. "I found I got a first cousin here in town. She's coming to pick me up. Give me a place to stay."

"Name?"

"Lorraine. Lorraine Raguzi. She married some two-bit college professor. A real douche. Got divorced."

Chip finally let him struggle to his feet. He stood there unsteady, trying to get his equilibrium. Chip hooked his ankle and tripped him one last time.

Chirburg fell with a big crunch on his right shoulder. Let out a wail of pain.

"You got pro wrestling goin' on in there?" asked the cop.

"Rowdy clients," said Boo. He made a claw of his hand, fuming get off the phone.

Now Chip was helping Chirburg up. Telling him he needed to be more careful at his age. Was liable to break something. Did he often have fainting spells?

Chirburg was crying, wiping snot off his lip with his sleeve. He staggered outside where a van had pulled to the curb.

"Jeezus, what is that stink?" A real Yankee broad voice.

"I just farted," Chirburg wept. "I'm about to take a two-day dump. You gotta get me to a commode."

"What do I look like? A sanitation service?"

Boo noticed Quinn had gone to the window, divided the blinds to stare at the woman driving the van. There was a look of shock on his face. Shock and something else. Dismay? Worse than that. Horror?

■ ■ ■

"You have ruined football spring practice," fumed Cherry, hands on her hips. She was spitting mad.

"Me?" went Samantha. "I didn't break their arms."

Word had gone through the school that three football jocks had had their arms broken by masked hoodlums. Both arms. Six total. They were at home afraid to leave their houses. They had talked to the coach by phone.

Cherry had a spray tan that made her look orange and a t-shirt that read "It's All About Me." Truer words were never written.

"You may as well have. You must have told them to do it. Poor Coach Wade. The winning-est coach we ever had. His career ruined. You and that skanky little friend of yours and her dyke mother."

"Skanky?" Sam was furious. She grabbed Cherry by the throat. "You listen to me, you hot-pants slut—"

Cherry slapped violently at Sam's hand. "Slut? You're the one in his room every night, you . . . you whore!"

In a high school, kids will swarm around a fight, and a girl fight is best of all. Soon there was a packed circle, everyone straining to see. Egging them on, shouting "fight, fight!"

But it didn't get very far, because Dru appeared, shoved her way through and demanded: "Did you call my mother a dyke?" And pasted Cherry one right in the eye.

Cherry ran screaming down the hall to the principal's office. And it was only a matter of time before the intercom ordered Sam and Dru there as well.

Principal Peevey was terrified. Sweat sat on his forehead like BBs. Anyone would be scared of Dru's mother. And Cherry's father was prominent in the town Chamber of Commerce and president of the football Boosters Club. It was a lose-lose situation.

Sam was the one he figured to hang it on.

"Up to our old tricks again are we?" he crooned, eying her with unconcealed hostility.

At that moment, Randall breezed in. "Cherry called Dru's mother a dyke. She's in complete violation of our civility and respect rules. And we all know how essential those rules are for a tolerant, caring environment."

The principal exploded. "What? Who invited you in here?"

"No one. I'm here to represent Samantha." He turned to Sam. "Don't answer any questions. They'll just try to get you to lose your temper."

The principal's face was bright scarlet. "You little bullshit artist . . . !"

"Bullshit . . . artist," murmured Randall, taking notes on a yellow legal pad.

"You can't take notes in here. This is a . . . a closed proceeding."

"Is there an established procedure for that? Is it enforced

system wide? And has the State Department of Education approved it?"

Peevey was completely flummoxed. His sweaty hands made a vague beckoning motion at nothing. When he thought it couldn't get any worse, Coach Wade bulled in.

Wade's ribs were taped so he stood in a funny posture and had trouble breathing. "Yew cain't even control your own office. That's why I'm up shit crick. We were going for the state championship next year. And now look at us. All caus'a yew and them two!"

"Samantha and Dru have done nothing wrong," Randall insisted calmly.

Coach Wade roared at him, "Yew little four-eyed pissant! That one there that dam' Samantha left my boys down in the woods to get their arms broke. Din't even call the cops nor nothin'."

"There's no duty to rescue," Randall asserted coolly. "Sam had no obligation to do anything. And as I've learned from the police report, all three of your gallant lads were carrying paintball guns. A reasonable inference would be that they were about to paintball the Jaeger home." He straightened his glasses. "Have you questioned them about who put them up to the stunt? Was it perhaps Cherry?"

"Me?" squealed Cherry in alarm.

The coach bellowed: "I'm gone wring yore little scrawny neck is what I'm gone do!"

Randall raised his eyebrows. "Do tell. Do you think you'd enjoy doing jail time?"

"Hell-l-ooo?" said Dru. "May I get a word in edgewise? I mean I am the one who hit Cherry."

The room fell silent.

Dru's voice was an acid sweetness. "Coach Wade? Remember the magazine my mother took from your office? Just because she didn't hand it over to the police doesn't mean she won't. She's taken it to a lab so the testing won't be bungled. There's all manner of your—I guess the polite term would be to call it DNA—on it. And she's having it photocopied. In color. I'm sure our dear Cherry will really enjoy seeing her entry. She's such a big fan of yours."

Cherry was doing a "What? What?" Agitated hand movements. Indignant.

The coach turned as white as a man after a heart attack. Skin like sun-faded parchment.

The principal put his face in his hands. His shoulders shook like he was crying.

"You know," said Randall, "with the complete disregard of procedural due process in this school, you could find yourself deep in civil litigation. It might take years for the school district to dig its way out."

Chapter 35

The weather was getting nice. Dogwoods blossoming white in the woods.

Quinn sat on his front porch, barefoot, madras shorts, a red polo shirt. Drinking iced tea. Reading a book on Sumerian mythology even though he knew it all by heart.

The Hebrew Abraham came out of Babylonia bearing their creation myths which they in turn had gotten from the Sumerians. In each, a god or gods deliberately created man from clay.

Adama in Genesis was Adapa to the Sumerians, the first man. The first woman Ninti means "Lady of the Rib."

The Sumerian twist was that Adapa was created by Ea and was so loyal to Ea that the god decided to make him immortal. Sent him up to the great god Anu who dwelled on Nibiru. But Adapa refused the Bread of Life, thinking it poisoned.

And so man through his own folly was condemned to a life of pain and toil.

Far in the distance Quinn saw the small girl jogging towards him.

For a time he had felt that nothing mattered but the one

thing. Samantha Fitzhugh. He had to possess her or all was lost in life. She was his rejuvenation fantasy.

But now there was a second thing. And she seemed to represent life's meaning as well. But a darker side. One that took him down to confront his subconscious.

She arrived breathing heavily, flinging sweat off her forehead.

Quinn asked if she would like an iced tea? She said yes. Would be deliriously grateful. Fanned herself with her hand. Wagged the hem of her t-shirt up and down to let in air. Showing her hard, brown belly. Navel a vertical slit.

He fetched it from the kitchen. She was sitting in a rocking chair. Reached up to take it, and their hands brushed. She drank the tea gratefully. Said it was a life-saver. Rolled the glass over her face and chest.

"You know," she said, "have you ever seen the photos in the newspapers of the coeds demonstrating against coal-fired electric plants?"

"Yes."

"There's always one—just one—wearing a Peruvian Indian hat."

She was playing with him. Being whimsical. "That's true," he agreed.

"And if you see a rock band—kind of wastrel guys in their twenties—there's always one—just one—in a plaid flannel shirt that's way too small. So he doesn't button it or tuck it in his pants. Just wears it over a t-shirt. Something his mother bought for him when he was fourteen."

Quinn laughed. "You're right again."

"Is there like some national protocol at work? And how do they agree on who the one is?"

Quinn knew she had planned this, but still wondered what brain-power this girl had. Was she a MENSA member?

"You know," she said, "I think you're majorly misunderstood."

"How so?"

"Living here all alone. It's bucolic, sure. But you've isolated yourself from women. From love."

Quinn knew the drill. Women always probed for weaknesses. They did it instinctively from the earliest ages. Get you to blubber and then feel shame that you had.

"I had a bad marriage," he said shortly. "And I will say no more on the subject. I'm not capable of suitable comment. And by the way, Dru, I'm thirty-two."

She fanned herself with her hand. "Say, do you mind if I take a shower? I am really sweaty."

Quinn paused. Then told her the bathroom was next to the kitchen. Fresh towels in the closet. She walked off, shedding her t-shirt in the living room. Dropping it on the floor. Her back was bare. No bra.

After a moment, he heard the shower run. Was she expecting him to walk in and join her?

That was when his ex-wife Lorraine came driving up the road leaving a faint trail of dust behind her van. Parked at an angle in the front. She was arguing with some middle-aged man who got out of the van with her. It was that dirtbag that Hog Man had smashed into the wall in the broker's office.

Chirburg was wearing a clashing madras shirt and shorts outfit. Looked like Quinn's old clothes. Holding a manila envelope. He saw Quinn and stopped short.

"Are those my clothes?" asked Quinn.

"Oh holy shit!" Chirburg exclaimed in recognition. Looking like he wanted to disappear into the earth.

"Go on," ordered Lorraine. "Touch him with the papers. Then he's served."

"Oh shit, you lied to me," he protested. "You said this was some real estate sale property you were looking at."

Lorraine exploded. "You needle-dick bug-fucker! Just touch him with it. Then your role is over."

Chirburg stared at Quinn in stark terror. "I got nuttin' t'do wit dis. Nuttin'. I swear t'Jezus."

He threw the envelope on the ground and got back in the passenger seat of the van. Slammed the door.

Lorraine picked up the envelope, waved it after him. "You numb-nuts! I try to save some money on a process server . . . !"

Quinn smiled grimly. "Are we engaged in fruitless litigation again? Let me save you a nickel. I accept service." He took the envelope from her hand. Tore it open. Pulled out the Family Court pleadings.

"Now comes the Petitioner who alleges and says . . ."

He scanned down it. The usual bullshit. Re-open the issue of alimony. Hidden assets. Expedited discovery. Specifically asking for records of a brokerage account in the name of El Macho Buggaron.

Quinn sighed. "You know, Lorraine, I've always wondered about that old concept of 'throwing the man out of the house.' We used to hear it growing up. Like the woman had the power to just order him to be gone. Stand there like Nemesis.

"The man was supposed to stuff some underwear and socks in a brown paper bag and slink away to the YMCA or somewhere. A buddy's couch.

"I never quite tied into it. How did she have that authority? You and I never tested it because we had a rental unit, and you stalked out. Got a moving van and cleared the furniture out while I was in morning classes. I came back to find bare rooms. You gleeful. Going to find yourself a real man."

Quinn went on perfectly calmly. "But let me tell you this. I'm going to go back in the house, put on some shoes and pick up a hockey stick I have. And I'm going to start breaking the glass on your van. And I doubt you have the money to make the repairs."

Lorraine gaped at him. He had a new authority she had never known.

"And you tell that shit-heels who's with you that I'm coming looking for him."

Chirburg could hear him. He put down the locks.

At that moment, Dru came out of the bathroom wrapped in a towel. Little bare feet tracking wet footprints. Shapely calves.

". . . the fuck?" said Lorraine. "How old is she? Twelve?"

■ ■ ■

Sam said, "And you just got dressed, and he took you back to town on the motorcycle?"

"That's pretty much it."

"Why?"

"Because he told me to."

"He told you to? That doesn't sound like you, Dru."

"Well, the witch had pretty much shattered the magic of the moment."

"You weren't repulsed by the scene?"

"No. It was right out of a fairytale. Handsome prince put under a curse. Me coming along to redeem him. The young girl pure in spirit. Positively Jungian."

Sam never doubted the sincerity of her friend. But Dru seemed to savor danger without comprehending the magnitude of it.

"What had you been planning before she showed up? Just drop the towel and stand there?"

"Isn't that what you do?"

"No rehearsed statement? No come-on?"

"I was stumped there. What does one say? I want you to pop my cherry? Teenage vulgar. I want you to be my first time? Rather cliché. I want you to make me a woman? Sounds like a hot-house novel from the 1920s."

"But you were ready to do the whole thing right there and then?"

"Sure. Why not? It's a romantic spot. Surrounded by acres of trees. Rippling brook behind. Birdsong. Rustic cabin. Nice decorations. Very tasteful paintings."

"Are you in love with him?"

Dru looked at her visibly puzzled. "No."

"Why then?"

Dru's voice took on a dreamy tone. "Because it will be delicious. Like being possessed by a figure from my subconscious. Some sinister Heathcliff. A fallen angel."

Sam was uneasy about Dru's use of the future tense "will be."

Chapter 36

Lorraine's lawyer, "Skip" Bufton, had a solo office above a shoe store in a strip mall. He was that kind of two-bit. When the secretary left at five o'clock, Quinn, Skeeter, and Hog Man pushed through the door wearing Hillary Clinton masks.

Skip looked up from his desk where he was snorting cocaine up a rolled dollar bill. Wild glint in his eyes. Crazy looking. Feeling bulletproof.

"Man, do you boys ever bathe? There is such a thing as soap and water, you know."

Quinn said, "That white dust really makes you stupid, doesn't it?"

Skip's nose was running a bit. He sniffed like he had a cold. Wiped it with the back of his hand. "Did Halloween come early? Or is this Mardi Gras or something?"

He was young, late twenties. Feeling cocky with the dope in his system. Getting a nice buzz on before he went out for the evening. Prowl the bars.

Quinn looked around the little office. Framed diplomas. Bar license. Admission to the 4th Circuit Court of Appeals. Group photo in front of a frat house. Fraternity paddle for beating the pledges, Greek letters on it. Duck stamp prints. Duck decoy on top of an old gunmetal gray filing cabinet.

"So how do you get into a solo practice? Fucked around in law school. Sat in the back hunkered down hoping the professor wouldn't call on you. Grades put you at the bottom of the class so there were no job offers. Even the public defender didn't want you. Am I close?"

"What is this shit?" Skip demanded. "A society roast?"

Hog Man moved around behind the lawyer's chair, making him twist around to see what was happening. Realization starting to seep in that something was out of whack.

"You know," said Quinn, "I'll bet there's kind of a moment there when you file a lawsuit. A big rush of exhilaration on the level of snorting coke up your nose. You feel so masterful. Knowing you've turned someone's life upside down. He'll be paying an attorney by the hour. Wincing at every bill. Lying awake at night twisted up in sweaty sheets.

"You know the rules of court and the poor shlub doesn't understand what's coming at him. You get to do pretrial discovery. Plunder his personal records. Demand he hand things over. He can't believe that he has to. Gets into the first spat with his lawyer. The bills go even higher. Delightful. At last you've got the big score.

"But then a solo practitioner like yourself, something always turns around and bites you. You get up against the big firms where they got a specialist in every little area. You're trying to handle whatever comes in the office. Flying by the seat of your pants.

"They beat you like a drum. Judge chewing your ass for being unprepared and late to court. Having to go back and explain to your client the case is lost on a motion for summary judgment and won't even go to trial. Client files a complaint with the state bar. You've got to go through that rigmarole of explaining to them. Living in terror of disbarment.

"So you inhale a few lines. Everything seems right again. You're on top of it all. Just like you felt when you went off to law school. Hook-up culture getting into high gear. The girls all thinking you were going to be rich."

Skip was halfway up out of his chair when Hog Man grabbed his wrists and held his hands flat on the desk. Skeeter brandished the nail gun.

Quinn said, "I know you don't have many clients, so you won't have much trouble guessing who the message is from."

They nailed his hands to the desk with about seven nails each. Left him screaming.

"Hey *nolo contendere*," said Hog Man as they went out. "Ain't that what they say?"

With the door closed, the lawyer's shrieks could barely be heard.

Chapter 37

After watching Kurt teach karate, Sam walked home with him the long way around the law school. They saw Randall's father and waved. He waved back.

The road bordered a pleasant old neighborhood. The pair sat on a dry-stone wall that was characteristic of the campus, built a century before by a professor homesick for New England.

Sam said she was tired, had had an exhausting dream last night of crossing a snowy mountain pass. Climbed and climbed.

Kurt said, "A pass is a known symbol of transition. You're changing from an old attitude of mind to a new one." He laughed. "Or you could just be dreaming about Switzerland."

Sam hung on his arm with both hands, put her head on his shoulder. "Tell me about Switzerland."

"It's green and clean. The Alpine terrain is the most beautiful in the world. All of Switzerland, a piece of France, Southern Germany, Northern Italy with the Lake District. I could live there and never leave."

"I want to go there."

He hugged her. "And so you shall."

"Will I have to wear a dirndl and yodel?"

"No, but you'll have to walk up a lot of steep hills in hiking boots and stand on a green summit with enormous vistas. And eat the food we've been serving you. Except a lot more of it. Because a relative will be shoving it at you. Urging you to fatten up. Does it appeal to you?"

"I feel like I would be safe from this . . . whatever is happening to me."

"I don't think you will ever be fully safe from it."

"Why?"

"The Jaegers believe in fate," he said.

Sam lifted her head. "Really? And that means you too?"

"It's not that everything is utterly predestined down to the iota. But Jungians believe we behave according to our archetype. Our need for children, great deeds, social supremacy—whatever the prime motivation is. So our lives, work, ambitions, and loves are all according to that form. And can probably be found in an ancient myth."

"We have no control over it at all? No free will whatsoever?"

"Oh but we do. We can do these acts positively or negatively. Be loving or cruel. Generous or selfish. All within the archetype."

Sam rested her head on his shoulder again. "Will you kiss me at least?"

"Yes. I think that's safe."

She held his face in two hands and kissed him slowly on the lips. Then slid her arms around his neck and did it more deeply.

He was so strong. It was like being absorbed into a giant force.

Sam had never had a father to hold her. Never as a small child gone running to him and been swung around. Never known the male force.

She could hear the voice of Enkidu to Shamhat. "I am the mightiest! I am the man who shakes the earth!"

"Stop it, Sam," Kurt said.

She drew back, her eyes glazed. "Stop what?"

"You're summoning the goddess. I can feel it. You'll start peeling off your clothes next."

Sam rested her head at his throat, breathed deeply, and tried very hard to be just boring Samantha Fitzhugh.

Chapter 38

"Did I say that?" said Boo. "I don't recall."

The cop Wally Butts was back on the phone, and Boo felt hunted. Cop asking where Trey had stayed. Boo having said it was a motel.

"Wal now, did he stay at a motel or not?"

Boo knew he was trying to trap him. They had checked the motels. Had to keep vague. "I don't know. He might have stayed with me. It was really pretty much of a nothing event. One, two days. Then he was gone."

"Wal, so he *was* at your place. Did he leave anything there? Anythin' at all?"

Boo thought of Trey's overnight bag. It was right smack in the middle of his living room. He walked around it each morning.

"No," he said. "Nothing. He had one of those wheelie bags you stow in the overhead. Traveling light. He had it with him when he left."

"Jes kind of a nothin' event for you. Like you said."

"Yes. I think that's accurate."

"Up in New York City, they's all riled up. Unnerwear

in a crack. They think he's daid. And they think you know somethin' about it."

"That's absurd," said Boo, trying to do a weary voice.

"They claim he was after some real valuable art. They think rival dealers would kill to get it."

"Is the art world that violent? I had no idea."

"Wal, you think on it."

Boo hung up. Squeezed his hands in an isometric exercise. Chirburg had been gone for two days now. He didn't know where. No calls from the home office. Maybe he was checking in. Maybe he wasn't and they didn't miss him.

Boo hadn't slept well. Had dreamed of his father. He had been lying dead in a pool of blood. Then got up and began fussing about the mess, blaming it on other people than himself. Suddenly turned and went into his lecture mode. Asked Boo if he had developed any follow-through. Found a project he had actually completed.

"You giving a sigh of relief?" said Chip. "Sleuthing cops at bay for the moment?"

Boo stared at his computer screen. The constant presence of Chip. Maybe he needed to give Quinn Shaw a hint about ridding him of this thorn in his side. But he couldn't have another death in his proximity.

Chip raised his voice like he thought Boo hadn't heard his first remark. "You recovered your poise after the third-degree grilling? Cop doing a Columbo on you?"

"You know, I actually work for a living. Could you leave me alone?"

"Unyielding professionalism. I love it." He held up the photocopy of Samantha Fitzhugh. Smirked.

Boo tried hard to keep the shock off his face. Chip had been snooping through his desk. The guy was a completely treacherous swine.

"So," Chip said. "She was right to be concerned. The corporate psychologist." He crossed his sharply creased pants. Swung one foot a bit. Suede bucks.

Boo tried to change the subject. "Do you get to send out laundry on your expense account? Get your pants pressed like that?"

"I can see why the dear woman is fretting. Your interest seems a little on the sinister side. Kind of like the strange disappearance of your school chum."

Boo cocked an eyebrow. Said nothing.

"You look nonplussed. Is that the word? Or what's the old expression? Don't know whether to shit or go blind."

"Would you mind going and fucking yourself somewhere else?"

"No reason to get short with me."

"Oh I'm tewwibly sorry," Boo said in an affected English voice.

"Tell you what. I'll lay you a little wager. I'm going to have me the dark babe before you do the fair one. You take the high notes, I take the low. What do you think? Fifty bucks?"

"So what evidence will there be?" said Boo caustically. "Other than your sophomoric boasting?"

"I'm going to knock mine up. Have her come whining and begging around here. But I'll be gone back to New York."

Boo snorted. "Or I might give her your address so she

can sue you for paternity. Or worse. Do you realize that in this benighted state they still have a civil action for debauching a virgin?"

■ ■ ■

Outside, a light rain fell in the night. Quinn ignored Dru's little teasing texts that came five minutes apart.

"redy 4 bed mmm."

"cuddlin pillow a'tween legz purrrr"

He wasn't about to leave that kind of electronic trail. The folly of infatuated school teachers drawn into a web by some little minx.

Quinn was reading about ancient Egypt which got its civilization from Sumer about 50,000 years later. The passage of ancient time seemed uncanny really. Fifty thousand.

But their gods and creation myths were derived from the Sumerian ones. The devout made a pilgrimage to a temple at Heliolopolis to worship the *ben-ben*—an obelisk—a long pointed pillar. A representation of the object in which the gods had arrived on earth before the memory of man.

Obelisks—like the Washington monument—are so much a part of the landscape that we forget the origins. The Sumerians called them NA.RU—stones that fly. To the Hittites it was *hu-u-ashi*—a firebird of stone.

At last Dru called around nine at night. Quinn was having a single malt Scotch—Talisker with the strong peaty flavor. Stretched out on the couch with his book. Music playing low.

"Hey, you," she said softly.

"Hey yourself."

"Is that Beethoven?"

"Yes."

"You have good taste. One doesn't see a lot of that among professors."

"True."

"You're not the kind of man to wear male bracelets are you?"

"No. No matter how macho they're designed—braided horsehair—buffalo head nickel Western styling—hook and clasp closure—it's still kind of prissy. A needless vanity."

"Good. I wouldn't like to think of you like that."

"I'm relieved we're on the same page on that issue."

"Did you used to canoe alone on dark, primeval lakes in Maine lined by brooding forests?"

"Yes. As a matter of fact, I did."

"Did you ever make love to a girl in the forest? Lying on fragrant conifer needles. A bed made of your clothes."

"No."

"No teenage girl amorous and available?"

"I was never that blessed."

"That is the word isn't it? The act of love is a blessing."

"Yes."

"Like the Sumerian divine marriage."

"Yes."

"Or Enkidu and Shamhat."

Quinn said nothing.

"What do you think?"

"I find myself incapable of suitable comment." But he knew the story and knew where she was going.

"You know the tale," she purred. "Enkidu was a wild man sent by the gods to counter the great epic hero and demi-god Gilgamesh. Gilgamesh was oppressing his people by demanding a *droit de seigneur* of every young girl before she was married.

"Enkidu was a true wild man covered in hair and living with beasts. Gilgamesh convinced a temple prostitute Shamhat to seduce this wild beast. She lay with him for six days and seven nights. Afterwards, his old friends the wild animals were afraid of him and fled him at water holes.

"Shamhat convinced Enkidu to join her in civilized life in the city of Uruk where Gilgamesh was king. Enkidu and Gilgamesh became great friends and went on many adventures together."

"Sounds rather like 'Beauty and the Beast.'"

Dru stretched and sighed. "A recurring personal myth for every young girl. The belief that her love is so pure she can redeem an enchanted beast."

Chapter 39

During first period, the texts were buzzing that Cherry's dad was in the principal's office with the three injured football players. And Cain was being raised.

The intercom summoned Sam and Dru to the office. Randall sauntered along like being a school ombudsman was a newly assigned role.

As they came into the outer office, the principal was heatedly saying, "Mister Stobbs, I have done everything humanly possible to get this scandal hushed up and save Coach Wade's career."

Every university town has a distinct divide between town and gown, and Roscoe "Bubba" Stobbs—hands in his pants pockets scratching his balls—was living evidence of it. Stobbs was Kiwanis, Chamber of Commerce, United Way, high school booster club and Mt. Moriah Baptist Church.

He was green pants, yellow sport coat, tie with Tweetie Bird on a purple field. Big comb-over and paunch he was long comfortable with. A big man of big appetites. Today he was pissed, and he was making that clear.

"Well it's not near 'nough," he pronounced, not caring who heard. "I want their little pert fannies expelled from this school for the good of the whole. There shouldn't ought to even be such a thing as a genius class. Little brainiac fucks ought'a be mainstreamed with everyone else so their damn egg-head shit would be bullied into the silence it deserves."

"Bullied?" queried Randall, eyebrows raised in question marks.

Stobbs jerked a thumb at Randall. "Who is this little dink?"

"He's . . . um . . . his father is . . . Mister Stobbs, we . . . you and I need to have a talk in private."

Stobbs couldn't take the hint. "I am taking time out of a busy sales day for this. These fine young scholar-athletes have important information to impart. Tell the man, Bo."

Bo stood there with both arms in casts and slings. Sullen and resentful at the taste of reality he had been dealt.

"One of 'em knelt down and called her 'm'lady'. Samantha knows who they are. The cops need to be told about this."

"Really now," said Randall acerbically. "And did he say 'zounds' and 'gadzooks' and 'forsooth' as well?"

"You don't make fun of me, you little four-eyed bestuhd. I get these casts off, I'll jam a two-by-four up yore ass."

"Really? Anything else?"

"That's just for starters, zit face."

"And what," Randall directed at the principal, "are our anti-bullying rules again?"

Stobbs' mouth gaped open. He was accustomed to bossing a car lot of high school dropout salesmen. Setting high sales quotas and making the boys sweat. Firing some at the end of every month. "Hit it and git it" was his motto.

With the booster's club, he was the hail-fellow, back-slapping "y'all know who the hail I am, and know I got the money to put where my big mouth is. I got me the purtiest daughter, the sweetest wife, and the ugliest dog this side of the Pearly Gates."

And whatever he wanted, he got big time. Couldn't remember when someone had dared talk back to him.

"Son, you are a piece of dog shit, and you heard it here first. Now get the hail outta heah 'fore I drop kick yore ass plumb through the goal posts of life."

"I suppose it's ethical for me to inform you I'm taping this on my cell phone," said Randall coolly. "I think I started it at about the 'pert fannies' part. I know I got 'braniac fucks'."

"You can't do that," the principal flared. "It's . . . it's against the law."

Randall could always stay just an inch to the safe side of insubordination. Never sassing. Just blandly stating fact.

"Actually it's not. There is no privacy right to not be recorded in this state. The only bar is an attorney taping someone without informing them."

"Who the hail are you?" Stobbs demanded.

"Possibly your worst nightmare."

"Are you threatenin' me?"

Randall said, "It's funny how people always say that. 'Are you threatening me?' Like they know something about the law, and you better back down. What would the tort be exactly? Assault? Duress? I have trouble seeing either."

"What are you talking about with your lying allusions and dee-lusions and bull-shit?"

"Wasn't there some investigation of you about a year ago? Paying bribes to Ford reps to get the volume and make of cars you wanted?"

"What does that got to do with . . . ?"

"The statute of limitations hasn't run on it yet. And the Attorney General is having dinner at our house on Saturday."

■ ■ ■

Boo sat behind his desk confounded by the super self-confident high school girl who had come by after 3:15. Beth Bolek's father taught finance at the business school. Extremely high-powered consultant. Flown around in client jets. Made an absolute racket out of academe.

The girl probably did finance problems in her sleep.

"You want to short the IPO of Chit-Chat?" said Boo skeptically.

"I want to sell it forward five days after the IPO at $45 a share."

"And you think the price will be lower than that, allowing you to pick up the shares on the market and deliver them to the buyer and make a profit?"

"Very good," she said, a tad condescendingly. Just like her father.

Boo shook his head. "CNN Money calls this the new Google. A cultural icon."

"The valuation's way too high. It's being launched at $40 a share. It would have to have insane financial growth to justify that price. Forty dollars is over a hundred times its actual earnings."

"It's projected to go to $60 the first day," Boo argued. "Five days from then it could be $120."

"Word on the street is the early investors are dumping their stock on the day of the IPO. They're insiders. They know it's a dog. The price will drop like a stone."

"Who's going to cover the loss if it goes south?"

"My daddy. He's got his account with JP Morgan in New York." She speed-dialed her phone and handed it to him.

"Speak to me," said Ransom Bolek at the other end. Crisp voice. All business. Time is money.

Boo got that immediate sinking feeling he'd have when the man would call on him in class. "Um . . . Townsend Radley," he said. "Your . . . um . . . daughter's here in my office. Wants to short Chit-Chat. Are you familiar with this?"

"Of course. I'm behind her on this. And she's dead right about it. I should have shorted Abercrombie & Fitch when she told me."

"She's . . . um . . . under eighteen. I can't contract with her."

"I'm only too aware of that."

"Um . . . when can you come in and . . . cough . . . um . . ."

"Be at my office at eleven tomorrow morning. Bring the paperwork. And don't dither any more please. You used to do that in class. Drove me crazy."

Boo closed his eyes against the insult. Did the man remember all his students that clearly? "Um . . . how many shares?"

"Ask Beth. I want her to call the shots. Get her toes in the water on this thing."

When she told him a hundred thousand Boo nearly got the vapors.

"Sir, this is not for the faint of heart. This thing will trade without rational evaluation. School kids. Hair dressers. Personal trainers. They'll all be buying. In five days the price could be through the roof."

Bolek sighed. "Radley, there's a reason why you're a retail stock broker in a one-man office and my Beth is going to U-Penn and become a hedge-funder. Try to think about that will you?"

Chapter 40

Dru and Sam were partners in the chemistry lab right after lunch. The class was allowed to use fairly dangerous stuff like an oxygen tank. The rest of the school were shown the lab once a year but never allowed to touch anything.

Each team filled a plastic baggie with oxygen. Mixed a beaker of dish detergent and water. Using a pipette, blew a bubble of oxygen into the beaker. Then moved the air bubble around with a strong magnet to show magnetic properties in oxygen.

Naturally, they all wore safety goggles.

"You would not believe last night at my house," Dru grimaced. "Mom hosting her Goddess Group. Lumpy old women, sagging fat butts standing buck naked around an incense burner chanting to goddess." She rolled her eyes.

"I locked myself in my room. But the next thing I knew, there was a cop at the door. So I came out. No warrant. Just wanting to come in and have a little chat about things. Take possession of the *Hustler* Mom got from the coach's office. Let drop the word 'larceny.' That kind of veiled threat."

"And?"

"So Mom just jerks the door wide and gives him a full view. Must have frightened the man out of several years of his life. Whew. Apologizing and backing up. He actually said 'Whoa, Nellie.' First thing out of his mouth."

"You think Cherry's behind this?"

"Probably. But certainly Coach Wade."

Dru went on with the experiment.

"Is there something you're holding back?" Sam asked.

"Yes. Mom had a lawyer deliver the original *Hustler* to the school district attorney this morning. And she had a courier—some bearded dork on a racing bike—drop copies off at the homes of all the girls who were found inside. With a personal note about the Coach's artistic creativity. We didn't send one to you. Didn't want to disturb the Jaegers. Mom likes you for some reason. She's never liked any of my other friends ever."

A commotion arose in the hall. Strident female voices calling someone a "barf-face yuck" and "dick breath."

Coach Wade suddenly exploded into the chem lab like a charging bull. Wild bloodshot eyes. Thick eyebrows tangled like seaweed. Plum-red face. Slobber flinging out of his mouth. A crazed beast that had escaped its cage.

"I'm gone fuckin' kill yore ass, yew little twat!"

Completely out of his mind with fear and wrath, he chased Dru around the lab. Knocking kids aside. Smacking over stools and glass objects.

Dru scrambled under a table, but he was amazingly quick. Grabbed her ankle with hands like catcher's mitts and dragged her back. Jerked her up by the hair. Got both hands on her throat and lifted her off the floor. Her feet kicking in the air.

He squeezed while she feebly gripped his thick, hairy

wrists. Fought against the pressure that was surely taking the life out of her.

Sam flooded with panic. Realized she didn't have a knife. About to fling herself at him, but beakers began to explode with the noise of firecrackers all over the room. Students shrieked and covered their heads against flying glass. Pow pow pow pow!

In split seconds, Kurt had taken his stance and rammed the heel of his hand square into Coach's nose. Coach's thick tongue shot out of his mouth, and his head jolted like it had met a cinder block.

Coach dropped Dru to the floor in a heap.

Stood there holding his face, eyes bulging, blood oozing through his fingers. Pain searing through him, addling his brain. Squealing like a pig.

Slowly, like a tree girdled by beavers, his knees buckled and he fell to the floor. Lay flat.

"Woo is he ever going to need an ENT surgeon!" Francie enthused.

Kurt reached down and scooped Dru up like a child.

She seemed to be feeling the heat of his body. Her nose twitched. She was breathing normally.

The room was a cacophony of voices. Marveling at the explosion, the berserk coach, Kurt's taking him down so smoothly and thoroughly.

Sam suddenly felt exhausted as from a great exertion. "The oxygen tank," she moaned. "It might have gone off and killed us all."

"Not really," said Nasar. "It's an oxygen concentrator. It pulls oxygen out of the air. It won't explode like the old cylinders." He paused. Seemed puzzled. A deep furrow in his forehead. "Why did all those beakers explode?"

Randall said to Dru, "I'm texting your mother the names of major personal injury lawyers in the area. This is going to be some seriously big bucks. Might even pay your way through college and then some."

■ ■ ■

Once more, the school day became cop cars and EMS. Safety inspectors scratched their heads over the glass debris in the lab, ultimately denying reality and deciding the coach had caused the carnage.

All the volleyball, basketball, soccer girls, and the cheerleaders and parents were in a furious knot in the outer office of the principal. Demanding an explanation for the *Hustler* scrapbook.

Bubba Stobbs was in full rage. "You sorry shit-for-brains fuck-haid! Lettin' my baby girl get huh-miliated like this! I'm gone kick yore ass from hell to breakfast."

Principal Peevey was a portrait of futility, shaky hands waving in the air, a mess of fear and anxiety. "I had no idea Coach Wade had made this thing and kept it in his desk. I knew there was an incident with a girl's mother but . . ."

Stobbs reared up. "*Coach* Wade? He ain't the coach here no more. His ass is fired. Like yesterday."

"Yes, yes, immediately. But . . ." Here the old engrained bureaucratic caution exerted itself. ". . . there are procedures we have to . . ."

"You get his fat ass out of this school house this skinny minute!" Stobbs bellowed. "He's a sex predator on a level

I ain't never heard of before. I'm comin' for him like a armor-piercing shell!"

"What is your role in this?" a shrieking mother demanded of the principal. "Why have you been covering for this scuzz-ball?"

All the others began shouting questions, waving their arms. Pushing towards him in a menacing unity.

The principal's face seemed to be melting like candle wax. He fled into his inner office and locked the door. Stobbs and other parents began hammering on it.

"You gutless weasel! You open this door or we'll kick it in!"

"Yellow-back coward!"

"Scumbag!"

"Toad sucker!"

"Half-ass bastard!"

Daddies will be violent in defense of their daughters' honor, but the mothers were shrieking like banshees.

No one announced the end of the day, but the teachers agreed everyone should go home. Dru's mother drove over to pick her up.

Dru strutted out, the heroine of the moment, to the admiring applause of the genius class. She waved an acknowledging hand in queenly fashion. Her throat was a solid stain of red choke marks.

Francie tut-tutted over her. Said she really needed to go to the hospital. There was clearly capillary damage and some subdermal bleeding. She could have more serious tissue damage, a fractured hyoid bone at the base of the throat.

Dru insisted she was fine. Then suddenly turned back, jumped up on Kurt, wrapped her arms and legs around him and gave him a big wet kiss on the mouth. Shoved her tongue right in.

Then sashayed down to the waiting car. When she opened the door some barely audible muttering came from the mother.

"Mom, he saved my life. Let's not be a shrew about this."

Chapter 41

Boo made a tremulous call to the New York office and got Skipper van Dine. Skipper belonged to the Round Hill Club in Greenwich. Was on the board of the Westchester Classic golf tournament. And of course he never failed to inquire about Boo's father and then act surprised when told the man was dead.

Boo asked whether he would be allotted any of the Chit-Chat IPO shares.

"Of course not. Only our big producers get those for their clients."

Boo thought about the Buggaron account. Fitzhugh. Pfiezer. He really did merit a few measly shares. But that wasn't the intended pecking order of things.

He wasn't really supposed to have those accounts. His was designed as an office where you were driven crazy by professors and students from investment courses. Nickel and dime-ing you. Professors with their pathetic mutual funds.

The home office hadn't figured on affluent retirees. Or organized crime.

But the numbers didn't matter in the minds of the van Dines. They were supposed to be important and you weren't. And if he made an issue out of his numbers, they'd transfer him to Broken Switch, Texas. Make him start scrabbling all over again there.

"I suppose you'll be taking the plunge," said Boo.

"As a matter of fact I am. Thinking of going a half-mil. The wife is bugging me about a Hamptons' rental for the summer. This ought to swing it. Ship her and the kids out there. Stay in the city and boff girls in vampire makeup from the dance clubs."

"Sounds jolly."

"It is. And the bet's a lead pipe cinch."

"I have heard otherwise."

There was a long pause. "You know, Radley, there's a reason why you're in a one-man retail office while I'm getting in on an IPO. Think about it."

■ ■ ■

When Sam got home, she felt really strange and lay down on her bed. Another violent mess. Her palms were damp. She closed her eyes and clearly saw Cherry talking to Kurt.

"Kurt, I'm so humiliated." Fake sobs. Covering her eyes to conceal there were no tears. Little heaving of the shoulders. "Put your arm around me."

"You weren't the only one in the magazine."

"But it's like everyone saw me naked."

"No they didn't. It was a magazine that a dirty old man concocted."

"You're always so sweet. So reassuring." She took his hand and pressed it against her face. Her voice became concerned. "Kurt, is she giving you all you need? I mean . . . physically?"

He bristled slightly. Pulled his hand back. "Let's not talk about that, please."

"That means she's not." Giving him the watery eyed baby doll look. Up from under. Winsome. "I'm so sorry for you."

"Cherry . . ."

"I understand a man's needs. My mother said if I learned it young it would serve me for a lifetime. A man's dick is like a dog. It has to be taken out at least once a day and played with."

Kurt laughed in spite of himself.

Now she was hurt. Little downward cast at the edges of her mouth. Vulnerable. Longing to please. "I know your needs. I understand them like she can't. She doesn't even try to make herself attractive."

"I'm really doing all right. Thanks for the concern."

"Kurt, professors don't make a lot of money do they?"

He looked around distracted. "No. Everyone knows that."

"I'm an only child. Daddy says my husband will get the Ford dealership. You could work there summers. Learn the business. Daddy would love you as much as I do. You could join the Key Club next year and then be inducted right into the Kiwanis."

"I really don't see myself selling cars, Cherry."

Moment of prolonged silence.

She moistened her lips. Leaned forward. "Kurt, we own a lake house. I want to make love to you. Naked. On a bed."

Samantha sat up with a start. She found it difficult to swallow. She hadn't heard his answer.

■ ■ ■

"Well, what did you tell her?" Sam demanded, hands on her hips.

"About what? And who?"

"About the freakin' lake house!"

Kurt stared at her in amazement. "You're going to be as unnerving to be around as my mother."

"I'm not your mother!" Sam railed. "I'm your girl-friend. And you've got every little harlot in the school ooz-ing around you."

"Just Cherry."

"Just Cherry? Dru wrapping her legs around you and tongue kissing you. Her sudden interest in Jungian philosophy."

She tried to give him a ringing slap in the face, but he blocked it with ease and she cracked her wrist on his.

"OW! That really hurt."

And now he was laughing at her. It made her furious.

"My gosh," he said. "Bulging eyes. A face of wrath. I've seen the love goddess emerge from you. When the goddess of war comes out, it's going to be terrifying."

"This is not some joke!" she shouted at him. "Did you see what I did in the lab? It's like I'm in some interactive dreamscape. I never know what's going to happen."

Chapter 42

Afternoon shadows were growing long. Quinn sat on his porch with his iPad reading about space aliens in biblical times, his interest sparked by a conversation with Tyndall Cranmer.

He was getting things out of Tyndall painfully slowly. Certainly painful for Tyndall. Complaining about anchovies on the pizza. The real problem was his joints getting so seized up he could barely straighten out.

There was a Tiffany stained glass window in the front of the bungalow. Angels going up and down a ladder while Jacob half roused himself from the ground in wonder.

Near Mt. Moriah, Jacob slept outdoors with a stone for a pillow. He woke in the night to a vision of angels going up and down a ladder that led to heaven.

He named it "Bethel" meaning the House of God.

"Did you put that window in?" Quinn asked.

"No," said Tyndall, "but when I saw it, I knew I had to have the house. The members of The Circle would meet here and watch the sun go down in a blaze through that window. It never ceased to fill us with awe."

"Symbolism seems pretty obvious," said Quinn. "Don't

tell me this was an alien visitation. Flying saucer with a ladder coming down."

"Symbolism that resonates should pop up a lot of places, a lot of different cultures. Tell me where else you find angels and a ladder."

Quinn scrolled down the screen. Tyndall was right. That imagery was unique. And there was more.

The Hebrews at that time had no belief in heaven. The dead went down to a shadowy place called Sheol. A place of darkness and silence. Dust returns to dust. You didn't join the angels and play a harp. The resurrection of the dead came into the Torah during the Hellenistic Age.

Abraham's concubine Hagar was addressed by angels from the air. Sodom and Gomorrah were destroyed from the air.

Cherubs were not plump winged children, but fantastic flying craft. Chariots of the gods.

Elijah and Ezekiel went up in chariots of fire.

Quinn's phone beeped. A text from Dru. "Nearly got killed today."

Quinn sat staring at it. The best come-on she'd done yet. He thought of her big, challenging violet-blue eyes with their exceptional brightness. Her smooth teenage flesh that hid the steel beneath it.

He tapped in her phone number. Knowing she was pulling him down. And thoroughly enjoying it.

"Hey, you," she answered in a soft voice.

He said nothing.

"You're not the kind of man who drinks flavored vodka are you?"

"No, just Scotch."

"Single malt?"

"Yes."

"Do you come from money?"

"No, we were the servant class. Rich town. Bar Harbor. And I'm observant."

"I believe that." She thought a moment. "You've seen me in the buff. Tell me a detail about myself others would overlook."

He took his time, looking at the latest pencil drawing by Jake Milroy. The detail was extraordinary.

"Your navel is a sharp vertical slit. And there's a tiny mole just to the upper right. Upper right from my perspective. It's actually in the shape of a heart."

Now she was quiet. Finally she murmured, "That's very good."

"I'm not going to stay on the line long. You got my attention by your message. So tell me about it."

■ ■ ■

Boo sat alone in his office at the end of the day thinking about shorting Chit-Chat on his own account. He knew that people made money like this. Knew the theory and how it worked. But it was still a mystery. And a frightening way to be swallowed whole by the market.

He really only understood inherited money that you gave to U.S. Trust to manage. Visit your trustee once a year in his tasteful office with the fly fishing prints. Listen to his soothing lecture on your prosperity. Then go to lunch at the 21 Club.

There was all the Fitzhugh money just sitting in a cash account earning a pittance. Ten million dollars just sitting there idle. Begging to be put in play.

Bolek was convinced of the soundness of the bet, and the man was a genius. He made so much money consulting and investing that he refused to teach the MBA students. Said they demanded too much of his time. He'd do one undergrad course and terrorize the kids into shying away from him.

Boo could make the trades and not have to use the Fitzhugh money except to cover losses. And if he won . . .

He could hear his father's voice. "Have a backbone for once."

His father, even in death, made him tremble with fear. Whenever Boo did a major screw up he'd run to his mother. She would shield him.

Boo closed his eyes. Something swam into view. It was Samantha's friend. She was whispering to him. He strained to hear.

"He holds her womb . . .

She holds his 'stones' . . .

The virgin is made to conceive and bear."

Boo sat up and looked around wildly. Was he hallucinating?

Chapter 43

The school had joined with Rhoda Shelley to get Coach Donny-Mack Wade hauled in cuffs from the hospital to the county lockup. When he finally made bail he had to walk home to find Bubba Stobbs had repo'ed his loaned Lincoln.

He was reduced to driving his beat-up old F-150 pickup out to a country store where he sat drinking Blue Ribbons, pouring some Old Setter from a pint bottle in with each can. Salting the rim of the can. Trying to forget the hell his life had turned into. Worse than his third divorce.

Cackling old hicks had heard all about the school events. Nudging each other. Saying "choking the chicken" and "Momma Thumb and her four darters."

"I just made me my own yearbook," he argued, belligerently drunk. "Little honeys come and go—come and go down—wah-hah—I like to have a memory of 'em.

"Shore I get plenny of teen tail. You win the big game and the cheerleaders compete to see who'll blow you. Want it put up their ice-hole so they don't lose their virginity."

At closing time, he staggered in the dark out to his truck muttering. "Bunch'a toothless hicks. What'a they know? I bin to collich. Put some numbers up on the board playin' ball. Got my Sports Management degree."

His truck was out back next to the store dump. Garbage fire smoldering. Some men were standing in the shadows. One of them grabbed him up with incredible strength and threw him headfirst into the truck bed. Got in and sat on him.

They fished his keys out of his pocket, cranked the truck, and drove off. One of them had a hob-nail boot on his neck.

Donny-Mac was bad drunk and couldn't accept the world of pain he was about to enter. "Hey mind the merchandise!" he yelled.

There was no response.

"Why won't you tell me what's goin' on? You're affecting my confidence level."

They drove for quite a ways before stopping. Hauled him out bodily. He had a sudden horrible thought.

"Were you hired by them bitches' daddies? Put the fear of God in me? Is that it?"

He turned around wildly. They looked like outlaw bikers. Braided pony tails. Beards. Biker colors on their denim jackets. Staring at him with flat empty expressions.

"It was just some ol' pitchers in a skin magazine. Din't hurt no buddy until that dyke bitch got hold of it. I mean can't a man unwind?"

They still said nothing.

He started desperately bargaining the only way he had ever known how.

"Y'all like football don't'cha? I tell you what, high school ball is a hum-dinger of a game, ain't it? You don't need no opinion poll to know that. Friday night lights. Young kids playing their dam' hearts out.

"College ball is way too professional. And pro ball, oh

man, don't get me started. It's all rigged, fixed, and zebras bribed to the finish. May as well watch pro wrasslin'. I mean how could it be otherwise? The betting line's big-gern' a ol' dinosaur."

One of the fifteen-acres-over neighbors of Lucifer's Legion was a hog hunter. Go out anytime, anywhere, any weather to hunt feral pigs. Chase them on horseback with a pack of mangy dogs that hamstring them while he leaps off a horse, ties their legs, heaves them in a trailer. Take them back to fatten up and slaughter.

The vicious brutes breed in litters year around. Root up crops. Invade suburbia. Some suburban soccer kids get chased by a big old tusker, the yoga mat and SUV car pool-ing moms panic and call him in. No sentiment, no animal rights nonsense, no concern about how he handled it.

He had a new batch he hadn't fed for a couple of days. Hairy brutes covered in mud. Smelling of feces and rank soil.

Quinn Shaw stepped closer so Donny-Mac could see him. Nylon shell warm-up jacket. Cross trainers. Appar-ently not a biker.

"Who're you?" Donny-Mack demanded. He was blink-ing rapidly, trying to get his head straight. "You look like a Yankee. But some university coach. Soccer or lacrosse or some such shit. One of them girl teams they gotta run 'cause o' Title IX."

"I'm a guardian of someone you ill-treated."

A moon was rising in the sky, breeze riffling the spring leaves.

Donny-Mack squirmed under Quinn's glacial gaze. "They done push me over the edge, I tell you. Sassy little bitches. You don't know the shit of being a high school coach. Them big university dudes with millions in pay. Even the low level Division III coaches, after the game, the reception in the Holiday Inn private rooms, ever-body goin' 'good game, coach.' Liquor flowing. You go up to your room and find a high-class hooker waiting. All paid for. Free night in a whore house.

"In high school you ain't got jack-shit. No gratitude. Bunch'a pikers. Parents nagging you to play their kid. Getting up petitions to have you fired.

"But every day you got them little bitches struttin' round all full up with temptation. Shaking their tits and ass. Knowing they got the pussy and this is the beginning of their moment of power. Get their periods all at the same time. You can smell it in the air.

"Alls I did was go in the locker room and look in their cameras. They got these self-shot pitchers of theyselves letting it all hang out. That little cunt Dru bitch Shelley, she makes it out a federal crime. Claims I was stealing money and sniffing undies. Puts it on the whole fucking World Wide Web."

Donny-Mack was weeping now in despair and fear and drunkenness. "Ever-body laughing at me. I just snapped my cable. Just like with my first wife. Little gal working concessions when I was playing collich ball. Wouldn't put out unless I married her. So I did. Church and everything.

"Then she still wouldn't put out more'n once a month. She was bloated. Her cooze hurt. Her head hurt. I told her I'd hurt her dam' head.

"Then come to find out she was ballin' my players. She

weren't but about a year older'n them, but that ain't no good reason. I'd been to collich. Had a stellar career ahead of me.

"I had to smack her around. Just hit her a little too hard was all. Plumb broke her neck. Had no idea it was so easy. So I dropped her down the stairs. Said she tripped and fell.

"I was starting my coaching career strong. Little county high school with some big ol' boys. Dumb as dirt, but they could sure run the triple-option. Won ever-damn game the first year. Cops wanted to talk football. Weren't real interested in the crime scene."

"Well, if it helps to unburden yourself," said Quinn, "then so be it. But our evening's entertainment needs to continue."

Four motorcycles flipped their headlights on a six-foot by five oil painting on an easel. Donny-Mack gaped at the spitting images of Samantha and Dru. Was he looking at a photograph of them both buck naked? There was a lion and some owls in the picture.

"That there's that Sam Fitzhugh," he blurted. "That gal's got a corncob up her ass. Little Miss Pristine Priss-Pot. Not mixing with the other girls. She needs to be fucked until her nose bleeds.

"And that little nasty cunt Dru Shelley, she's like something spit up out of hell. Somebody oughta tear her head off and shit down her throat!"

Hog Man threw him to the ground. "Show respect." Then shouted over his shoulder. "All of you!"

The Legion all knelt on one knee.

Donny-Mack spit dirt and grass. "This is who you're

upset about? I thought it was the cheerleaders. Bubba Stobbs had put you up to this."

Quinn kicked him hard in the head.

"Ow goddammit shit!"

"These are the children of Nibiru," Quinn intoned to all. "Direct descendants of the Annunaki. They are goddesses descended to earth."

Donny-Mack sniveled, "Please don't do whatever you're planning to do to me. It ain't right."

"We don't have a real protocol on this one," said Quinn. "So let's just get it done."

Hog Man stepped on Donny-Mack's back to keep him still.

"You cain't do this to me!" he wailed. "I'm a winning coach. What will you do come fall next season?"

Skeeter chopped Donny-Mac's hamstrings with a machete in quick slashes. Then two of them tossed him screaming over the fence to flop in the mud and filth of the hog pen.

He tried to stand and couldn't. The pain was excruciating.

He heard a snuffling noise out of the dark. Saw little piggy bright eyes.

"What are you doing to me?" he screamed.

Hog Man said, "Ever hear the expression 'went to shit and the hogs ate him?'"

Chapter 44

Boo couldn't sleep the night before the Chit-Chat IPO. Twisted and turned and turned some more. Finally took a sleeping pill and zonked out, slept until nine a.m.

He leaped out of bed, and the first thing to catch his eye was Trey's overnight bag. This had been eating at him as well. Were the cops watching him? See him heave it in a dumpster? Was it better to have it in the house or the car if they got a warrant?

He compromised by bringing it in to work. Openly. No suspicious plastic bag. It was ten by then.

"Going somewhere?" Chip asked.

"Maybe."

"I need to know if you're going to be out of the office."

"Why? You might have to do some work?"

"Where's Chirburg? I miss using him as a punching bag."

"I'm not his minder. I guess he's with his cousin."

Boo put Fox Business news on his computer. The Chit-Chat IPO had been a disaster, investment banks stuck with millions of shares they had guaranteed to sell.

Institutional investors who had bought, dumped it immediately they realized it was a dog, sending the share price through the floor. The only holders were several million college kids and dumb-ass high school teachers.

One of the teachers, some wild-haired nut from Chicago in a teacher's AFT union jacket was interviewed ranting about the evils of capitalists. He had cashed in a big part of his retirement to buy shares.

"Thieving greed-head blood-suckers!" he railed, both fists punching the air. "Ought to be strung up by their (bleep)!"

Then came the MIT dropout twerp who had designed Chit-Chat. Black jeans and a black t-shirt that read "Gen-Y Intern." He sounded like he had an allergy. Insisted the product was merely misunderstood. All the buyers should hold and watch. It was ready to take off. In fact, now was the time to get in and buy while it was cheap.

"And next up—why can't business apps be more professional."

Boo shut it off laughing nervously. The little teen genius had been right. One day down and four to go. He looked up at the ceiling prayerfully. Chip had retreated behind his *Wall Street Journal.*

"Man, the unedited rants of idiots," smirked Boo.

Chip said nothing.

The market for Chit-Chat had slid towards the gutter. Boo couldn't believe his euphoria. Felt like he had taken a sniff of amyl nitrate.

He began going through his big accounts, just a reassuring procedure he did each day. Everything in its place, all was right with the world. And Chit-Chat had a stake driven through its heart.

He stopped in shock at Buggaron. It was three million

light. His head snapped around at the hidden Chip. Jumped up and smashed the newspaper down on the desk.

"You didn't!" he accused.

Chip tried to look nonchalant. "What?"

"Did you buy into the IPO? How did you get the shares?"

"An hour after the opening bell, there were a lot of them on the market."

"By whose authority did you make the buy? Did you sign my authorization?"

Chip wouldn't meet his eyes. Began straightening out his newspaper. "It was a sound bet. With the information I had, I'd do the same thing again. Skipper van Dine bought in."

Boo was spluttering. "The unmitigated arrogance . . . the stupidity . . . !"

"Money comes in every month. They won't notice."

"Won't notice? How can anyone overlook three million?"

"They wanted investment. We made a bet for them. They've got the shares in their account."

"*We? We* made a fucking bet?" Boo took his squash racquet and cracked Chip in the head with it.

"YOW!"

Kept bashing him as Chip tried to get under the desk to avoid the blows. Cracked him in the shins again and again.

"You stupid, presumptuous prick!"

■ ■ ■

Quinn placed a bookmark and closed Carl Jung's *Man and His Symbols* as the cop car drove up. Black and white Crown

Victoria with the narrow, flat light on the top. Quinn thought it was funny how police fashion changed. He could remember the big revolving bubble lights.

The cop got slowly out like he was stiff from sitting. Quinn slowly rose up out of his chair on the porch. Not acting anxious. Merely curious at the visit of a minion of the law. When asked, agreed that he was the right Quinn Shaw.

The cop's little brass name tag said "Lt. Butts."

Cop put one foot on a step, shook his head in wonder. "Man you married a right piece'a work. That Lorraine could outdo any wet hen I ever seed."

"Did you encounter her professionally?"

"Yeah, she was down at the station raising all kinds'a Cain. Says you nailed her lawyer's hands to a desk."

Quinn smiled faintly. "She would say that. If we had children, she'd claim I molested them."

The cop rubbed his jowls. "Yeh, lying bitches ever'one." He looked around curious about the house, clearly wanting to go inside and search things. "What exactly do you do out here?"

Quinn shrugged. "This is where I live."

"Yeah, but I mean what do you do for a livin'?"

"I'm taking a sabbatical from college teaching. Doing research on Sumeria."

Quinn immediately wondered if the cop knew words like "sabbatical" and "Sumeria."

"Yore wife says you're involved in a criminal enterprise."

"So is she. She's a realtor."

The cop laughed. "Read about her lawyer in the paper? Skip Bufton?"

"As a matter of fact I did. Although it was light on details."

"I worked that crime scene. Man, what a mess. EMS completely stumped. He was so completely nailed down they had'a get a skill saw and cut out chunks of the desk. Take him to the hospital for surgery with the wood stuck to his hands. Jabbering out of his mind about Hillary Clinton. Man, she's a scary woman, but that seemed a bit over the top."

"I remember him from the divorce. I think he has a bad drug habit."

"S'matter of fact we found a baggie of cocaine in his desk. Lookin' forward to asking him about it when he comes out of surgery. State bar will be innerested as well."

The cop hitched up his gun-belt which immediately went down below his gut again. "Man, it's been a long morning. You mind if I come in and have a drink of cold H20? Maybe a Diet Co-cola, if you got one?"

Quinn gave him a sympathetic smile. "Much as I support the Fraternal Order of Police, I'm really too busy to jaw about life."

The cop looked regretful. Like he thought they could be pals. "Yeah, I can see that. Perfesser with impo'tant readin' to do. Well, I'll let you get on with it."

Quinn gave him a two finger salute like a Cub Scout. "Nice making your acquaintance."

The cop turned, then paused and looked back. "Man, them coeds'll give a man a boner, won't they? I don't know how you perfessers stand it."

"Most of the faculty are women now. And the men don't have dicks. Ponytail men. Men who wear t-shirts that say 'this is what a feminist looks like.'"

Cop chortled. "Yeh, I can buy that. Bunch'a juice-box suckin' lib'rals. But how 'bout yourself? You get a fair share of coed poon? Gal failing the course comes up and says she'll make it worth your while to improve her grade?" He cupped his hands in front of his chest. "Big ol' rack on the gal. Wearing pyjammy bottoms to class, her thong unner-wear showing through them."

"Nice daydream. But it's never happened."

"I su'spose not. That's a shame. By the way, you don't happen to own any masks do you?"

"Like a hockey mask?"

"No more something for a party."

"You mean like the Lone Ranger?"

"Yeah, or full face."

"No, can't say as I do. Haven't done Halloween since I was a kid."

Chapter 45

"Nasar cracked the code," said Dru. "It took him about five minutes."

"He's read the diary?" Sam asked.

"I only gave him one line, but it's got the entire alphabet. This is it. This is the address."

Dru looked around the 1930s bungalow neighborhood heavily shaded with trees. Narrow houses with deep front porches from before air conditioning.

"Dru, the Milroy house is about three doors up."

"Duh."

The one they faced had Craftsman details. Beams showing. Wood shingles. Diamond pane windows. A stained glass window. Biblical scene of angels climbing Jacob's ladder.

The front door was predictably locked. They walked around to the back. Yard overgrown with weeds. Fallen down bird feeder. Clothesline with wooden pins on it. Automobile tire planter with dead plants. Metal shed with the door hanging by one hinge. Rusty push lawn mower inside.

"Does Kurt really believe in fate?" asked Dru.

"Yes. All our behavior can be found in ancient myths. You just have to identify the myth. And there you have it."

"And you're so smitten that whatever he believes, you believe."

"That's the way of the world, isn't it?"

"You know," said Dru, "Erishkigal was imprisoned in the underworld by the dragon Kur. I kind of feel like that's my mother. And I'm the Queen of the Dead."

She was trying the windows, finding them locked.

"So what is your primary desire in life?" Dru asked. She grunted at a window that wouldn't give.

"I want to bear Kurt's children," Sam replied. "I want the Jaegers to be the grandparents."

"The naive maiden talking. All girls go through this. It's like wanting to be Queen of the Animals. Be a veterinarian. Heal the puppies."

"No," Sam said stubbornly. "I see myself in a chalet in Switzerland. Deep glistening snow on the ground and covering the roof. Three rosy-cheeked children. Two girls and the youngest a boy. I'm baking bread and cake for them. Their father is . . . well, doing some man thing. Climbing mountains maybe. But he will be home soon. And we are all expectant."

"Good grief."

"So how do you see yourself, Miss Cynicism?"

"I think I'd like to be a siren luring sailors onto the rocks."

And with that, Dru took a brick and smashed the glass of a window.

Inside, the house was totally silent. Old chicken buckets and pizza boxes on the surfaces. Empty Scotch bottles and Coke cans. Dust everywhere. Ratty old furniture. "What a dump," said Dru.

"What do we say if we're caught?" Sam whispered.

"Leave that to me, Heidi," Dru answered in a normal tone. "You just keep your hand on your knife."

"Who's out there? Who is it?"

The voice came from what seemed like a bathroom. The knob was jammed with a straight chair.

"You gotta let me out. I'm tied up in here." He kicked the wall.

"Who are you?" said Dru.

"I'm . . . who are you?"

"Hansel and Gretel. We followed a trail of breadcrumbs. Is this the witch's cottage? And which way's the oven?"

"Very funny. Open the goddam door and let me out."

"Say pretty please."

"Are you, like, fucking kids? Have you come here to vandalize a vacant house? Let me out or I'll have the cops on you."

"So why don't you call them?"

"Because my goddamn hands are cuffed."

Dru kept searching the room. Almost immediately she put her hand on the book of photos. "Uh-oh," she said. "What have we here? Is this a trophy book of all Tyndall Cranmer's fornications?"

"What're you . . . ? How did you find that? How do you know my name?"

"Your little hidey places are pretty obvious. My gosh, what an array of skanks. Liberal intellectuals every one. Oh, and here is Cressie."

"What? What do you know . . . ?"

"We've got her diary. We know all about the hush money you paid her. And other things."

"What? What other things?" He sounded like he was choking.

"You must have wanted her silenced very badly."

"No! You don't think I—!"

"You're certainly a prime suspect."

"I didn't do it. I swear to God!"

"Do you even believe in God?" Dru asked. "Weren't you a professor?"

Then Dru spotted the light socket with a piece of masking tape over it. Peeled off the tape and flipped the switch. The secret compartment in the wall sprung open. Inside was a skull at least four times the size of the typical human. And it was elongated towards the back. The brain had been huge.

Sam and Dru exchanged looks. Both awed. Both realizing something portentous lay here.

"We'll carry it in a Hefty bag," said Dru.

"Carry?" Tyndall yelled. "Carry what?"

"The skull of course, silly," said Dru. "Don't tell me someone is keeping you prisoner here looking for this. His detecting skills are fairly pathetic. But of course I am a goddess."

"Goddess? What are you talking about?"

"I am Erishkigal, Queen of the Dead."

"You're nuts, that's what you are."

"Perhaps. But I'm the nut outside the bathroom."

"Lemme outta here," Tyndall whined, kicking the wall, "I'll give you money. That's all you thieving kids want. Money to buy weed."

"No," said Dru firmly. "I think you will remain in Hades. While we waltz away."

They left him wailing like a sick dog.

Chapter 46

Skipper van Dine was on the phone blistering Boo. "You find Chirburg by five o'clock today."

"I don't have a bloodhound," Boo protested.

"Let's get straight about my mood, Radley. It's beyond lousy. I lost a half million on Chit-Chat. When my leech of a wife finds out, I won't be able to go home. I am looking for an ass to kick, and yours seems like a good place to start. Five o'clock!"

He hung up. Boo shrugged. He had more immediate fears. Lucifer's Legion. There was no survival guide for dealing with them.

He turned on Chip and demanded, "What are you going to do to replace the Buggaron money?"

"Nothing," said Chip stubbornly. "What are you talking about? They made a purchase. They lost some money. The Chit-Chat shares are in their account. They may rise in value."

"What does your father do? He's going to have to back-stop you on this."

"I'm not talking to you about this."

"You damn well are," snarled Boo, smacking him in the shin with the squash racquet.

"Owww shit," went Chip, falling out of his chair to the floor.

"What does your father do?"

"He collects Early American folk art for the Metropolitan Museum of Art. It's all philanthropic."

"What? He's a trust-funder? Did he drop out of some serious financial firm? JP Morgan? US Trust? Announce he wasn't cut out for office warfare? Needed to spend more time with charity work?"

"Of course, he keeps up appearances, but there's next to no money."

"How did you go to Saint Paul's?"

"Generation skipping trust. You know about that."

"You shithead. You just developed all your hard-charger personality and fantasy on your own. No ancestral genes. I'll kill you!"

Boo struck Chip on the shin again and again. Chip writhed in agony on the floor.

"You have put me in Dutch with these desperadoes. When they find out, they'll eviscerate us."

■ ■ ■

Randall caught Samantha outside after school. She felt a debt of gratitude for his defense of her before the principal, but she knew he was sweet on her. And it was really hard to get beyond his acne and motor-mouth.

"You know how Dinorah is always classifying people in subcultures?" Randall began. "Well she thinks our class has defensively isolated ourselves from the rest of the school, and this is a big mistake. We're denying our-selves participation in the high school rituals, and we'll look back with regret."

"Somehow I don't think so. But go ahead."

"Anyhow, she's organizing a big group of us to go to the Junior-Senior Prom. It's not like anyone is actually dating or having the gut-wrenching experience of phoning a girl and asking for a date. We're just kind of pals. Like we are normally."

"And?"

Randall looked incredibly nervous. He had sweat stains in his pits. "And I know Kurt wouldn't be caught dead at a prom. So I thought maybe . . . maybe you'd go . . . with me."

"I don't really dance, Randall."

"Nor do I. But it would be a classic memory if I could be a wallflower with the prettiest girl in the school."

He looked like an earnest puppy dog. If puppies had glasses and acne.

Sam closed her eyes and took a deep breath. Why me? she thought.

Then she thought Randall's father was the law dean. He was invincible. Which made Randall nearly so. And she needed all the help she could get in life.

She opened her eyes, looked straight at Randall. Forced a smile.

"Yes, Randall, I will go with you. You may pick me up in a car. I presume you have a driver's license. And then you will pick up as many nerds and geeks as the car will hold. We will all go together.

"I will walk into the prom on your arm, and we will prop

up the wall. We will drink revolting punch. No sneaking a hip flask. We will boogie faintly if the beat is strong enough. We will walk through the school ring prom arch and have professional photos made. And we will go home early. No after-parties. We wouldn't be invited anyway."

"And?"

"And I will kiss you goodnight on the doorstep, and tell you I had an enchanting evening."

Randall looked like he was going to faint.

Chapter 47

Carrying the giant skull in a Hefty bag, Samantha and Dru walked through the swaggering streams of students on the university campus. All of them glued to social media even as they walked with friends. Joyful in their four-year fantasy of love and irresponsibility. The grass was fresh-mowed and smelled sweet.

Sam remembered Anthropology from when she was a little girl and her mom worked there. It was a ratty old building, one of the oldest on campus, water-stained ceilings, ill-heated and cooled, all showing with a perfect clarity the lack of status of the department.

Inside, a cultural shift into the world of digging in dirt in arid lands. Glass cases of bones. Bulletin boards of summer expeditions everywhere on earth. Bearded male professors in trousers with cargo pockets, bush shirts.

Professor Pru Gardam was tall and cadaverous. Bony cheeks. Gray eyes, gray hair, cracked lips. Stringy neck. Big feet in tennis shoes with mesh nylon uppers. She wore a bird skull necklace with a sharp beak all cast in pewter.

It would be easy to picture her manning the searchlight on a tower in a concentration camp. Brisk and efficient. Acknowledging the Fitzhugh name. She waved at the one chair.

Sam sat down, the bagged skull on her lap. Dru remained in the background.

For such a tiny room, the ceiling was disproportionately high. And it was cluttered with the detritus of academic life. Photos of Pru in a bush hat under a hot sun. Stacks of books and papers—the well-guarded interest of her scholarly niche.

"Your mother," said Pru, "is a woman of strong character who likes to have her way in the world. Our experience with her was . . . disagreeable."

There was no response to that.

"And you wish?"

"Your expertise," said Sam.

"I do have my reputation," Pru said with a touch of grandeur.

Sam gave a faint smile. "The pleasures of scholarship."

Pru sat up straight, looking quite formidable. "Is your demeanor frivolous?"

"Not in the least."

"Very well. I will revert to civility. Now come, come. Don't waste my time."

"We have something for you to examine."

Pru made an imperceptible nod. Waited in an expectant silence.

Sam set the skull on the desk and unwrapped it.

Pru seemed in a condition of deep shock. Her face sagged. Her sinewy bare arms quivered. "A child of the Nifilhim," she whispered.

"So, you know what it is."

Her eyes squinted as though in pain. Her fingers hovered as though afraid to touch it. "What are you doing with this? Where did you get it?"

Samantha hesitated, "We found it."

"Have you been in Ireland? Is that it? Where is your mother? I mean where is she right now?" Her voice was indignant, vociferous. And then deeply suspicious.

"You're playing some deep game with me. Sybyl disappeared. Toby disappeared. Tyndall disappeared. You know something about these mysteries."

"Not at all. We . . . came across this. Thought you'd know about it."

"You tax my patience. Don't you get evasive. Did your mother find this?"

Sam reached to gather up the bag. Pru slapped her hand. "This stays here."

"It's ours," Sam protested.

"We're taking a measured approach to this. I keep the skull, and you go away."

"No," Sam argued stubbornly.

Pru's voice turned whispery, oozing a sense of danger. "And what will happen if I refuse?"

"Far worse than you can ever imagine," said Dru, suddenly making her presence known.

"Who are you? What are you doing here?"

There was fear on Pru's face. She seemed to be seeing a vision that Sam couldn't. Was the color of Dru's eyes darkening?

Then Sam spotted the small glass case on Pru's desk.

There were various votive statues, all of the sort sold to tourists in the Cycladic Islands of Greece. But there were Babylonian ones as well. A copy of a bas-relief with Ishtar—who replaced Inanna—raising her skirts to show her sexuality. Flanked by owls. Standing with bird feet on a lion.

And next to her was Ereshkigal whose name stayed the same across the centuries.

Pru's eyes never moved off Dru's face. "You stay away from me. You don't ever come here again."

Dru wrapped up the head and pulled Sam out the door.

"Don't you ever come back! Do you hear me!"

Chapter 48

"Now put your hands down," Quinn instructed. "You only get to grab the rope when I kick out the crate. Make things sporting."

It was early morning. Deep in the woods behind Quinn's house, mist seemed to breathe out of the ground.

Chirburg and Lorraine were standing on upended drink crates, nooses around their necks, ropes looped over a big limb, tied to a tree trunk. But their hands were free.

The members of the Legion were way back in the trees. Quinn wanted these last moments to be intensely personal. And he continued to marvel at how much violent crime one could get by with if you had sufficient gall.

"Okay, pencil dick," sneered Lorraine. "You've made your 'effing point. Now cut the shit and let us down."

"He's got our ass in a bear trap," Chirburg whined. "Don't provoke him." He lifted his chin and twisted his head inside the noose. The crate wobbled.

"Fuck face here? He won't do jack-shit. Couldn't find his dick with both hands. Nose stuck in a book. Foot-noting his way through life."

"You really were the complete package, Lorraine," said Quinn shaking his head sadly. "Sarcasm. Eye rolling.

Dismissiveness. Patronizing. Mocking, sassing, ridiculing. When you walked out, you were going to find a real man. Remember that? So how did it work out? Realtors with blow-dried hair. Always saying they were about to separate from their wives. Always got a house for sale with the owner moved out. Hump you on the wall-to-wall carpet."

Lorraine spat, "You stole the sunlight out of my life. Every goddam' day. All your damn journal articles I was supposed to make over. That dumb-cluck alien planet thing in *The New York Times*. I actually had relatives who heard about it. Phoned up wanting to know if it was true."

"That I had an article in the *Times*?"

"No. If there was some wild-ass planet coming for us. I mean you were such a Mister Know-it-all. Talking down to my mother at Christmas dinner."

"I told her that dinosaurs and cave men didn't exist at the same time," said Quinn. "Seemed like something she might like to be aware of. Although it had no bearing on daytime TV."

"I got nothing to do with this!" shouted Chirburg. "I swear to God I barely know this woman!"

"You really need to stop interrupting," said Quinn.

Chirburg was crying, his mouth turned up in the hideous smile of grief, his voice rising in a wail of misery. His shoulders seemed very narrow. "You inbred peckerwoods. I knew you lynched innocent men like this down South. I hate you people."

"Actually, I'm from Maine," Quinn explained. "But you probably think we're inbred too." He raised one finger in warning. "Now I've told you not to interrupt."

He turned back to his ex-wife.

"You know, Lorraine, I wanted to make the marriage work. Tried to overlook your common behavior. Throwing beer cans out of car windows. Saying 'fuckin'-A' to the Dean's wife. Your dirt-bag relatives always wanting us to invest in some cockamamie scheme."

"Yiz should'a been so lucky. My brother Vinny was in on everything that came down the pike. First pinball, then video game arcades, then poker machines in bars. Offered us a chance to get in, and I had to tell him we couldn't afford to gas up the junker car. My important intellecshual husband."

"Vinny's got poker machines?" said Chirburg.

"You really are the limit," said Quinn, totally exasperated. "You know that?"

"What? What're you . . . ? No! No please!"

Quinn kicked the crate from beneath Chirburg who dropped and grabbed the rope all at the same time. Swung kicking in the air. Trying desperately to haul himself up so he wouldn't have his air cut off.

"Grrrg . . . unk . . . whuff."

Quinn turned back to Lorraine. "I actually read self-help columns in the women's magazines. 'Shameful, yet pleasurable tricks to do under a sheet.' 'Put the sex back into your marriage.' That kind of thing. Trying to get inside a woman's mind."

Chirburg's arms were tiring. "Hep me, hep me," he gurgled. His face suffused red.

"Cut him down, you asshole!" snarled Lorraine. "He's going to strangle."

Quinn shook his head in despair. "Lorraine, Lorraine. Though you grow older, you never grow wise."

"He's my goddam' cousin. Now cut him down."

Chirburg's arms dropped, and he hung there, mouth open, eyes wide in a look of surprise, feet toes down, maybe a foot off the ground.

Quinn turned to admire his handiwork. "You know that expression 'twisting in the wind?' I've always wondered about it. But now it's all clear."

Lorraine was aghast. "You son of a . . . you've killed him! You won't get by with this!"

Quinn held her eyes with his.

"You were always watching TV. I thought I married an Italian, I'd at least have an attentive wife, a homemaker, great food. 'There's cold cuts in the fridge,' you'd say. And as I walked in there, you'd yell: 'Hey, Quinn, beer me.' A voice like some sandhog in a union jacket. Expect me to wait on you."

■ ■ ■

"You're going to the prom with Randall?" Kurt accused.

"It's not like you'd take me," Sam answered.

"It's not like you ever expressed any interest. And you might have told me. He's bragged about it to everyone at school. And I have to hear it from Cherry."

"I felt sorry for the poor geek. That's all."

"Randall can do just fine with his little secret fantasies about you. He shouldn't be encouraged."

"Why? So you can continue to take me for granted?"

"What is it I'm not doing? I don't have a lot of experience with this boyfriend business."

"No, it's so much easier with Cherry. You just go right to the rutting goat phase. Can skip the wooing."

"Wooing? What is it you want me to do, Miss High Maintenance? Recall when you read *National Velvet*?"

"I don't know," Sam said stubbornly. She knew she was being stupid, but she wasn't going to back down.

"You don't know."

"That's right. You think of something."

"Well, we have our SATs coming up. And AP exams. I suppose I could spend each hour gazing at you with longing and throw away my future."

"You don't need to be rude about my going to the prom. You could be nice about it."

"What would that consist of?"

"Quit being so damn logical. I can't take all this questioning."

Kurt chewed on the side of his mouth. He was steamed, and she could tell it.

"My parents have discovered where your mother is. She's in England."

Sam was shocked. "How did they do that?"

"The usual way. Mom talked to the spirits."

Chapter 49

It took Boo over an hour to find a phone number for Chip's father. A home number in Cold Spring Harbor on Long Island. One of the fanciest communities on the Gold Coast. He dialed apprehensively. Not knowing what he would encounter.

"No pithy critiques, please," said the voice from the other end. An effete voice. "I'm suffering combat fatigue."

There was momentary confusion over who Boo was, the father, Leland Trafford, thinking he was from the Metropolitan Museum of Art. Boo explaining his relationship with Chip at the brokerage.

"Chip works? I had no idea."

Boo had never met the man and had to listen to fifteen minutes of a Colonial wind vane collection he was trying to get donated to the museum. The "hysterical tinkering" on the part of museum directors. Talk about self-absorbed.

"Chip did a major unauthorized trade," he said finally. "He lost three million."

"Dear me. That's quite a lot."

"Exactly. If the money is replaced, however, I won't be obliged to report it."

"Curious. I would think you'd be obliged to report it no matter what."

"Well, technically . . . but I like Chip. I'm willing to bend a point. Try to not cripple him so early in his career."

"Really? So few people do like him."

"Well . . . I was his age once. Did foolish things."

"I don't doubt. And I suppose there's the whole question of how trades get authorized. Sure, the client didn't do it. You don't have the written authorization. But who's to say you didn't make the trade?"

"What?"

"And even assuming you convince your superiors, there will have to be an audit of the office. Are you sure everything is completely in order? Hmm? Never cut any corners yourself? Never churned an account?"

Boo was furious. God the rich were so infernally cunning. Just turned the whole thing around on him.

"Okay, that's it. I'm damned one way or the other. Chip's going down."

"I really don't care what you do to Chip. I've never liked the boy. Not even sure he's actually my son. His mother was extremely promiscuous. I spoke to her about it more than once. But she was deaf to all pleas. Said it was her passion for self-expression."

■ ■ ■

Sam was walking back from fencing when Bubba Stobbs pulled to the curb in his Lincoln and flipped open the passenger door.

"Hop in. I'll give you a ride."

"I'm just going over there." She nodded towards Kurt's neighborhood that bordered the campus.

"I just want you to know there's no hard feelings on my part."

"On your part? For what?"

"For all that went on."

"I didn't . . . fine. Okay."

"No, don't walk off. I need to talk to you about muh darter Cherry. I think she's out of control."

"I don't really know anything about her. Sorry."

"I'll tell you 'bout it. I need a teenager's perspective."

Afterwards, Sam couldn't believe she had been dumb enough to get in the car, but she did. She put her fencing bag between them on the seat, but she couldn't get out her sword cane easily.

Immediately he drove off at a growing speed, shot past her turn despite her protests. Down the wooded hill faster. Ran a red light at the bottom. Honking horns of cars slamming on brakes.

Three miles out of town he just pulled over to the side of the road. Sam tried to open the door, but he had the child's lock on.

He put his right arm over the back of the seat.

"I think my darter's turning into a little whore," he said in a confiding voice.

Sam's lips were tight together. "I don't know anything about it."

"My wife's a whore. Cherry gets it from her."

Sam said nothing. She stared out the windshield, refusing to make eye contact. Then she saw the copy of *Hustler* poking out from under her seat. Folded to the picture with her face on it. The woman did have big jugs.

Bubba had laced his fingertips through her hair. She jerked her head away.

"How would you like a brand spankin' new car?"

"I don't think so. What would I do with it?"

"What would you . . . ? Why drive it. How do you get to school?"

"I ride my bike. I'm ready to go back now."

"What would you like? I'll buy you anything." His belly was quivering. Sweat on his forehead.

"I'd like to get out of the car."

Sam was frightened but also filled with a growing anger. All these creep men coming at her. Now this one. "I can't believe this is happening to me! You are disgusting!"

"I swear you and that little friend of yours . . . it's like you give off some kind of musk. You're making me plumb crazy. I ain't responsible for what I'm about to do."

"Stop! Let me alone!"

He leered, "I want to take your inventory."

Sam had her sword out of the bag, but she couldn't draw it from the stick. She poked bubba in the eye with it.

"OWWW goddammit!"

She kept jabbing him viciously again and again. "Open the damn door!" she screamed.

He yelled and dodged back, grabbed the cane. She pulled the sword free and sliced him across his gut.

She could feel it cut through his shirt and flesh.

He looked down in shock at the growing red stain. Then started wailing.

"Let me out, or I'll run it through you!" she threatened.

"I'm gonna kill you!" he roared.

He came up with a handgun from the side pocket on the door. Sam rammed the sword through his wrist and up against the window.

Pain seared through him like an electric current. The gun fell to the floor. His lips moved soundlessly. Then he began squealing like a pig. "Inh-eeee-inh-eee!"

He tried to free his wrist, but it went farther up the sword. Blood splattered and smeared across the glass.

"I'll let you outIswearitJesusmotherfucker!" he vowed.

"Use your other hand."

He undid the locks, and Sam tumbled backwards dragging her bag with her. She ran across the road and stuck out her thumb. A car flashed past.

Then right behind it came a motorcycle. Sam waved frantically. It pulled over. Dru was riding behind a man Sam knew, arms tight around his waist.

They both did a double-take at Sam's bloody sword. Bubba staggering out of the car holding his wrist against the throbbing pain. Screeching.

Sam slung her bag across her back and climbed on behind Dru. "Talk about *deus ex machina*," she said.

Bubba got out in the road ahead of them waving his arms. "Halp me! Halp me!"

Quinn kicked him with his boot as they roared by, sending him cart-wheeling into the ditch.

■ ■ ■

Quinn let the girls off two blocks from Dru's house. When Rhoda heard about the incident with Bubba Stobbs, she immediately got her lawyer to come over with a rape kit.

"No one raped me," Sam explained. "I stabbed him through the wrist."

Rhoda stared with glowing admiration in her eyes. "I think you've just written the definitive work on feminism. Written it in blood."

The woman lawyer, Lois Trefusis, looked like a bulldog covered in a tent. Tote bag. Rubber-soled shoes. Butch haircut.

Sam felt remarkably calm as she told her story. She had been in complete control of the sword and her reasoning the whole time. The thrust through the wrist was a necessary one to disarm him.

"You are an inspiration in your frankness," said Lois. "When I think of the lying dirt-bags I usually have to deal with."

Lois-the-lawyer's eyes turned hard as obsidian as she outlined her strategy. "We're going to do a preemptive strike. Sue Bubba for defamation of Dru in trying to get her kicked out of school. At the same time we file against him on your behalf. Defamation. False imprisonment. Assault. Battery. We will load him up."

Rhoda took Sam's shoulders with two very powerful hands. Looked her in the eye so close they almost touched foreheads. "Thank you for being a fighter. And thank you for being a friend to my daughter."

Dru rolled her eyes. "Allow me to play my insignificant role."

She dialed her phone. Randall answered.

"Randall," she said. "Pull the trigger."

Chapter 50

Quinn was in the diner at the end of Chastain Street having a cheese omelet and coffee when the cop came in. Sat on the stool beside him at the counter.

Took his hat off, put it on the vacant stool. Said, "Seems like there ain't a man alive who takes his hat off indoors no more. Manners just up and died."

Quinn nodded in agreement. Held his coffee mug in two hands, looked straight ahead over the rim.

The cop said his name was Wally Butts. Ordered two eggs over easy, grits, sausage links, white toast, and coffee. Started in eating the moment the plate came to him. No fussing over salting anything. Ate the toast dry, drank the coffee black. It reminded Quinn of someone who had given up smoking but didn't have his taste buds back.

"What's become of yore ex-wife?" Wally asked with his mouth full.

Quinn shook his head. "The less I see of her the better."

"Ain't that the truth. We had her checkin' in ever' dam' day there for a while. Wantin' yore ass in the calaboose. She done finally relent. Cut us some slack."

"It's odd how women want you as an ATM machine, but then want to ruin you as well."

"Yeh. I think it's kinder like a pincer movement. They'd be happy with either result."

Wally ate some more. "You know it's funny, that lawyer boy what got his hands nailed down. Says some men in Hillary Clinton masks did it. Told him it was a message from somebuddy he done pissed off. But you know what I figger?"

"What?"

"The boy din't have a whole raft of clients. My bet is he got by dealing coke to the credentialed set. But one of his few clients was the high school football coach. Donny-Mack Wade. Got himself a winnin' record that ol' boy. Ever' year the Ford dealership lends him a brand spankin' new Lincoln. Gas charge card. Week in a beach house. But he had a run-in with a kid whose mom runs Women's Studies at the University. Somebody Shelley. Lawyer got involved."

"And?"

Wally put down a three dollar tip. Got up to go. His gun belt creaked.

"Wal, I talk with the campus chief. He says his men cross the street to avoid that shemale. She is yore original bad news diesel. Carries a *bocce* ball as a weapon."

"Seriously? So you think . . ."

"Yep. Yore hairy-legged dykes. Some of them're built like they load cement trucks for a livin'."

"I can see that. Yes."

■ ■ ■

What magical pull Randall had with the Attorney General must have been pretty powerful because Roscoe "Bubba"

Stobbs was indicted the next afternoon for commercial bribery by the statewide grand jury.

When Bubba got the bad news, he was in the hospital after major surgery on his wrist which he might never use again. Francie reported that he roamed the halls in a bathrobe offering residents and interns "whatever bucks it takes" to be diagnosed with a major coronary problem or "the big C."

"He's getting ahead of the game," Randall pronounced. "They usually wait until they're convicted and facing sentencing before they try for sympathy."

Federico quoted Simon Bolivar's deathbed statement: "From heroism to ridicule is but a single step."

Dru and Quinn had just been riding around the county when they saw Samantha in the road.

"It was nothing big," said Dru. "I'm not in the mood for earnest criticism."

"I tell you," Sam insisted, "he's part of a motorcycle gang. They're the ones who broke Bo's arms."

"I saw that as poetic justice."

"They don't play patty-cake, Dru. They are dangerous people."

"I don't know about the rest of them. But Quinn's . . . beguiling."

"What?"

"Well, more like an avenging angel. I can't think of a more dramatic rite of initiation for the nubile maiden. It will make the event an enduring classic."

"You can't be serious."

"I suppose now you and my mother are such fast friends you're going to rat on me."

Sam was exasperated at the accusation of betrayal. "Of course not. But I would expect you to have some common sense."

"Getting in a car with Mister Stobbs? That was a real commonsensical move."

Chapter 51

"Man, this lil' ol' peaceable burg has gotten some weird shit going down of late," said Lt. Wally Butts, legs stretched out from his chair in Boo's office. "Perfessers disappearing. Art dealer gone missing. Lawyer with his hands nailed to a desk. Frat boy scalped. It all lands on my desk."

"It's a right bitch," said Boo.

"I keep trying to get the chief to designate me a detective. Let me wear civvies. Black polo shirt and slacks. My Glock kind of high on my hip. Badge clipped on the waist. It's a pretty sharp look."

"That's true," said Boo, staring at his computer screen, trying to act like he was busy, fighting back his nervous tension.

Two days post-IPO, and Chit-Chat was down to twenty. The profit would be enormous. If it held. If nothing turned it around. What was the point at which to cover the sold shares? He got no answer from Bolek or Beth. Wouldn't answer his calls. The greed for greater profit battling the fear something will cause the price to lurch upward.

Now a cop snooping around.

"You know the way barbershops have done disappeared,

college kids not cutting their hair. I have to go to some styling salon. Cost me a small fortune. But they got little honeys can talk you into most near anything. Got my nose hair waxed. Shove that gunk in it, let it set, then yank it out. Wooo. No nose hair. Even let her trim my eyebrows. She said you got a briar thicket growing here."

"Life's full of new experiences," said Boo.

"The goings-on in this town. Durn if Coach Wade—he's the local football boy—ain't jumped bond. Disappeared like he done gone up in smoke. He kind of publicly hit the skids there. Royally pissed off the Ford dealer. Which was why he was in jail.

"I'm sure he'll be found working as a security guard at some casino in Mississippi. He's not my problem at least. Those bail-skip tracers are like bloodhounds.

"But man, the shit I got on my plate. That scalped frat boy's parents are on our case. Calling state legislators. Demanding SLED get involved. I would'a said it was a fratty boy stunt, just look for some drunk fool to crow about it on Facebook. But those Guy Fawkes masks were meant to deliver a message. Who was Guy Fawkes anyhow?"

"Tried to blow up Parliament way back when," said Boo, eyes on the screen but seeing nothing. "The Brits have a bonfire night for him in November instead of a Halloween."

"I thought it was some Occupy Wall Street thing."

Suspicion in his eyes.

"They use the mask too. Rebellion against capitalism."

"Hmmm. You know we got all this crazy shit on the

campus now. Organized militant dyke and fag groups. Crazed left-wing professors. We used to call them comm'unists. I wonder if there's some anti-frat movement out there."

"Wouldn't surprise me."

"An' them New Yorkers keep buggin' me about that missing art dealer. Never met one before. Are they all total twinkies?"

"No, some aren't."

Wally looked dubious.

"Anyhoo, I go by this art perfesser Jake Milroy's house. The one our disappearing act was supposed to meet. He's on some kind of dope. Just drooling and jabberin' about a planet Nuhbooroo or something. Not a lick of sense in him. And, funny, he's the one whose daughter got killed.

"And get this." He slapped Boo's knee. "He's got this painting of two buck naked gals, like yin-yang. And one of them is the spitting image of a gal here in town we had some run-ins with.

"And the other one, was the little gal the coach tried to kill. Dru Shelley. This is so dam' complicated I've set up a photo board with lines connecting clues with all that's going on. Got my mind racing in all directions. Good thing I'm comfortable with confusion."

He stood up and arched his back, stretching out. "Man, I wish they paid me what I thought I was worth."

"Don't we all."

"You sure Trey din't leave nothing with you? Might be

something you don't think is a clue, but to the professional investigator it's something else."

Boo realized with horror that Trey's overnight bag was no longer beside his desk.

■ ■ ■

Dr. Clearwire's literature class was the usual shambles. A big rant on the evils of genetically modified food. Then how fracking for natural gas would destroy our water supply. The evil of "blood diamonds." Dangers of off-shore drilling. And he got in global warming.

Nasar began reciting aloud the periodic table of the elements and their atomic numbers. His memory was phenomenal. Clearwire glared at him.

To get the class' attention, Clearwire slammed his *Gilgamesh* book on the desk. He was so rattled he couldn't get his thoughts in order.

And then it really started. Kurt disputed him on the snake and threshold imagery which did not go down well.

Clearwire told Kurt he had a PhD and was published in peer-reviewed journals.

He then tried to explain deconstructionism, and Sylvie, whose mother taught in the French Department of the university, had to correct his pronunciation of Jacques Derrida.

Then Emily, whose dad was in English, corrected him on the difference between a meme and a trope.

Clearwire looked like a boxer who has been punched repeatedly into the ropes. In a daze, he went to the Shamhat story. He couldn't stay away from sex.

When he called on Dru to read aloud, she brazenly stood up rather than sitting hunched in her seat mumbling. Her neck still bore red streaks from the strangulation by the coach.

She had started to wear miniskirts with cleanly shaved legs despite her mother's disapproval. Her hair was sister-locked with beads and antique coins. All the boys were suddenly lusting after her.

"Shamhat stripped naked
and settled herself on the ground,
touching her flower with legs spread.
Enkidu smelled her musk and approached carefully.
She took hold of his strong penis,
and pulled it inside her, flexing her loins."

As she read, Dru swung her shoulders and hips. Rattled her braids. Spoke in a saucy voice. Making a joke of it. Not the least embarrassed.

"She used her love arts to show him
the power of woman.
He kept his erection for seven days
And made love to her tirelessly all the time."

Clearwire was staring at her face, breathing heavily through his mouth. The cords in his neck showed like vines climbing a tree.

The entire class burst out laughing at him.

He leaped up, knocking off his cap in the process. "What's so funny? What is wrong with you people?"

The cap lay upside down on the floor in front of his

desk. A plastic baggie of weed and rolling paper had fallen out. And the front row of students could see the picture of Dru from the year book pasted inside the crown of the cap. Stained with sweat, but still clearly visible.

Clearwire's mouth gaped like a fish that's jumped out of an aquarium.

Chapter 52

When Quinn came into his house in the late afternoon he found the magic marker note from Dru on the table.

"Down in the creek. Join me." Signed with a one-inch straight vertical line and a tiny heart at the upper right. Representing her navel.

Couple of sweat drops on the paper. She had run out here.

He stood on the back porch looking down to the little winding creek which flowed gently over rocks leaving eddies and pools. Buzzards were circling way back in the woods where the two bodies hung. Her running shoes and clothes were scattered across the leaves.

Picking up a canvas and wood lawn chair, he walked down slowly, wondering what he would do. Knowing it would be based on emotion rather than reason.

The water was clear and the air was warm and filled with spring. She was lying back against a rock braiding her hair into a single plait. At the last moment, she got a bit abashed and pulled up her knees to cover her little breasts.

"Hey, you," he said, stealing her line.

"I don't have any clothes on," she said complacently, giving him her little impertinent smile. "Really hot running."

She looked like a small furnace was burning inside her body. The water should be sizzling with contact.

Quinn opened the chair and sat down. His eyes went up and down, admiring her sleek beauty, the firmness of youth and a long distance runner. She knew he was noticing. How could he not?

She lay back against the rock, displaying her breasts, burnt umber nipples. They seemed to beckon. That was the role of breasts, wasn't it? There was something in Sumerian about that.

"You know," he mused, "my first semester teaching at the university, my wife and I were invited to the studio art department Halloween party. Lorraine was young and hot. Dressed as a gypsy which was easy for her. I was . . . I forget.

"Anyhow, the party was in an old house back of Chastain Street. Apartment on the top floor. It was an artsy party. Really creative costumes and wild revelers. Professors like big kids. Same mentality as the students, and there were a slew of students there. A maelstrom of hard partiers.

"Booze was a big washtub of Purple Jesus set on a table. When you came in, you were given a straw. The food was nonexistent. And a mob surrounded a little spectacle.

"Rolling on his back on the floor absolutely raving drunk was a sculpture professor. You may have seen his work a couple of places on campus. He's quite good. You can tell what the object is. Vegetable, animal, or mineral. Not just an amorphous blob or welded scrap metal.

"Well, riding his chest was a drunk coed. Falling out of her clothes. And she was telling him in a loud, slurred voice—that if he could manage to struggle to his feet, stagger down the stairs, and reel down the street to his apartment—all the special things she would do to him. Quite explicit.

"And I can remember like yesterday thinking to myself 'man, this college teaching is going to be a lot of fun.'"

Dru laughed lightly, revealing straight, white teeth. "And was it?"

"No. Maybe I should have been in studio art."

The leaf shadows made dancing patterns on the rocks and water. Dru gazed distractedly at the buzzards circling on an updraft. "Something dead back there."

"Must be."

"It's absolutely amazing," she said with sudden enthusiasm. "The Gilgamesh Epic. The very first piece of real literature in history, and the symbols are all there. The great flood. Tree and snake. Quest for profound knowledge and immortality. Gilgamesh, the first demi-god hero.

"Part of your subconscious Jung called 'the shadow.' It appears as dark figures in dreams. It's the job of the ego to tame the shadow and bring it into line.

"Enkidu the wild man was a symbol of Gilgamesh's shadow. Shamhat tamed him through sexual intercourse. The symbolism just resonates with you. And this all erupted from the Sumerian soul."

Quinn knew this was all just innuendo for his arousal. But still, he wondered what woman of any age he could be having this conversation with.

She stood up dripping from the water. She had a thick black bush when all the girls were spending hours shaving their mons pubis bare. Her torso was a smooth uniform brown with no tan lines.

"Jung," she said, "called the 'anima' the woman within the subconscious of every man. This symbolic figure personifies all feminine aspects of the male psyche—irrationality, prophetic hunches, sentiment, link with nature, ability to love."

Quinn tried to gather his thoughts, sort them in coherent order. Discern the future. But it was impossible while looking at her.

"Yes," said Quinn. "A longing for unreal romantic love. Erotic fantasy. And the anima takes the shape of the *femme fatale*, a death demon. Sirens. The Lorelei who drown men in the Rhine. A poison damsel. Mozart's Queen of the Night."

She smiled. He smiled in return.

She walked towards him step by step. Sensuous. Magical. Radiating mythical powers.

Her lips puckered seductively. She wet them with a tiny pink tongue tip.

Boldly, she straddled his legs, ran her hands through his hair and began to kiss him deeply on the mouth.

He touched the curve of her lithe back, gripped her hard little buttocks.

Dru said, "I think we can say my legs are having an amicable split."

Chapter 53

Boo was on the phone with Wally Butts who was saying, "I got SLED in here this morning, setting on the edge of my desk, telling me I'm a dry hump. Their little idea of a performance appraisal. He did have a nice pair of boots though. Ankle holster. Boot-cut pants. Would love to dress like that.

"Anyhow, after he finished giving me a raft of shit, he says 'You're beyond self-parody.' What the hell does that mean?"

Boo didn't want to tell him.

"I tell you what. This town has become like the Bermuda Triangle. Folks disappearing left and right. Now I got your New York office calling saying somebody name of Chirburg was down here, ain't come back. You know anything about that?"

"They've been bugging me too. He went off with a cousin of his named Lorraine Raguzza—Raguzzi? I can't remember. I think she's a realtor in town."

"Wal now I will sure 'nough check that out. Many thanks for the tip, good buddy."

"I try to be a good citizen," said Boo.

"Hey, hang on. Lemme run something past you. I got a frat boy scalped by Occupy Wall Street masks; I got a lawyer's hands nailed down by Hillary Clintons; got football player's arms broke by Nancy Pelosi. Can you make the connection?"

"All wearing masks? Um . . . all Democrats? I give up."

"Yeah, I'm having trouble with it myself."

Boo hung up. At least he didn't have to feel guilty about Chirburg. Hoped he had gone down the rabbit hole.

New York had been bugging Boo as well. Wanting to know about Chirburg, about the Buggaron account that seemed to grow a couple hundred thousand a month. How much had Quinn hauled down to the Caribbean?

Chit-Chat had dropped to ten, so Boo bought the shares that had been sold forward. $4,500,000 minus $1,000,000. Profit of three million-five. Not bad for a little high school girl. Not bad? Jeez-a-reee.

Boo himself had laid his bet for 500,000 shares. His profit was $21,500,000. He could scarcely believe it. Sat down in a chair marveling at the figure. That was what he needed. Sicily maybe. Taormina. Palm trees. A walled villa.

He knew he should be ecstatic except for the missing Buggaron money Chip had thrown away. He didn't want to replace it with his newfound wealth. It wasn't fair. He had made that money. And besides, a transfer like that would link him to the Buggaron account.

Chip came in complaining about not being able to get decent Italian pizza in the South. The lack of a food truck culture.

"Why don't you go find Chirburg? Get the home office off our backs."

"Off your back. Nobody's on my case."

"Then why don't you go back to New York?"

"I prefer it here. Up there I have to look busy all day long. Some midlevel jerk coming around and asking me about the numbers."

His eyes were roving the side of Boo's face.

"What?" said Boo.

"I suppose you're wondering about Trey's suitcase." Smug.

Boo's heart leaped. He pressed both thumbs on the edge of his desk. Didn't look around. "What suitcase?"

"The one you had beside your desk. The one with your fingerprints all over it."

Steaming now, Boo jerked his squash racquet out from under the desk.

Chip raised a warning hand. "Whoa there. If I were you, I'd put that squash racquet down. You see, I've peeked inside. Wearing plastic gloves of course. There's a photo of a painting which sold for major moolah. A painting of that Samantha girl . . . your romantic yearning posing for a nude portrait. It just—" he shook his head "—it just pulls things together in such an intriguing way. Kind of heightens the reality of our little contest with the teen queens."

Boo put the racquet back under the desk slowly. His brain trying to assess this new development. He had twenty-one million. He could just bug out. But he couldn't leave Samantha. He wanted her too much.

"Say," said Chip. "Now what's the name of the colored girl? I don't think these girls are all innocent."

■ ■ ■

"You did what?" said Samantha, completely aghast.

"I got naked with him," Dru replied with complete nonchalance. "Well, he didn't. Just me."

Dru described in detail her little seduction at Quinn's cabin. Her voice was dreamy. She touched on small details of nature. The creek and woods that were both bucolic and brooding at the same time. The flicker of light among the leaves. The distant buzzards like a reminder of mortality and the live-for-today urges of the flesh.

"You dry humped him?"

She answered with a child-like honesty. "Isn't that what teenagers do? I know you do it with Kurt."

"Did you . . . climax?"

"Majorly."

"And then what?"

"I lay my head on his shoulder and wept. I felt like I had melted down into a puddle."

Dru could read the distress in Sam's face. "Sure, there's a big age gap between us. It wouldn't have seemed that way in the nineteenth century. I was always struck by Princess Natasha in *War and Peace* who was seventeen when she married Prince André. Knocked up immediately and then died giving birth to the child."

"Is that what you want?"

"Of course not. But it's like in *Gilgamesh*. You create a balance. Gilgamesh is civilization; Enkidu nature. Shamhat transforms Enkidu so he can become one with Gilgamesh.

"But it's not just sex. All animals bang each other, but very quickly. Shamhat was a priestess of Ishtar, or Inanna, if you will. She gave Enkidu sex as a holy ritual. For six days and seven nights."

Dru quoted from the epic. "'His mind expanded. He knew more than the animals.' You see, he had joined with the goddess and known religious ecstasy. He became beautiful like a god."

"I'm lost," said Sam. "Is this some charitable act for you then?"

"No. That's just a side effect. I am experiencing the goddess inside me. My mom carries on about this all the time. It's delicious."

Chapter 54

Samantha was on her way with Kurt to take the SAT. They couldn't help but be tense, society made such a big freakin' deal out of it.

Distracted, she answered her phone without looking at the caller. It was Dr. Wilhelmina Shattuck of the University of Michigan.

She talked hurriedly, establishing who she was. Said she had the grant money and a team of ethno-biologists who wanted to look at Sam's DNA. She was quite insistent. Pushy.

"Why is anyone interested in this? Why do you keep bothering me?"

"Look, just tell me this. Do you have green eyes?"

"Yes."

"Is your hair some variety of red?"

"Sort of." Sam was getting guarded.

"Do you . . . have an extra rib?"

"I'm not answering any more questions," Sam said firmly. She was suddenly wondering if she had enough pencils for the test, irritated by this nuisance of a woman.

"Please hear me out. If your parents are both some

variety of Celtic, it is possible . . . well, you might have the DNA of a vanished line of humanity. This . . . this could mean a great number of publications for us and an ongoing series of grants that—"

Sam clicked off. Publications. Grants. It sounded so like her mother that she wanted to scream.

■ ■ ■

Tyndall Cranmer's house was perfectly silent in the early morning until Quinn dragged him out of the bathroom and unlocked his thumbs. Then the complaining began.

"You can't keep me like this. I'm a state of nerves. My gums hurt. I got hemorrhoids bleeding. The seat of my pants is soaked."

"Who did this?" Quinn demanded, gesturing furiously at the vacant hidden compartment.

"Teenage vandals. They broke in and taunted me."

"What were they? Some dope smoking skate-boarders?"

"No. A coupl'a teen girls. One of them totally sassy. She located the hidden compartment in under five minutes. Made me feel like a nitwit."

Quinn was pale with anger and shame that he had been bested like this. "And you kept me hanging, and now I've lost it."

Tyndall was crying. "I knew you'd kill me if I told you everything."

"Let's tell me everything now."

Tyndall talked volubly, desperately, as though thinking he could bargain his way out. "It was a giant skull.

Elongated. One I found in Turkey near Mount Ararat. The Turkish authorities took the rest of the skeleton. I could have gone to prison for life for stealing it. Locked in some pesthole with heroin smuggler animals and lunatics."

Quinn didn't seem particularly impressed.

"You know what happened," said Tyndall. "The Annunaki came down, built space ports, created mankind to mine for gold. They created man in different places so he'd be divided, unable to rebel. And they bred with some of the women. Giants were born."

"What are those pictures Sybyl had of mutant looking creatures?"

"You don't create man out of nothing without some slip-ups. Plus the Annunaki were amphibious themselves. Maybe that was the prototype."

"What? What was Sybyl Colfax up to in Ireland?"

"There are some of them still alive. The screw-ups. They're called Fomorians in Irish legend. She made contact with them. Communicated. She was compiling a dictionary of words. She thought it was the core language of mankind."

A wave of uncontrollable anger passed over Quinn. "My natural impulse is to strangle you right here. But I've brought the gear for something more creative."

Tyndall's expression was vacant, fatalistic, almost that of an imbecile.

Quinn regarded the filthy room mournfully. "You know, this house has a stunning absence of taste. It's like you lived a grad student all your life." He shoved Tyndall back in the bathroom.

He threw stout twine over the shower rod and put the prepared noose around Tyndall's neck.

"What we're going to do is arrange an autoerotic hanging. If you're intellectually curious, here's how it works. You shut off oxygen to the brain, it induces a near-hallucinogenic state called hypoxia. You jerk off, and it gives you a huge high.

"Now, the fail-safe mechanism is you just let go of the rope. Air is restored."

Tyndall clutched at straws. "You mean I get to live?"

Quinn turned a lazy, charming smile on him. "No. You'll be dead. Because I'll be holding the rope. Now take your clothes off."

Tyndall seemed stupefied as he obeyed. Hands trembling. Fighting his clothes that stuck to him as though glued. His body was scrawny, sinewy. He stank from his captivity.

"You know what's funny," said Quinn, "is in other centuries, doctors thought this was a cure for erectile dysfunction. Know why?"

Tyndall was sniveling like a punished child. "W . . . why?"

"They see a public execution, the villain would get a boner. Sometimes shoot off. But the erection would last for hours. They called it the 'death erection.'

"Now I've got the album of your conquests. All your old fuck slaves. Do you want to pick one as your final lover?"

"I can't. I can't," Tyndall wailed.

"You could cooperate a little," Quinn chastised. "I mean

you've been a leech and a shit-ass all your life. Don't you want to go out pleasing at least one person?"

"I'm sorry," Tyndall wept in complete submission. "I'll do what you want."

Quinn made him put on women's fishnet stockings and black silk underpants, garter belt, even a bra.

"You ever see that old movie *The Blue Angel*? Where Marlene Dietrich humiliates the old professor? That's what you look like. I've even brought a movie poster of it to tack on your wall. Kind of set the stage of your mindset at the time of death."

Tyndall was fighting tears and snot. Then he cut loose and wet the floor in a splashing yellow stream of urine.

Quinn frowned, regarding him steadily. "Try to muster some dignity here, will you?"

Chapter 55

"Blue M&Ms really should be abolished," Dru pronounced. "They just have no place in the traditional color mix."

"Do tell," said Samantha.

"The browns and greens have a comforting effect. I can look at them with deep contentment. Earth colors. Like me."

They had just taken the SAT which was a huge event in their lives. Now they were out and feeling liberated, giddy, full of nonsense. Meeting friends for lunch like college kids.

Chastain Street was the old business street of the town. Beloved of realtors who were selling the "authentic" university town experience.

Bubba Stobbs was out with his wife against her better judgment. His life seemed to be experiencing a slow, painful death. Rhoda Shelley's lawyer had gotten her lawsuits served, and the treble shock had him tranquilized under the care of a shrink.

His lawyer had called Lois Trefusis with wild threats of suit for battery against Sam. Lois had laughed. Asked do you really want your client in front of a jury?

Now he was buttonholing people he knew on the street. Talking randomly. His wife fumed. He was being a major embarrassment.

"They ain't got nothing on me. Just small stuff."

Dru and Sam were right in his path. "Let's cross the street," Sam urged.

"We're not going to hide from that sleaze-bucket," Dru argued, dragging her along. "Just keep your knife handy, Zorro. You may have to kill him."

"Don't even think such a thing."

Bubba was saying, "They claim if you stand up while working, there are major health benefits. I'm on my feet on the sales lot all day long. Ought to be healthy as a horse. I sure eat like one."

The other man pulled out of his grasp, walked rapidly away.

"I jes' want to get back to normal," Bubba called after him plaintively.

He turned and confronted the girls. Raw longing in his eyes. "I dunno what you two do to me. I ain't responsible. It's like witchcraft."

And then as they watched in horror, he unzipped his pants and exposed himself. And grabbed Sam and Dru in a bear hug.

"Love up to me," he ordered.

"Gross me out!" Dru yelled.

"I want me a fusion of flesh here. Obey me."

His wife was hitting him with a pocketbook. "Stop it, you dam' tom-fool ee-jit!"

That was when a stranger gave Bubba a good crack to the head with a squash racquet. "Take that, you villain," he said in mock drama.

"OW mully!" Bubba yelled.

His wife dragged him away, hissing at him to shut up and zip up his pants.

"Sum-bitch cold-cocked me!" he yelled.

The whole street seemed to be watching. And this guy wasn't a stranger. The girls had seen him in Boo Radley's office. He was wearing a suit and striped bow tie.

"Chip Trafford," he said by way of introduction. "My first day as a knight errant."

"Dru Shelley," said Dru, holding out her hand as if to have it kissed.

He shook it gently. Squeezed just a tad.

Sam couldn't believe the sultry way Dru was looking at him. It was like some secret voice in her uterus was whispering directions for seduction.

The goddess was truly inside her.

■ ■ ■

"It's imperative you locate Chirburg," ordered an angry Skipper van Dine.

Boo couldn't win. He either had the Chirburg dirtbags who hated him because he was educated, or the Ivy Leaguers condescending to him because he wasn't educated enough. He was prep n'er-do-well to Skipper. An object of contempt.

"I can't believe the company is so hard up for talent we have to employ a man like Chirburg," Boo argued.

Skipper sighed. "I don't know why I'm bothering to explain this to you. Chirburg came from a family of bookies.

Numbers are second nature to him. And he's a dirt-bag. He talks the language of our typical broker. He can gang boss them, and they don't mutiny like they would with me. And my bonus depends on him making them productive."

Boo made a bunch of lame excuses and hung up. Chip had been grinning through the conversation. Wearing a Paul Stuart suit and an English Speaking Union bowtie.

"Van Dine," he scoffed. "Stays barricaded up on the sixth floor with the rest of the Ivy elite. Planning the grand vision."

"Yeah. Gets Chirburg to ride my ass for sales. That's grand."

"The company's completely schizophrenic. When they saw your background, they probably had you interviewed by van Dine's crowd. I got the treatment too."

"Yes. One of them had a stuffed owl in his office. Another had come back from gambling at Baden-Baden. I thought, these are my people."

Chip laughed. "You figured you'd rapidly leap over the riffraff. Join your natural element. Let me tell you a secret. Other than that tiny group, the whole company's riffraff.

"Think about it. The 'Main Street' brokerage all across the nation. And what is Main Street like in Dayton and Sandusky? We're talking snake-skin print trousers. Matching white belts and shoes. Has there been no pressure on you to join the Jaycees?"

Boo realized Chip was dead on. At least they had put him in a college town and not Bentonville, Arkansas.

Chip was still grinning at him.

"So, the cat swallowed the canary?"

"I have met the girl in question. Dru Shelley. Stage one is achieved. How are you coming along with Samantha? I mean we do have a competition, don't we?"

"What will you have in common with a sixteen-year-old girl?"

"We have a shared passion for Caffè Vanilla Frappuccino Blended Beverage. As long as the beans are ethically-sourced, of course. You see, we actually had what in this lax age might be termed a 'date.' And it's pretty clear she is a hot-to-trot little mulatto."

Chapter 56

"Man, you forget about the resources you got in your own backyard," said Lt. Wally Butts. "I went over to the campus and found some random psychology professor in her office."

Boo sat behind his computer, all ears, but pretending to work.

Butts said, "Suspicious of me? Lemme tell you. The original beady eyeball. I done tole the chief to let me wear civvies—folks around here don't respect uniforms—but oh no. But eventually she came around to talking with me."

"And?"

"Well, that's what's incredible. I laid out my dilemma. All them masks. And she made the connection right off. Just amazin'."

"Don't keep me in suspense."

"She said the masks are important, but first you got to focus on the victims. Football heroes. Frat boy. Lawyer."

He paused expectantly.

"Yes?" Boo asked.

"Don't you see? They're all like big symbolic male figures. The kind of men who run things. High school. College. Workplace. Somebody's really got a hard-on for them.

That's not her words, but you catch the drift. And then we get to the masks.

"Clinton, Pelosi, the street trash." He was getting excited, referring to notes. "Man, this is like one of them psycho killer movies where clues are being left. I'm being taunted. Catch me if you can.

"The street trash—they hate exclusive clubs, social privilege, the rich—scalps the frat boy. Clinton—she's gonna be the woman president, break into the old boys' network—nails the lawyer to his desk. Pelosi—she's like Title IX or equality for women in sports or something—breaks the jocks' arms."

Boo stared at him, half wondering if this could be true.

"Nails, scalping, broke arms, that's all got to mean something too. But that stumped her. She said she'd think on it."

"Did she have any thoughts on who the perpetrators might be?"

"Well, of course, she didn't want to venture because it's got campus commies written all over it, but I got it more narrowed down. This is wimmen for sure. Your diesel-dykes."

"Did the victims say it was women?"

"Naw, but you can't believe most of what victims tell you. You got nails in your hands, your imagination kinder rips free of its moorings."

■ ■ ■

"I'm making my move," Chip boasted. "Went over to Dru's house after she got out of school. Just rang the bell. She had warned her mother was a holy terror, but the old dyke wasn't around."

House full of strange goddess art. Weird cubical furniture. A dildo lying around in plain view.

"So did you have a pleasant visit?" Boo asked, disgusted.

"She's a sensual young thing. I actually got a little tongue."

"I can't believe how perverted you're being."

"Hey, you've got the hots so bad for Samantha, they're concerned about your mental stability back in the home office. That's why I'm here. Corporate concern."

"How very empathetic of them."

Chip slapped his palms on the arms of his chair. "Been a nosy-Parker, have we?"

"I need an interpreter around you."

"I understand you talked the manager into letting you into my room at the University Inn." He looked at Boo who maintained a poker face.

"And of course the suitcase wasn't there."

Boo had learned that to his despair.

"You know Trey was real preppie. Had everything monogrammed. Even his silk boxers."

"They will do that."

"I may start mailing things to the cops. One at a time. I know they're dumb, but they might be able to figure out what the initials stand for."

      ■ ■ ■

"Samantha . . . ?" began Mrs. Jaeger gently.

Sam looked up from her homework.

"I know this is personal. If you'd prefer to not answer . . ."

"I'd tell you anything," Sam said fervently.

"You had an unusual DNA test, didn't you?"

"Yes."

"My husband got a call from someone in Michigan. Quite adamant that you should be examined. As a professor, he was supposed to understand their need to develop a line of research that would result in a continuing series of publications."

Sam pressed her temples. "I'm sorry he's being bothered. My mother told me to do nothing until she returned. It was the last thing she said to me."

"It's not a bother. We're on your side in all things. But . . . you don't know your father, do you?"

"I've never seen him. But he's not a bum," she added defensively. "He sends us money. Quite a bit actually. It just sits in an account. My mom won't touch it. And he sends me a knife each year in some kind of cryptic message."

"What was your mother's maiden name?"

"McAlpin."

"So you are more or less pure Celt. Descended from the most ancient people of Europe."

"Yes," said Sam. "And I had a tail. I'm some kind of reptilian creature."

"No, Samantha," Mrs. Jaeger soothed. She hugged her, held her close and smoothed her hair.

Sam felt so completely relaxed, she wondered if she was asleep. She could see a wind swept grassy hill with a stone circle on the summit.

Chapter 57

Lt. Wally Butts was eating a bag of Doritos, the crunching amplified over the phone. Boo held the phone away from his ear, wished he'd stop chewing. Boo had called up, casually asking details about the mask felonies.

"All the witnesses said they stank to high heaven. But I figure that's meant as a distraction. Like a man robs a bank wearing a red bandanna around his neck. Teller looks at the red instead of his face."

That was when the bell went off in Boo's head. When he realized who was behind this. Quinn and Hog Man. That gave him trouble concentrating on his scheme. "Well . . ."

"Wal, whut?"

"I just . . . I'm pondering the timeline when these things began. If there's someone new in town that came about that time."

"Hmmm."

"I mean it might not be dykes. It might be . . . I don't know. Somebody you'd never suspect. Got the world by the tail. Money. Big future. Fancy tailoring. But a screw loose in his head."

"Well, that would narrow it. The business community's not real big in this town. And most'a them dress out of JC Penney's."

"So who does that leave?"

"I dunno. A few lawyers. Bunch'a doctors at the medical school."

"Or . . . maybe a stockbroker?" Boo suggested. "Just come to town. Maybe on temporary assignment."

"What are you driving at?"

"Have you ever seen that movie *American Psycho*? You ought to get it on Netflix. It's an eye-opener."

■ ■ ■

Quinn walked into Starbucks utterly lost in thought.

What was The Circle? A doomsday cult? Or just some constipated academicians? Sitting and watching the sun set through a stained glass window of Jacob's Ladder.

Everything that he knew—everything that he put in that stupid article that ended up in the *Times* was based in fact. And it led inexorably to aliens on the earth. Twelve elder gods each with a celestial body. Just like today.

And the tradition held. The Greek Pantheon only had twelve gods. No more, no less. When the cult of Dionysus emerged from Asia Minor, the Greeks shoved Hestia out so he could be seated at the table.

But there were gods in the heavens and gods on the earth. The Sumerian invocation to prayer:

"Hear the gods of the Heavens,
Hear the gods of the earth!
Hear the mighty olden gods!"

The gods on the earth were the Annunaki who shaped man out of clay. Taught him architecture, writing, technology, agriculture.

Then he saw Dru.

She waved gaily. "Hey, you."

She was with that shit from the brokerage. Chip somebody. St. Paul's and Yale.

She was sitting back in her chair, one leg stretched out with an ankle resting on Chip's knee.

Quinn knew she was just so pleased to make him jealous. So female.

Dru started to make introductions, but Quinn told her they were acquainted. And he certainly hoped the brokerage was more discreet about his account than they had been with Chirburg. Looking Chip straight in the eye.

"That was Boo running off at the mouth," said Chip all blasé. "Not me."

"Chip is going to teach me squash," put in Dru. "He says I'll need it for Oxford."

"You're Oxford?" Quinn asked Chip. He still hadn't sat down. And Chip was too cocky to stand up.

Chip said he went to college in Connecticut. Quinn knew the code. Too modest to mention Yale. Which left a snobbery spectrum between Trinity at the top and U-Conn at the bottom.

"U-Conn?" Quinn said deliberately.

"No, Yale," Chip replied, vaguely irritated. "Trumbull College."

Quinn knew he was going to enjoy doing this one. To the last gasp.

Chapter 58

Wally Butts was animated as he walked with Boo across the campus. "You were sure right about *American Psycho*. Watched it last night and it all kinder shaped up in my mind. Damn if it ain't got a nail gun in it. That must be where he got the i-dear. You know about copycat killings?"

"That's the point really," said Boo carefully. "I could swear this weird stuff just started up about the time Chip got here. I don't know what friends he has down here. But I'm sure you have methods of asking."

Wally looked smug. Like he knew all about using a rubber hose in a jail cell.

Boo told Wally that Chip drove a leased Porsche. Had it parked at the University Inn. The colonial styled building was right ahead, aged alumni drinking cheap white wine on the lawn. Some kind of fundraiser.

They walked around the back, and there was the car. Gleaming wax job. Chip had had it detailed. And Boo had gone by the leasing agency, shown his company credentials, and gotten duplicate keys made.

"He's always going in the trunk, rummaging around in there. Kind of secretive. Keeps stuff he won't leave in his hotel room."

Butts rubbed his chin. "Durn."

Boo said, "You know, to get into cars and rooms and such you've probably got to have a warrant. And that means probable cause and some judge giving you trouble. But . . ."

"But?"

"If I were to just open the trunk . . . and you were standing right here and saw something . . ."

"You'd do that?"

"I try to be a good citizen."

Boo popped the trunk. And there was Trey's suitcase. And a Hillary Clinton mask. And a nail gun.

Wally Butts' face stretched in amazement.

"Jackpot," he said softly.

■ ■ ■

At four in the afternoon, Sam sat at the kitchen table as Mrs. Jaeger made dinner. Searing a piece of beef before covering it with vegetables, potatoes, and beer to slow braise in the oven.

Mrs. Jaeger pulled out a chair and sat down opposite her. "Samantha, I've been reading about the name 'McAlpin'. It was originally Alpin or Alpen. A Pict name. The oldest known people to inhabit Scotland. Your lineage goes way back."

"I don't want a crest or a coat-of-arms," said Sam wryly.

Mrs. Jaeger folded her hands in her lap, thinking how to proceed. "Jungians believe in racial memory. It's called 'genetic memory' now. It exists at birth. Common experiences of your ancestors become part of you. Jung called it the 'collective unconscious.' It is probably encoded in your DNA."

"Yes?"

"Parapsychologists believe it includes subconscious memories of actual historical events. I believe this myself because I have visions."

Sam closed her eyes and breathed out. "So have I. But of recent events."

Mrs. Jaeger asked if she could do a little test and led Sam into the living room. She placed a straight back chair in front of a particular picture among all those on the wall. It was a watercolor of a big stone lying on its side, carved with Celtic spirals such as one sees on jewelry.

"This is an entrance stone to the prehistoric monument of Newgrange—a gigantic circular mound with a stone passageway shaped like a very long cross. It is 5000 years old, older than Stonehenge and the Egyptian pyramids. Now I want you to sit quietly and look at it. And tell me what you see."

Sam did as she was told. Kurt had said they went to these ancient sites and made paintings of them as a way of absorbing the past. Mrs. Jaeger would go into intense trances.

Three spirals coming out of a center. The Triskelion. They represent harmony.

The vision wasn't long in coming. A thrill ran through her like a mild shock of electricity. And she was standing in torchlight hearing singing and strange music of reed instruments and tom-tom-like drums. Heads were mounted on stakes. A slave girl was being dragged by Druids towards an altar stained with blood.

Sam stood up a panic fear, fist jammed between her teeth. Her face was twitching violently.

■ ■ ■

"What the fuck have you been doing down there?" Skipper van Dine bellowed over the phone.

"Um . . . business?" said Boo. He had gone back to the office feeling euphoric. Now he had to get his ass reamed.

"Don't get cute with me, you moron. You've been doing naked short selling."

"Um . . . sort of."

"Sort of? Chit-Chat blew up in everyone's face on Wall Street, and you're down there shorting the thing without borrowing the stock from someone before you sold it forward. Do you not think you've been noticed?"

"Well . . . there was really no stock to borrow. The insiders wanted to dump theirs on the opening day."

Skipper was screeching. "So you just go blatantly illegal!"

"Yeah, but plenty of people do it."

"What do you think we are? Fucking Lehman Brothers? We are the Main Street brokerage. Big-cap stocks. Buy and hold. We don't help clients go on speculative binges. Who is Beth Bolek?"

"A high school kid. Very insightful about the market. It's okay. Her old man would have been good for any losses."

"A school kid? We've got the SEC all over our asses, and I've got to tell them it was an underage kid. Who made the twenty-one-five million?"

"Um . . . I did."

"*You did?* You, Townsend-fucking-Radley made twenty-one-five? You don't make that kind of money ever! I barely made a million last year, and that was with my bonus."

"That's it, isn't it? I'm supposed to be nobody so you can feel good about yourself. Know you're higher up the food chain."

"My soul-sucking wife is on me night and day about a house in the Hamptons. You can't buy—you can't *rent* a house in the Hamptons on my income. Even on the North Shore. And you clip twenty-one and a half million. You're fired! You lock the door on that office and get out of it!"

"You don't have the authority to order that."

"Well I'll get the authority in about fifteen minutes!"

There was no time to lose. Boo wired a lawyer in Curaçao to open a Swiss bank account for him. Sent him the money in his personal account to Curaçao immediately after for forwarding.

Paused and thought. No, there was no time for contemplation. He wired all the Buggaron money as well. It was just for safe-keeping. He'd give it back. Eventually.

■ ■ ■

Quinn sat on the dry-stone wall with a biker named Sweathog. One more dumb brute who cheerfully did his bidding.

Harley parked next to a stone monument to the Daniel Boone Trail.

The sun was setting, and the trees were filled with trash birds. College kids going past yacking into cell phones. The biggest decision they faced each day was who to eat dinner with.

The biker was linebacker size, shirtless underneath his denim jacket. Iron cross tattoo on his chest. A permanent malevolent look on his face. He had once been in a duel where each man was given a ballpeen hammer and their left wrists handcuffed. Hooked his opponent's hammer and disarmed him, shattered his skull in one blow. All under five seconds.

No one could keep track of the pills the man popped. Rainbows, blues, leapers, purple hearts. He'd wake up with the shakes each day, chew aspirin, and shoot speed into a vein.

Quinn aimed a finger at him. "I think it's time for you to do your thing," he said.

The biker revved his engine, bounced up a couple of stone steps and took off up the brick path onto the campus.

Chapter 59

Boo was throwing some personal things in a cardboard box. He knew there was to be an armed private security guard at the door in the morning. He answered his cell.

"Um . . . it's Chip. You know that one phone call you hear they give you? Well this is it."

Now this was pure pleasure. "What are you doing in jail? Get caught with an underage girl?"

"It's crazy. I don't understand it. I'm being framed for all kinds of berserk crimes." His voice dropped to a whisper, "They've got me in a cell with some drug meltdown biker. The guy's got fingernails like bear claws. The cops just laugh at me. Say if I want to talk about anything, they might find me another cell."

"So why don't you talk to them?"

"About what? I haven't done anything. I don't even understand all the shit they say I'm accused of. I had Trey's suitcase. Big 'effing deal. You know where that came from. Call them and tell them."

"I dunno. I'm kind of busy right now. I just got fired."

Chip didn't seem to hear. "He says he's going to gouge my eyes out!"

"That would be a problem."

Chip was pleading. "Man, don't leave me here with this biker. He is a total lunatic. I'm afraid to go to sleep. He says he's going to *gouge my eyeballs out.*"

"Maybe I'll take a swing by the jail later. See if you need any reading material or anything."

■ ■ ■

Quinn was back at his house, a light rain pattering on the roof. It was 7:30. Dru called.

"Hey, you," she said in almost a whisper. "Thinking about you."

"Oh?"

A bit of silence. "You're not jealous I played squash with Chip are you?"

"Not in the least."

"I was re-reading your *Times* article on Nibiru," she said. "Do you really believe it?"

"I didn't at the time. It was meant as a joke. But now I wonder."

"Why?"

"Because all the evidence points in that direction. It was not just the gods on the earth—the ones the Sumerians called Annunaki—but the big gods from the heavens made state visits. The Temple of Anu was called 'the pure sanctuary.' It was a house to receive someone who descended from Heaven. And when Anu came there was great panoply. His wives and daughters were paraded to a part of the temple called the House of the Golden bed of the Goddess Antu.

"A feast was prepared. An astronomer-priest mounted to the topmost tower and watched in a particular place in the sky for the rising of a planet named the Great Anu of Heaven. He would then recite a liturgy 'To the One who Grows Bright.'

"And throughout the land, there were bonfires and feasting in celebration. He was the father of the Annunaki gods and had brought man the art of brick-making, the building of cities, metallurgy, agriculture."

Dru purred like a cat. "It soothes me to hear you talk. I'm imagining I'm touching your lips with my fingertips. Can you feel it?"

"Yes."

"Did you like my naked body?"

"Very much."

"Are you afraid of me?"

"Cautious is a better word."

■ ■ ■

"Hello?" said Samantha.

"This . . . is your broker. Boo Radley. Please don't hang up!"

Sam closed her eyes in exasperation. Her experience with Mrs. Jaeger had left her feeling drained. And now this bozo.

Boo paused a breathless moment.

"I'm here," she said.

"Thank you. You're exercising admirable restraint. What I am about to tell you is truly important."

"Okay. What?"

"Do you have pen and paper? I want you to write something down."

"Okay."

"It's the name of a bank. And then a twenty-digit number. Are you ready?"

"Yes."

He gave her the numbers. Had her read them back.

"You know I'm obsessed with you . . ."

"I gathered."

"I'm going out of the country. If something happens to me, I want you to have this as a legacy. I'll explain later."

He waited a time. "Good-bye."

Sam hung up. Looked at Kurt. Showed him the paper.

"Is that a Swiss bank account number?" asked Kurt.

■ ■ ■

Quinn had dozed off for a moment. His watch said eight o'clock. Time to think about his usual solitary dinner. He had bought a monkfish filet. Would steam it with celery and fennel.

He poured out a neat Scotch in a squat glass, looked out on the dark trunks of the trees. A faint tremble of lightning appeared on the distant horizon over the pasture.

Dru called again. Speaking in a low voice.

"I'm writing my *Gilgamesh* paper on the wild man Enkidu."

"Oh?"

"Enkidu is seduced by the temple prostitute and becomes civilized. She is a conduit of divinity. A mystical connection to the life force, to the love goddess Inanna."

"I see."

"Gilgamesh had built the great city of Ur. Ziggurats and all. But he's a tyrant who bangs the wives and daughters of his subjects. The new reformed Enkidu comes, and they wrestle. I can see the scene. Sweaty bodies. Rippling muscles. Like the wrestling scene in D. H. Lawrence's *Sons and Lovers*. Kind of homoerotic.

"At last Enkidu prevails. And Gilgamesh becomes not merely a noble person, but such friends with Enkidu that they are as one. And it's Shamhat's doing that the duality is joined."

Quinn thought about her lithe little body. Desire burned in him like flame crawling up a newspaper.

"I want to play that role for you," she whispered.

■ ■ ■

Dusk had given way to darkness as Boo walked down Chastain Street past a noisy bar. The unrelenting revelry of college kids. Smoking cigs back in fashion. The moral scolds never could understand equal and opposite reactions.

Everything seemed tickety-boo, as one used to say. He

would get into another line of work. Being idle rich. And yes, he was going to indulge in the luxury of a little gloating. Old Chip was in a place that St. Paul's and Yale had not prepared him for.

The town police station was an old firehouse brick building with paint peeling metal bars on the windows and wire reinforced glass behind it.

Battleship gray interior. Padlocked rack of pump shotguns and AR-15s. A countertop with Lt. Wally Butts behind it on the phone, a half-eaten package devil egg sandwich in his free hand.

Wally Butts hung up the phone and folded his hands over the contour of his stomach.

"Oh man, I just got finished with one of them true-crime TV shows. I mean they are pissing their drawers to get going on this. This is big-time lollapalooza. 'Preppie Mayhem', they're calling it. They say it's a working title. Woo-doggies. I'm gone have to control the media rush."

"How's Chip taking his new celebrity?"

"It's like there's an electrical short buzzing inside his head. Circuits not connecting."

"Who's that in the cell with him?"

Butts laughed. "That's purty funny actually. Some wigged-out biker. Drove his Harley right onto the campus lawn. Came up to a campus cop, stopped, and hocked a big loogie on him. Just sat there with a mule-eatin'-briars grin on his face."

"And?"

"Cop tased the shit out of him. Hooked him up and

brought him in here. We'll prob'ly kick him loose in the morning. After he's had an accidental fall and hit his head a couple'a times."

Uncontrolled screaming ripped through the building. It rose and fell without a break. A banshee wail out of hell that stood Boo's hair on end.

Wally's lips formed a tight line. "What the fu—?"

Boo followed him as he leaped up, grabbed the key ring to the cells and hustled into the back.

Wally's jaw dropped in disbelief.

In that horrifying moment, Boo knew he wouldn't have to wait for an afterlife. He could be punished right here.

The biker was crouched on Chip's body like a feeding baboon. He had ripped open the chest, cracked the ribs, torn out the heart. And was eating it.

His head turned towards them. His eyes were empty of any human emotion. And his face was dripping red with gore.

Boo bit his lips until they bled. He knew he was screaming, but his ears were filled with a roaring sound.

Wally was turning the key in the barred door.

"No! Don't!" Boo bleated.

■ ■ ■

"Is that Mozart?" asked Dru.

"You're certainly knowledgeable about music," said Quinn.

"My mom listens to it. She says it makes her 'one with

goddess,' even though a man wrote it. Which pisses her off. And in school, Evangeline's dad teaches music theory at the university. We all exchange information. Push us along in life."

"That's helpful."

"So what are your plans in life?" asked Dru over the phone. "You've seen that academe sucks."

"I think I'm about finished here. Think I'll go back to Maine. Buy a sailboat to live on. In winter go down to Martha's Vineyard. It's cold, but you don't get iced-in like Maine. In summer, maybe sail as far up as Newfoundland."

"Have you ever thought of sailing the Atlantic?"

"I could do that. I'm used to loneliness."

"You could come see me in England. Take me up into the Shetlands. Southern Norway. Maybe as far as the Faeroes."

"You're going to England?"

"I've decided on Worcester College, Oxford," said Dru. "There's a lake and a canal and cricket fields on the grounds. Mix of Medieval and Georgian buildings. I'll have an old black 'push-bike' as they call it. Buy books at Blackwell's on Broad Street across from the busts of Roman Emperors. Maybe take up Field hockey like Kate Middleton."

"So beyond that, have you formulated any life ambitions?"

She spoke in a low voice. "I think I'd like to be lethally beautiful."

"You've achieved that."

A long pause. "And I want a serious date with you."

■ ■ ■

Boo watched in horror as the biker beat Wally Butts to the floor with his fists, took the Glock off him and hammered him unconscious.

Sweat-hog grabbed Boo by the necktie and dragged him out the front door. His bearded face was smeared with gore, his eyes empty of all human meaning.

"I'm late for somewhere," he said.

It was the only coherent thing the man said the whole time.

A cop car stood there. The biker flung Boo in the back behind the wire grill. Jumped in the front. Gunned the engine and put on the siren and lights.

He must have hit ninety going up Chastain Street, drunk college kids scattering. Boo tried to talk, but his voice was strangled.

Boo knew he was flying on the outer edges of life. He was losing his hold on reality and would soon be a flame passing into the afterlife to be snuffed out.

He could feel Dru cup her fingers inside his. She was drawing him into the depths. Her eyes were soft and understanding as though she had seen this so many times before.

"You will pass through the seven gates," she said. "I will be waiting." Then she lowered her eyes and was gone.

Two cop cars sat nose-to-nose blocking the streets, lights flashing. A bullhorn barked something incoherent. The biker smashed into the two engine blocks with a gigantic WHAM!

Boo hit the grill, crashed to the floor, lay there numb like a fire was dying in him. Slowly he pulled himself up like he was rising from a watery deep towards the light. He couldn't breathe or even whimper.

The biker's head had gone through the windshield. Slowly, he pulled it back out, leaving a clean round hole. He shook glass from his hair and painfully climbed down from the wrecked cruiser.

Officer Buck shot him in the crotch with a pump shotgun, blowing him onto his back where he twitched and shivered and struggled. Blowing bloody saliva out of his mouth.

"He's doin' the 'Funky Chicken'," said Buck, and all the cops laughed.

"That is not the least bit funny," scolded a rotund woman wagging her finger. Butterscotch hemp dress with a rope belt. Birkenstocks. Tote bag a giveaway from an academic conference.

She was surrounded by a knot of faculty members who had come out of an Ingmar Bergman film festival in the little art theater. They seemed unmoved by the gore. More interested in vindicating their dislike of the police.

"You're trained in this," shouted another. "Do something!"

Buck shrugged. "He's DRH."

"What does that mean?"

He grinned big. "Dead Right Here."

"I'm telling you, you've got to do something, or I'll have your badge!"

He looked into space, then bent down and made the sign of the cross. "In the name of the Father, the Son . . ."

They burst into self-righteous fury.

"You jack-booted neo-Nazi monster!"

"Cold-blooded fascist killer!"

"Storm-trooper goon!"

Chapter 60

Boo knocked himself out with alcohol, but woke up at first light. Showered and started frantically packing a light bag. He had skedaddled for Italy many a time as a teenager with his Mom. Father in a rage, probably because some swindle hadn't panned out. They'd just get the hell out of Dodge.

Mephisto shoes for walking. Espadrilles for the beach. Roll-up Ecuadorian straw hat. Doing a mental checklist, he realized his passport was at the office.

And there were liable to be cops there. And a company man from the next town going through his computer. He phoned Wally Butts, asked how he was getting on.

Wally was in high spirits. "Woo, I done forget how bad it hurts to get pistol whipped. But my face'll provide good visuals. Docs say brain damage remains a question mark, but I'm thinking I'm okay. Can do the sobriety field test."

"It was a night to remember."

"And how. Man, things have gone nucleer. Economic realities done turned bright. True-crime writers. Reality TV. Some of them already at the airport rentin' vans. Got me a Noo York agent, lust went bat-shit crazy over the biker cannibalism angle.

"Talking to this movie-maker on the phone, ask him what we do first. He says—get this—he can't 'dissect the long process of development.' I ask you, who talks like that?"

"Hollywood simoleons. I love the smell of it," Boo enthused.

"Lordy, I need me a financial shot in the arm something awful. We ain't got what you call a generous incentive program here on the force."

"Well, you deserve all the credit for cracking the case."

"Chief'll be nosing around trying to horn in on that. You bet'chore bippy. But, hey, I figger' maybe midafternoon on going out to a rough and tumble local bar and celebratin' if you want to join me."

"Thanks, but I have to make a business trip. Um . . . has there been anything else? Anything you're supposed to attend to?"

"You mean like locking yore brokerage and puttin' yore ass on the street? Yeah, they been calling. Like we're some security guard service."

"And?"

"And nothing. Ever'body's got his own legal issues. When my ex-wives hear about my change of circumstances . . . not good."

■ ■ ■

Boo unlocked the silent office at eight o'clock. He didn't seem to be on anybody's radar. He opened the bottom drawer of his desk and found the passport right where he expected.

He was condemned to be free. Who said that? Some Frenchman?

What would he do first? Go to Milan and order a custom pair of Louis Vuitton shoes? Select the heel height and stitching? No, the cobbler would be in no hurry. He'd have to keep on the move.

And the uplift was he had cheated death. Evaded the dark goddess. He felt bulletproof. Or charmed, living in a story with mythic contours.

He'd buy a nondescript Fiat and drive south in search of the sun. A chameleon blending with the landscape. Happy to be on earth. Following a fresh and inspiring path.

And however unlikely it had seemed before, he knew Samantha would come to him. Close the door on their pasts. Synchronize their dreams.

He looked up with annoyance to see Marvin Pfiezer struggling in with his walker. This was new. He used to use a metal cane. Swollen bare ankles with some kind of scaly eczema on them.

And behind him, Mrs. Adele Ader in a big Jackie-O style sunhat.

"I got some ideas to turn this investment climate around," Marvin announced. "I hear you got Adele in annuities. What made you do that?"

"We're dating," she beamed. "I think he's brilliant. And we're so well matched. He likes an olive in his martini, I like a twist."

"She's sure put a spring in my step," he said, beaming back. Looking up from his hunched over posture. "I think she ought'a be the face of Revlon. I'm getting' my tattoo removed by laser surgery. She thinks it'll make me more distinguished. She's Southern gentility, ya know."

"Look, the office is closed, and I'm heading out."

"Whadda ya mean heading out? You looted the accounts and bugging out?"

"Of course not."

"Not so fast," said Adele. "My late husband, the judge, said I was a master at spotting a shifty-eyed character. And there's something distinctly fishy about a closed office on a weekday."

"What? I thought I was 'dear boy'? The word-of-mouth phenomenon."

"Not no more," snarled Marvin. "Not with this level of customer disservice. Call the cops, Adele. We'll show this ass-wipe some shock and awe."

Boo tried to push past, bumped Marvin who fell with a clatter over his walker.

"You've hurt him!" Adele shrieked. And pulled a small .32 caliber revolver out of her purse.

Boo gaped at it in horror. But she was fumbling for a cell phone. Boo smacked her to the floor with a flat hand blow, kicked Marvin who was clutching at his ankles, but got tripped up in the walker and fell himself.

And Adele Ader sunk her dentures into his hamstring just above his heel. Bit in hard.

It felt like the teeth were made of titanium. Boo screamed in agony. She was chewing through his flesh.

He screamed and screamed.

"You got a navel ring?" Sam said, astonished.

"Look." Dru lifted her shirt to show the little glittery bangle. "Sexy or what?"

"What did your mother say?"

"I told her you liked them, and I had a girl crush on you. She said 'okay then.' She has big hopes of me being a lesbo with you. Last night I got the lecture on how the gender ratios were so skewed in college that the girls were all claiming to be lesbians until graduation. She said they'd learn to prefer it for a lifetime once they found how awful men were in the sack."

"Your mom talks to you about sex? Mine doesn't talk to me about anything."

"Well, she's usually bustling at something. Kind of lecturing over her shoulder. It embarrasses us both. But that doesn't stop her."

Dr. Clearwire came out of the principal's office. He was wearing his cap and a t-shirt that said "Moral Relativist." It wasn't the wisest choice.

"I don't have the slightest sympathy," said Principal Peevey coldly. "I would think the example of the coach should have sufficed as a warning."

"I can't help myself," said Clearwire, in a trembling voice. "The two of them together are some kind of synergy. I lose all rational thought."

"I can certainly agree with that. And I can also tell you've lost all control of the class."

"Did that vicious Emerson . . . ?"

"Emerson didn't say anything. He's very in charge of his life that young man. But word is all over the school about your sex obsession with the girls. And the students are mocking you on social media. And the sheer stupidity of having marijuana on your person. I'm going to have to suspend you pending an investigation."

"But you can't. I've . . . I've got a PhD."

"I have no other choice."

"I've got journal articles."

"I'm not impressed."

"It's because you've been accused of not being in control of the school, isn't it?"

"I don't see any need to talk with you about this."

Sam and Dru looked at each other.

"Is he talking about us?" Dru asked. "The synergy?"

■ ■ ■

At the counter in the diner, Lt. Wally Butts ordered Salisbury steak, mashed potatoes and gravy, green beans, sweet tea. He said, "Aw man, it just gets messier and more fucked up. I mean ol' Marv opens up with the .32, parks four rounds in Radley, but catches Miz Ader square in the head with the fifth one."

"Sounds unpleasant," said Quinn. He had the barbecue plate with coleslaw and fries. Smoky hot sauce.

"Not half like the night the biker ate the heart out of another stock broker. I mean Hollywood is jes' lovin' ever minute of it. It's the South the way they want it. Only problem is we're not down in the Mississippi Delta or somewhere. It's too upscale 'round here for them. Too New South."

"Too many professors around."

"Yeah, they'd prefer hillbillies with moonshine jugs and rifles."

"What will happen with Marvin?"

"That's up to the DA. His doctor says he's got pre-dementia. There was evidence of a fight. Miz Ader had a bruise down on side of her face. And she had chewed clean through that Radley's hamstring. It was when he tried to get up and run, fell flat down, that Marv shot him."

"This used to be such a quiet town."

"Tell me about it. Other than the fake rape claims outta the coeds, there was nothing else. All'a sudden I'm in the middle of a shit storm. But I have to say I'm enjoying the Hollywood money angle."

"Money's always helpful."

"Say, did your ex-wife ever turn up?"

"I sure hope not."

But on the subject of money, what was really concerning Quinn was where his money was. Still snug in the broker-age account? Or had something fishy indeed been going on with Boo.

Chapter 61

With Mr. Clearwire gone, Professor Jaeger came and gave an hour lecture on the symbolism of *Gilgamesh* that had the class utterly enthralled and the girls in love with him.

"Man as authority figure," gushed Dru afterwards. "Wearing a suit and a polka dot bowtie. Oooo, baby. That just gets to my vitals. Do you think Mrs. Jaeger would mind if I slept with her husband?"

"I think she'd mind a great deal," said Samantha.

"I am trying to be funny."

"Ha-ha."

"Why are you in a sour mood?"

"I can't help it. I'm so in love, sometimes, I can't stand it."

"What's wrong with that?"

"I want something to happen with Kurt. And instead it's like a shadow is hovering over us." Her eyes started to water. "The Jaegers are waiting for some magical powers to come out of me."

"What on earth are you talking about?"

"I made the flag fall over. I blew up the clay heads and the lab beakers. I can change the path of a knife with my mind. I . . . see visions . . . of things that really happen."

Dru stared at her. "Ooo-kay."

"You don't believe me, do you?"

"Um . . . no."

"I saw Cressie Moonchild's spirit the night she died. I'm convinced if I walk past her murderer I'll know who it is.

"My spirit left my body and passed through doors. During a thunderstorm the love goddess came out of me in the most devastating way. And now the war goddess is emerging. I'm certain I'm going to kill someone."

"You know," said Dru, "I'm not real good about other people's delusions. I mean I have plenty of my own. Why don't you talk to the Jaegers about this."

"I do talk to them. Mrs. Jaeger is psychic. We did a séance, and my voice emerged from her. My voice begging Kurt to . . . to do me. She sees and hears everything." Sam started crying. "I can't handle this stress."

Dru was looking at her warily. It was too much information in a rush.

Sam said, "I want to show the Jaegers the skull."

"Why?"

"I don't know. It's just part of the mysteries that are wrapped around me to the point I'm smothering."

■ ■ ■

"What is this? An art gallery?" said a uniformed Lt. Wally Butts, coming into the Lucifer's Legion clubhouse.

Quinn had had the gang scatter, knowing the visit was inevitable. He and Hog Man were the sole occupants of the building. And the paintings of Samantha and Dru were stashed. Leaving the multiple ones of the cosmos.

"How's about a PBR?" said Hog Man from behind the bar.

"Don't mind if I do," said Wally. "Although I'm old enough to remember when they were called 'Blues.'"

"You are dating yourself," said Quinn. "This is now a hipster drink. It's considered ironic."

Wally wandered the dingy building looking at the paintings of the zodiac, eclipses of the sun, black holes. "I don't get it," he said.

"I've tried to raise the tone of the club," said Quinn.

"Man, ain't he ever," said Hog Man. "We get lectures on ancient myths and shit. It's opened our eyes to things."

"The art is Jake Milroy's. He rides with us sometimes. It's kind of an overflow from his house. You know Jake? The one whose daughter was murdered."

"Yeah, I know him." Wally looked utterly stumped. "And you, Quinn Shaw are part of this?"

"I like to ride a hog. Hair in the breeze. Joy of the open road. We get together and ride to Myrtle Beach for the biker convention. Sometimes go 'cross Alabama all the way to the Redneck Riviera just for the hell of it."

"So what do these ol' boys do for a living? Boost cars? Deal meth?"

Quinn laughed. "Most of them got day jobs. Mechanics and such. A few are on disability." He laughed again. "Probably mental disability."

"I'll say," said Wally. "That one we had in the jail couldn't have held down any job except animal in a cage at the zoo."

"Sweat-hog was a tragic case," said Hog Man sadly. "Got blowed up in his tank in Desert Storm. Heard a constant ringing in his head. I don't know what controlled substances he imbibed, but he shore done some of them."

"Yeah," said Wally, looking sly. Kind of kidding them along. "I imagine there's a little dope dealing going on here and there with these boys."

Quinn sighed. "I know where you're headed. You're thinking RICO, that racketeering statute. I got a patchy knowledge of it. Prosecutor's wet dream. Find a mere two crimes in a ten-year period, and you arrest the whole gang. Seize their bank accounts. Get them to roll over on one another.

"You're thinking you got Sweat-hog's rampage. If you could find something else. The problem with that, is none of these boys has a bank account."

He paused and drank from his beer.

"And with all those crimes on that lengthy RICO list—murder, arson, rape, all of them—you know the one that's missing?"

"What's that?"

"Cannibalism."

Chapter 62

"You're going to the prom with Emerson?" said Sam astonished.

She and Dru were in the Goodwill where Dru did all her shopping.

"Mom had to say 'yes.' You remember what Emerson said. Race always trumps gender."

"What on earth are you going to wear?"

Dru held up a tiny dress icy-blue dress on a hanger. Spaghetti straps.

"That . . . you're petite, okay? But that was meant for a ten-year-old. It doesn't even cover your tush."

"I think it's perfect. What are you going to wear?"

■ ■ ■

Right in the middle of fencing with an opponent, Samantha began to get the buzzing that said a vision was coming on. She felt dizzy, dropped her foil and staggered off the mat and Hopped down on a bleacher.

She waved off people asking what was wrong. Bent forward and hugged her knees. Stared at the floor blankly. The blood hummed in her veins.

She could see Cherry talking to Kurt. Acting pitiful.

"I'm feeling so low. Daddy just sits around the house in his underwear drinking and talking to a stuffed deer head. He believes if he talks to the deer, the state Whitetail population will regenerate."

"Well, he has a lot to worry him," said Kurt.

Sam wanted to spit. He was being sympathetic.

"Aren't you just ready for school to end? I'm so sick of it."

"It's not been a good year."

"We don't really have to go to college. Daddy didn't, and he's done really well in life. All that wasted time with books that have nothing to do with earning a living. You could go to work for Daddy in sales. I'm sure you'd be great at it."

Kurt was shaking his head.

"They say it's best for girls to have their children young." She was looking straight into his eyes. "We could get married at eighteen and make a baby."

"That's nothing I want to think about now," said Kurt. He was trying to edge away.

Cherry slid her hands into Kurt's waistband and held to him. Her bosom was nearly touching him, her face slanted upward.

"Oh, I'd never try to trap you. My momma has Norplant in my arm. She says prom night is always dangerous for girls. If you're not going to the prom with Samantha, you could take me."

"I don't see myself in a rented white suit with pink piping around the lapels."

"You could dress any way you wanted. I wouldn't care.

It's just you I want to be with. And we could leave early. Normally Daddy hosts one of the big after-parties, but he's not this year because he's feeling so miserable. But we could drive to our lake house. No one expects me back before dawn anyway."

She tugged his shirt-tail out and ran her hands along his waist, feeling his flesh. "I would make it worth your while."

"Sorry, Cherry. That's generous, but I have a girlfriend."

Cherry burst into tears. "You are so mean! I hate you! I love you. I hate you! I hope you go blind from jacking off!"

Cherry ran away, and the vision abruptly ended like turning off a TV.

Sam stood up slowly. Her mouth opened and closed. She felt contaminated. She hated Cherry so much she could kill her. And yet she was relieved. Kurt had been faithful.

She knew she wouldn't tell Kurt. She couldn't have him thinking she could spy on him like that. But despite the wringing-out experience, she was starting to feel better.

Chapter 63

Quinn and Hog Man told the brokerage secretary to take off early, and slid quietly into Boo's old office where Skipper van Dine sat hunched over the computer.

"So, what's become of all the big money? Like say the Buggaron account?"

"It's vanished. That why I'm here." Van Dine looked up. "Who the hell are you?"

"I'm the agent of the owner of that money. You've received verification from a lawyer in Curaçao. And, you're going to track the electronic trail and find where it went. And one more thing. We're not supplicants here."

Quinn could feel van Dine giving the once over to his two-button linen-and-cotton blazer, the tie with crossed squash rackets.

"We've got the full resources of the brokerage on this. Now I don't answer to you. Is that a Dartmouth . . .

"No, Hamilton."

"Oh," he sniffed with a faint note of disdain. "Do they have a decent bar in this town with cask ales and oysters?"

"We're inland, so no oysters. Plus it's May. Remember? And it's a college town. You can't avoid kids. Beer-slinger dives."

"I feared it would be a desert. NASCAR re-tards. But I'm right busy, so if you'll excuse me."

Quinn rubbed his chin thoughtfully. "You know it's funny how just out of the blue things change up on you. Have a stroke. Get hit by a car. Wake up in the hospital paralyzed. Suddenly nothing's ever the same again. Well in your case, change just walked through the door."

Hog Man clamped van Dine's shoulders and pinched in with powerful fingers. Van Dine squirmed and squealed.

"Oh, I know. In your understanding of things, if I let you walk out of here, you run to the cops. Or getting no satisfaction there, you flee to the airport, stay in the crowds, afraid to even use the men's room, fly home.

"But we are called 'Legion' for a reason. We know where you live, where your kids go to school, where your wife gets her hair done. You'll never be able to trust a repairman, the pool boy, an electrician again. Anybody in a van might just spirit you away to pain you never dreamed of."

"No! Don't. We know the money was wired to a bank in Curaçao. And from there to Panama. They have fucking corporate secrecy in Panama. They can't divulge the names of the owners of a corporation. It's a dead-end."

"And your big brokerage doesn't have any pull down there? Any inside whatever?"

"Well, we might. I don't know yet." He was stalling.

"Now that you're having a special moment of clarity, I suppose you've claimed his cell phone from the cops. Seen what calls he made the last days of his life."

"He . . . he only made two calls. One to an airline. Tickets to Italy. The other was to a Samantha Fitzhugh. She seems to be a client."

"Well, you keep working on the problem and don't go home to New York until you've solved it. And keep what I said in mind. Because we're going to give you the first installment on pain."

Van Dine struggled frantically. "What? What do you mean?"

"Man, you are the squirmiest dude," said Hog Man. "Now, you'll prob'ly pass out from the pain. But don't worry. You won't bleed to death."

Hog Man held van Dine's hand to the table and snipped off his little finger with a Leatherman Multi-tool.

Van Dine screamed himself into unconsciousness.

■ ■ ■

"We're going to have a séance, and I get to spend the evening drooling over Kurt and Professor Jaeger," said Dru all excited.

"You really find Kurt's father alluring?" said Samantha, a tad jealous that she felt the same way.

"Oh lord, if he were my father . . . I would be such an obedient girl. No smart mouth. No backtalk. No arguments just for the hell of it like I do with my mom."

"Your mom's okay with a séance?"

"I didn't tell her. If she knew of Missus Jaeger's powers, she wouldn't leave her alone, badgering her to display woman power. It would be Dyke Central at the Jaeger house."

"So what does she think you're doing?"

"Having a romance with you."

Sam gaped at her.

"Mom's highly pleased I'm staying over the night and sleeping in the same bed with you," said Dru. "Can you imagine a parent like that?"

"Am I going to have to kiss you in front of her to continue this charade?" asked Sam.

"I don't know. We'll just play it as it goes."

Dru gave Sam the bag with the giant skull. "There. Now you owe me big time. And I intend to collect. Prom night I'm telling my mother I'm spending with you. And you're going to back me on this."

"What are you planning? Emerson?"

Dru gave a mysterious smile. "Emerson's a beard. I'm going on a journey of descent. To discover my realm."

"What? Surely not with that man. Have you even made a pro-and-con list?"

Chapter 64

"The Great Flood," said Prof. Jaeger, "was a punishment for the Nifilhim having intercourse with the women of the earth. They were rebellious angels. Cast out of heaven. Their children were giants."

Kurt, Dru, and Sam listened intently. The skull sat on a coffee table in the living room. Outside, leaves clicked in a light breeze. Blossoming dogwood was white down in the park.

"It is only a fragment in the Bible. Just before Noah and the Flood. The *Book of Jubilees* is a Hebrew work not recognized by Christians save for the Orthodox Ethiopian Church. It tells the story of Genesis in greater detail. Particularly the fallen angels who mated with mortal women.

"And in Sumerian myth, it is also quite explicit. Their Noah is named Ziusudra. The gods held a council and voted to destroy mankind. The god Enki defied them and saved Ziusudra, his family and the animals.

"Elongated skulls have been found all over the world. There was a custom of binding infants heads with fabric and leather straps to grow into the elongation. The Flathead Indians were famous for it in America. UFO buffs claim that gods descended from the sky. Giants with these sorts of skulls and massive brains. And that humans tried to imitate their appearance. 'Cone heads' are found in museums throughout South America.

"But giants, now that's something to ponder. I have heard of these tucked away in museums. We should have it DNA tested."

What bothered Samantha most was she suddenly realized questions would be asked about where she got the thing. Would she admit she had left a man tied up in a closet? And she knew Mrs. Jaeger was reading her mind.

■ ■ ■

After dinner, they lit a single candle, held hands around the table, and watched Mrs. Jaeger go into a trance. Shortly, she began to speak.

It was a purring voice, but clearly Dru's. Voicing her carnal desires with an almost religious fervor.

"I would so bang Professor Jaeger. Right here on the table with everyone watching. Starkers. My ankles on his shoulders. Clutching his biceps."

Sam stared at Dru who had her eyes closed, completely unmoved by the revelation of her private thoughts.

Mrs. Jaeger began to twitch. The blood drained from her face. She trembled and shivered as if in the grip of a strange force. Her voice became guttural, and she spoke in a language that Sam had never imagined. And as she talked, Sam's head began to swim. Lights went off behind her eyes.

Sam had entered a dark world that seemed utterly forbidding.

Black trees dripping with rain. Boggy ground.

Hooded crows filled the trees cawing in baleful cries. Corpses lay everywhere. Broken weapons. Spears, swords, shields. Men face down in the bog water. Headless bodies. Heads mounted on stakes. The crows were drifting down from the trees to peck the eyeballs of the dead. Eating the softest part first.

Dru was with another girl Sam didn't know. They beckoned to her. And Sam knew who they were. The trio of Celtic battle goddesses called the Morrigan. Badb, Macha and Nemain.

She was Badb-Catha—the Battle Raven. The battlefield was the land of Badb.

A hideous wailing filled the air and died away.

Sam blinked her eyes, awake to the dining room.

Dru, Kurt and Prof. Jaeger had their eyes closed.

Mrs. Jaeger had fallen silent, exhausted, and breathing in the pattern of someone asleep.

Chapter 65

"Please don't hurt me," whimpered Skipper van Dine. He was unshaven, unwashed, his Paul Smith shoes badly scuffed. He'd spent the night in the hospital. Refusing to say how he lost his finger. Now spaced out on drugs. Left hand a big bandage wad.

"We think it's only too reasonable for you to restore your client money that was stolen," said Quinn in a reasonable tone.

"I've been on the phone with the CEO all day. He won't budge. He says it's an insurance matter. And they think the . . . um . . . origin of the money might be a sound defense."

"Is this what you do with any money that comes from the Caribbean? I can't imagine it's very good for client relations."

"I don't know." He was crying now. "I don't know what's wrong with them. Chirburg disappearing . . . it's all just weird."

"I mean we can't make the firm replace the money. But perhaps you have a personal fortune . . ."

"What? I don't have that kind of money! Do you know what it costs to live in Manhattan? Nagging cunt of a wife like a vacuum cleaner on my wallet."

Quinn shrugged. "Well, I'm fresh out of ideas. I guess

we'll have to leave it in your capable hands. Whatever is left of them."

He nodded at Hog Man. The Leatherman appeared.

"No!" van Dine shrieked. "I tell you, he was obsessed with the Fitzhugh girl. Our psychologist was following it. He sat staring at her picture on his computer screen all day."

"So?"

"He must have told her he was going to bug out. He must have given her the account number as a backup. She's got to be in on this with him. Don't you see it makes sense? Hot pants little teenager just make him go off his rocker."

"Well, that's an avenue to investigate. But in the meantime, I think you ought to concentrate on the normal solution which is the firm better put the money back."

Since the left hand was bandaged, they clipped the little finger off the right. Van Dine wept and screamed, crawled under the desk as though it would give him protection.

"You shithead!" he shrieked. "I knew Hamilton College people were like this! You belong with Colgate and Hobart and those . . . those other places! Animals every one of you!"

■ ■ ■

"So it's all, like, real," said Dru, still in a bit of a daze from the séance.

"I told you," Sam replied.

"I thought I'd shit a brick when my thoughts came out of her mouth."

"I warned you about that."

"What was that language she was talking in?"

"Kurt says it's an ancient form of Erse. She's done that before. Tapes of it have been sent to linguists in Ireland, but they can't fully decipher it."

"Did you have a vision?"

"Yes. And you?"

"A shadowy man was leading me down a moonlit path above the sea," said Dru dreamily. "I knew he was going to rape me, and I was frightened but thrilled at the same time. He held my wrist firmly so I couldn't escape. But I didn't want to escape. I had no clothes on. I could feel the sand beneath my bare feet."

"And?"

"It ended. With a huge feeling of loss. Like that world was so much better than the one we live in." She looked at Sam. "What was yours?"

"I saw a battlefield. Covered with dead and dying."

Chapter 66

"Samantha, we must talk," said Mrs. Jaeger. She looked grave. "We are bonded, and I want to help you."

"Have I done something wrong?"

"No, not at all. Because you were studying Gilgamesh, because I heard you recite the Love Song of Inanna and Dimuzi . . . I just assumed . . . Were you . . . that night when we returned . . . was the sculpture of Inanna in the room?"

"Yes. We ate dinner with it between us."

She paused and took a deep breath. "This is difficult. People are so skeptical. But primitive people believe there are spirits or souls in all things. Rocks, trees, rivers. I am unable to verify that one way or another.

"I do know that humans, through their emotions, leave a residue behind. Things that can be read. I do this all the time. Old cities, antique objects whisper to us. Anyone can feel the past. Some of us, you and I, hear it vividly.

"And I think you were channeling the sculpture. You were, in your erupting subconscious, being Sumerian."

"I can't believe I'm reincarnated or something," said Sam.

"No. It's not that. The goddess comes in many different guises. But yours properly comes from your racial memory.

There were very few clan mothers that were the origin of humanity. They were clustered in Greece, Syria and Anatolia, giving rise to the Garden of Eden story and Noah's Flood. The growing population spread out of Anatolia east into Mesopotamia and west across southern Europe.

"We know of as many as five Ice Ages. The last one ran from about 30,000 to 10,000 BC. As the ice sheet retreated, Neolithic people in Iberia and southern France moved north.

"The great flowering of civilization in Mesopotamia began around 4000 BC. Your ancestors were already in the British Isles. I can be certain of that because of your blood type."

"Yes?"

She seemed to be struggling with emotions. "You see, I was confused by the whole business of Sumeria. When the truth began to dawn, I did the séance. What I saw . . . what I learned . . . oh, Samantha!" She hugged Sam close. She was trembling.

"I saw a field of dead," Sam whispered. "Hooded crows cawing in the trees. Pecking their eyeballs." Now Sam was shivering.

"When the goddess of battle emerges," said Mrs. Jaeger, "I fear it will be quite terrible. Worse than anything we have imagined."

"I've stabbed people," Sam said, weeping now, tears running freely. "I don't want to kill people. To go to prison. Please stop what is happening to me. Please."

"Our son loves you," Mrs. Jaeger said. "We will never abandon you. But you have a destiny that cannot be avoided."

Chapter 67

Kurt wasn't around when Randall came to collect Samantha for the prom. She looked for him, but he was deliberately absent. She felt as though some bond had been broken and questioned for the nth time why she was doing this.

They picked up a gang of kids from the class, sitting on each others' laps, laughing with the strange relief of trying to be like normal teenagers. The school parking lot was already jammed with cars. The wilder guys sneaking booze, getting a buzz on.

Behind the gym stage was a loading ramp with a roll up metal door. This was the planned entrance to the prom. You walked up the cement ramp, and there you were.

Samantha wanted to leave almost as soon as she arrived. It was tacky like all senior proms.

You walked across the stage through a crepe paper over chicken wire class ring, paused for professional photos to be made. Randall was beaming as though he had been completely redefined as high school stud with a trophy date and a brilliant future as a major litigator ahead of him.

The theme of the prom was the 1967 "Summer of Love" in San Francisco. Which no one their age could really understand, but it seemed romantic with its '60s counterculture, hippies, and flower children, and the backdrop of the war in Vietnam.

Julie Huang had dreamed it up. Her grandparents had fled Vietnam with the boat people. Her grandfather hated her band and always left the house when they practiced. And he thought the prom theme thoroughly disrespectful of the travails they had been through.

Julie's college professor parents shrugged, said: "What can we do? She's an American teenager."

A projector flashed changing giant images of psychedelic posters from the Fillmore Ballroom for concerts by Big Brother and the Holding Company, the Grateful Dead, Quicksilver Messenger Service, Buffalo Springfield, Jefferson Airplane. These alternated with hippies and iconic photos of the war—naked child burned by napalm, police chief of Saigon blowing out the brains of a Vietcong captive.

Julie's band "Saigon Sally and the Mekong Steamers" were dressed like bar girls in navy blue with white stars hot pants and red and white stripe halter tops. They were playing the old Jefferson Airplane hit "Somebody to Love."

Julie, lead guitar with a pink Gibson—lead vocalist, front woman and visionary—her voice perfectly capturing the legendary rocker Grace Slick's wail. Beth on bass doing back-up vocals. Evangeline on the drums, gluing it all together. The amps so loud music pulsed through every object in the room, through the floor and walls.

"You gotta find somebody to loh-oh-ove."

And every boy in the room fantasized about having a special treat at the end of the evening.

The ten cutest girls in the sophomore class were selected each year as prom servers. They got to cute around and flirt with the older boys and whisper about which of the senior girls would go "all the way" that night.

Leonard Clearwire was hanging around the giant tub of punch wearing a t-shirt printed like a tuxedo. "What are you doing here?" demanded Principal Peevey.

Clearwire gave him a stupid smile in return.

"You've been smoking something," Peevey accused.

Clearwire grinned stupidly again.

Bubba Stobbs drove a big limo into the parking lot transporting all the cool boys and girls. He steered with one hand, the other having healed into what was pretty much a club.

"Ain't nothin' gone stop my baby girl from having a big time prom!" he roared, as they all piled out.

He was wearing a televangelist pink tuxedo with black piping, a frilly front shirt and a black bow tie so big it seemed to surround his fat face.

Officer Buck was off-duty security. Dressed as a cowboy in boots, Stetson hat, and yoke front black shirt with red roses.

As Cherry sashayed by, he touched the brim of his hat and said, "I'm Officer Buck. Spelled with a 'B' and not an 'F.'"

She looked at him.

"I've got some Dickel in the car if you want a little sweetner in yore drank." Gave her a big wink.

Cherry told him he was a creep.

■ ■ ■

Quinn had put candle stubs all over his house. Lit them each in turn. He sat down on his front porch with a Talisker, the house glowing behind him like some Thomas Kincaid cottage painting you'd see for sale in *Parade* magazine.

A platoon of Harleys drove slowly up, shut their engines. There must have been twenty of the Legion, Hog Man at their head. Ruining his planned evening.

Hog Man had a quid of Skoal in his jaw, running down his chin. Took a big drooling spit.

"You know it's funny," he said. "All that money disappearing. Not that I figger you took it for yourself nor nothing. No, what I wonder about is that gal Samantha. Yore intended goddess." He scratched his filthy head. "Well, it just gets all complicated."

Quinn realized Hog Man was wearing a leather cord around his neck with van Dine's two fingers hanging on it.

Hog Man leaned against one of the stripped cedar posts. "I mean you've made a major contribution to the club and all. Ever'body likes the name 'Lucifer's Legion'. Hail, we get compliments at bikers rallys. Gals admiring our colors.

"We got yore buddy Milroy decorating the place. Really brings a touch of class to things. Proud to have a Hell's Angel or a Satan's Disciple in for a drink.

"You bring us all this deep shit to think on. Chariots of the gods. Planet of death from outer space. The coming doom. Man, outta sight. But I'm jes wondering on one little thing."

"What's that?" said Quinn.

"Why is it that you get both them goddesses?"

Quinn stared at him. Had it finally come? The end that he had expected the first time he walked into their club?

"You realize," he said, "that Dru's the goddess of death."

"Yeh," Hog Man chuckled. "I kinder like that aspect of her."

■ ■ ■

Randall and Sam walked down from the stage in the wake of the cool kids. Sam really, really wanted to go home.

Bubba Stobbs bulled into the gym like he was prom Big Daddy. Announced he got "hisself a whale of a thirst hanging with the young folks." And drank down a Dixie cup of punch. Then, right out in the open, poured hooch from a silver hip flask into a second one.

He took a deep drink, wiped the back of his mouth with his wrist.

"Woo!" he said. "That'd scour out a clogged drain."

The band had gone into the psychedelic drug song "White Rabbit."

"One pill makes you giant, one pill makes you small."

Clearwire reeled over and lurched up against Sam, grabbing onto her to steady himself.

"I have to talk to you," he slurred.

"Why?"

"I . . . I want you."

"What for?"

"I want you. Can't you understand? I want to possess you. I want to fuck you!"

"You're disgusting. Get away from me."

Randall shoved him away.

"Go ask Alice, when she's ten feet tall!"

Francie came at her next. "There's something in the punch. People saw Clearwire pour it in. A big jar of something."

Randall looked down at his empty cup.

On the floor, the dancing had become totally frenzied. It wasn't in time to the slow rhythm at all.

"Look at them," said Nasar. "Totally wigged out."

"And you've just had some kind of mushroom . . ."

Bubba Stobbs stripped out of his tuxedo jacket. Then the cummerbund. Then the shirt, ripping it off so studs popped out like seed pods bursting.

He grabbed one of the tenth grade prom server girls and ripped down her strapless dress to expose her small, quivering bosoms. She fled screaming.

Bubba chased all the prom servers as they scattered like geese. Bobbing and weaving after first one and then the next.

"I'm gonna get'chew, yew little dickens!" he shouted.

"And the white knight is talking backwards,
"And the red queen's off with her head!"

Principal Peevey had stripped off his jacket and tie. Now his shirt was coming off.

"I need you," he breathed to Ms. Frissel. "Now."

"Yes," she hissed back. "An authoritative man. I've longed for one. All the years of whipping spineless, sniveling men. Fuck the shit out of me."

Sam pulled Randall up on the stage out of the scrum, wondering how to get him to take her home. He talked about the composition of the state Supreme Court and the politics of getting appointed. Touched on the grandeur of his ambition.

That was when Sam saw Dru tippy-tapping across the dark parking lot to climb on the back of a Harley with a big hoodlum, then they roared away.

Sam had an image of her shoes and her tiny little dress. Her back hunched around the driver.

The little knot of genius class kids huddled in a corner while the rest of the school staggered and reeled, their voices deranged. Some were on their hands and knees, long strings of vomit hanging from their chins.

Cherry was hysterical. "Who are these people? Why are they laughing at me?"

Randall was in the middle of boring Sam to death, telling her he would skip his senior year in college and go right into Duke Law. And then it changed.

He was standing very close and began to rub her behind. His hand went up under her dress. Squeezing.

"Randall, what are you doing? Stop it."

He had his hand up the front of her dress into her underpants.

"Randall! You can't do this without even kissing a girl!"

Cherry ran out and down the ramp. "I'm going to kill you, Samantha Fitzhugh!"

Sam looked after the running figure. The sight made her breath catch.

Three Harleys with two riders each roared across the lot headed straight for the gym ramp. Then the limo fired up. Its lights came on.

Officer Buck was standing on one foot trying to get his pistol out of his ankle holster. A Harley flew by, the rear rider slashing him across the face with a heavy chain, tearing bone and flesh. Spinning him in a twirl of blood.

Sam was kicking away Randall who was on his knees trying to lick her legs.

She jumped back against the wall as the bikes blasted past and around the class ring. Went airborne and crashed on the gym floor still upright.

Right behind it came the limo, Cherry hunched over and peering through the wheel like a demented person.

The band stopped dead. Anyone in the room not in a stupor stared in horror.

Julie Huang's grandfather was a former South Vietnamese paratrooper colonel. He and his wife had gotten out on a raft, spent twenty years working their donut shop to put a son through college to become an embarrassing peanut-ball child psychology professor. In his old age, he now had to live with the boy and hear his drivel every day.

He had been home fuming about his disrespectful granddaughter and had decided to take direct action. What he saw in the gym infuriated him.

The principal and a teacher were actually doing the unmentionable on the floor while kids stood watching.

The rest of the room was high on drugs, and his grand-daughter was dressed as a Saigon bar girl.

And now an invasion of motorcycle hoods.

Any thought that it might be a student escapade was banished when he saw Bubba Stobbs take the lash of a chain that split open his flesh from shoulder to belly. He windmilled his arms and fell backwards.

In the old colonel's world, failure of nerve was never an option. In keeping with that, he had a concealed carry license and a .44 Colt Peacemaker beneath his traditional Vietnamese silk brocade tunic. An American general had given him it, as they sat drunk and despairing when they learned the US Congress had cut off military aid to South Vietnam and handed the country to the communist wolves.

He threw down on the lead cycle and drilled both riders with one shot, following with two more before the bike reared on its back wheel, slammed down and spun across the floor.

Cherry behind the wheel in the limo ripped through the class ring, went airborne, crashed down and spun around to bounce the second bike, crash through the punch and food table and smash Clearwire into the wall.

Principal Peevey raised his head from what he was doing. The students ran hither and yon in a panic stricken rout. Others, dazed on the drug, stood rooted to one spot.

Sam jumped down from the stage, opening her clutch bag to take out her throwing knives. All six of them held in her left hand in a flat stack as she threw down the bag.

The riders from the second bike were on their feet, but

Col. Huang blasted both of them with deadly aim. And was out of ammo.

Sam was running hard across the gym as the third bike chased the colonel, chain whirling like a cowboy lariat. The mob of students parted shrieking giving the biker a split-second view of Peevey and Frissel copulating right in his path. The bike struck with a fleshy thud, spilling the riders and dropping 565 pounds of metal on the amorous pair.

The bikers got to their feet unharmed. They spotted Sam. Fixed her with a menacing stare.

She came to a halt. The way they held eye contact, Sam knew they had come for her.

She stared back with grim determination.

A surge of wildness, violence coursing in her blood, making her nostrils flare. The rest was pure instinct. No gray areas. No doubts. Just the imperative to kill.

She was Inanna, owner of the Tablets of Destiny, driver of the seven lion chariot. She was Badb, terror of the battlefield.

She let fly. The first she dropped with a knife straight into his chest. It hit with a thunk, penetrated his heart. He collapsed to his knees. Fell over.

The second tried to dodge, but she focused, followed him with the throw and caught him under the armpit. Then put one straight into his eyeball.

He shrieked hideously, the noise largely drowned by the jabber and braying of the drugged teenagers.

Sam stood surveying her handiwork, not sure if she was

asleep or awake. She had killed two men. But her pulse was extremely calm.

Kurt was standing there, his hand on her neck. "I intended this as a gift when you got back. But mom said you were in trouble."

He held up a cloth bandolier with all her knives snug in cloth scabbards. The Gurkha kukri fitted behind her right shoulder blade with the hilt positioned for an easy draw.

Meanwhile, the band had burst into a triumphant "Volunteers for America."

Behind the wheel of the limo, Cherry was gibbering soundlessly. Clearwire was splattered against the wall in a big starburst of blood.

The drug was powerful and those under the influence continued their galloping insanity. Braying, mooing, barking. Many in some atavistic mood, attempting to breed.

Col. Huang, having noticed that Julie had arranged a Vietnamese portion of the buffet that had not been smashed by the limousine, was sampling the beef noodle soup called Pho nuoc. Gunning down four men had calmed his passion.

When they finished the song, Julie came over to join him.

"Who is the girl who throws knives?" he asked.

"That's Samantha," Julie gushed. "She's wonderful. But not as wonderful as you." She threw her arms around him and kissed his bald head repeatedly.

The Colonel smiled for the first time that evening and seemed to be reevaluating the offspring of his pathetic professor son. She had watched men killed and was unfazed.

She realized his stories of war were true, and her eyes were ablaze.

Kurt and Sam stood on the stage looking at the writhing zoo down below.

"They've got Dru," she said. "We have to go find her."

"How do we do that?"

A distant portion of her mind seemed to take over. "I know the way. I can see it."

■ ■ ■

Dru got off the back of the motorcycle and walked into the open door of Quinn's cabin. Candles big and small were on every object. Flickering in a yellow glow.

Dru slid the thin straps over her shoulders and shimmied the dress down over her hips into a puddle on the floor.

The light caressed her flesh, accented highlights in her hair and made her radiant. Alluring in her promise of surrender. Infused with heat, she squared her shoulders and thrust out her small breasts. The goddess was in her, and she was unrivaled in her beauty.

Quinn would make love to her in straightforward yet tender fashion. Until she became accustomed to it and could take his vigorous rhythms. And rise mewing and moaning into a soaring orgasm.

She walked towards the bedroom. The door was ajar, the room candlelit as well.

The bed sheets were turned down, just as she had known they would be. The bower of enchantment.

The goddess whispered to her:

"She exposed her naked body
and they did as man and woman do
embracing hotly and climbing into the bed."

Above the bed was a painting of Sam as Inanna and Dru as Erishkigal. The painting they had seen in the Milroy house. In a ghostly glow of flickering light.

It no longer seemed to hold the promise of erotic romance. The painted image was neither an enigmatic beauty nor a time traveler from a time of ancient gods. Its gaze was piercing. It was diabolical. Malevolent.

She sensed danger. Then she saw Hog Man and a slew of other bikers.

"Come awn in, honey," said Hog Man. "Make yourself at home."

Quinn was in a corner tied to a chair.

And Dru knew for sure at that moment of clutching fear that she was in way over her head.

■ ■ ■

"Turn here," said Sam, and Emerson turned the car onto the dirt road.

In the distance they could see Quinn's cabin, lit up inside like a fairytale cottage.

There was a car ahead of them, its headlights slicing the night. It pulled up at the house that glowed from inside. Rhoda Shelley got out, head down, and charged through the door.

"Momma!" they heard Dru scream.

Rhoda swung the *bocce* ball with lethal accuracy, simply exploding their heads left and right in a welter of gore. Two of them were finished, but little Skeeter jumped on her back, driving her to the floor. Sat astride her, hand twisted in her hair, bashing her head into the boards.

"Momma! Momma!" wailed Dru.

"We've got to kill them all," said Kurt. "I'll give you a field of fire. I've got your back."

Sam put the Fairbairn dagger right between Skeeter's shoulder blades. He seemed to wither as he died on top of Rhoda.

Sam sprang through the door, tense, senses alert. She registered the scene in a second.

Dru was naked, arms twisted behind her back. Her mouth wet and open, a welt on the side of her face where she had been slapped. Big bikers in a semi-circle. Coarse faced. Some flabby, some with flat bellies, ridged with muscle. Men strong enough to break a baseball bat across a knee. A smell of reefer smoke and b.o. and sweat.

When they saw Sam's face, their grins collapsed.

"Sunny-bitch," one gasped.

Sam was filled with a battle ecstasy. A maniacal blood lust. A grim determination to exterminate them all.

She held the Russian Spetsnaz knife by the point. Let fly.

She caught the first one in the chest, snapping his head back, sending his sun-bleached ponytail swinging wildly.

A weird keening came out of Sam's throat. It was the blood freezing sound of the Morrigan, bringing terror and confusion to the battlefield.

One lunged at her, but before he could close the space, she threw. Squinch! Caught him in the throat, making him gag, iridescent bubbles of blood coming out of his mouth. Gurgling. Hands quivering with palsy inches from the lethal blade.

Sam was suffused with blood rage. The knives seemed to vibrate in her hands, lusting to kill. And she whipped them through the air one after the next.

The onslaught of steel was terrifying. They actually made a whistling sound.

The terrorized bikers cowered in a bunch into the corner and she picked off the outermost ones. Faces remodeled with agony, clutching at the hilt of a knife embedded in their chests, feebly reaching behind for one stuck in their back.

Groans and screams and death rattles.

Only a brief respite before she began the storm of steel again.

And then she was out of knives. And Hog Man remained standing alone among the dead and dying.

"Man, you are good, honey," he said admiringly. Then he advanced on her like a Goliath.

In a whirling blur, Kurt kicked him into a sack of broken bones. The last blow, when Hog Man was on his knees, snapped his neck. He went down with his mouth spitting blood and his head twisted at an impossible angle.

The stench of death clung to the air. Sam had gone silent.

Quinn was gone. Dru had cut him free.

"My baby my baby!" Rhoda wept, cuddling Dru, the blood from her head lacerations smearing them both.

Cops came. EMS wrapped Rhoda and Dru in blankets and put them in the back.

Dru said, "Momma, if I keep my grades up, do you think I could go to college in England?"

"Anything, my baby," Rhoda cried, stroking Dru's head.

Chapter 68

In the aftermath, Lt. Wally Butts blathered incoherently in front of the TV cameras.

"Aw, I mean someone done went DEFCON 1 on them boys. Bodies ever'where. Dead and more dead. Like cordwood."

He got so twisted around trying to explain things that he just gave up and let the screen-writers try to unravel a plot out of it. They said it was good, but needed some car chases.

SLED came and told Butts he was a total dumb-ass. It was obvious there had been a war between rival biker gangs. Lucifer's Legion had gotten the "shitty end of the stick." They didn't care what some crazy teenagers said about it. The whole gang of them had been on drugs any-old-how.

Cherry said she didn't remember a thing about the night and if stupid old Mr. Clearwire had stepped in front of her car but she didn't remember it, well then it just hadn't happened. Anyhow—arguing in the alternative, as Randall would say—he had doped them all up and got what he richly deserved. She was just glad her poor loving daddy was alive and back moving the inventory.

And on the subject of Bubba, many people believed he had valiantly stepped in front of a motorcycle to try to protect the kids rather than being in a drunk and blundering frenzy. As a result, the Attorney General figured he couldn't get a conviction and dropped the bribery charges against him. Bubba had four hundred stitches in him, but he came out of the hospital swearing he was a new man.

He wanted to present a Ford Dealership Order of Valor to Colonel Huang at a school assembly. The new principal Ms. Wibbing didn't just decline, she refused in very harsh language. They should have called the police and let them handle the matter.

Bubba was incensed. "So tell me how we were supposed to just stand around sucking our thumbs waiting for the cops. I mean a lot of kids might have bought the farm."

"That's not the point," she said forcefully. "We don't condone heroism."

Bubba looked like he had had ammonia thrown in his face.

He spluttered and shouted abuse at her until he came to "I can guarantee you won't have a dam' football program come fall if I don't get behind the search for a new coach."

"That's quite all right," she answered with utter disdain. The prim mouth smiled tightly. "I'm eliminating contact sports. They encourage the worst in the male animal."

Bubba looked like he had suffered yet another near-mortal wound.

Bubba awarded the Stobbs Ford Dealership Order of Valor in front of the local TV cameras at his car lot. It was a corporate-looking wood plaque with brass inscription, something he had made up, but Col. Huang was still pleased. He wore his old uniform and medals, among which was the South Vietnamese gallantry cross with bronze star. Julie was super proud of her grandfather.

There were a lot of aged American and Vietnamese military men in attendance. Some got into the liquor too heavily and shot out windshields on the cars in the lot.

"Aw, hail, I don't care a toodle," a drunk Bubba avowed. "I don't need possessions. I can get up each blessed day and look in the mirror and say praise the Good Lord I am alive."

Col. Huang was feeling like he belonged in America for the first time and offered to organize a pistol club for the school. Ms. Wibbing said absolutely, positively, under no conceivable conditions no.

"Guns are the tools of the devil," she spat. "Not that I believe in the devil. Or in hell. But the metaphor is apt. I believe in Darwin and in the ultimate taming of the male species guided by the sure hand of the administrative state. The eradication of violent male instincts is my primary mission at the school. I trust you follow my line of reasoning." All smug and self-satisfied in tone.

He said fine, he'd just do it on his own. It was a free country. Or so he had believed when he came here.

When she furiously declared that she could and would control the behavior of the students outside the school day, she got her first encounter with Randall and was left a very shaken woman.

He told her a legal clinic at the law school was organizing the class action against the school district for injuries from the prom debacle. He would be more than happy to add the new right of free association issue to their enterprise with her named for joint and several liability.

"I trust you follow my line of reasoning," he added blithely.

When Dru brought home the gun club news, Rhoda Shelley turned wildly enthusiastic and announced it should be a joint project with the university. Her Women's Studies girls needed to learn their way around a diversity of fire-arms. She bought Dru a Ruger .22 as a starter, promising to upgrade to a .38 when she could place all her shots in the head or heart of the target villain.

Rhoda herself took to carrying a 9mm Glock 17 with a seventeen round mag. She also wore a variety of t-shirts: "A Woman's Place Is Behind the Trigger," "Yes, I Shoot Like a Girl," "Why Aren't You Pro-Choice When It Comes to My Self-Defense?" and her favorite "Samuel Colt _Really_ Made Women Equal."

Suddenly, every boy and most of the girls in the school were talking muzzle velocity, stopping power, and maga-zine capacity. AR-15s hung in the back windows of trucks in the parking lot. Ms. Wibbing walked the halls in dread, feeling like she was at an NRA convention. She had trouble sleeping at night and developed a spastic colon, requiring an adult diaper.

■ ■ ■

In so many ways it just went back to being high school. On the AP exams, the genius class had all placed out of two semesters of college US History and two of chemistry.

Likewise they had knocked the top off the SAT with Nasar and Dinorah making the unheard-of perfect scores.

Naturally this brought the Educational Testing people down on them convinced of fraud.

They engaged in prying conversation rife with traps. Nasar lectured them on the origin of the atomic weight system, and Dinorah gave them an overview of the early history of sociology from Auguste Comte through Durkheim, Spencer and Max Weber.

After a week of fruitless snooping, the educrats went away pronouncing the genius class one of the top four high school programs in the US.

And then the new kids came.

"Holy shizzle!" enthused Randall. "Have you seen the new girl? Talk about a smoke show."

Her name was Parmita which means "wisdom," and her father was an astrophysicist. She was taller than Sam and astoundingly beautiful. Honey-colored brown eyes, jet black hair, and a walk like a super-model. According to Jasper, whose father was in the film department, she was the spitting image of Shakira Caine in John Ford's "The Man Who Would Be King."

A friend to the world, Julie Huang was the first to step forward and introduce herself. By lunchtime, Parmita was settled into the class.

It was after chemistry when Parmita confided to Julie that she seldom met a boy taller than she. And she went weak over brilliant boys. Yes, she had Nasar in mind.

Ever the matchmaker, Julie introduced them. Parmita cast her eyes down modestly as she had been taught, and Nasar was beyond hopeless, stammering, and actually chewing his shirt collar.

Dinorah was the child of sociologists, and as such, a master busybody. She took the baton from Julie and brazenly called the mothers to point out the obvious synergy. By the time she hung up, she practically had an arranged marriage.

Nasar was invited to a dinner of *ram ladoo* and chicken *malai* kebabs and a fun evening—as Sam had once predicted—of working equations. It all went so well, that Parmita was invited to Nasar's house for a dinner of *murg makhani* and a Bollywood movie about star-crossed young lovers.

The other newby was a Scottish boy from St. Andrews whose father would be a visiting professor for the next year in the university English Department. His name was Ian, and the sight of him made Dru's heart pound like a jack-hammer.

He looked like a character in Harry Potter, talked with a beautiful burr, and went to a boarding school called Fettes in Edinburgh. He had come with his parents to have a gap year in America before starting at Worcester College, Oxford.

He went out for the last day of spring soccer practice and completely dominated the field, bending it like Beckham to score twelve goals against a defense so flummoxed, he seemed to be playing against traffic cones.

The coach of the now premier sport in the school began to babble about state championships.

Dru sat in the bleachers enthralled, absorbed in a romantic coma.

The goddess had not abandoned her. As the practice ended, she fixed Ian with a sultry stare that stopped him dead in his tracks. They were seen walking home together talking.

■ ■ ■

Lt. Butts took Sam and Kurt to visit the Legion headquarters where the woods were being searched. Sam identified the paintings as having been done by Jake Milroy. Denied having posed for them.

The cops were searching the woods, a place of rats and rooting hogs and vile rubbish. When Sam saw the rotting skeleton spiked to the tree she stiffened, struck by a sudden image of Cressie Moon Child being strangled, and was certain who had done it.

She threw up violently, but wouldn't tell the cops what she knew, Mrs. Jaeger had warned her against revealing her powers. Her life would be a series of ill omens from now on. The unscrupulous, the greedy, the evil, the pious do-gooders would all try to take advantage of her if they knew the truth.

Afterwards, they sat on Kurt's porch swing, Sam resting her head on his shoulder. They had killed people.

It was a wicked world, Mrs. Jaeger had said, and death was the Great Certainty. We all moved on predestined lines towards it on the grooves of our character and the virtue of our deeds.

There was no alternative to what they had done.

Azaleas were blooming along with the dogwood. Dusk settled in bringing the lonesome hoot of the owl in the park.

"It will never be the same," Sam sighed regretfully. "The past no longer relevant; the future a vast question mark."

"No," he agreed. "But some people get polio. Some leprosy. At least yours won't be visible. And most people won't believe the evidence when it's right in front of them."

"Thanks for the bucking up," she said sourly.

"You have a force for good in you. The images that are now so easily unlocked."

"You and I could make a fusion of our efforts," she ventured.

"We're going to England to find your mother. Dad bought the tickets. We'll be together . . ." He let the sentence trail away.

She brightened. "No matter what?"

"For better or for worse," he vowed, in an echo of marriage vows. And then he kissed her very deeply.

About the Author

ALLEGRA DRAKOS was born to a London-and-Athens based Greek family of wine and olive merchants. She was educated in the US and at St. Catherine's British Embassy School in Athens, Greece.

Defying a Greek girl's imperative to marry at 18 and became a baby machine, she studied archaeology at Worcester College, Oxford, and the American School of Classical Studies in Athens.

Her research among dusty ruins has convinced her the once-great empires of Atlantis, Lemuria, and Mu were destroyed by a cosmic impact in 10,200 BC with earth crust displacement, volcanic eruptions in the Ring of Fire, and the near extinction of all life.

Allegra spends much of the year on the island of Hydra in the Saronic Gulf. She believes in the Oxford comma, documents regional differences in Greek cuisine, raises Kotsifali grapes, and lives very much for each day.

Because the next great cataclysm approaches from beyond Sirius, the Dog Star.

www.ingramcontent.com/pod-product-compliance
Lightning Source LLC
Chambersburg PA
CBHW062103290726

48975CB00001B/93